Thorn Boy

Printed by CreateSpace, An Amazon.com Company

Made in the USA, Charleston, SC

To learn more about, or to contact John visit his website:
http://www.centerforfloralstudies.com

ISBN: 1492815934
ISBN-13: 978-1492815938

DEDICATION

To Dad

NONFICTION TITLES BY JOHN KLINGEL

THE FRUGAL FLORIST®: DO-IT-YOURSELF FLOWERS ON A BUDGET

THE FRUGAL FLORIST® DESIGN TABLE GUIDE

CONTENTS

AUTHOR'S NOTE

The *Thorn Boy*, also called *Fedele* or *Spinario* (cover picture), is a Greco-Roman Hellenistic bronze sculpture on permanent display at the Palazzo dei Conservatori, Rome. Its image has been reproduced world wide in various sizes and compositions.

My Father served in the United States Military's liberation movement of Nazi Germany. As children, he shared with us his experiences. When Dad returned home, he carried a war souvenir, a small ceramic copy of *Thorn Boy* taken from an office of the Third Reich. After his passing, I became its guardian.

An authentic, true blue rose does not exist; however, in October, 2009, Suntory, a Japanese manufacturer of beverages and its subsidiary, Australian based Florigene; introduced "APPLAUSE". It has been publicized as the first ever blue rose.

The town of Belle Glade sits on the eastern shore of Lake Okeechobee, and, I hope, authentically described, but it is used fictionally in this novel. The same is true of certain businesses, bars, restaurants and other places mentioned.

In 1990 Danny Rolling, known as the Gainesville Ripper, brutally murdered and mutilated five university students as they slept in their apartments. Rolling had moved on after the murders in Gainesville and was eventually arrested for armed robbery in Ocala, Florida.

In all other respects, however, this book is a work of fiction. Names, characters, places and incidents are either the product of the author's imagination or purely coincidental.

This book required research in several fields, and I am grateful to the experts who took the time to direct me. I'd like to acknowledge James M. DelPrince Ph. D., AIFD; Mississippi State University; a highly respected professor for his advice and knowledge in plant science.

I would like to extend a heartfelt thanks to Dr. Jan A. Ganesh, PSY for her expertise in multiple personalities.

I would be deeply remiss if I didn't acknowledge a special, long-time friend, Vincent C. Petrovsky AAF, AIFD, for his suggestions, guidance and knowledge in two totally unrelated areas: soil study and genetic karma.

While I do not consider myself in any way an authority on The Family Karmic Inheritance I believe that there is a deeper reason why we feel what we feel. The quote below sums it up best.

"If we could read the secret history of our enemies, we would find in each man's life a sorrow and a suffering enough to disarm all hostility."
—Henry Wadsworth Longfellow

Nationally renowned astrologist, Elizabeth Spring offers an expert's viewpoint on this topic which can be found at www.elizabethspring.com

All of these people have provided valuable information. All errors, exaggerations, omissions or fictionalizations are entirely the fault, and the responsibility, of the author.

I would also like to extend my gratitude to a couple of new friends: Authors Diane A.S. Stuckart and Jeffrey Hammerhead Philips, members of my writers' critique group, for kicking my butt—figuratively speaking only. This book wouldn't be what it is without their ideas and suggestions.

And lastly, I would like to acknowledge Bonnie Wade for her editing talents, contributions and endless support. Friends, like these, are truly above the price of rubies. Thank you.

Prologue

The European Theatre of World War II was coming to an end. As Allied Forces advanced on Germany, the bloody Battle of Berlin raged on over their heads.

APRIL 29TH Midnight-

She stood stoically, dressed in navy blue, before the SS officer who was to marry them. An unsettled, nauseated feeling called upon her every morning and confirmed what she'd suspected: pregnant.

A frequent blood donor, Eva Braun was thought to be 'generous' because she had O-negative, a type that can be assimilated into any person's body. The fact was she had to because of a genetic decease, Hemochromatosis, in which her intestine absorbed too much iron. If left untreated, excess iron accumulates in vital organs, particularly the liver, pancreas and heart. All of her organs could become irreversibly damaged, and cirrhosis, diabetes and heart failure could result. Blood-letting was a simple way to manage her condition, as well as supply the troops.

Flickering candles offered the only light in the small library map room located on the lower level of the Führerbunker. Moments later, Adolph Hitler, Chancellor of Germany, entered through a side door. Hair slicked to one side and wearing a brown, full dress uniform with the Nazi Party's ubiquitous swastika arm band, he stepped to her side. His dark, piercing eyes meet hers briefly in exchange for her slight smile.

In a simple ceremony they become man and wife. The event was witnessed by Joseph Goebbels, who soon became the next Chancellor of Germany, and Martin Bormann, Hitler's private secretary.

Hitler often bestowed gifts upon Eva: various items which were stolen property of wealthy, European Jews. Their favorite was a small, white statue of a young boy sitting on a stone removing a thorn from his foot. The object intrigued Eva because of her fascination with Greek culture and art. She often imagined herself as a goddess who beheld unparalleled beauty.

To the Führer, the statue was a symbol of his "Master Race". Lean, impressively built, the subject depicted what every German should be in Hitler's view: pure. This was proven in the publication of his political beliefs, 'Mein Kampf' (1925). In it, Hitler wrote that those of unpolluted German birth, Aryans, were superior to other peoples of Europe. Acting on those beliefs, the Führer authorized that sexual relationships between Germans and ethnic groups, such as Jews, was a crime punishable by death.

On the day following their wedding at approximately 1:00 pm, the couple said their farewells to the staff and the members of the government's "inner circle". They returned to the library's map room; later that afternoon a gunshot was heard. Rushing to the locked door, Hitler's valet, Heinz Linge, and Hitler's SS adjutant, Otto Günsche, broke into the small study and found the leader of the Nazi Party slumped over his desk. A large pool of blood encircled his head.

Eva was found in a fetal position on the sofa wearing the dress she was married in. A cyanide capsule lay broken on the floor just below her feet. Her hands covered her delicate face; she was still and lifeless.

A few inches away, the only witness, their cherished statue, *Thorn Boy*, sat.

How can something as beautiful as a rose create so much terror?

--Derrick Stabb

Chapter 1—A Woman Named Tchelet

FRIDAY THE 13th 1950

AALSMEER

THE NETHERLANDS

Cornelius Hicks and the Docent worked side by side diligently for months in the subterranean laboratory located beneath the largest flower auction house in the world. As a young, driven botanist, he labored industriously to make his mark in the world of floriculture. While they labored, the thunder of huge trams intermittently whisked by overhead carrying millions of sold stems to markets in Europe, Russia, Africa, South America and the United States.

He whispered over the bubbling flasks perched on the stovetop. "Mr. Hicks, your destiny is predetermined, proven by your talent. From that first day in class I could see that you had a gift. You understand the quatrains' meanings which is why I chose you to carry forward the mission, as my Docent had chosen me."

Since he returned from service in World War II, at the youthful age of twenty-two, Cornelius resumed his passion...create a new cultivar by way of his unorthodox theories in horticultural science. The only ingredient lacking was funding; his limited resources had run out expressing concern from his Docent. "This project could run into tens of thousands of guilders. What are you going to do?"

Cornelius stared at him through the steam and responded, "I've met a woman; a few weeks ago at the museum. Since then, we've formed a bond. I think she's attracted to me. I saw an opportunity and told her about my work and financial dilemma; hoping she'd take the bait. She expressed an interest in helping."

The Docent responded, "And what does she want in return besides your affections; there's always a bigger price."

Cornelius smiled back at him and confidently answered, "She wants the rose to be named after her and her sister. I thought it was a fair exchange, rather romantic." Then, he returned his focus to his experiment.

"Houd uw handen regelmatig vast, geef aan uw ongeduld niet toe," commanded the diminutive man standing at his side, as Cornelius cautiously poured the grayish, smoking liquid. "Hold your hands steadily; do not give in to your impatience," he repeated forcefully in English. The edge of the flask clinked gently against the beaker. Minuscule bubbles of oxygen trailed one another slowly as the mordant fluid gradually entered the glass holder. This was it, the moment he had striven for.

In this highly flammable and toxic state, Cornelius had to slowly elevate the temperature of the liquid and then cool it down again prior to uniting it with a solid substance of uniquely prepared soil combined with human tissue and blood. He carefully transferred the final blend to another gas burner.

"We'll need another flask. There's more in the cabinet across the hall. Wait a moment, I'll be right back," the Docent ordered and then left the laboratory. Cornelius turned away from the flasks and watched his teacher's shadow drifting quickly across the Van Gogh painting they both admired, as he departed.

Four containers of solution at various stages of temperature were on the stove top. His type-A personality compelled him to disobey the Docent's strict orders and accelerate the process. Failing had not crossed his mind.

A steam spewed into the air and filled it with a corrosive odor which forced him to put on his protective face mask.

Three of the previous mixtures were nearly ready to be removed, but the fourth was taking longer than expected. Checking the fuel source, Cornelius realized the gas was spent. Frustrated, he yanked off his protective mask and gloves threw them on the floor and retrieved a second tank from the storage cabinet below.

Determined to immediately resume his progress, Cornelius, with wrench in hand, turned the nozzle counter-clockwise. He hurriedly disengaged the empty tank and reconnected the full one. Unaware, he failed to secure the proper bond. He slammed the cabinet door shut beneath the burners, stood hastily and turned the front burner to high.

A sudden flash ignited the four beakers of acidic fluids and sent an explosion through the laboratory. He was knocked backwards off his feet and was slammed to the floor. His face was on fire as the toxic liquid bubbled on his flesh. Hand towels were left on the shelf where he landed; he frantically reached for them.

The Docent and a staff member down the hallway heard the pounding blast and came running into the lab area horrified at the sight displayed before them. The staffer grabbed a fire extinguisher from its wall bracket and quickly sprayed the retardant foam on the blackened stove top. The Docent tended to the defenseless, young Botanist supine on the white, gritty concrete floor. Smoldering blood rushed from his wounds. He rushed to an ice machine in the hallway, returned and immediately applied the frozen cubes wrapped in a towel to his severely burned face and hands. Inches away the Docent smelt the stench of burning flesh as he heard Cornelius mutter the words, "Cornelius is strong, Cornelius is worthy, Cornelius is powerful."

The staff member threw the spent extinguisher to the floor and dialed an emergency number. Minute's later, sirens from a dispatched ambulance pierced the tranquil night. The scientist's heart had stopped.

Fearing depletion of oxygen to the brain, the Docent applied chest compressions working feverishly attending to his protégé while the driver quickly transported the seriously injured man to Saint Lucas Andreas. ER physicians stabilized him as he fought for life.

In his lab jacket's front pocket was a thin, leather wallet seared from the blast. The Docent found a hand-written card; a poetic verse on one side, on the other the name and number of a woman...Tchelet.

Chapter 2—The "Master Race" Features He Sought

AMSTERDAN ONE YEAR LATER

Gauze bandages thin as rose petals delicately covered his severely burned face as Dr. Cornelius Hicks faintly sighed. The frigid cold soothed the tender skin underneath them while he studied every inch of the shivering young woman. His eyes paused briefly on the rose tattoo etched into her shoulder's skin. She crouched in the corner of the dimly lit walk-in freezer, the single incandescent bulb behind him illuminating her like a plaster saint. The reflection from the crackled, aluminum walls revealed her shimmering blonde hair and sparkling blue eyes, watering from fear as much as from the cold air. He nodded. These were the Aryan traits he sought.

She was the perfect specimen.

Now, Hicks' sigh held a note of gratification as he eyed her trembling hands bound behind her back. Trussed up like a Christmas goose...though, unfortunately for her, she would not be there to celebrate that holiday the next time it came around. Abducting her had been childishly simple. He had wooed the trusting teen with compliments in his halting, phony Dutch accent that made her laugh, had plied her with cheap beer to which he surreptitiously had added a little something extra to render her groggy. She hadn't protested as he had walked her out of the popular night club; she had only giggled as he helped her into the back of his van and then bound her, hand and foot, with rope. But the drug had worn off by this time, and the teen was no longer a willing victim.

Eager to get on with it, he ripped the tape from her mouth in a single motion. She shrieked; small dots of blood now encircling her perfect lips where the strip's adhesive had torn her flesh. Even as he admired the effect—rather like a rose, he told himself—she struggled forward and spit in his face.

Hicks jerked away using the back of his hand to wipe the spittle off his cheek. He could easily tolerate blood, but painful memories of early boyhood when classmates would hold him down and take turns coughing up phlegm on him, he'd never been able to stand the sight or feel or sound of spit.

"You're hurting me!" she shrieked, falling back against the wall again. "Where in the hell am I? Who are you?"

"They call me the Botanist. I am your friend." He said as he stared directly into her pool blue eyes.

"Friend? I've never seen you before. No, wait, I remember. The club...you were there."

"Of course, I was there. I was looking for you...waiting for you." He made his smile deliberately gentle though he knew the attempt could not disguise the flat expression in his single dark eye that made even the boldest, young tough on the street swiftly look away.

She saw what the rest of them saw, and she screamed—the sound streaming from her blue lips and visible to him in the frigid air. He came closer, so close he knew she felt his warm, tobacco-laden breath wafting against her cheek. Hicks saw her cringe as he gazed at her nipples protruding behind the thin, cotton blouse that was no protection again the freezer's arctic chill.

She took a deep gulp.

Her fear turned antagonistic. "Are you one of those sickos who gets their rocks off having sex with cold bodies?"

He threw his head back in a deep, guttural laugh.

"Rape! You misunderstand my intentions. You're not here to satisfy some basic, primal desire. Your offering is much more significant than that."

"Then what do you want with me?"

"My dear, it's not what I want with you. It's what science wants with you."

"Science? What am I, some sort of weird experiment?"

"No need to be angry, young lady. Experiment, no. I would say, more accurately, that you are having *an experience*. The experience your life was created for...making an important, beautiful contribution to the world. Your reward is immortality; mine is redemption. We're a team."

"I know you're confused, but you must have faith. You see, with your genetics and my expertise, it's a perfect match. I've watched you for a long time."

Hicks reached out caressing her face and hair then his fingertips gently danced over her tattoo.

"Besides this obvious mark, I know you inside and out, literally. Luminous blue eyes, silky blonde hair, pure dietary regimen, and most importantly, the right blood type, O-negative; my associate at the blood bank has been most thorough. You should feel honored. You're the first. This amazing Aryan body of yours holds the right combination. The *Master Race* qualities, indicative of supremacy, make you vital to my project. I feel that I have unlocked what nature has kept concealed."

Terrified, she jerked back again. "You're mad! What combination; what in the hell are you talking about?"

Hicks was irritated. "I'm talking about the science of humanity, you stupid girl. Something you obviously wouldn't understand, let alone believe in. It's what each terrestrial being possesses—a direct connection to the Earth."

He took a deep breath and regained his composure. "My dream isn't original, no, no, no.

There have been other scientists before me, but they don't possess the knowledge, the courage, and the gifts. My dear, you and select others like you are the gifts!"

The effects of hypothermia had begun to take hold, her eyelids became heavier and heavier. Hicks pulled his insulated jacket tighter around his neck and left the freezer to warm himself with a cup of hot tea and a smoke.

He returned thirty minutes later. She drifted into a peaceful slumber. Her life ended. His concept of immortality had begun. Smiling, satisfied, the scientist checked his watch. Amsterdam was a city where nearly everyone speaks English, and freedom of expression was visible everywhere, two of the reasons he had chosen to live there. Another was it was the flower capital of the world: perfect. He could access everything he needed to see his work to fruition and explore his, not to be denied, creative feminine side, as well.

The scientist frequently wore lingerie under his lab coat. But when he was out for the evening, a womanly, dressier look seemed appropriate. He loved the soft fabrics and how they felt against his rough skin. It also made for a less fearful and somewhat natural disguise.

After a quick change into his favorite female attire of a lacy floral patterned blouse and pleated skirt, he headed out the door grabbing his paisley print eye patch dangling nearby on a hook. Next to his keys hung a laminated card; he snatched it up. On one side was a female friend's phone number; on the other side a short verse. It read:

"The sky is blue and calling your fate

The time is now you mustn't wait

Sacrifices made are surely justified

After all, their names will be immortalized"

Hicks couldn't escape his superstitious nature; he confidently slipped the good luck verse into his wallet. His first stop was Studio 80, one of the city's largest underground discos. It's rather neutral interior of pale green and blue couldn't be more in contrast to the rest of the vibrant, touristic Rembrandtplein Square.

Tonight he would meet up again with a young lad he met there before, one so attractive and friendly with the "Master Race" features he sought.

THE FOLLOWING MORNING—Amsterdam News Channel 5 A.M. Report:

Dutch police are baffled by the disappearances over the past three days of two teenagers from a popular Amsterdam night club. The only connection was each had a blue rose tattoo. We'll bring you more as this story develops.

Chapter 3—Another Gainesville Ripper?

FALL TERM

UNIVERSITY OF FLORIDA, GAINESVILLE

SEPTEMBER 1990

6 AM

Ugh that alarm clock...

Derrick Stabb thought as he rolled over and hazily smacked the snooze button with the palm of his hand making a half-hearted attempt to catch a few more minutes of sleep. This was his first week of classes as a college freshman. A couple of minutes later, he sat on the edge of his bed, scratched his thick, blonde scalp and wondered what today would be like. So far, campus life had proven to be a very different atmosphere than what he had experienced back home in Belle Glade.

Mature beyond his inexperienced age of nineteen, Derrick had grown up in the small, farming community on the shores of Lake Okeechobee, in western Palm Beach County where migrants came and went during the winter harvest season. Neither the son of a field worker nor a land owner made his childhood unique. He and his younger brother, Rodney, were raised since toddlers by his sweet, doting grandmother after their father was killed in Vietnam and their mother abandoned them. Grandma Ma said, "He has the wisdom of his grandfather, the passion of his father and the intuitiveness of all of the Stabbs before him." She managed, alone, to put food on the table, clothes on their backs and pay for schooling from their father's life insurance policy.

During high school, he had mostly peripheral relationships with members of the student body. Instead of playing sports, which he was suitably built for, he'd rather have spent time with his grandmother in her rose garden.

The window unit in his dorm room rattled away barely cooling the cramped space. The air was still, warm and heavy. Fall has not yet arrived. That musty odor that is so common in old Florida buildings hung in the air.

Derrick labored with an uncomfortable feeling—a sensation he'd never experienced before, not anxiety; it was deeper than that: a premonition. It was as though he knew something sinister had unfurled.

He rolled out of bed, stood and headed for the bathroom deciding on the best method to remedy his queasy stomach. Inside the medicine cabinet were antacids his Grandma Ma had sent along knowing he'd need them. Derrick popped open the cap, cocked his head back, and tossed two in this mouth. Momentary relief.

Rifling through the drawers in his discount store dresser composed of pressed fiber board covered with beige, vinyl laminate, he pulled out one of his black, loose- fitting favorite tees with a beer logo in gold on the front. Fortunately for him, he didn't need a lot of time to get himself ready and out the door. With little time to waste, Derrick grabbed a pair of denims slung over the desk chair, pulled them up his well-built legs and headed out the door. At a brisk pace, he started across campus to his first class putting his gut feeling that something was terribly wrong in the back of his mind.

Fifield Hall, where Derrick's classes took place, was on the other side of the campus from his dormitory room. The University of Florida was Derrick's first choice because of its nationally recognized horticultural program. His guidance counselor at Glades Day School recommended U of F. She recognized Derrick's exceptional intelligence after he aced his SAT's and the university's entrance exam. His success would have earned him a quick acceptance into any college's plant sciences curriculum. Horticulture was his first love, history was undoubtedly his second.

Although he had many talents, a sense of direction wasn't one of them. Most of orientation day he had spent lost. It didn't provide nearly enough time for Derrick to figure out which way was what. Huffing and puffing just after he got through the door of Fifield Hall, Derrick was met by a huddle of students gathered in the foyer. The chatter among them focused on the news that one of their new classmates hadn't been seen in the past three days.

Julie Rose was a pretty, petite blonde with a bright smile and vivid, blue eyes who recently moved from Pensacola. She sported a small blue rose tattoo on her right shoulder. "Did you get the tattoo because your last name is Rose?" Derrick inquired in the book store line. Coincidently, she was the first person Derrick met when he registered for class. They talked about growing up in different parts of Florida and how a state varied so much in vegetation from region to region. Obviously, they were both in the right class since the conversation centered on plants and flowers. Derrick connected with her; he was impressed by her knowledge of south Florida's vegetation and was looking forward to seeing her in his class.

"No," She responded with a timid smile. "A bunch of my girlfriends got together and decided to do something crazy to celebrate our womanhood. This is what we came up with. I know my mother's not going to like it one bit."

The situation before him reminded Derrick of his high school days where he was disconnected from most of the crowd. Now, on the outside again, he observed the conversation within the group. He didn't like what he was hearing about Julie.

One macho looking guy, wearing a sweatshirt with the impressive Olympic Swim Team logo, laughed and said, "I took her for a slut. She probably picked up someone at a bar."

Derrick immediately stepped into the group. He towered over them and, in Julie's defense, said, "I don't believe that! I spent time with her in the book store, and my take was that she was OK—yeah, better than OK!"

The swimmer immediately backed down from the strapping six foot Derrick Stabb. Then, he made an about face and headed for the entrance.

The human theatre on the college campus was tense. The university was still reeling from the murders of five students in their dorms a week earlier. Hundreds of students had returned home until Danny Rolling, known as the "Gainesville Ripper", was arrested and charged in the heinous crimes.

Now this, thought Derrick; who would want to hurt Julie? Could there be another serial killer out there, an accomplice to the first crime? Or, maybe she decided to go back home and not let anyone know.

Class assembled in room 2318 on the second floor of the Horticultural Sciences Building. The room was spacious with big windows that flooded it with light. Derrick started to settle down from the altercation. His attention was drawn to the oak trees just outside the building, draped with Spanish moss, swaying softly in the breeze. He loved the Florida skies, which are usually clear and allowed natural daylight to substitute for the harsh glare of florescent tubes above. This time of year, the sun bathed his face in a warm glow as it rose into the southeastern part of the sky and cast long shadows through each pane.

Derrick took his seat in the front row. He didn't want to miss a thing. Moments later, his professor slung the door open and entered the classroom with ramrod posture. He tossed his brown, leather bag on the desktop, turned to the class and, without expression, introduced himself.

"Good morning students, I am Stanley Hicks; *you* may call me Dr. Hicks." He spoke in a soft, breathy voice that could easily have been mistaken for a woman's.

Tweed must be the standard fabric for college professors thought Derrick taking note of the professor's jacket. He passed several other teachers in the same coat on his way to class.

Stanley Hicks looked the part of a Doctor of Philosophy in Plant Sciences—a tall, fit, distinguished man with graying temples and thick sideburns indicated he probably had tenure. He looked familiar, too. Then Derrick realized it was Dr. Hicks he saw earlier that morning when he was looking franticly for his classroom.

The professor appeared to struggle with some boxes from his car's trunk.

Addressing the class, Dr. Hicks was clear that he detested—or, more accurately, feared—the smell of smoke: cigarettes, cigars, even campfires. The sight of smoke or the crackling of the flames sent him into an immediate panic. "This is the only time I will get personal and only because I do not tolerate gossip. It's a waste of precious time and energy. Many years ago my twin brother and I were in a house fire. After countless surgeries, what you see is the after effect. Any questions? He paused. "Good now we can proceed."

He didn't crack a smile, which commanded a certain measure of respect and control. He wasted no time and got right to work giving the students an overview of the course. Derrick's stomach started to churn again. He had hoped the first class of the day would present a more relaxed atmosphere, but quickly realized it wouldn't be, not with Stanley Hicks at the helm.

Concern for Julie faded in and out of Derrick's mind as he worked focusing on what Dr. Hicks was teaching the class. With so much on his mind, Derrick barely noticed the time as the bell sounded class dismissal.

After he returned to Fifield Hall following break, Derrick noticed a black, official looking sedan parked in the circular driveway outside the building. He paused for a moment, shifted his back pack and observed the students he conflicted with earlier. He dealt with the misery in the pit of his stomach as he inched forward to find out what was going on. It appeared that some of the students were being questioned by an investigator regarding Julie's disappearance. Derrick hoped the nasty comment made earlier about her wouldn't resurface. He stood a reasonable distance from them. The official spoke determinedly as he followed up on a missing persons' report. *Obviously, she didn't go home*, thought Derrick. The officer now made eye contact with Derrick. The knot in his stomach was racing upward to completely disable any coherent sound from his throat. He held his badge as he stepped up right in front of Derrick popping two more antacids.

He extended his hand. "I'm Lt. Robert Waites. I understand that you know Julie Rose."

Waites was a forty-forty man; he had a forty inch waist and was forty years old. The investigator joined the force as a rookie eighteen years ago right after he graduated the police academy. His stocky physique resulted from too many lunch favors from locals. The boyish faced lieutenant quickly developed his skills into that of a seasoned professional after the horrendous "Gainesville Ripper" case unfolded before his eyes. Gainesville was a quiet town. Waite's first big investigation was the Danny Rolling's case. Now, a week later, he still battled the gruesome images that haunted his memory on a daily basis, nor had he fully regained his appetite.

In pursuit of this case, he had the same determination and a lot of questions to ask. Since yesterday, Julie's purse and school bag turned up in a secluded wooded area in Hendry County. In her bag was the usual identification: driver's license with a better than average photo of the stunning blonde, blue-eyed beauty, student I.D. card, library card and cash. Obviously the motive wasn't theft. Julie was a regular blood donor, too. She carried a card that indicated so with her blood type, O negative—one of the rarest and most sought after because others with any blood type can received it.

"Yes, I met her in the bookstore," Derrick swallowed hard and responded.

"What did she talk about: her interests, relationships, work experience?"

"We just chatted about school life and how excited we were to get started."

His interview with Lt. Waites was brief. "If you think of anything, please don't hesitate to call me," he said handing over his card.

As he started for the door, Derrick recalled something Julie had told him that seemed unimportant, until now. "Sir, she said she was renting a cottage from this guy, a scientist, I think, who was involved in some sort of secret plant project. She said her landlord traveled a lot, so he didn't usually collect rent in person until recently. In the past, she mailed it to a post office box in Belle Glade, but, this time, he asked her to meet him where he worked."

Waites, suspicious of everybody, listened to Derrick as he continued with more of the conversation. He wasn't sure what to think of the young man who seemed to have an amazing ability to recall details. "In his lab, located in some old barn outside of town, she was fascinated by the hundreds of culture dishes she saw. Julie said it was really interesting. I told her that I grew up in Belle Glade. Maybe I could meet him, too and see his lab. But I don't know if she ever mentioned it to him."

"She went on to say that she told him her contribution to mankind was donating blood. And it was especially important because she had this rare type. Her landlord seemed oddly interested in that particular piece of information. She said that it was kind of a weird, awkward moment, but he was pleasant, so she didn't think too much of it."

"Did she mention his name?"

"No, no I don't think so."

Waites continued, "We didn't find any contact information for him in her purse. Oddly enough, her parents didn't know who the guy was either. Seems to be lots of non-communications here; you'd think that if their daughter was going off to college, they'd want to know who she was renting from. Well, if you think of any other details, you have my card."

Waites took a deep breath; the kid's story sounded pretty far-fetched. He paused for a moment and curiously raised his eyebrows just as his mind again flashed back to the blood splattered dorm room of Rolling's victims.

Chapter 4—No Place Is Totally Isolated

BELLE GLADE

WESTERN PALM BEACH COUNTY, FLORIDA

An old, faded blue van caked in dust raced passed the sugar cane mill's four gigantic and ominous stacks. The billowing, white steam possessed a deafening sound not unlike that of a lion's roar as it spewed forth. The fall harvesting season was rockin' and rollin' in The Glades.

A rusty, metal sign designated GOLDSTEIN SUGAR CORP hung loosely from two chains as it swayed back and forth on a wooden post near the main highway just off Torry Island Road. In a remote location bordering the shallows of Lake Okeechobee, the sturdy barn could not be seen from the main road. Built generations ago, many of the antiquated buildings that dotted the farmland in the lake area were torn down, this one different, though, from those. Still standing, it was perfect for many functions: it housed a priceless car collection, sheltered clandestine experiments and accepted late night deliveries.

As the rust-eaten van skirted along on the fringes of Belle Glade's city limits, tiny pings, which sounded like buckshot, darted at the wheel wells from bits and pieces of the shell rock road. Steadfastly, the driver sped ahead toward the barn sitting stoically in the distance silhouetted by a bright pumpkin moon. The fixed, eardrum-shattering clamor from a generator inside impelled the driver to temporarily cover his ears after slinging the van door open.

After emerging from the vehicle, Dr. Cornelius Hicks struggled to get something out of the back. Whatever or whoever was in the large canvas bag was still flailing about making it more difficult to manage.

Hicks had a companion who scooted off the passenger seat. A figure, shorter and much stockier than he, revealed a woman's shape. She grasped an L-shaped implement, a tire iron. As she propped herself against the side of the van for support, she limped around to the back and raised the instrument. The sound on impact was like the splattering of an over ripe watermelon becoming one with the side walk. The squirming immediately ceased inside the heavy duty body bag.

The two carted the bag up to the side door. He fumbled with a large ring that held an inordinate amount of keys jingling about. Finally, finding the right one, he unlocked the heavy-duty pad lock and forced the rusty hinges open with a creak. A pack of startled rats scurried away into the darkness. Once inside the pitch black barn, they cautiously walked the uneven shell rock ground.

He turned back as they edged closer to the silhouette of a geometric shaped box and informed her, "My lab was moved to this location a few weeks ago. One of my tenants couldn't keep her promise. She was too mouthy, but her soul will live on in the beauty of a rose. In the future, I'll have to be more careful about letting my guard down."

Each at one end of the bag, exerting a great deal of effort, they carried it through a vast, open space toward a small aluminum sided freezer sitting at the far corner. Cornelius picked up the heavy industrial cord and plugged it into the outlet on the side of the silver-sided, prefab, cube structure. The area was instantly flooded with incandescent light. He removed two heavy jackets from hooks along side of the door and handed one to the woman. He reached inside the pocket and retrieved a pair of gloves. As he slowly opened a solid steel door, the cold air rushed out; mixed with warm it created a fog that tumbled onto the floor. They dragged the heavy, canvass bag inside. Moments later each returned outside the freezer holding several packages neatly enveloped with white freezer wrap secured with masking tape. Carefully, Hicks and his assistant undid each parcel as he methodically recited three times. "Cornelius is strong, Cornelius is worthy, Cornelius is powerful."

"I have almost everything I need in place to start the process," he said in a forceful voice as he gestured toward the long, narrow bundles laid out before them.

"This is the beginning of a very a complicated process, and you must follow my instructions carefully. I have worked on this theory for decades, but without your assistance in obtaining these victims, the project would have taken more valuable time. There's much to do."

He walked over and flipped the switch on a large wood chipper. The sound gradually rose until the decibels reached a nearly intolerable intensity.

She acknowledged his remark and nodded through her surgical face mask. Then, she had begun to feed the frozen, solid substance into the opening illuminated by a single, powerful flood lamp. After a few minutes, the grinding halted. Her arthritic fingertips carefully combed each gray, frizzy strand as she picked bone slivers from her hair. After accumulating several in her small palm, she tossed them back onto the pile of shredded flesh. Exposed to warmer air, the particles had begun to thaw emitting the stench of death.

He continued, "We have a shared mission here. I trust you. Others may not understand, but then how could they? The world largely doesn't accept new ideas. I've experienced that. You do understand?"

She nodded again.

"Good," he responded. "But we are not the only two who believe; there are others. See."

He handed her a coil bound note pad with entries scribbled in it. Ungloved, she accepted it.

"Read them; they're stanzas delivered from a higher power. Signs from beyond, channeled through an oracle. He understands, too." She tightened the muscles on her forehead while struggling to comprehend their meanings; she read the cryptic verses out loud to him.

"Her enamored view supports your plan.

With contributions made you know you can.

Although challenges ahead may beset,

A position she holds is your best asset."

"An unearthly goal is yours by right.

Clouds in the heavens are blue tonight.

A bright young man creates an illustrious text.

He holds the knowledge; you'll see what comes next."

The following morning, two young grade school boys played outside the pecky cypress walls of the monstrous structure. A NO TREPASSING sign was poorly hammered in place diagonally across from a weathered sign GOLDSTEIN. It was understood that the barn that sat at the edge of the open field was strictly off limits. It was surrounded by acres of short prairie grass and a few melaleuca trees, which made it a perfect location for football practice. The team from Christian Day School met there on Saturdays to practice. Their teachers took an active role in student life after class and on weekends supervising games.

They used this isolated property at the end of Torry Island Road near Pelican Point because it was away from the noisy, cane harvesting machinery. However, lately an unusual sound resonated from deep within the ominous structure. On most Saturday afternoons, there would be a team or two practicing ball, not paying much attention to the activity coming from inside. Today was different. Curiosity captured two youngsters' interest and drew them closer to the old barn. Between the weathered boards, there was a tiny crack where a pair of sentinel rats appeared to stand guard at ground level. The boys ignored the warning. One of them threw a rock in their direction and watched them wiggle their grey, furry bodies back through the opening. After the coast was clear, they pushed and shoved each other for their place to peer through. The curious sound surrounded the building but originated from the west side. Drawn in, they listened closely. Above the piercing, grinding sound, someone shouted instructions. They became more intrigued as children do with the forbidden.

Surrounded by an enormous amount of darkness was a single, free-standing flood light, which illuminated a lone area.

There, a daunting contraption ground away as a tall, slender figure systematically fed something into it.

Small chunks spewed from the opposite end. Ground up tree branches and trunks typically created a fine dust that filled the air. There wasn't any dust. Instead a prism of color, a rainbow, danced in the beams of artificial light. Water crystals?

Suddenly the machine fell silent, and the operator walked to the receiving end where a shorter, solidly built woman stood. She utilized a flat edge shovel and had begun to mix another material with the particles spread about on the concrete floor. She limped around the hefty mound of organic matter in a semicircle and slowly added another shovel full, and then another. She paused and pulled a cloth from her coat pocket, then wrapped her excoriated palms—tender from gripping the rough wooden handle—and resumed turning the mixture over and over again as it had begun to thaw. Gradually, a fetid odor filled the air, foreign to the young boys; it drifted through the cracks in the wall and burned their nostrils. As it had grown stronger, the stench didn't seem to deter her from her job. The boys with mounting curiosity took turns pushing and shoving each other to the side while they contended to get a longer look. After a while, the inquisitive adolescents relented to rationed time at the narrow opening as each tried to figure out the activity within.

Inside, the sound went from a deafened, nerve-racked pitch to nearly total silence in a few moments. Without the pulverized noise of the equipment, peace dominated. Birds innocently chirped in a nearby podocarpus hedge while the occasional buzzing echo of cicadas could be heard in the distance—late for this time of year.

The summer had been unusually dry because most of the seasonal rains missed this area. Small plants in the midst of shallow roots were brittle and struggled to stay alive up against the barn walls. The larger of the two lads stepped backwards onto a dried branch. A sudden loud crunch caught the attention of the man inside. He paused, turned and at a steady pace headed for the door on the other side. By the time he reached the narrow entrance, he stepped outside shielding his eyes from the bright sun; the boys had disappeared into the grassy field.

Certain he had heard something, he had no choice but to dismiss it; his time was limited.

He returned to the wood chipper inside and his waiting accomplice. She stood leaning against the shovel breathing heavily through the cloth securely fastened behind her scraggly salt and pepper hair that covered her mouth and nose. He paused, lit a cigarette, then motioned for her to continue her efforts. He appeared not to be a very patient man, intolerant of any behavior which would hinder his progress. She immediately resumed her activity carefully shoveling the reddish, moist mixture into seedling trays neatly spread out on the floor before her.

Chapter 5 – A Plan For Vengeance

The young artist, protected by his canvas apron splattered with paint, entered the sitting room. His jet black hair glistened in the early morning light filtering through the impact-resistant windows. Dabs of acrylic colors had dried on his smooth, tanned, hairless arms. He approached her as she sat in her desk chair with a smile of gratification after finally completing the hundred or so hours of labor creating the Venetian garden of marble columns and hanging vines on the dining room walls. "The work is finished Mrs. Goldstein. I'm eager to get your approval," he said with a bright, even smile.

She stood with perfect posture, smoothed the pleats on her skirt and followed him into the dining room. He made a quick about face nervously anticipating her response. "Beautiful!" she proclaimed as the corners of her pink painted mouth turned upward. "I see why you were recommended so highly. The detail is remarkable. I feel as though I am in Italy again." She approached the wall to get a closer look and leaned in, her nose inches away from the art work. "Amazing, just as I had requested; these tiny blue roses you painted are almost life-like. I can nearly smell them."

"I'm happy you're please, Mrs. Goldstein. Here is my final invoice. I will pack up my brushes and be on my way." As he turned she said, "I'll have your check ready. Please see me in the sitting room before your go."

Approximately twenty minutes later, he respectfully stood next to her looming over the gold and black lacquered, ornate desk. In one sweeping motion she ripped the document from the leather covered binder and handed it to him. He took it from her small hand and glanced down.

An ear-to-ear smile crossed his, handsome face observing the generous amount. "Mrs. Goldstein, this is much more that the invoiced amount."

"When I'm happy with results, I believe in rewarding. You did exactly what I had requested—hence the bonus."

"Thank you, thank you very much indeed!" he exclaimed continuing to study the gold trimmed, embossed name handsomely printed on the elaborately decorated check. Then, he wrinkled his forehead and questioned reverently, "I'm not familiar with the pronunciation of your first name. May I ask what is it?"

"Tchelet, pronounced **Ĉhet**-let, it means *blue* in Hebrew." she answered.

He nodded approvingly, "I see, well, thank you again. I'll be on my way."

"My house man will assist you out." she replied just before he turned and left the room.

"Come see the trompe loeil, Varda. He did a fabulous job!" She said with enthusiasm to her sister seated across the room.

"In a moment," she responded struggling to take a deep breath. "Do you think we will ever find it, Tchelet?" Varda asked in a weak, yielding tone. The petite, frail women languished as she adjusted herself into a more comfortable position in the overstuffed, silk upholstered chair. The ocean view from their well-appointed Palm Beach penthouse was exceptionally spectacular on this clear autumn day. A few puffy clouds traced the Atlantic Ocean's horizon line as they drifted across the vibrant blue sky. Tchelet, who sat at her Louis the 15th style, antique desk inches away from the bank of floor to ceiling windows, gazed at the white caps of rolling waves. To her, they resembled blue sheets trimmed with white organza she slept on as a child, flapping in the distant breeze. The Gulfstream was only a mile off shore. Warmer than regular ocean water, the current was elevated; it appeared like a perpetual wave that never reached the shoreline.

"I hope so," responded Tchelet as she drummed her fingers on the leather cover of her checkbook. "I feel we're getting close. It's just a matter of time before we find it, Varda.

Now you must get some rest; remember what the doctor told you. All of this activity is wearing on you."

As she spoke the words, Tchelet knew time was running out for her sister. If she was to find Thorn Boy, she needed to do it fast.

Her parents expected so much more from her than her sister. Growing up in Berlin, Tchelet matured quickly and had more of a passion for business. She was the aggressive one.

Recently transplanted last season from Philadelphia, Tchelet and Varda Goldstein had finally settled into their luxurious, new, seaside condominium after months of spectacular renovations. No cost was spared: gold facets, inlaid onyx floors, recently completed trompe loeil paintings of Italian gardens on the wall to trick the eye into seeing three dimensions, and Tiffany chandeliers adorned the ceilings of every room.

Head of the family's farming business empire, GOLDSTEIN INTERNATIONAL; it was Tchelet's idea to move permanently to Palm Beach. She felt it would be easier to manage their Florida farming assets, most of which were located near or in Belle Glade—translated it meant a beautiful open space.

Palm Beach was only twenty-one stop lights and fifty-five minutes east from Belle Glade, but worlds apart. The communities were two polar opposites in every way imaginable. Palm Beach was one of the richest islands in the U.S. and a hypothetical stone's throw away from what appeared to be a third-world country. The mere idea of them living there surrounded by that black muck, they called soil was ludicrous. Palm Beach was the perfect spot.

The unwritten rules of the island were distorted to her and, on occasion, held a double standard, depending on who you were. Self-made millionaires or heirs to family fortunes, as in their case, were typically the ones who made up this prestigious group of blue-bloods.

Tchelet filled her days raising money for charity and hosting teas, luncheons and cotillions. She was determined to gain a prominent place within *all* of Palm Beach society. Many of their friends were also from Philadelphia, which guaranteed their speedy acceptance into the island's Jewish community, but that wasn't enough for Tchelet. She wanted more.

Although the entitled, glamorous twosome came from one of Europe's most prominent Jewish families, and they attended the best finishing school, discrimination met them right away at the base of the bridge to the exclusive island. As she stood at her desk facing away from her sister, Tchelet gripped the crumpled rejection letter in between her perfectly manicured fingers. Her sponsorship into the Beach and Racket Club, Palm Beach's most restricted society group, had been denied because of who she was. She attempted to save face, but the rejection quietly ate away at her consciousness. She struggled daily to bury the hatred exacerbated by years of blatant bigotry. She turned away from Varda, ripped the letter to shreds and tossed it into the gold trimmed waste can. Several pieces fluttered onto the cream marble floor.

It didn't matter that she married well. Her husband had been very successful in his own right. His family cultivated the richest tobacco ever grown in Israel. The need to expand their farming enterprise brought the company to south Florida, a region that provided perfect year-round climate conditions and rich soil. It was during that time he amassed a fortune. With extreme wealth came extreme toys. He kept one of the largest collections of vintage Bentleys in the U.S., which were safely locked away in an old barn on the Goldstein property.

Tchelet barely tolerated the prejudice she experienced daily in small, inconspicuous ways. Who were they to judge her? Most certainly her secrets were concealed—covered up in designer gowns and crowned by diamond tiaras. The recent scandal involving prominent names circulated the Island exposing tainted love. It gave her a clearer idea of how Palm Beach treats women who secretly desire other women.

It was bad enough that she'd been denied the best tables in Palm Beach restaurants and obligated to take the less premium spot in the ballroom during a charity function, even the ones she helped organize. Despite all that, she held on vehemently to her provincial, Jewish traditions and ancestry and guarded her secrets.

Now widowed, neither sister had ever had children, Tchelet by choice, Varda due to physical complications. Tchelet devoted time to her passion, gardening, and became heavily involved in the Pennsylvania Horticulture Society. Varda was the gentle, artistic sister who conceded to the intolerance.

Tchelet was haunted by their history and feared that if others knew of her constant nightmares of their parents, who were gassed in one of Hitler's concentration camps, it would show weakness.

She was strong, but the past ate away at her.

All of this hatred because she didn't fit the blonde and blue eyed mold of the Master Race,

Seldom did she sleep a night through. Haunting nightmares made frequent visits, the vivid images from so long ago replayed over and over again in her head. Tchelet struggled to understand the cruelty in her past. In particular, one night long ago as young girls, she and Varda hid in a large closet in their home while SS officers stormed their neighborhood of predominately upper-class Jews. It was the horrible sounds of that night that haunted her repeatedly—the shrieks and guttural cries as the Nazis picked and chose who would be next. It was inevitable that their home would be violated, a thought she couldn't bear, reflections that were still with her to this day.

She stared at the tattered pieces of paper that surrounded her feet. The flashback in Tchelet's mind was vivid. It began in the middle of the night, October 1941. There wasn't time to pack anything; they left with only the clothes on their backs. Their cherished little thorn boy statue was left behind along with the final memory of their father. Tears welled up in Tchelet's eyes remembering as he grasped the figurine. In seconds, she and Varda were whisked out the door to safety under the cloak of darkness.

More and more horrors of The War plagued them. Hitler's senseless gruesome experiments on victims—who could have likely been her family—imprisoned in a make shift hospital, once a Berlin asylum, were beyond Tchelet's comprehension until now. Now, she had the upper hand; now, she could take action, and finally, now, she could seek retribution.

They discovered later though a few surviving friends that during the occupation of Germany, the family's home was looted of all its prized antiquities, as were most of the wealthy Jews and European blue-bloods who lost their fortunes. History revealed that priceless heirlooms were scattered to the wind; some ended up in the hands of Nazi officers. Varda, sweet Varda, had hoped for the return of their statue after she read an article in the Jewish Advocate that, at the end of the war, liberating soldiers recovered a variety of articles as war tokens, possibly as a remembrance of where they had been during those awful times.

She prayed that, as an act of humanity, the fighters' consciences would guide them in finding the true owners.

Fortunately, they were able to reclaim much of the fortune their father had hidden in a Swiss bank account. However, all of the treasures they loved were gone. For nearly fifty years, they had been on a quest. Their prized possession, a gift from their father presented at the girls' Bat Mitzvah, was the one thing they wanted to see and touch again. *Thorn Boy* was the only tangible connection to their parents and childhood.

This afternoon, the newcomers to Palm Beach society would prepare for their first fund-raising event of the social season. Every winter season, which extended from November to Easter for seventy decades, Palm Beach hosted over a hundred galas that benefited a wide variety of charities.

Tchelet left the room to fetch a pair of blue Manolo Blahniks from her closet. She returned to her sister's side and said with heart felt love, "We can't ever give up. Father and Mother would finally be able to rest in peace knowing that their most precious gift was home with us, where it belonged. We'll have *Thorn Boy* back again."

This charity event was especially important to them since Varda was diagnosed with Cystic Fibrosis. Their money bought the latest drugs and treatments, but time was running out. Tchelet's desire was to do something wonderfully unique for her sister, whom she deeply loved. Finding the statue would be wonderful, but there was something else she wanted for Varda, too. There wasn't any material gift Tchelet couldn't give her. They had everything except *two* things she wanted most for her sweet sister. What could she do, with her days numbered, for the most important person that remained in her life?

Varda loved roses; they were her favored flower and blue was her signature color. Although the artist masterfully created their images on the dining room wall, Tchelet had found a solution to her challenge in a young, brilliant scientist she met at a Van Gogh exhibition in Amsterdam shortly after The War. His dream would become her dream: creating the world's first, authentic blue rose and naming it after them.

But unforgiving, cunning Tchelet had other intentions. She had a plan for vengeance, and Cornelius Hicks' science was instrumental in that plan.

Chapter 6 —The Blue Rose Bride

UNIVERSITY FLORIST

GAINESVILLE, FLORIDA

"You call this a bridal bouquet? This is the worst looking mess I've ever seen!" She screamed as she snatched the bouquet of dyed blue roses and limp sunflowers from the young designer, threw it on the floor and stomped on it until it was an unrecognizable mashed glob of blue and yellow.

"Can't you understand what I want? Why is this so difficult?"

"CUT," shouted the director. "That was great! I think you captured the drama of the frustrated bride's feelings perfectly. This opening scene will really grab the viewers' attention."

On the other side of the flower shop's front counter, facing the bride, stood florist Emily O'Sullivan, a part-time student at U of F. These early morning tapings were rough. She struggled as her eyes adjusted from the blinding camera lights; it was 6:00 a.m. Only a week into filming, and clearly she started to regret that she agreed to portray the florist who designed the bouquet. Feisty and fed up with the rigors of taping an experimental TV pilot, Emily thought, *Bitch wouldn't know a nice bouquet if it bit her in the ass.*

Emily's second thoughts surfaced as she faced the director. In her raspy voice, she informed him, "When I decided to audition for this project, by the way, appropriately named BRIDAL HORRORS, I had no idea what I had gotten myself into."

"Then why did you agree to do this?" he responded in frustration.

"Well, after weeks of pressure from my friend who's enrolled in the university's film program, I must admit it was the money that finally wooed me." She sighed as her eyes shifted downward. *What have I gotten myself into?*

After the shoot, Emily pulled her unmanageable curly, red locks back with a rubber band revealing her freckle-faced, Irish grin. Weddings had become her specialty because of her attention to detail and willingness to make people happy. She told everyone how much she loved the romance that surrounded the happy occasion. The truth was weddings were big business and Emily loved the money, too. Besides, everybody else in the shop hated dealing with the brides.

From what she had experienced in her three years as a designer, an appointment with a real bride was never this dramatic, but she had been warned; reality TV sold drama. And if she were to admit the truth, it was the *drama* that drew her into watching *Survivor*. But she had discovered that the reality of reality was too much reality.

During the break, in between shoots, she contemplated her appointment the following day with an authentic "horror-bride" named Regina Ball. *This one should be a real doosy.* Emily referred to her as "the screw ball."

Emily struggled with this particular bride's obsession and choices over the Florida Gators football team colors—blue and orange—as her wedding's color palate. God forbid if a friend ever forced her to wear a bright blue bridesmaid's dress accented with an orange sash. She would approve of a sophisticated navy blue or chic periwinkle, but Gator blue? One *large* plus about the wedding, however, was the huge budget, biggest the shop has ever had—twenty thousand dollars, just for flowers and décor. She had already picked out her new car with the bonus.

The thought replayed over and over in her mind: *God, I dread painting all of those roses.*

Emily munched on walnuts during the break while she fumbled through the pages of her script. Folded neatly next to it was the fabric swatch from the bridesmaids' dresses that her real "blue rose bride" mailed earlier. She normally wouldn't strongly object to what a bride chose for her wedding party, but this time would be a real challenge. She had to find flowers that complimented the dress, not harass it. Her reputation was at stake.

She glanced over the counter and watched the director's assistants as they continued to scrub the floor. As hard as they tried to get the paint residue from the dyed blue flowers out of the shop's Astroturf, it remained fused to the plastic bristles.

She prepared the blue dyed flowers for the shoot the old fashioned way, and it was a disaster. The can of spray paint Emily used had become clogged. She pushed a toothpick to unblock it, and paint shot all over the shop's ceiling. She couldn't get the spewing paint can into the trash fast enough. Then she tried to dip the flower heads in dye. The color dripped all over the shop's floor and her, new, white sneakers.

Yesterday, she had read an article in one of the trade publications about a company named Azure, which was based in Melbourne, Australia. There in the lab scientists' worked toward the goal of genetically engineering colors of flowers, particularly roses. She had seen pictures of their success in creating unique, new hues such as violet, purple and mauve in dianthus, what the public knew as carnations, cloned from the purple gene in petunias. The results had given those flowers a revitalized presence in the market place. But roses—very popular with brides—proved to be a more difficult flower to alter because there wasn't a blue color gene in the DNA of a rose.

The actress approached Emily with her attention buried deeply into her lines and said, "This flower business is more than meets the eye."

Emily glanced up and responded, "Flower buyers spend over seven billion dollars annually, and the demand for new colors is increasing especially with blue flowers, which are some of the rarest found in the color spectrum."

Emily reached under the counter and pulled out the trade magazine she had read earlier. She flipped to certain pages that showed rose varieties and pointed to one. "They are not actually blue but a lilac color. Without painting, which I detest, obtaining the exact blue hue is seemingly impossible."

Emily flung one last fist full of walnuts into her mouth while she recalled yesterday's horticulture class lecture. She was eager to impress the actress with what she'd learned. "The primary plant pigment, delphinidin, gives blue hues to flowers, such as hydrangeas, violets and delphinium. It's also an anti-oxidant. Delphinidin is pH sensitive and is affected by the acidity in the soil. Pink hydrangeas turn blue with the change of the pH balance in the soil. When I was a little girl, I remembered my mother pushed rusty nails, or poured pickle juice onto the soil at the base of her hydrangeas to alter the acidity and keep the color blue.

"It sounds like the science of flowers is pretty intense."

"Ooookaaaay break's over," shouted the director. "Let's get the next segment."

Emily hesitated for a moment and returned to the counter staring face-to-face with her, already geared up for their next altercation.

"This doesn't come close to matching my colors," yelled the pretend bride. "Now what are you going to do?"

Eyes rolled to the back of her head, she thought *Jesus H,* as Emily contemplated what she would like to do with those flowers, and it wouldn't be pretty!

As she clicked the lock in the flower shop door, Emily glanced at her watch, 6:00 PM. She loved working in the business of flowers but was glad this day was behind her. The show taping sucked the very life from her. She looked both ways then darted across the street to her waiting car.

Emily's hippie dad had given her his second car to use in Gainesville. It was an old, bright blue Volkswagen Beetle that sounded like a lawn mower as it chugged down the street. She had fondly named it 'Janice'. Thank God the car was generally reliable. Her father had secured a bike carrier to its front near the storage area, where she kept her helmet and pads. After a nasty fall several months ago, she had become much more safety minded. To keep fit, Emily peddled to the shop on nice days.

She hurried to meet up with her boyfriend, Derrick. Emily fumbled impatiently with her macramé key chain, finally unlocked the car door and tossed her bag onto the seat.

She was keen to hear about his first day at school.

They met when Emily was touring the university six months ago. She had just left the brick, two story, admissions office when she observed the strikingly handsome lad from about twenty yards away as he exited his pickup truck. It was one of those smart, compact pickups that was sporty and functional. A vehicle said something about its owner. This truck said "fun and smart".

A little insecure, she chose to ignore her feeling and reacted on impulse. She smiled and gave a slight wave across the parking lot. She fully expected no reciprocity. Much to her surprise, he approached. His features that appealed to her from a distance were enhanced as he came closer and allured her even more. The palms of her hands began to sweat, a nervous reaction she fought and detested since sixth grade. Her automatic reaction was to fold her arms tightly under one another as she tried to hide her pollen-stained fingers, but it also sent a false signal—disinterested. Quite the contrary, Emily was enamored.

His high cheekbones and strong, square jaw presented the young man's face as perfectly symmetrical, one of the hallmarks of beauty. His nose was long but wide creating a balance of both the rugged and the elegant. As though he'd just stepped out of Greek mythology, Derrick's exquisite, Aryan-like qualities were exceptional.

Hand extended, he breached the awkward moment. Emily relaxed her straight-jacket stance as her hand made contact with his. His powerful, callused hand enveloped her dainty fingers. It was as though he was handling a baby chick, so *gentle*. He had put her immediately at ease. She loosened up and enjoyed their first touch.

Unable to take her eyes off him, she didn't want to relinquish the moment. She wanted to invite him for coffee, brunch, a beer...something? Emily abandoned an old idea—let the boy ask first—and blurted out an awkward request. He accepted.

An unmistakable chemistry occurred between the two of them. It had always been her motto to date several boys at the same time. The time had come for her to rethink her motto now that her heart has spoken so clearly.

Darkness had fallen; thank God Derrick's dorm wasn't too far from the shop.

She loved the evenings. Even though it was still warm, the changing season had settled in with shorter days. Two speeding tickets in the past three months struck a chord and told her to slow down. She was excited about seeing him but was mindful of the posted 35 MPH speed limit. If she got one more ticket, her dad was taking the VW Beetle, and she would be biking to work and school everyday.

Emily pulled up in front of the dormitory building a half an hour later and slammed into the concrete car stop. The little car jerked back. She clicked the ignition off and yanked the emergency brake. With purse in hand, she flung the door open, bumped it shut with her hip and darted up the three flights of concrete stairs her skirt flapping about.

She banged on the door with the open palm of her hand. Embarrassed, she noticed the green crud under her fingernails and wished she'd taken a few minutes, back at the shop, to scrape it out. She doubted Derrick would care about her nasty fingernails if he shared her feelings at all. He eased open the door.

"Where are we going tonight?" she asked, and then realized that Derrick's mind was elsewhere. His eyes were focused on the floor rather than making contact with hers. His expression was not the typical joyous one she loved so. No bright smile, no embrace, something was eating away at him. He told her about the sweet girl with the pretty smile and a rose tattoo he met at the book store that had now disappeared. At first Emily was a little jealous. Derrick seemed a little too captivated by his new friend; then she realized that he was only concerned about what could have happened to her.

He said, "No one at the administration office has heard anything. Today a lieutenant from the Gainesville Police Department told me her rented cottage looked as though she'd left for the day. The bed was made and all her clothes and personal items were in place. The obvious things were missing: her purse and school supplies she needed for class."

Emily said in a meek tone that occasionally faded in and out, "This is really creepy. How could someone just disappear?"

Derrick shrugged his shoulders and responded, "I have had this very bad feeling in my gut since this morning. From what I could tell, there wasn't any reason anyone would want to hurt her."

Emily added, "And if she's okay, what's the explanation? Hey, maybe she's part of a cult like Patricia Hearst and the PLO, abducted by the groups' leaders and brainwashed."

"What? Where do you come up with this stuff?"

"Well, most people don't tell you their life story when you first meet them, sweetie. Maybe she's an heiress. If she had something secretive going on in her life, it's not going to be broadcasted."

"Hey, listen to this," she rapidly changed the subject without taking a breath. "I had this wacked-out bride in the shop who wanted *blue* roses for her wedding. Couldn't believe how much meaning she placed on those hideous, dyed flowers especially since there are other *natural* blue flowers. Besides, there's something about a blue rose that doesn't seem quite right, unnatural. I can only imagine she has plenty of issues. I pity the poor guy marrying her. He's probably in for a lot of surprises."

Emily tilted her head to one side and turned the corners of her mouth upward as she worked at capturing his attention with the distraction, but it was in vain. Obviously, the matter had consumed Derrick. It pained her to see him fretting over a situation that might resolve itself in the next day or so when the missing girl could show up. Then, the thought crossed her mind that she really didn't know everything about Derrick. She had only seen him in happy times. This was another side, and she had to take his feelings seriously if she wanted to remain in the relationship. She detected that he wouldn't tolerate insensitivity. In a move to show him she cared, Emily stood on her toes and put her arms around Derrick's broad shoulders. "Let me take you out for dinner. I know there isn't anything I can say to make you feel better, but us being together, especially when you're feeling down, is all I have to offer."

She did it. She managed to get a little grin out of him even if his mood change was only temporary. It was unrealistic of her to think that there wouldn't be any bumps in the road during their relationship. She needed to show him that she was there in spite of what could happen.

Chapter 7 —The Business of Death

"I don't understand why you'd want to be a funeral director," said Bernice Johnson to her only daughter in a fit of exasperation. "There are so many other *nice* careers out there."

Judy suppressed a sigh. She'd had this same conversation weekly with her mother for almost a year now. Once more she turned to her mom and attempted again to explain why she felt this was her calling. "Mother, I want to be there for people when they are most vulnerable. Remember when Daddy died, and how you felt?"

Bernice's eyes looked initially at the floor, but then she slowly raised them and made contact with her daughter's. She was gradually coming around, but not without concern. "Judy, I don't think being with people in mourning all the time is best for someone with your, well, condition."

Judy struggled with periodic bouts of depression preceded by panic attracts. A learned skill—she had it drilled into her head by her mother to keep her illness to her self. One of her coping techniques, Judy would lock herself away in her bedroom in a fetal position holding her knees against her chest as hard as she could. "Is it time to refill you prescription? I'm making a trip to the drugstore today." Her mother taught her that complaining never solved anything as she preached, "Judy, it's nobody's business. Do you hear me complaining? Its part of life, deal with it." Her mother seemed especially adapt to that popular cliché of brushing issues under the rug.

Judy Johnson had always felt that she was a unique person. She didn't want to fit in at school with the popular crowd.

Judy's view on life drove her to hang out with, actually seek out, the underdogs. When she was on her medication, she had no problem conversing with just about anyone; she was aware that she had great social skills.

Judy acknowledged, but wasn't vein about, her striking features: long, luminous, blonde hair; piercing blue eyes surrounded with thick eyelashes and smooth, silky skin. But she'd rather have been appreciated for her quick wit, sensitivity and intelligence.

Mortuary school wasn't her first choice. Her boyfriend, Ben Freeman, suggested it. At first, she thought he was kidding. But when he pulled out the literature, she realized this was a serious conversation.

Judy grew up in a well maintained, Boca Raton enclave consisting of people mostly from northern European ancestry disparagingly referred to as WASPs—an acronym she detested. She hated labels and defended each person's individuality fiercely. Judy freely accepted those around her. She relocated from the hustle and bustle of Chicago with her parents when they moved to South Florida. She was only two. Her mother was comforted by the people who were much like themselves. Nearly everybody in the neighborhood was tall, blonde and blue-eyed—collectively, an interesting ethnic contrast of people nestled amongst the many exclusive, Jewish gated developments.

Judy's tomboy behavior was one more facet of her diversity. She filled in nicely for the son her father never had by spending time with him at Slim's Fish Camp. One weekend a month they celebrated father/daughter time—without her mother—as they cast their lines from the shores of Lake Okeechobee. Her favorite moments was of her father laughing at her struggling to get the night crawlers onto the hook.

Judy loved to spent time on the beach reading romance novels when she wasn't with Ben. After a while, his suggestion to attend mortuary school made sense. She figured, with all of the seniors moving to Florida, the funeral business would be a good way to stay employed. That kind of thinking, that she would even consider this notion, alone made Judy different from most.

"That tattoo, Judy. What possessed you to mar your beautiful skin with that ugly blue rose tattoo?" Bernice questioned Judy trying to understand her daughter's seemingly uncharacteristic deed.

"A group of girlfriends at school decided to get them. It's so small, Mother, hardly noticeable," said Judy as she rubbed the tiny artwork scored into her arm just above the elbow. "I purposely got the smallest one available, so it wouldn't attract so much attention. It could have been bigger, Mother, *much* bigger."

Bernice took in a deep breath and mumbled, "Stubborn girl."

Judy excelled in school. There were only a few months left to the program, and already, Judy had begun her internship in her boyfriend's family-owned mortuary. It was a perfect opportunity because few family-owned funeral homes were left in South Florida. Most were bought up by national conglomerates, which left out the personal touch Judy thought was so important.

She darted up the stairs frustrated with the same "doting mother" conversation and called Ben.

"What a bummer you have to work this weekend," she protested.

"I know, but I should still have plenty time to spend with Derrick and meet his new girlfriend," Ben replied. "Dad doesn't need me both days, all day long; it's just for a few hours on Saturday afternoon."

"Yea, but it still throws a wrench into my weekend birthday celebration," she replied.

"That's the business. When duty calls, Freeman & Son answer," retorted Ben.

The sacrifice was minimal. Ben enjoyed his work. Judy knew that he truly admired his dad, and so did she. Mr. Freeman was an extremely compassionate man. It was obvious when Judy observed him speaking with bereaved family members while they made pre-need or at-need arrangements. Mr. Freeman would tell Ben and Judy. "It takes a special kind of person to do this work."

Ben admitted to Judy that his life had changed in an instant. He fell in love the minute he saw gorgeous, tall Judy Johnson enter the front door of the Central County Blood Depository office to fill out a job application. He was there working part-time.

Ben was certain their relationship was meant to be because, while most of his girlfriends cringed at the idea of him working in the funeral industry, Judy totally accepted it.

Ben would tell everyone in her presence, which had become a little embarrassing, "Judy has eyes you can dive into. They're like giant pools of water surrounded by white sandy shores."

"Well, I gotta run," Ben said.

"I'll wrap up at the funeral home around four and call you," he comforted Judy. "We will have plenty of time to drive up and meet Derrick. Besides, they were driving down from Gainesville late last night and probably will want to sleep late and spend time with Grandma Ma."

Judy, with some reluctance, agreed.

She returned the receiver to its cradle of her Princess Anne phone on her bedside stand. Judy was proud of her professional choice, and it showed. As she apprenticed in the funeral home with bereaved parents, she realized the service value of being a funeral director. She had a special gift that brought comfort when it came to the loss of a child or teenager.

"Where're you going tonight, Judy?" Bernice Johnson questioned her daughter after she retuned down the stairs.

"Ben and I are meeting his buddy, Derrick and Derrick's girlfriend, Emily. They drove down from Gainesville last night to spend time with Ma."

"So you're going to Belle Glade?" Bernice said doubtfully.

"Yes, as soon as Ben is finished at the funeral home. He'll stop by here and pick me up," responded Judy.

"What are you going to do in Belle Glade?" Bernice said with a raised eye brow.

"I don't know, Mother, just hang out I guess. Here we go again with another interrogation. First, it's my career choice, now it's my social life!"

"I'm just concerned, Judy. You know how much I love you." Bernice reached inside the closed kitchen drawer and handed her daughter a box festooned with a balloon motif and wrapped in primary color ribbons. "Happy 20th Birthday, Judy!"

Judy's defensive mood immediately turned receptive. "Oh Mother!"

Beaming, she graciously accepted the beautifully decorated box. Judy's delicate hands danced over the chiffon wired edge ribbon carefully untying and removing the wrapping. Inside was a blue silk scarf, exactly the color of Judy's intense eyes. Judy removed the scarf from its box to embellish her ensemble.

"Beautiful, Mother; I love it! Thank you. Now don't you worry; I always feel safe when I'm with Ben," Judy said eye-to-eye as she attempted to reassure her mother, then sealed it with a hug.

Judy knew her mother liked Ben. He was a handsome kid who came from a good family and was dedicated to the funeral business. However, every time he shook her mother's hand, she would later express her uneasiness to Judy about it saying, "Where were those hands today?"

"Now, Mother, any other stipulations?"

Ben's black Cadillac Fleetwood pulled into the driveway.

"Well, we always ride in style," said Judy as she turned away from the window and giggled.

Always the gentleman, Ben called for Judy the old fashioned way—at her door.

"Good evening, it's nice to see you again, Mrs. Johnson," said Ben as he smiled and extended his hand politely.

"Good evening, Ben," Mrs. Johnson responded, then prodded for more information.

"Judy tells me you two are off to see a high school friend."

"Yes, he's my best buddy. We met while playing high school football. He's a Belle Glade native raised by his grandmother. Derrick started school at the University of Florida, but he's home for a weekend visit."

"We'll be fine, Mother," Judy chimed in. "I'll call should the evening go later than expected."

The sun started to set as it left golden, yellow streaks against the sapphire sky. A few stars gradually twinkled in the east. Ben held the passenger door for Judy as Bernice Johnson watched from the living room window. Judy glanced up and gave her a quick smile and wave. She lowered the vanity mirror on the sun visor and flipped her hair over her shoulders. Her long, golden tresses, accented with her new scarf, were stunning against the camel colored, leather seats of the luxurious automobile. Ben steered his way down the driveway in the shiny, sleek sedan.

They were committed to make a difference in the business of death.

Chapter 8 –Blue Roses and Muck

After all these years teaching at the university, Stanley Hicks's passion adorned him daily. The students who began each new school year were always special to him; although sometimes they'd never know it by the way he acted. A few referred to him as being apathetic; however, he knew nothing could be further from the truth. He grinned as he heard them quietly in the halls. Stanley was firmly dedicated to his students, and as each one of them understood him better, that became more apparent.

With his back to the class, Stanley began writing notes on the black board with broad, sweeping strokes, as though he was conducting an orchestra.

Lined up like soldiers along the edge of Stanley's desk were jars of soil neatly labeled from different counties around Florida. He turned and carefully held each one up to the light as it streamed through the windows. Stanley tilted each jar from side to side as he directed the students' attention to the small samples. There were so many types. He defined them. The coastal area had a sandy texture, composed of millions of years of shells that washed onto shore and compressed into shell rock.

As Stanley proceeded to the next sample labeled MUCK, Derrick, seated in the first row, raised his hand. "Dr. Hicks, may I offer to the class what I know about muck?"

Surprised by the invitation, the professor invited him to the front of the room with a single hand gesture.

"Go ahead."

Derrick proceeded, commanding attention as he stood with perfect posture before the assembly of students. Each pair of eyes focused directly on him.

"The center of the state is rich, black muck—a pure organic matter that is the product of years of accumulation. It contains no mineral content. Muck soil oxidizes and disappears when exposed to air. Sand can be added to give it stability. In Belle Glade we refer to as 'Black Gold'. The lake region is one of the largest for producing winter vegetables like corn, green beans and sugar cane. It's no wonder that anything planted in this muck grew like a weed. At one time, nearly the entire region was underwater. It was formed over millions of years, and the 'River of Grass' covered an area almost coast to coast flowing into the Florida Bay. Unfortunately, our generation will have to deal with urban sprawl and farming, which has had a devastating impact on the Everglades. Politicians, environmentalists and locals are battling it out to restore what once was and still farm the land. Actually, I believe, it will never be what it once was."

Derrick took his seat. Stanley stood at his desk and applauded him. The class followed. "Derrick, I'm impressed by your detailed description of the jar's contents, as well as your unbridled passion for the environment."

Derrick responded, "Is this sample really from the lake region, Dr. Hicks?"

The question seemed to startle the professor as he abruptly turned around and made eye contact with his inquisitive student.

Yes, I gathered it myself two days ago. Why do you ask?"

"Well, sir, my grandmother has this beautiful rose garden in Belle Glade where I grew up. She has just about every color rose you can imagine. I mentioned to her that it would be amazing if she could grow a blue rose, that I'll bet, if we put the right combination of elements together in that rich muck, we could do it. Scientists change the color of flowers all of the time by influencing the soil with different elements, which happen to be the same as in our bodies. There must be a way. She just laughs at me.

She says what in the world would someone do with a blue rose.

A blue rose doesn't mean anything; it's not like red or white. We would have to come up with a whole other reason to give someone a blue rose. But, my girlfriend is a florist, and she says customers ask for them all the time. For weddings, funerals and a lot of other reasons, so blue roses could be popular if they existed. But sir, I've spent many an hour working with her in the garden, and I don't ever recall the soil that I shoveled around her bushes having that reddish color."

Stanley countered, "My twin brother is a horticulturalist; he lives down there near Belle Glade. Actually, it was *he* that provided *this* particular sample."

Hicks scratched his chin and said, "Well, Derrick, you've just given me an idea for the whole class, one that will start out the school year with a challenge. I want each of you to write a report on how soil affects plants focusing on how the elements in soil affect the color of flowers, particularly blue, since its thought that they would be so popular with the public."

Stanley Hicks turned and faced the board, immediately digging into the subject of the day, horticultural cornmeal. A jar of white, flakey material was introduced to the collection. The product, a natural disease fighter, was a solution for black spots on roses.

As he passed through the room, he held the containerized example close up. Derrick noticed what looked to be a fungus under one of his fingernails—a condition called onchomycosis, associated with people who had their hands in water or moist soil. The fungus spores attach themselves beneath the nail and begin to feed on the nail's cells. Difficult to get rid of.

Derrick, perpetually inquisitive, piped up, again.

"Get your nail fungus from digging in the garden, Dr. Hicks?"

The teacher quickly curled his fingers inward and studied all four nails, then remarked, "Why, yes."

"Maybe the horticultural cornmeal can treat that, too."

The class chuckled.

Stanley smiled, remarkably amused.

The bell sounded.

After Derrick departed from the classroom, thinking about his blue roses, he noticed a group of students huddled together in the hallway. They were rallied by the one he had the altercation with defending Julie's reputation. They seemed to be having their own private session, and it was clear that he wasn't invited. This time the topic he overheard was Professor Hick's horrible deformity. Derrick hated it when people gossiped about others. A feeling he shared with his Professor.

Derrick approached reminding them. "Remember what he said, that he and his brother were in a terrible fire. Their home was burnt to the ground. They barely escaped alive. That explains his fear of smoke. You should be glad that you don't have something like that to deal with everyday." The group disbanded, some with their heads down. However, he noticed their ring leader sporting a jacket with the Olympic logo emblazed on the sleeve looking back over his shoulder, smirking in Derrick's direction.

Chapter 9 – A Blue Moon

"Hurry up!" Emily shouted to Derrick. "It's nearly a five hour drive; by the time we get down there, it will be time to turn around." She was anxious about her first introduction to Derrick's grandmother, who surely must have been a saint in a past life. Emily hoped that she would meet Grandma Ma's expectations. According to what she'd heard her boyfriend told his grandmother about her, Emily had a lot of measuring up to do. Her insecurity resurfaced again. She didn't want to sabotage the relationship with obsessive questioning and look like a pathetic, neurotic school girl. She needed to do some self-evaluating.

Her past experiences didn't help, though, because guys can be such jerks! Especially when it came to lying, she couldn't deal with it. Derrick certainly wasn't a liar, just the opposite; he always did what he said he would do. She hated the insecurities that she harbored, justifying that life's a bitch at times, and its' lessons can sometimes better your psyche. *Just remember this is a new guy...shed the fear and go forth, a challenging concept*, she thought.

"You can't stuff too much in 'Janice,'" she told him.

"I don't intend to. I just have a few cloths to take back." Emily was entertaining fantasies of the two of them sharing an apartment next term, but she didn't want to push it. Too soon.

"Sorry I was running late today. I decided to take a CPR class and this was the only one with an opening. I've had it on my mind with Ma getting up there in years, and well, you just don't know when you'll need to know it. One of the instructors mentioned saving someone life in a restaurant a few night ago.

The guy stood and then keeled over having a heart attack. If it weren't for my coach he'd been a goner."

See, she thought, what a great guy; always thinking of how he can help others. Why do I buy into this insecurity nonsense?

Derrick said to Emily as he shoved another box into the tiny car, "We're going to have a great time. I want you to meet a couple of fantastic friends of mine who are attending Dade County Community College."

"What are they studying?"

"They're in mortuary school."

"What?" she responded, horrified.

"Yea, they're going to be funeral directors. Ben's family has been in the industry for generations. They actually live upstairs from the funeral home in a pretty swanky apartment."

"Creepy," Emily remarked. "I don't care how nice the place is."

"Ben met Judy where they worked. Judy actually changed her major after they started dating."

"Let me guess, at the blood bank?" She joked with a nudge to his side.

"Right, how did you know?" Derrick answered.

Emily threw her hands up. "That figures. Well, this should be an interesting weekend hanging out with two vampires. Maybe we should rent *Love at First Bite*."

"That movie was over ten years ago."

Derrick gave her a disapproving look. She decided not to push the subject with her distorted sense of humor. Emily was sharp enough to realize that he was a gentleman choosing to ignore her mockery.

"It's truly amazing what one college guy can fit into a VW," announced Derrick standing proud with his hands on his hips. The entire back seat and small trunk area in the front of the car were filled with his duffel bag, a suit case and two over stuffed garment bags.

"Why are you bringing all this?"

"These clothes need to be mended: some are missing buttons and my pants are too long. Ma will fix them."

Engine rattling away, with Emily behind the wheel, the two U of F students hit the road.

"I heard a rumor about you yesterday just after leaving class."

"Rumor?" said Derrick puzzled. "And what did you hear?"

"Crazy, really, as most rumors are; you're being linked to some sort of campus cult, like you're their ring leader or something."

"Cult...what!"

"I said it was crazy." She hollered over the rattling engine.

"There's a group of kids, one in particular, circulating this. Something about an Aryan League; did you do something to piss off someone?"

"The only thing I can think of is defending Julie Rose's honor to a group of idiots who were running her reputation into the ground without knowing her. Obviously, they don't know me either if this is the kind of nonsense their spreading."

"That Rose girl was mentioned, too. She was part of it, or you were recruiting her, or some crazy crap."

"Yea, that's crazy for sure."

"Well, that's what I said when I heard it, but you know how rumors go; it's like guilty until proven innocent. You're going to have to find this guy and put a stop to it."

"I think he's jealous because Dr. Hicks showed interest in what I was sharing with the class. Well, when I see him again, we will have a nice chat; man-to-man...you know what I mean?"

"Great, well enough of that; let's go see this amazing rose garden you keep telling me about," she said as the little blue car pealed out onto the highway.

Southbound traffic on I-75 was heavy as usual on a Friday evening. Emily, with both hands firmly planted on the wheel, felt every car that raced passed them as her diminutive 'Janice' shimmied down the highway.

Derrick shouted over the clamoring engine as she steered the rickety contraption down the freeway, "You'd be a goner if something larger than a motorcycle hit you."

"Hey, don't complain; besides it's just until I become a TV star, and I can afford a bigger and better car," Emily yelled back.

At that second, Emily saw in her rear view mirror a driver coming up behind them with blazing head lights nearly forcing them off the road. The reckless driver passed them on the left side with such force the wind violently shook the little Bug. It happened so fast, but Emily felt the van clip the oversized bike rack mounted onto her front bumper.

"Asshole!" screamed Emily fearfully as she struggled to keep the car under control. "That maniac scared the shit out of me!" Her heart pounded against her rib bones.

The last thing she wanted was for her family to get a visit from the cops.

"Let's just take it easy," he said. "Remember those old Florida tags 'Arrive Alive?'"

"Yea, I'd like to find that guy and bang one over his head," she said clutching the steering wheel with a white-knuckled grip.

By the time they arrived, still unnerved by the near incident, it was late and very dark. "There aren't any street lights in this part of town," Derrick remarked as she pulled onto the gravel driveway. The only light before her had come from a small porch lamp as mosquitoes buzzed around it. The moon was a bright, gaseous bubble that hung low in the night sky.

Even in the dimly lit field, just to the side of the house, Emily could see the gorgeous, rose bushes Derrick bragged about. As a florist, she appreciated exceptionally beautiful flowers.

"Wow! Look at those!"

"I told you," Derrick said. "Everything out here grows like crazy in this muck."

As they walked up to the white, wood, frame house, the sweet fragrance filled her nostrils. "I suggested to Grandma Ma that she enter those in the Palm Beach County Fair. They would take every ribbon the judges handed out."

"Now, Derrick, stop bragging," came a sing-song voice from the other side of screen door.

"Ma, this is Emily."

Emily grinned as the door's spring retractor creaked open. Before her was a matronly, full-figured woman in a floral print dress. Her hair was styled in a 60's classic bouffant. She still had her apron neatly tucked around her from preparing supper.

"We don't shake hands here, dear," she announced as Ma threw her generous arms around Emily's neck giving her a kiss on the cheek. "You're family as far as I am concerned." Her crisp, clean fragrance drifted up Emily's nostrils easing any doubt she'd be welcomed.

"You must be tired, come in and rest."

Emily followed Derrick with two bags in hand through the doorway into the front parlor. An areca palm in a large cachepot graced the corner of the room. Its fronds waved in harmony as each blade of the ceiling fan passed by. Each piece of immaculate, French provincial furniture was strategically placed within the room. A bowl of fully opened, white roses loosely arranged graced the coffee table. The open windows allowed a breeze flapping through the informal, lace curtains. Their heels tapped against the wooden floor as the three made their way toward the kitchen.

"Just put your bags in the hallway. We'll take them upstairs later. I've got a meal about ready to be put on the table. You must be starved."

Emily was charmed. She could clearly see why Derrick missed his home and his Ma. After her stomach was filled with seconds, Emily pushed back from the table tugging at her blouse. "No more for me. This is the most I've eaten since last Thanksgiving." She was self conscience of her abdomen's protrusion and thought it was unattractive.

Derrick rubbed his belly in hearty satisfaction. "That was great, Ma."
"Glad you enjoyed it dear. I still have your favorite dessert, apple pie-a-la-mode."

"Oh, I don't know if I can eat one more bite," said Emily as she discreetly reached under the table and released the top button on her slacks.

"Well, take a few minutes and carry your things upstairs. Later you can come back down for a little treat."

Alone in the guest room, Emily could hear Derrick in the room next door as he opened and shut the dresser drawers. Enveloped in a comfortable feeling, she tended to her needs searching through her travel bag for makeup remover and toothpaste. Moments later she approached the bathroom, thinking it was vacant. She stopped. Through the slightly ajar door she saw Derrick; his naked back was toward her. Her eyes delightfully followed his spine, deeply inset between beautifully defined trapezius muscles. She traced his backbone all the way down to the crevasse separating his buttocks. She stared as if hypnotized; a tingling sensation came over her body voiding any guilt of spying.

His golden hair grew so quickly. It caressed his neck in such a way that would make any woman envious. So handsome...so beautiful, she pinched herself, finding it hard to believe this man thought so much of her that he wanted her to meet his grandmother.

Emily waited patiently back in her room until she heard Derrick's bedroom door handle click shut. As she entered the bathroom, the first thing she noticed was the claw foot tub. Its sturdy form sat securely on tiny, black and white tiles. A curtain rod encircled it overhead repeating the oval shape. Steam from the hot water tap rose and framed the mirror above the sink. She scrubbed the road dirt from her face until her shiny complexion reflected back. The stress of the trip down was now a distant memory. She returned to her quaint room. Its floral print, wallpapered walls reminded her of her grandmother's house. Emily climbed into the twin bed. Her body sunk protectively into the down mattress.

She took comfort in knowing that Derrick was on the opposite side of the wall. Emily cushioned her head on the delicately scented pillow case and drifted off.

The next morning, she watched from her bedroom window as Derrick stepped out onto the small front porch surrounded by a freshly white painted railing, down the steps onto the rock driveway. He was still in his pajamas. He turned, looked up and waved to her as she peered from her perch. Emily could feel the cool morning air as it rushed through the thin screen tickling her upper lip. She felt like Rapunzel at any moment casting her imaginary locks below for her prince to climb.

Derrick called up to her. “Wake up, sleepy head.”

Emily smiled back.

Coffee percolated on the stove top; its aroma filled the upstairs and captured Emily’s attention as she drew several deep breaths. *One could get real used to this*, she thought.

She had grown up in a house with five sisters, and each morning they fought to get into the bathroom much like grappling the last seat on the bus at rush hour. What a luxury to be able to take as long as you like. The thought lasted only a few minutes however, interrupted by the clanging of pots and pans in the kitchen below. She suspected Ma was putting a hearty breakfast on the table. She should offer to help.

“She may be up there in age, but she can still down a full meal,” Derrick whispered into Emily’s ear as her wooden chair creaked after she sat down.

The radio was on in the kitchen just loud enough to hear it from the dining room. “I like to get my news in the morning,” she said as she turned to both of them and handed over a basket of piping hot biscuits. The steam was rising from beneath the cloth napkin. “You’ll need a good breakfast to get the day started off on the right foot,” she said. “My husband always had a good breakfast. ‘The most important meal of the day,’ he always said.” Emily took the basket from her acknowledging the advice with a nod.

“You know, dear, Derrick’s grandfather was a Congressional Medal of Honor recipient. He died in WWII close to the end of the war. He almost made it home, but now he’s buried in a military cemetery just outside of a small town, Epinal, located in Eastern France, almost to the German border. Derrick promises that someday we will go there."

Emily glanced at a magnificent, framed tribute of the old woman's much-loved husband. It hung in the dining room just over a side board. The elaborate collage displayed the ornate medal, a photo of Ma with Derrick's grandfather, a newspaper article publishing his disappearance, his wallet, dog tags and the last handwritten letter she had received. Framed, hanging to the right of the tribute, was a certificate of valor and an aerial photo of the cemetery.

Emily was captivated by the nostalgic remembrance lovingly displayed on the wall. It appeared nearly everything in the house had historical significance, each item beholding a story. A small white statue displayed on the side board, just below the collage of her husband's memorabilia, seemed especially endearing. It was of a young boy sitting on a rock picking a thorn from his foot. The grandmother must have noticed her staring at the statue, and her voice turned serious.

"My husband made his army buddy swear on the battlefield that if anything happened to him, it would be delivered to me after the war." Emily diverted her eyes back to her hostess and responded, "Really?"

"Yes, he's called *Thorn Boy*. As you can see his request was honored," she said as she pointed to the statue. "My husband knew about my affinity for sculpture. I would drag him to every antique show in the county when we were dating. I was told that this was acquired on a raid of Nazi Headquarters, but he must have had it with him when he died. See, it has traces of his blood on it." Her attention turned back to the breakfast table.

"As you can see, I don't believe in skimpy breakfasts," said Ma. "And when I don't have visitors, I still serve up the same for a couple of fellas who help me maintain my garden. It's a labor of love, but I couldn't handle it alone.

After breakfast, Derrick will have to show you his handy work; it's quite impressive," she added.

"We could see the roses in the moonlight as we drove up; they are so beautiful," Emily said before she gobbled up another fork full of scrambled eggs.

Moments later the calm was broken by a static filled broadcast over the tiny radio in the kitchen window.

A second missing student from the University of Florida in Gainesville was discovered late yesterday.

"Oh no, another one gone!" gasped Derrick.

Ma stood up and ambled into the other room making an attempt to tune the radio in a little better. As the three listened in astonishment to the vague news report, Ma shook her head and said, "What is going on up there?"

"We'll be okay, Ma," Derrick answered nervously.

Ma scooted back from the table and stood. She reached over for Derrick's plate and carried it to the kitchen. "You two go ahead and enjoy your day; I'll take care of these".

Hand-in-hand Emily and Derrick strolled toward the impressive, stone grotto about two hundred feel from the house. Its details had become more remarkable as she got closer. "This is amazing! You built this all by yourself?"

"I sure did," Derrick said proudly as he stood tall, blew on his finger nails buffing them against his outward extended chest.

"Does she walk all the way out here daily?" whispered Emily as she brushed next to Derrick, feeling a strong sense of pride in this exceptional man.

"She said she does. I can tell that she's less confident about her footing in the loose soil, though. I suggested that she only walk this distance when her helpers are within calling distance."

They sat in silence on one of the benches that flanked each side of the niche that towered over head. "You know, you could have weddings out here!"

Derrick turned to her in amazement. "What?"

"Sure. It's perfect: gorgeous roses, a beautiful backdrop. I could see a fabulous arrangement perched in that niche. The guests chairs could be arranged in a semi- circle, and the ceremony could take place right here," she suggested pointing.

Derrick gave her one of his looks, the one she recognized when a sermon was about to follow.

"Is making money all you think about?" he blurted out.

Emily returned the expression.

"Where would people park?" He continued.

"They would have to traipse all the way out here dressed formally. Besides, I don't think Ma would appreciate strangers as they meandered through here and pinched off her rose buds."

"Don't be so negative. All I was saying was what a beautiful place this would be for a ceremony. I didn't consider the logistics. You know how I love to romanticize," Emily cooed as she ran her fingers through Derrick's thick, blonde hair and dreamt of her own wedding one day on this very spot.

"Remember that crazy bride I had this week?" Emily broke the silence, "the one with the blue roses and the Gator's theme?"

Derrick strained and then shook his head yes.

"Here's another crazy thought for you as long as I am coming up with these 'doosies' for ideas. What if you had a garden filled with blue roses, real ones?"

"*You* sound like the horticulturist," Derrick remarked. "It's really weird you brought this up. Yesterday, in class, I got off on a tangent about how a soil's elements can affect plants. Well, afterwards, the professor assigned everyone in the class to write a report on the subject. Mine is specific to how the soil affects the color. So I have that to look forward to when I return."

"I'll lend you a trade magazine with an article in it I read last week. There's a company, Azure, based in Melbourne, Australia that figured out a way to get carnations to accept the purple color gene from petunias.

I heard they are working on a blue rose; so far the results are only producing lavender ones, not nearly as exciting. Supposedly, they have collaborated with a company in Japan that is actually growing test samples.

Imagine, it would be like the *Wizard of Oz* when Dorothy and her friends skipped through the field of poppies! You could charge a fortune for people to see a garden of blue roses, not to mention what crazy brides would pay to get married here. With the money you'd make, you could build a beautiful paver stone walkway through the garden leading to the grotto and a parking lot!"

"You are too much!" Derrick expressed grinning broadly. "Will you keep me posted on this amazing, scientific process? In the meantime, I don't recommend you quit your real job. Oh, look at that." He glanced down at his watch.

"It's getting late, we'd better head back."

"Hey, that's what makes life exciting, dreaming about new ideas," Emily retorted in defense of her vision.

Derrick took her hand once more as they stepped high over the rows of bushes. He said turning back to her, "Well, watch out...sometimes dreams can turn into nightmares."

"Maybe we should head to the coast tonight. Let's go to Palm Beach and have dinner," Derrick remarked to Emily, who was still excited about the blue roses.

Right then, Ma called from upstairs, "There's a mighty fancy car coming up the road."

"Wow, we're traveling in style tonight!" Derrick shouted with enthusiasm as he ran toward the front door. Derrick met Ben and Judy on the front porch wrapping his muscular arms around them. He hadn't seen his best friends in months.

"Come on in; I want to you meet my sweetie."

Nervously, Emily arose from the sofa and extended her hand to Judy. She then uncomfortably repeated the gesture to Ben.

"Never mind the handshaking," said Ben as he ignored it and embraced her in a big bear hug.

"Derrick has told us how talented you are."

Growing up in a non demonstrative atmosphere, Emily felt her back stiffen, uneasy with all the hugging that people seem to do around here.

Emily turned and gave Derrick a surprised look, "He did?"

"You're a floral designer, right?" Ben said.

"Yes, I work part-time in a shop while I attend classes at U of F. I love it. Everyday is different. People are a little crazy sometimes, but it's great."

"I can tell you stories about crazy people!" said Ben interrupting Emily. "Just last week we had this very wealthy family in; they made funeral arrangements for their grandmother."

At that moment Ben turned to see if Ma was within ear shot. He quickly lowered his voice to just above a whisper and continued on:

"They had this special dress they wanted to put her in for the viewing so we told them to drop it off the day before visitation. They did. It was beautiful, beaded with tiny crystals hand sewn into the bodice, pricey no doubt. It really looked more like a wedding gown we thought, but whatever. So after the viewing hours ended, the son approached my dad and said, 'We'd like to have you take the dress off and put this one on her.' Dad looked at the guy like he was crazy and said, 'We can't. Besides, why would you want to change her burial gown?' The son replied, 'It was very expensive and we want to return it to the department store'."

"I heard Dad as he continued. 'Let me explain something to you, sir. When we dress the deceased, we have to cut open the back of the garment and slip it around her.' I thought this guy was going to faint. 'That was a $10,000 gown!' he roared. 'It isn't now,' Dad replied."

Ben continued. "Add that little figure to the cost of the funeral arrangements, and the family spent over $35,000. I guess they thought the salesperson in the store wouldn't know any better. Apparently, they saved the tags and planned to return the dress the next day just before the store policy deadline expired. No pun intended."

"Gross!" said Emily. "I'll never look at a department store dress the same way again; from now on *all* my clothes are coming from Goodwill."

"Who knows where those came from? They don't ask any questions," said Derrick, followed by hearty laughter.

Judy turned, taking notice of a small ivory colored statue on the side table in the dining room. Curiously, she slowly made her way toward it.

"This looks like it has a story connected to it," she remarked, suppressing her emotions. "May I?" she requested from Derrick, as she reached for it, which he acknowledged with a nod.

July carefully picked up the ten inch, delicate looking statue and held it close to her chest. Seconds later, tears formed under her tightly sealed eyes and tricked down her cheeks. Her trembling became visibly concerning.

Derrick approached placing his hand on her shoulder, "Judy, what's wrong?"

She took a deep gulp and opened her watery eyes, "I can't explain this. Sorry."

Derrick smiled at her and leaned in closer whispering, "That's okay, Ma gets emotional too when she holds it. She says it has powers. We've just placated her. Guess there is something to *Thorn Boy's* mystique."

Judy returned the statue to its rightful place as Derrick continued, "You see, my grandfather's army buddy brought that back after WWII. We were told that it was with my granddaddy when he was killed. See the traces of his blood on the base. Ma treasures it."

Derrick glanced down at his watch. "We better get on the road. I can fill you in on the story while we're out."

"I definitely want to hear this," Judy responded wiping the last of her tears away.

“What are we doing?” Derrick inquired from the group.

“I thought we’d have dinner in Palm Beach,” replied Ben. “I vote for Taboo Restaurant on Worth Avenue. Dad gave me bonus money for my extra hours this week when I told him we were celebrating Judy’s birthday.”

“Sounds like a plan to me,” Derrick responded.

By then, Ma made an appearance in the living room. “Now be safe tonight, you know how many crazy drivers are on the road out there.”

“Believe me, you don’t have to remind us,” Emily piped up. “Last night driving down 75, this jerk flew up behind me with his brights on. Then he whipped the van over to the left lane and passed us like a bat out of hell.”

Emily noticed a glance of disapproval toward Derrick from Ma. She continued, restrained, “Sorry, I think he clipped my bike rack.”

Derrick’s grandmother slowly took one step at a time as she descended the carpeted stairwell and entered the living room.

“What are you doing tonight, ‘Grandma M’?” inquired Ben.

“Oh dear, this old lady is spending a quiet evening at home reading her Bible. I’ve had a full day working around here and probably will go to bed early.” They gave the family matriarch a good night wish and waved.

The two couples walked outside into the quickly changing, evening air. They approached the little blue car that sat in the front of the house. By now it was dark and hard to make out the damage on the front left side of the bike rack affixed to ‘Janice’s’ bumper.

“Poor Janice,” said Emily as she rubbed her fingers along the scraped surface in a half-hearted attempt to conceal it.

“Your car’s name is Janice?” Ben asked.

“Yes, I named it after my father’s second wife. In his divorce he got two of the three cars they owned. My sisters didn’t want this one, so he gave it to me to use while I’m in school.”

Ben popped open the trunk on the Cadillac and produced a flashlight. He shined it on the scratched area. "There's some blue paint imbedded into the chrome finish."

"That won't do me much good. We didn't get a tag number. It all happened so fast. I'll see if I can get one of the guys at the body shop to fix it."

They piled into Ben's choice wheels and headed for SR 80 east, the asphalt conduit directly linking the Glades with the coast. A golden, full moon gradually ascended into the clear, night sky. It was the second full moon this month, a blue moon.

Chapter 10 –Ma and Her Memories

There weren't too many five-generation Floridians left in the state. As people retired, they sought refuge in cooler climates with fewer crazy drivers. Grandma Ma, or 'Ma' as most people called her, loved Florida and continued to live in her home of fifty-six years. There, she had survived hurricanes, droughts and waves of insect infestation.

In the far corner of her rose garden, Derrick had created a grotto for her in memory of his father and grandfather. Built as a summer project while he was in high school, Derrick was inspired by the grotto, Saint Mary Star of the Sea, he and Ma discovered in Key West during one of their road trips. Ma was captivated by the shrine.

His ambitious nature was clearly demonstrated as he toiled to complete the project. Ma was proud as she watched him persevere in the relentless, Florida sun.

He'd worked steadily for twenty-eight days as the job neared completion. Derrick added a few finishing touches to the grotto; it stood a towering fourteen feet above the ground with a base twenty feet wide by ten feet deep. The niche alone was six feet tall. He rejoiced to Ma when the work was done.

Now that she was less able to go anywhere, Ma spent early morning hours and late evenings in the garden, often praying her rosary. She was deeply moved that Derrick spent most of his summer income from odd jobs to create a place of peace and quiet reflection. Somewhere she could cherish the memory of those she lost.

Later that evening Ma slowly submerged herself into the steaming, sudsy water. The aromatic, bubble bath consumed the bathroom.

Her old claw-foot tub had been in the house since the killer hurricane struck back in 1928. Now, all that was left were her roses and her memories.

As she dribbled the silky water over her shoulders, a smile crept across her face. Her wedding day: Mr. and Mrs. Clarence Stabb were pronounced man and wife June 6, 1939 in a small Catholic ceremony at St. Mary Queen of Peace.

Her smile dissipated: A few weeks later Clarence, everyone called him "Stubbs", left for training camp in Kentucky, then off to Europe. 'The War', as Ma referred to it, was a recipe of many emotions: fear, joy, pride, sadness and courage all mixed together with a dollop of romance.

She refused to change anything in the house after the war ended. The times reflected their happiness. She wanted to remember everything just as it was when they first moved in as newlyweds. The pain was still as real as it was when she received word that "Stubbs" was missing in action in December, 1944.

After the war, she returned home with her son to plan a memorial service. At the service, one of the visitors brought her a white rose bush. She suggested Ma plant it in honor of her fallen soldier. That rose bush began her on a new journey and passion. She knew that if he were alive, he would be so proud of the home she kept and the garden she tended to so lovingly.

America's involvement in the Vietnam Conflict had begun in the late 60s. She said her goodbyes, once again, this time to her son. They stood along side the other drafted young men who gathered in the early, morning hours at the American Legion on Avenue D before departing town on buses headed for boot camp.

The moment remained crystallized in her memory when Derrick and Rodney arrived home from grade school, just before the Christmas holidays, to find a young military man in the front parlor. She was sitting on the sofa with her hands cupped over her face obviously in tears. The boys ran up to her and discovered that their father had been killed. Now, with their mother abandoning them, they were technically orphans. She remained strong. She knew the two young boys would need her, and this was her reason to keep on going.

After a half hour, the tub's water had begun to cool her skin. She emerged; the only sound was the water that trickled off of her back into the tub.

Tonight, like most evenings during the fall, the windows were raised just a few inches to allow the fragrant fresh air to waft through her bedroom. She looked forward to enjoying a warm cup of tea before retiring.

She propped up her pillows against the headboard. The soft mattress swallowed her as she crawled into bed, fluffed the comforter, and opened her Bible, but struggled to concentrate on the passages she read. Ma glanced over at the bedside clock displaying eleven pm. The evening breeze created a "swishing" sound as it cut through the screen in the bedroom window. Her eyes lids grew heavy, but Ma dreaded another night knowing that sleep was only temporary. Her mind was haunted with the burden of so many worries. She wondered what Stubbs would do if he were here. Her heartache was exacerbated by every waking moment as she lay in bed staring into the twilight. Gradually her eye lids closed again. The weighty book that rested in her lap gently closed and tilted to the side. At last peaceful slumber was hers, but not for long.

She awoke from a hazy sleep as tiny stones intermittently pinged against the windowpane. Hail? She turned to check the digital clock, one am. Curiosity lured her from her warm bed, carefully down the stairs through the screen door onto the front porch. No inclement weather. Strange, what woke her?

Hazily, the resplendent sky's misty, soft azure color with swirls of feather shaped clouds cast a blue hue onto the rose blossoms below, transforming the flora and fauna into a wonderland of mystical images.

Nightingales sang in the garden. Beckoned by their song, she followed along the cool, sandy path beneath her bare feet. Inching along, step-by-step, she eventually reached the grotto and knelt. Ma rested her elbows on one of the stone benches; typically, her rosary was intertwined between her fingers. She had begun to pray.

Fine water droplets collected on her cheeks and hands as she held them tightly together, silently reciting the Hail Mary. The nightingales sang more sweetly, which drew Ma's eyes toward the niche above her. A beautiful image, an illusion unclear at first, was surrounded by blue light and appeared from nowhere, smiling gently.

Unafraid, she had begun to pray aloud feeling its holy presence.

Blue roses lay at her feet as she raised her arms outstretched, supine hands in a divine gesture. The shimmering white garment tied with a blue, sheer sash and a blue veil waved gently over her angelic face. Ma felt a peacefulness. She bowed her head in prayer knowing that the beautiful apparition was there to guild her though difficult times. Ma waited faithfully for a message. The apparition stood in the niche as her robes and sash waved gently in the night breeze.

Ma believed that surely she was sent by God. No one else knew about her precarious, financial situation. The beautiful being must hold a message that was to be her salvation. Ma waited, and then she heard the words. "You have earned your reward." Ma bowed. She heard the words again. She lifted her head to gaze once more, but the apparition had faded away. A thin sheet of paper gently drifted back and forth as it made its way to the ground and came to rest before the grandmother's knees. On it were two verses.

"Beds of blue roses,"

"Blonde hair so fine,"

"Look to the sky,"

"She is divine."

"A sweet grandmother's garden is a delight.

She holds a secret, you've created her plight.

Your success will soon be realized.

In the end her flowers will be prized."

Clinching the folded paper, Ma's face rested in the palms of her hands. She sensed that it would not be the last visit from her spiritual messenger.

Chapter 11 –A Night They'd Never Forget

The black Fleetwood's powerful, eight-cylinder engine cut through the damp, night air as seemingly thousands of mosquitoes splattered against its windshield. Ben pressed the windshield wiper button spraying a sudsy solution as the rubber arms waved back and forth clearing his view. Thick smoke rode the thermals from the scorching flames as it drifted over parts of State Road 80, a direct route through the fields, east toward Palm Beach.

This time of year, burning cane sent blazes high into the air. Torched by the harvesters, the vegetation was easier to cut with the dense growth thinned away. As the fire inched toward the road, the long, incinerated leaves from the plants filled the air with gray snowflakes called cane ash. *Like a snowstorm,* Derrick idly thought as the flakes fluttered by inches from his face.

Ben remarked, "Judy, are you okay? Something seems to be bothering you. Since we left Ma's, you've been very quiet."

Judy took a deep breath and confessed, "Sorry, I got such strange vibes from holding that statue. Give me a minute, I'll be fine."

"I'm here for you Judy," Ben said glancing over. A few moments of silence followed then Judy perked up. "Tell me more, Derrick." she requested, turning her head over her seat back, glancing in his direction.

"Well, after the war ended, an army buddy of grandpa's brought it back for Ma. His name was Cornelius. Ma called him Corny. I remembered because how many guys named Corny do you know.

"Corny!" exclaimed Emily.

"Anyhow, this is the story I head from Ma when I was a little boy.

Grandpa was part of the liberation movement chasing after Hitler. They were a special military envoy that saw a lot of casualties. His unit stormed the offices of the Third Reich in Berlin. Grandpa picked up the statue, which was in the Nazi's office...you know, like a souvenir. Sometime later, he was killed. According to Ma, the red stains on the bottom of the statue are Grandpa's blood. She said that because of the sentimental reasons, she could never bring herself to try and clean it. It became a 'relic'. "

Judy gave an exaggerated shiver. "Gross, but that is interesting."

Derrick continued, "The story gets better. It's called the '*Thorn Boy*'. You see, I've got this thing for history, so when I researched the original statue for a high school paper, it gave Ma's statue more intrigue. It's a Greek bronze, also known as *Spinario,* displayed in the *Palazzo dei Conservatori* in Rome. It dates back to 150 B.C. When the Romans conquered Greece, I guess they got the art as a bonus, too."

Judy asked, "What about those mystical powers you mentioned earlier."

"Actually, *Thorn Boy* is the inspiration from which Ma got her little nickname for me as I cleaned those thorny rose stems cut from her garden. And Ma said that the little *Thorn Boy* brought many good things into her life; me being one of them, she said. But the best part was the fact she claimed that every time she held it, she could feel the warmth of Grandpa as though he were with her. Once, when she was coming down the stairs for some tea, she noticed a soft glow coming from the dining room. She couldn't believe her eyes. The image next to the *Thorn Boy* was Grandpa. He was smiling at her... it only lasted a second. I guess you could call that mystical."

Ben said, "Well, who knows what's possible or not. We have no idea what mystical experiences may lay ahead for any of us?" He glanced over at Judy, "Are you sure you're alright?"

"I'm fine!" She snapped back taking Ben off guard.

"Sorry, I didn't mean to upset you," he responded.

"I'm sorry Ben; I don't know what got into me."

As they approached the east coast, the first cool front of the season moved into South Florida shoving the warm, heavy air south, leaving a dry, clear, starlit night. Derrick put the window down a bit and felt the night air as it forced its way through the crack. It was the perfect Saturday night for a celebration.

Derrick remarked as Ben pulled the Cadillac up to the valet, "Wow, looks pretty busy. I'm surprised since the winter tourists won't be here for another two months."

Ben responded, "Well, Saturday night you know. And this place is pretty popular with the year-round residents. Besides, it's the busy places that have the best food. And, since this is Judy's birthday, we're not skimping. It's going to be a night we'll never forget."

Ben watched the busy staff of servers clad in white, starched aprons and button-down shirts, buzz attentively about the room. Excited about the evening, he heard sounds of prosperity harmonizing with the sounds of clinking stemware and plates. The tables were set and cleared under soft, incandescent lights that cast an amber glow which accentuated the newly tanned skin of the customers. He loved Florida.

As the plates were cleared from the table he announced, "I've planned another stop recommended by a friend from mortuary school. He said that it was a cool place, but I've never been there before. We all might be in for a big surprise."

Derrick asked, "What's it called?"

"Roosters on Belvedere Road; he told me that it was popular with a mixed crowd, whatever that means."

A mixed crowd, indeed, thought Ben as they entered through a side door. What appeared to be men in drag took the last two remaining seats next to him and Judy at the bar. He watched in amusement as the one, unskilled in walking with four inch heels, struggled as she made her way to the restroom's door marked LADIES. Her blousy floral print top made for an interesting compliment to the pleated, knee high blue skirt. The shorter, stockier companion nodded presenting a gray crooked smile to him and Judy. Her knitted scarf, neatly wrapped around her neck, created a violent conflict with the pastel yellow, silky shirt and blue men's slacks. She donned a fascinator of feathers in her hair, which fluttered in the draft of the air conditioning vent just above her. Ben nudged up closer to Judy and put his arm around her waist.

Affable Judy smiled back to the odd, little character. She inquired with the standard question to which no definite answer is required. "Are you from here?"

"No," replied the androgynous person, who now was beginning to take on more of the characteristics of a real woman. She was feminine in her actions lifting her pinky finger as she sipped from her cocktail glass.

Judy responded, "So few people are actually from Florida." At that moment the woman's side-kick hobbled back to the bar and carefully wedged her way in between Judy and the stocky woman.

Here is a person that doesn't need heels; it must be a guy, thought Ben. *Maybe this is a prelude to Halloween.*

He pointed over head, just within reach of the bartender, to a large stock of liquor displayed on wooden planks supported by chains that hung from the ceiling.

"Just ask, and they can whip it up," shouted the statuesque figure in a low, gruff voice over the music. He sported a wig, heavy make up and an eye patch. Ben noticed what was barely visible in the darkness; the man appeared to have a severe facial deformity. Maybe that was the reason for the disguise, Ben thought, *although nothing underneath the makeup could be worse.*

Ben turned to the corner of the bar, opposite the main door was a small stage painted black, dressed with a Mylar curtain. The bartender told him that karaoke night was on Thursdays. Saturdays nights offered drag shows much later in the evening if his friends hung around.

Ben's uneasiness grew; he'd have a *talk* with his buddy who recommended the spot without telling him that it was a gay bar. Was it some sort of weird joke? He reached over to Judy, pulled her shirt sleeve and gained her attention. Then he pulled her closer and hollered in her ear that maybe the group should move on.

Barely able to be heard over the clamor of *Elvis's Blue Suede Shoes,* his comments fell on deaf ears, but he persisted.

Eventually Judy got the picture, rounded up Derrick and Emily, and Ben led them to the door. In the parking lot's ambient light that hugged the narrow building, he turned back and noticed the two characters he was trying to elude following behind.

There was one final stop Ben felt comfortable which he suggested to his friends before heading back to Boca Raton. During his wild teen years, he frequented a dance club called Heartbreakers, situated in a desolate shopping center on the corner of Congress Avenue and Forest Hill Blvd.

"This is one popular place," Ben remarked. "There's hardly an available parking spot. We're going to need good parking karma."

The other three gave him a wide-eyed stare.

"What, haven't you ever heard that? Judy, I'm surprised. You of all people should relate to that. We used to say it all the time when scouring lots at the mall looking for a good spot."

"I do, but I've never heard of 'good parking karma'. Ben, where do you come up with this stuff?" Judy responded sounding a bit agitated.

After a few minutes of circulating the lot, Ben pulled into a spot situated on the fringe. "So much for good parking karma, we can walk off that meal," he joked as he checked his watch. They exited the car in the last available parking place and headed for the main entrance.

By now it was nearly midnight, but the bar was just getting busy. Crowded with people who appeared to be mostly in their teens and 20's, Ben watched the multitudes of partiers filtered through the massive club in an unorganized conga line. Always protective of Judy, he held her hand tightly as they made the rounds.

Revelers gyrated on the dance floor while the spinning mirrored balls and flashing lights zoomed across the large space. Derrick and Emily waved at him and Judy after they found a comfortable spot at the bar. Then, he and Judy headed for the inviting sounds of the dance floor; it was one of their favorite songs, *"True Blue" by Madonna.*

After the song was over, Ben pointed Judy in the direction of the ladies room while he made his way back to his two friends who waved from their perches. They chatted and ordered another drink and watched what appeared to be a group of under-aged, school kids standing and modeling. Derrick and Emily told Ben they were ready to head out.

"Judy should be back any minute," Ben shouted above the music.

After about twenty minutes had passed, Ben said, "Maybe she saw someone she knew".

As Emily and Derrick continued to finish their drinks, Ben made the rounds through the night club. He began to wonder how he could have missed Judy. At five foot ten inches, she generally rose above the crowd, especially in heels. He started to get a peculiar feeling. Ten minutes later, Ben approached his friends with a look of concern.

"Can't find her?" Derrick inquired.

Ben shook his head as Emily looked on.

"Let me check in the ladies room again," she hollered.

Ben looked at Derrick. With obvious concern in his voice he said,

"This really isn't like Judy. She would have come to get me if she had run into a problem."

By now the three were growing concerned. Emily returned from the ladies room and shook her head, no sign of Judy.

Ben, in frustration, said to Derrick and Emily. "I'm starting to get a bad feeling in my gut."

"Let's not jump to any conclusions; there's got to be a logical reason behind this," Derrick replied.

"I'll run out to the car and see if she's there." Ben felt it was a slim chance, but he couldn't think of anything else to do. He returned from the parking lot and shook his head no.

"It's two am! We should have headed home by now," Ben said in a panic. "I'm calling the police." He followed a group out the door and saw a pay phone near the street corner. He ran up to it, reached deep into his pocket for a dime and dialed Operator.

Ben paced back and forth along side of the Cadillac as the last of the partiers exited the club.

"A cop should be here soon," he said to his friends.

The Sheriff's cruiser pulled into the entrance and headed for the lone, well dressed, college students standing next to the Cadillac in the back of the lot. Deputy Bruce Sistrunk pulled up slowly behind them. His car's head lamps illuminated the distressed expressions on the two males and one female.

Anticipating a quiet night, he wasn't usually on duty for the graveyard shift. Tonight was an exception; he traded time with a fellow deputy. He got out of a squad car. With a bullet-proof vest, holster, night-stick and extra thirty pounds hugging his mid section, he struggled, gained momentum and finally exited the car. The leather holster and car seat crackled as the deputy placed his left foot on the asphalt. His first thought looking at the three people before him: *nice wheels.*

"What seems to be the problem?" he said as he approached the group.

"My girlfriend is missing," Ben responded with dread in his voice.

"Since when?" the deputy inquired.

Ben responded with beads of sweat collected on his stressed forehead, "Just now, tonight, we haven't been able to find her. We all came here together, and now she's nowhere to be found."

Emily chimed in, "I checked the restroom twice, and we walked all through the building."

"This isn't like Judy at all," Ben said as he choked on his words.

"In order to put out a Missing Person's Report, the individual has to be missing for at least 24 hours. In most cases, the person usually shows up during that time. I've heard all kinds of excuses. Could she have left with someone?"

"Not willingly!" Ben snapped back.

"I know you're concerned, but it's only been a few hours," the deputy remarked as he half way tried to console the nervous boyfriend.

"I have to head back to Belle Glade to take my friends home. Then my girlfriend and I would be driving back to Boca. What am I supposed to tell her Mother? I lost her daughter! For God's sake, this doesn't make any sense."

As Derrick turned away momentarily from the group, something familiar captured his attention.

"Look!" said Derrick pointing back toward the club. The four heads turned at once to the dark green, waste receptacle situated near the back entrance of the building.

A large Dumpster sat with one lid slung back exposing the debris within. Draped over the edge, fluttering in the evening breeze was a blue scarf. A chill ran up Ben's spine.

"That's Judy's! Her mom gave it to her before we left," he exclaimed and ran toward it. The others followed.

The deputy reached in with a gloved hand and gently lifted the blood stained, silk scarf placing it into a plastic bag. He noticed a small clutch concealed under part of the scarf.

"I'm calling in forensics, and I need to get a statement from each of you. Wait here." Sistrunk returned from his cruiser. Ben paced back and forth in front of Derrick and Emily.

"This is horrendous. Where did she go? Somebody must have done something terrible to her."

Derrick said placing his hand on his buddy's shoulder, "Ben, try to calm down. The scarf has gotten the cop's attention; he's taking this more serious."

The deputy returned. "Someone from the Sheriff's Office will be here soon to take the evidence and search the area. All of this information will be cross referenced with other data in the system. Hopefully there's a fingerprint on the hand bag that will match up with someone's in the data base. Is there anything else you can tell me as to why someone would abduct your friend?"

"Abduct!" The sound of the word sent Ben's stomach into knots.

"No, I can't imagine why any of this is happening. We were all out for a good time. What a nightmare!"

The deputy stated, as a matter of fact, glancing down at the plastic bag holding the scarf and small handbag, "Well, like I said, sometimes the person turns up in less than twenty-four hours. Go home and wait until you hear from headquarters. An investigating officer will contact you."

Ben pulled the Cadillac into Ma's gravel driveway. Derrick slung the car door open. Standing there in the bleak moonlight, he offered his friend comfort. "The police with do everything they can to find her, Ben. Do you want to come in and call Judy's mom?"

"No, I mean, I don't know what the right thing to do is. Let me head back and try to think."

Emily said, "I know this is tough, Ben. But, there's gotta be an explanation to all this. Let's pray that Judy turns up okay, and this is all just a big disconnection back at the club."

"But, the blood on the scarf, did she get into a fight with someone? Oh, God, what could have happened?"

Derrick put his hands on Ben's shoulders and said confidently, "She'll show up. The police *will* find her."

"I'm hoping they do," responded Ben starting the car as Derrick shut the Fleetwood's heavy door. The crackled sounds of the pebbled driveway were the only sound in the stillness as Ben backed away and steered his car to the main road.

He replayed the evening's events over and over in his head as he attempted to comprehend what had taken place. What in the world was he going to tell Judy's mother?

Later that night a police car's blue and white flashing lights quickly advanced upon the old, blue van and forced it to pull over. Prepared to deliver a lecture and citation, a Belle Glade Policeman shone his flashlight at the driver he thought to be a man wearing red acrylic fingernails. The officer was taken aback slightly.

Riding shotgun, his companion looked like a woman. She had gray, frizzy hair and matching costume jewelry—an interesting detail, considering nothing else coordinated.

The driver riffled inside a beaded and sequin handbag and produced a license with a photo that barely resembled him. Deep crevices and sagging skin indicated the scars of a burn victim. *No amount of make up would adequately conceal that fact, so obviously it was the same person just a little more colorful,* thought the officer.

No smell of alcohol. After he checked the driver's license, he wrote a citation for speeding as well as a broken tail light and sent the pair on their way with a stern warning reminding them, "Deep canals run along each side of the long stretch of highway. If you were to lose control, nothing would stop the van from plunging into the water, drowning you. Now, we don't want to be fishing you nice ladies' bodies out of there, do we?"

"Thank you, Officer," responded the driver nervously in a low, masculine accent.

"Where are you from?" he inquired as he handed the license back through the car window.

"The Netherlands," he answered just before dropping the license back into the handbag.

"Really, so far away, and what brings you to our little part of the world?"

"I'm doing research on the muck." It was a shrewd response as he hoped for a quick end to the inquisition.

"From what I know about Amsterdam, it is a city filled with canals, so you must feel at home here."

"Yes, sort of, but my stay here will be ending soon."

"Well, safe driving," said the officer as he stood and backed away from the van and ambled back to his car while the couple sat anxiously and watched. He opened the driver's side door, gave a single arm stroke wave back at them and got in.

The driver reached into his bag and pulled out a pack of smokes. He tapped the end of the pack against his palm, opened it and put the filtered end up to his lips, lit it and started the van. Cautiously, they edged away from the grassy roadside following the cop for a short distance. Their van made the first available left onto Belle Glade Road as the police cruiser's lights disappeared from sight.

The frumpy cross dresser in the passenger seat turned around to check on the woman in the back where Judy Johnson lay motionless.

Chapter 12—A Garden Of Blue Roses

"Rise and shine, my little Thorn Boy, You and Emily have a lovely breakfast waiting for you," Ma called out in her singsong voice the following morning. Derrick gently nudged his girlfriend, and then slowly fumbled for his glasses on the night stand.

How should they break this news to Ma? he thought as the two descended the stairway and entered the dining room. Emily's expression looked as though she just lost her best friend.

"What's wrong dear?"

As Emily and Derrick pushed the food around on their plates in a half-hearted attempt to eat, they shared with Ma the events of the night. After she listened attentively, without saying a word, the matronly woman got up from her chair and exited the room. The two young people gave each other a questioning look. After a moment, Ma returned holding her statue.

"*Thorn Boy* has always brought me hope, especially when I needed it most. As you know Derrick, your grandfather made sure this got home to me even though he didn't make it back. When I hold it, I know he's here for me, and he will be here for you, too." She placed the statue in table's center.

She went on to say, "Last night I had a beautiful dream. I was in the garden and all of the roses were blue. A lady appeared to me and spoke a message: 'You have earned your reward,' she said. I don't know exactly what she meant, but I do know that if we pray, we will get answers."

Emily exchanged a knowing glance with her boyfriend. The two were reliving her words spoken just the day before. "A garden filled with blue roses."

Derrick said, "Ma, are you feeling alright. Are you sure you saw someone? Maybe it was a dream."

"Well dear, do dreamy visions leave notes behind?"

Ma took the tiny piece of note paper, with the two stanzas scribbled on it from the drawer in the side table, and pushed it across the tabletop toward Derrick.

He studied the poetic verses and handed the paper over to Emily. "What could they mean?" she inquired.

Derrick took the paper back and said, "Blue roses, blonde hair, and a secret plight, Ma, it is way too weird. Or somebody is just messing with your head. You need to be really careful. Someone has you and your garden in their sights. Why, who knows, but there's gotta be a reason. And I sense the reason is not to your benefit. Promise me your will tell me if this happens again."

"Yes dear, I will, but I don't worry. I have your Granddaddy here to protect me."

Hands joined, Derrick, Ma and Emily shared a moment of silent prayer.

Perched on his stone, the little *Thorn Boy* studied the bottom of his foot, determined to find the thorn easing his discomfort.

After breakfast, very reluctantly, Derrick and Emily loaded their belongings back into 'Janice.' In the bright daylight, the scrape on the bike rack was clearer. Deep inside the fine gashes were thin markings of blue paint. The impact had pushed the fender into the body of the car.

Derrick picked at the embedded paint along the bike rack and said, "It's not going to do much good since the crazy driver responsible is long gone. Maybe I can find a body shop to fix this the next time we come back."

Emily nodded, threw her bag into the back seat and hopped into the passenger's seat. Derrick put the driver's seat back all of the way to accommodate his long legs and started the car.

"She'll be fine," Emily said to Derrick touching the back of his neck after noticing the worried look that wore on his face. "Her faith is strong and she's not a naive woman." Her words seemed to bring him some comfort as the corners of his perfectly formed mouth turned up slightly.

She'd do anything to help him feel better, but Emily kept her skepticism hidden. The garden of blue roses could only exist in a fantasy.

Chapter 13—The Blood Business

Ben shielded the early morning sun with the back of his hand. He approached the front porch of his girlfriend's mother's house and nervously rang the doorbell. He checked his watch hoping the hour wasn't' too early. Moments later, Bernice Johnson opened the door wearing a blue robe. "Ben! What are you doing here at this hour?"

"I need to talk to you, Mrs. Johnson."

"What do you mean *missing*?" she screamed inside the house, clutching the chair's arm.

Ben trembled struggling to keep himself composed sitting on the sofa facing her. "It all seems like a bad dream. We were all sticking close together, having a great time. Everything was great until we started to leave the night club to come home, and we couldn't find Judy. We searched the club over and over again. Finally, I got to a pay phone outside away from the music and called the cops. A deputy showed up, and that's when we spotted Judy's scarf, the one you gave her, in the trash behind the building. Her purse was underneath it. The deputy said we'd have to wait twenty-four hours. I can't believe this has happened."

"Where were you, what club?"

"In West Palm, it was on our way home. God, I wish we would have just gone straight home."

"Twenty-four hours? Is he crazy? Judy wouldn't have just vanished on her own; someone is responsible. Who is this deputy?"

"I don't remember; it all happened so fast. He told us an investigating officer will contact us after analyzing the evidence. "

"I'll call the sheriff's office now."

She leaped to her feet and darted into the kitchen, grabbed the wall phone and dialed O. "Operator, I need the number to the Palm Beach County Sheriff's Office."

"Is this an emergency?"

"YES, it's an emergency!"

"Alright Ma' m, I'll dial the number for you."

"Yes, hello, hello, I am Bernice Johnson. My daughter was reported missing last night. She and a group of her friends were at a night club. Her boyfriend just told me what happened. He said they found her scarf and purse. I need to speak with somebody, *now*."

"Hold the line, please."

Several agonizing minutes passed, they seemed like hours as she paced back and forth. The long cord had begun to wind itself together, then, a voice.

"Mrs. Johnson? I am Deputy Bruce Sistrunk. I need you to come to the station as soon as possible. We have some questions to ask you about your daughter and her friends."

"What! Why aren't you out there looking for her? Please don't wait twenty-four hours. Judy wouldn't have just run off on her own, something's happened to her."

"We will, Mrs. Johnson, but I need to speak with you privately, in person here at headquarters. And you need to bring as much information about your daughter if possible: medical and dental records, whatever you have."

"Why, why do you need those records? Officer, I demand that you tell me what's going on!"

"We have two missing victims in Gainesville that seem to match the same physical description as your daughter. It's a vague connection, but we need to look at anything and everything."

Baffled, she slowly hung up the phone. By then Ben was standing in the kitchen too. "The police want me to come in and bring Judy's medical papers. God, I just don't know what to do. Ben, I will call you later. Let me get this information together and drive up to West Palm."

"I want to go with you, Mrs. Johnson."

"No, he said alone."

Ben hung his head and approached the door. Just before opening it, he turned and said, "I feel awful. This is all my fault. Will you call me as soon as you can?"

"Yes, of course, Ben. Now let me get going."

All of her important papers were in a fire safe box tucked deep inside on her bedroom closet's floor. It was the most convenient place she could store the heavy, cumbersome thing. She searched through memorabilia of old photos and newspaper clippings bound together with rubber bands. She reached into the box, pulled out a stack of neatly folded papers and flipped through them for anything that she thought could be of help to the police. Although, she wasn't sure what that would be. Nervously, Bernice gathered up Judy's pictures, admission papers to school, medical information and anything else she thought would be useful. She paused and thought, Judy's medication, her panic attacks, what would happen if she suffered one and didn't have it?

In less than an hour, she was sitting at a desk in the West Palm Beach Criminal Justice Complex next to the deputy who was at the scene.

Deputy Sistrunk said, "It seems the similarities in the case of your missing daughter and those of two other missing girls are hair and eye color, as well as blood type. The facts are that they were all young with blue eyes, in school and regular blood donors. I assume because of their rare, adaptable type."

She directed a look of utter confusion at him. "What would that have to do with anything? I frequently give blood due to a medical condition."

"Medical condition?" he questioned.

She pointed and said, "Yes, it's in the records I brought. The excess iron in the blood is removed by donating blood; only it's done on a more frequent basis until the excess iron is removed. If left untreated, iron accumulates in vital organs, particularly my liver, pancreas and heart. All of my organs can become irreversibly damaged."

Sistrunk raised his eyebrows and responded, "I see, but we're talking about O-negative, one of the rarest types. Plus, people with any other type can receive it."

She continued, "It doesn't matter what your blood type is."

Sistrunk replied, "We think blood type has something to do with these three cases."

"We, who's we?" Bernice Johnson inquired.

"I have been collaborating with a Lieutenant Waites from the Gainesville Police Department. Over the past four days, three people, including your daughter, Mrs. Johnson, have been reported missing. Strange as it may sound, we think there is a connection although these disappearances happened over 300 miles away."

"Someone would go that distance to abduct someone for their blood type?"

"Like I said, not just any blood type, and not just anybody, specific people with specific traits; these are the pictures and descriptions of the two others who have gone missing up there. Oh, and one other thing."

"Something else?" she inquired.

"They all had blue rose tattoos. We thought that was strange since they didn't seem to know each other."

He handed photos to her. She couldn't believe her eyes. In comparison, all three were almost identical in everyway. Cloned.

Ben returned to his part-time job at the Central County Blood Depository in Ft. Lauderdale the next day, but struggled to keep his mind on what he was doing. A sloppily folded newspaper was placed on the coffee table in the waiting room. On the lower left column appeared the headline, COLLEGE STUDENTS ABDUCTED.

He stepped into the small cubical assigned to him that included a phone, desk and just enough room on it to display photos. He plopped down in his desk chair. An eight by ten of Judy gazed back at him. The twinkle in her blue eyes, her beautiful perfect smile, God he missed her.

Moments later a squeaky, high-pitched voice said, "Hi Ben, how are you doing?"

Ben raised his head from his folded arms across his desk and responded, "Struggling, Mrs. Craig, really struggling, I spoke to Judy's mom this morning. She's wreaked; I don't even think she believed what I was telling her.

"I saw the morning paper. I'm concerned about Judy's medical condition. Her Hemochromatosis; if she goes too long without discharging some of her blood, there could be serious medical problems."

Ben responded, "I didn't even think of that."

"Please keep me posted, Ben. And if there is anything that I can do for you, don't hesitate to ask."

"Thanks Mrs. Craig. The police are investigating, and for now, all we can do is wait. It's frustrating, but it's in their hands."

"Could you help me with some heavy boxes in my office, Ben?"

Happy to assist his boss, he stood and followed Hazel Craig down the hallway. She struggled with a limp, but managed fine as she ambled her way through the building. Her salt and pepper hair, crooked smile, and endearing charm amused him and patrons alike. She was an unlikely expert in the "blood business".

"I need to load these into my car. I'm taking a little trip to Gainesville. They're making some updates in the blood bank office up there and asked for my expertise."

Ben, only happy to oblige, grabbed the top box; the flaps weren't sealed. He noticed an envelope peering through the top with the highly distinguishable Olympic seal prominently displayed.

"Mrs. Craig, don't you want to tape these flaps closed? I'm afraid you'll lose some of the papers."

"Oh, thanks, Ben. How careless of me. You *are* a good guy to have around."

"This looks impressive," said Ben, as he called her attention to the fact he noticed the famous logo.

"Yes, the board of directors of the swim club in Ft. Lauderdale asked me to take some of the athletes' records up to the blood bank office there. Apparently some have rather rare blood types, and well, you know, they make very good donors."

"Oh, uh sure, well that makes sense," responded Ben hiding his confusion as he loaded the cumbersome box into the car's trunk.

Mrs. Johnson left a message on Ben's answering machine. It had been three days, and the phone conversations with Sistrunk were growing more and more frustrating. Who would harm her beautiful daughter and why?

Ben immediately returned the call as soon as he picked up the message. "I'm going up to see Derrick this weekend. I'm obsessed with the idea that the cases up there are somehow connected to Judy."

"What could possibly be the connection?"

"I don't know. I'm following my intuition," replied Ben. "I'm exploring the possibility it had something to do with Noetic Science."

"Noetic...what?" Mrs. Johnson questioned.

"It all started with someone claiming to be an intuitive healer who came to the blood bank a couple months ago to donate. When he met Judy, he told her that she had a beautiful aura with lots of blue in it, that she was balanced and relaxed and that she could be a healer, too, because her aura contained aqua."

"Judy became really hooked into this new science called Noetic; it has to do with intuitive consciousness, an 'inner knowing'. You know your daughter; she was open to just about anything."

"No, I don't think so, Ben. I know my daughter, and I have a hard time believing that she would play into something like this."

"I was there; the healer, he was really odd. A quirky little man who wobbled about with a cane; he wore one of those old hearing aids that occasionally shrilled; he really had Judy's attention, big time. She said it interested her because the science dealt with so many mysterious subjects: meditation, a global wisdom society and mind-body healing. I know it sounds heavy. Judy would share it with me as she learned. I have to admit I wasn't so convinced, but Derrick thought it was intriguing."

Bernice interrupted in a disbelieving tone, "It seems like some sort of a cult thing, but I'm sure Judy would never get herself involved in anything weird like that, at least, not by choice. She didn't mention anything about it to me. It's not like her to hide anything from me. And Derrick, from what I know that you've told me about him, this doesn't seem like anything he'd be involved in either."

"Oh, there's more. The healer went on to say that she was an "Indigo Child" because of her intense blue eyes. He said the light shines out and around them. Supposedly, Indigo children have high IQ's, are highly accomplished, deeply spiritual and tend to be rebellious and oversensitive. They also have heightened intuitive and psychic abilities."

"No, no, no, this isn't my daughter. This is all just a bunch of nonsense. Somebody trying to make a couple of bucks off naïve people; Judy is much wiser than that. She wouldn't buy into this. I know it. Maybe I should go with you up to Gainesville. I would like to talk to Derrick myself, in person, and see what this was all about."

Suspecting he would meet resistance, Ben cautiously chose not to push the issue with her.

"No, Mrs. Johnson, right now I'm just following a hunch; besides, the cops don't seem to be making much progress."

She began to cry. As she choked back the tears, Mrs. Johnson said,

"I'll have to hang up now. If I hear anything from the deputy I'll call."

She gently returned the receiver back onto the cradle and thought, *a cult...?*

Chapter 14—Turning Pink Hydrangeas To Blue

Not in the mood for work, Emily turned the key in the front door of the flower shop. The charming, tinkling sound of the chimes, attached to the door's frame, announced her arrival. The silk orange lilies and blue roses of University of Florida Gators displayed merrily greeted her. She was relieved that the laborious shooting for the reality show had wrapped up earlier than expected.

Emily thought, *if you were going to find real blue roses, Holland would be the first place they'd show up.* She wondered if she would hear back from her "blue rose bride". She wasn't thrilled with the idea of painting roses, glancing upward at the ceiling where the blue paint shot made its mark. After her last escapade with the spray paint, she preferred to avoid anything suppressed in an aerosol can.

The chimes on the front door jingled merrily signaling this time a customer had entered. With a broad smile, Emily politely approached the disheveled, corpulent woman. At first glance, Emily was amused by the odd, little lady as she approached the front counter. Her ensemble was quite unique. Some would describe it as vintage. The floral print dress she wore with tiny blue roses had to date back to the '50s. The woman's obvious knee high stockings sagged over her '60s style, scuffed, blue shoes with a low heel and over-sized buckle.

Emily has been known herself to comb through racks at the thrift store just down the street, and she certainly appreciated a good buy, but this lady, Emily thought, took thriftiness to a new dimension.

She anticipated a moth to come fluttering out of her coat pocket any second.

Politely, Emily followed behind the woman who waddled back and forth, with a slight limp, in between the metal buckets of vivid blue delphinium, corn flowers and hydrangeas. A couple of left-over, blue stem dyed, semi-fresh roses from an earlier shipment caught her eye. Emily was going to toss them earlier that day but decided that they still looked sellable. She was glad she reconsidered because the woman was delighted by their uniqueness. It just goes to show, Emily thought, *there is something for everyone*. A curiosity consumed her as to what type of recipient would be receiving blue roses.

Not unusual, she didn't have the exact address. It killed her when customers would send flowers and not have the necessary information. What did they think would happen when they tried to mail a letter under the same circumstances? Returned, that's what, but, no, not the way the florist deals with it; she reached under the counter while the odd, little lady stood by and pulled out the heavy cross-reference directory popular with florists, known as the "blue book." Emily's nimble fingers flipped through the pages for NW Southern Oak Lane and found the name Thompson. "Here it is, this book is a real time-saver. The house number is 8529. Let me write it down for you, so you'll have it the next time."

She smiled, displaying a disheveled upper row of teeth, and took the address.

Then, she reached inside her purse and handed over a credit card. The shop had just started taking credit cards. Emily pushed the owner stating that more and more people were using plastic now. After the printer spit out the receipt, Emily ripped it from the paper roll and handed it and a pen over the counter. "Sign here, please." It was then she noticed the large aquamarine ring sparkling on the customer's finger and commented.

"What a beautiful stone."

"Oh, thank you. I just love blue," she responded in a squeaky, high pitched voice.

No kidding, thought Emily.

"It was a gift from an old friend," she said as she dropped the receipt into her purse and snapped it shut. Without uttering another word, she turned and headed for the door, quickly passing by the elaborate display Emily proudly created of premium lucky bamboo, miniature table top fountains, pin holds and other recently acquired Asian-influenced gifts. Heading toward the door, she paused for a second to take a closer look at some silk roses accenting a plant garden near the exit. They were blue. *So much for Feng Shui,* Emily thought as the door shut.

As Emily leaned against the shop's front counter, she scratched her scalp. She couldn't figure out the customer's message on the card, "To My True Blue Beau." She had written some strange cards but this was original. Typically, the customers ask florists for suggestions. They have no idea what to say especially when it comes to romance. She got a kick out of these goofy guys who would come in, order flowers, usually roses, and then spend ten minutes trying to figure out what to say on the card. She kept a laminated list of gushy lines taped to the inside counter. Now she'll have a new one to add when the bona fide blue roses become a reality.

That morning there were bunches of fresh, color-treated roses on the supplier's refrigerated, flower truck, and some were that hideous dyed blue. Thank God she didn't have to paint anymore. After arranging the order specifically requested by her customer, Emily put the remaining flowers in the front display cooler. Later in the day, a high school kid with hair the same color blue bought them; *wonders never cease*.

It was a brisk day at the shop. Emily kept the driver out most of the morning. Her assistant, a budding new floral designer just out of flower school in West Palm, worked diligently processing flowers and cleaning buckets. The quirky, young lady was many in a string of apprentices that came and went.

The job did have its entertainment qualities. Since the driver would be out on a long run, Emily decided she'd get out and make the timed delivery herself.

The recipient was located in Thornhill, an affluent gated community in a heavily wooded part of town with phenomenal lawns, lush landscaping, mansions and residents with impeccable taste. Painted blue roses didn't quite fit into that scenario.

She carefully placed the vase on 'Janice's' front seat and cranked up the noisy motor. It was a beautiful day to make someone happy, she thought. Emily wound her little Bug through the tastefully maintained roads of Thornhill and came up to the house's gate. She pushed the CALL button. A voice came over the speaker. "Flower delivery for Thompson," she announced. Within moments the massive iron gates opened, and Emily made her way up the prodigious driveway toward the two-story, colonial style home.

She stood on the porch admiring the massive white pillars and pots of blooming petunias and salvia while she waited patiently for someone to answer the door. Suddenly, the door handle turned, the heavy, wooden door opened and a familiar face stared back at her. It was Brian Thompson. Emily remembered him as the guy in Derrick's hort class he had had an altercation with before they were being questioned by the police. Derrick pointed him out to her one afternoon shortly after the incident. She easily recalled it because of his polo shirt bearing the Olympic rings.

"What are these for?" he questioned with a snort.

She loved the remark; like she's supposed to know why people send flowers. It bugged her as much as when she would be making deliveries and every person she passed would ask, "Are those for me?" *People are so annoying sometimes*, she thought.

"I don't know; why don't you read the card," she abruptly responded pointing to the envelope.

He opened it as she stood exasperated holding onto the heavy glass vase. "Oh man, I can't believe *she* sent flowers. She was really a strange one. I was at a swim meet in Ft. Lauderdale s few days ago at the Swimming Hall of Fame. You know, Team USA won the gold medal at the Olympics," he announced with a protruded chest reminding Emily of a dandy rooster.

Derrick was right, this guy really is arrogant.

He continued as Emily bit her upper lip. "You know, my team members are like a brotherhood, and we frequently donate blood together."

Emily wondered if she had looked interested in his story because she wasn't.

"While we were there, we made a visit to the Central County Blood Depository. I do it all the time, but this time was different. I've never been drilled by someone with so many questions. She asked me about my nationality, my family's background? What's that got to do with giving blood? And then, she wanted to know where I lived. I told her in Gainesville. The last thing I needed was a stalker. I've had those crazies in the past. I didn't expect her to find me, but she did."

Emily fought a sense of guilt.

"As if this isn't bizarre enough, and this was really weird, she asked me my favorite color, and I said *blue*. I don't understand this card message, what does it mean?"

"A pure blue rose is yours to hold.

This gift is deserved, its pure as gold.

Because your commitment is unwavering,

You will pick the blossom of your favoring."

Hoofing back across campus, Derrick headed for his dorm room after class. As he climbed the stairwell, he heard the hallway phone ring. He tossed his book bag to the floor and scuttled to answer it. Ben's voice was always welcomed.

"Ben, hey, have the cops found out anything about Judy yet?"

"No, they're still following this hunch with the blood types. So far, it's the only thing they have to go on. I haven't spoken to the deputy since the night Judy vanished. I have his card. Maybe I should give him a call. I've got to do something other than sit around and twiddle my thumbs. All I can think about is where could she be? And her Mom, she's wrecked."

Derrick responded, "I'll give the lieutenant that questioned us last week a call although he makes me *really* nervous. Maybe there is a connection in the disappearances up here with Judy's. Don't worry, buddy. They'll find her."

Derrick sensed the words had little meaning to Ben immediately after he had spoken them. He hung up the phone, returned and looked around his cluttered dorm room. He searched through his papers on his desk for Lt. Waite's card. Finally, he found the black and white official business card under a pile of single sheets of paper and two study course note pads. He called the number. No answer. He left a message.

Careful not to misplace it again, Derrick slid the card into his wallet right behind his diver's license feeling that he would need it again.

He dug into his school work. Tonight he had some research to do for class. Every student received an assignment, a term paper due at the end of the week. He wasn't sure if he annoyed Professor Stanley Hicks or what with his cleaver comments, but the teacher gave him an assignment, a rather unusual one: how soil conditions impact plant life, in particular, flower color. Strange coincidence since his girl friend had brought up the subject of real blue roses earlier and thought that someone could make a fortune with them.

I guess if something is rare enough, there is always someone willing to pay, he thought as his mind started to wonder, *how much?*

Hours later, exhausted from the stress of school work and worrying about Judy, he laid his head on the small desktop. It rolled back and forth over the coil binding of the note pad creating discomfort. Derrick's head rose up, and he noticed a drool puddle that dampened the pages smearing the ink from the notes he had taken earlier. His arms were sprawled out over the pile of papers that was to become his report. Awakened by the obnoxious ring vibrating the black, wall phone next to his dorm room door, startled, he darted out into the hallway, grabbed the receiver, fumbled it and grabbed it again.

"I need to speak with Derrick Stabb," a voice said forcefully.

"This is he," Derrick responded hazily.

"This is Detective Robert Waites. I'm returning your call."

The all too familiar lump climbed up into Derrick's throat as he struggled to become coherent. "Oh, uh, thanks. Something has been haunting me. Last weekend, I was out with some friends back home. We went to West Palm for a birthday dinner. Some birthday dinner, the evening ended with my best friend's girlfriend disappearing. Seems eerily similar to what's been happening here."

"How so?" Waites questioned.

"We met with a deputy. He came to the night club where we lost track of our friend, Judy. He called in forensics when we found our friend's scarf with blood on it. Judy's mom called and spoke to a detective at the West Palm Beach Sheriff's Office. He was familiar with the missing students' cases here. He felt that there could be a connection."

"What is the officer's name?"

"Sistrunk, Bruce Sistrunk, I think."

"Really," Waites responded in a suspicious guttural tone. "And why is it that I haven't heard anything from this Deputy Sistrunk, you say?"

"I don't know; maybe he's trying to get more information. But, he said to my friend Ben that his girlfriend and the two people that have gone missing here all have identical descriptions—hair and eye color—right down to their rare blood type, O-negative, along with the fact that they were all regular blood donors."

"This all sounds really strange. Are you sure you haven't been smoking some 'funny weed', son?"

"Oh, no sir, I don't pollute my body with anything like that. I try to keep a clear mind all of the time. This whole blood issue has really got me puzzled. You see, I'm working on this report for my hort class; it's about how soil affects flower color."

"Hort class, what are you talking about; what's hort class?"

Derrick responded sheepishly, "Horticulture. I'm studying plant science.

I've got a pile of books on my desk I'm searching through looking for actual science that supports a theory I have based on blood meal, an organic fertilizer.

It's a byproduct of slaughterhouses, a nutritional soil amendment that's high in nitrogen used in promoting green, leafy growth. Nothing really to do with flower color, but maybe when various blood types are introduced to different kinds of soil, like muck, it can affect the plants grown in them. I know it sounds far-fetched, but I believe that there could be a link. I mean, we're all connected with the planet through the same elements."

"Bruce Sistrunk, you said? I'll contact him. Let me see what he has to say. And, son, leave the police work to the police. You focus on your studies. I'm sure that's what you parents are paying for, not to play part-time detective. O. K.?"

Click.

Derrick pulled the receiver back from his ear and thought, *well; he doesn't waste time playing nice,* as he stared into the phone's receiver. He returned it to the cradle, made an about-face, entered his room and shut the door.

His hyper-acidic stomach rumbled as Derrick pushed the small boxes and bottles around in his medicine cabinet. As he made his way back to his desk, Derrick noticed a dog-eared newspaper from a few weeks ago on an ottoman in his small bedroom. The front page photo glared back at him. It was Waites, grainy but clearly identifiable, with a handcuffed Danny Rolling. Derrick popped the antacids into his mouth. He was only trying to help. Waites was a serious man, no doubt. A crazy thought, but the last thing he needed was to be in the cross hairs of a cop with an ambitious agenda. Maybe he should keep his distance from all of this stuff about killers, disappearances and blood types. Really, what did he know anyway? Plants, that's what he needed to focus on: his schoolwork and his report, for now anyway.

He pondered, *where to start, where to start, as* he dug into the intimidating stack of books perched at the end of his desk with his new-found knowledge about soil from the samples on the first day of school. It began with soil, itself, which is very complicated. It contained air, water, dead organic matter and various types of living organisms. All those elements affected plant growth and development.

Interesting. Earth has various minerals including iron, which is the fourth most abundant element on the planet, mostly in the form of ferromagnesium silicates. However, most of the iron oxides and hydroxides are not readily available for plant use. So it must be manipulated by adding organic matter thus changing its color and consistency. Derrick's thoughts turned back to the first day of class and the jar of soil that had a reddish color. He pondered what organic matter could have been added to get that dark reddish color. Blood? No, crazy thinking.

Soil pH is the measure of acidity or alkalinity. A material which influenced iron availability and the pH must be added to aerate the soil and interact with the organic matter. When microorganisms decompose in organic matter, iron, previously tied up, is released in forms available for plant uptake. Mineral soil—soil derived from the Earth—is weathered rock. Organic material, Derrick learned, was how acid levels changed flower colors; Ma's sister, who lived up north, would pour pickle juice or sometimes push rusty nails into the ground around her pink hydrangeas to turn them blue.

Now he must research aluminum—the most abundant metallic element produced by the planet. Derrick pointed to the words on the page with his index finger as he read aloud to himself about its negative effects on plant respiration, "It says here plants assimilated carbon dioxide and oxidize organic substances in the cells with the release of energy while they released oxygen and other products of oxidation."

He scratched his thick, blonde scalp quickly seeing that he had his work cut out for him. His thoughts turned back to a conversation with Emily. She had mentioned, a few days ago, a company's quest to develop blue roses. Again, an interesting coincidence since they don't exist.

He wanted that A on his report from Stanly Hicks, a professor whose campus wide reputation was known to seldom give an A. But it wouldn't be anything less than astounding for him, as a student, to come across a breakthrough that lead plant science in a new direction and created the world's first authentic blue rose. Anything is possible in the world of modern science, but could he prove it, he thought, e*nough dreaming... get back to work.*

He refocused back into his research material. Time was running out. Only a few days before his report was due, and Derrick was determined to impress his professor.

After her delivery, Emily checked her watch; it was late. Her assistant could lock up the shop. Since she was close to Derrick's dorm, she could make an unexpected visit. Huffing and puffing, she scaled the flight of stairs then called though his dorm room door, "Hey Derrick, surprise, surprise, surprise."

The door opened to an embrace and kiss between them.

Emily said, "So how's your report coming along, sweetie?

"Okay, I guess," Derrick responded as he rubbed his forehead. "I was able to find pieces of information that affected vegetation, but putting them together into something that makes sense is a supreme challenge. Dr. Hicks knew he was presenting me with a big assignment. I hope I can measure up. At least I can say that I have expanded my knowledge on the elemental affects of iron, aluminum and pH balance on plants. Hey, did you know that arsenic contains cobalt? I've discovered that we are all connected together on this planet through our origins. Plants, insects, animals and humans all started millions of years ago and emerged into what we have today. It's anybody guess what will exist tomorrow. There are always new developments happening in the world of plant sciences."

Emily interrupted, "Derrick, I have another riddle for you to try and decipher. A customer sent flowers to that guy you had the argument with, Brian Thompson."

"Oh, yea, that arrogant jerk; I can't believe someone was sending him flowers."

"I took the delivery and stood there while he read the card. It was very strange only four lines.

It was in reference to blue roses again, just like in the one your grandma had. And there's a mention of gold."

"If they know what's good for them, they'll avoid him. Unless they need him for something, it would be great to see someone like him being used for a change. No doubt a guy like him has a history for using people."

"Well, like you said, someone has him in their sights. Derrick, don't get yourself worked up over it. He's not worth it. Hey, speaking of history, I just read this interesting story about a California hybridizer who developed the 'Stargazer' lily, an upright Oriental lily. Listen to this:

He mixed a bunch of plants in a field and let the bees 'do their thing'. Low and behold a new variety emerged; unfortunately the poor guy didn't protect his work. One of those passionate souls without much of a business sense, I guess. A whole bunch of growers made a lot of money, and all he got was a lily named after him. Well, that's not entirely true. He had his legacy. However, the moral of the story is, Derrick, if you find a secret formula for a new flower—one that people will stand in line for—protect it."

"I'll take your advice under consideration, but I think I have a distance to go. You know, Ben has a break in his schedule. He's coming up this weekend. We'll get together. Are you free?"

"Sure," Emily responded. "I don't have any weddings unless something unexpected, like a big funeral happens, I'm around. Certainly, he's not in the mood for partying with Judy still missing."

"Oh no," Derrick responded in Ben's defense. "I'm hoping he can help me out with my report. He's an ace in science, and I need all of the help I can get."

"Yea sure, well, I'll let you get back to your report. We don't want Professor Hicks giving you a 'black star' so early in the school year."

"Thanks for that," he responded with a grin.

Emily darted out the door of Derrick's dormitory building. The climate on the U of F campus was very guarded over the past several days. Glancing about, she noticed people stayed in groups to and from cars and buildings. And she heard that there were several of her friends who spent nights at a co-student's place if they lived alone. There was a rumor that all of the undergraduates removed their blue colored contact lenses. Sure, there may not be any truth to the stories, but why take any unnecessary chances. Emily thought, *really, what is so special about blue eyes anyway?*

Chapter 15—Specimen Number Four

The next day streaks of brilliant red sunlight clawed across the deep blue morning sky announcing daybreak. Runners took advantage of the cool morning running the wide, winding roads inside the prestigious community just outside of Gainesville's city limits. On this morning, an elegant lady wearing a velour jogging suit walked her Maltese dog in the grassy swale past the stately house. An unmarked, oxidized blue van with a busted tail light pulled up to the iron gates at the Thornhill Estates. Three lush acres separated the circular drive from the entrance marked THOMPSON, 8529 NW Southern Oak Lane.

The driver pressed the bright orange call button on the gray box. It rang inside the mansion at the end of the long driveway. A deep male voice rushed and out of breathe answered, "Hello".

"A. C. Service Techs here for your monthly pool treatment," responded the caller.

"Weren't you just here?" he replied.

"We found a leak in one of the hoses leading to the pool pump and we've come back to replace it." The gates slowly opened and allowed the service vehicle inside. *That was easy enough*.

The driver, one eye concealed behind a patch, slid from his seat and made his way along side of the van. He met his stout, female companion at the rear. Towering over her, both wore a cap and matching dark blue overalls with an indistinguishable logo on the shoulder. The cleverly disguised, plump woman pulled her cap down low over her eyes shielding them from the light as she barely managed a large duffel bag with wheels from the back of the vehicle. She sat it down onto the ground and pulled out the retractable handle. Limping awkwardly, she followed the driver around the back of the house toward the pool area.

A tall, athletic, young man with broad shoulders greeted them as he unlocked the arched gate. He was the picture of youthful fitness poured into his Speedo with the prominent Olympic logo exhibited above his muscular thigh. Peering just below the leg opening was a blue rose tattoo. His wet, slicked-back hair was now bleached nearly white from the sun. He had stunning blue eyes and was powerfully built. Obviously he kept in shape from repeated laps in the regulation size pool before them.

Water droplets trickled down his tanned skinned chest as it contracted and expanded with each heavy breath. The two strangers watched carefully and followed as he led them through the back gate into the pool area. The serviceman reached around to his tool belt and felt the handle of the heavy, pipe wrench. Once safely inside the pool area obscured by the lush Crape Myrtle, he unsnapped the leather binding and slowly lifted it.

With only a slight "thud," the young man's limp body hit the paver stone apron that surrounded the massive pool. His head, torso and limbs bounced twice in synchronization as the body came to rest chest up. Blood rushed onto the pool's tile apron from the deep split in the back of his head. Quickly his accomplice retrieved a gray, heavy-duty trash bag from the gear they brought. They wrapped it tightly around the head and neck followed by vibrating sounds of duct tape as it was dispensed and secured a seal.

The killers worked diligently folding his muscular arms and legs inward allowing them a better chance of getting the two-hundred-plus pound athlete into the sturdy carrier.

After they successfully contained their catch, the man walked over to the pool's edge and dipped the pipe wrench, stained with the O-negative blood they sought, into the water. Red thread-like streams trailed into the clear water and gradually dissipated in the current of the perfectly pumped pool. After he uncoiled a garden hose, his accomplice quickly rinsed the crimson liquid off the paver stones and down a nearby drain.

The two perpetrators grunted as they strained to make their way through the gate back to the waiting van. The driver looked about; the coast was clear. They loaded the duffel bag into the vehicle. He steered the vehicle down the driveway, paused and waited, tapping his index fingers against the wheel and recited, “Cornelius is strong, Cornelius is worthy, Cornelius is powerful,” as the gates slowly opened, and exited. Specimen number four.

Chapter 16—His Nickname Is Thorn Boy

Ma's gardener pulled up to the portico at Memorial Medical Center and opened the passenger side door on the rusty old, '57 truck. A slight squeak called for some attention. Gradually, one at a time, she placed her blue slip-ons onto the black top driveway while he held the door for her.

As she entered the foyer, the smell of disinfectant permeated the halls of the immaculate facility. The polished floor reflected her image—the hallway was so sterile. Artificial flower arrangements and commercially produced paintings all in the same color palates accented the greeting area.

She managed her handbag, a loose bunch of cut roses in one hand, and her cane in the other; Ma steadily rounded the corner at the centrally located nurses' station.

A set of secured, white, heavy, metal doors with tiny windows labeled PSYCHIATRIC WARD was a few yards ahead. On the right side of the doors, mounted to the wall, was a small aluminum box. Ma pressed the CALL button. A soft, female voice came over the speaker requesting I.D., authentication and a password. The grandmother leaned over closer to the speaker, announced her name and the last four digits of her social.

The doors opened simultaneously accompanied by a whooshing sound. She meandered down the hallway and greeted with a nod a few residents as they sat motionless in their wheelchairs. Some were coherent and acknowledged her back. Gradually, she made her way to room 136-A. The name STABB in bold letters was written on white card stock which slid into a small, metal frame mounted on the front of the door.

After a gentle knock, Ma reached for the silver handle and pushed down. The weighty door swung open and she entered the room. Restrained in his bed with grey, nylon straps lay a lean, young man, his blonde hair mussed from being pinned down. He turned his head slowly from the sparkling window and gazed at the flowers in her hand.

Rodney was admitted to the facility after his bipolar disorder became much more serious. His violent mood swings and manic behavior made it impossible for him to be at home with her or to be left alone. And to hold any job for him was unthinkable.

The medications he tried either had terrible side affects or failed completely as doctors treated his bizarre and mysterious condition. Ma struggled with her decision and guilt to keep him here.

The cost was staggering, nearly $7,000 a month. Initially, she thought his stay would be temporary. She couldn't have ever imagined that two years later she would still be visiting him here. All of her savings had vanished. Ma finally, reluctantly resorted to the equity in her home as a source of revenue, but that was running out quickly.

Over the past several months, the bank had called her on a regular basis. She had fallen behind on payments. Ma, for the first time in her life, was faced with a financial situation she didn't know how to deal with. There were many nights when sleep was interrupted by unsettled thoughts of being forced from her home. The only thing she could do was go to the grotto in her garden and pray to the mystical vision for guidance.

She stared into the blue eyes of her once beautiful grandson. *It had come to this*, she thought. In her golden years, she now dealt with a gravely ill grandson and the threat of foreclosure on her lovely home, beautiful rose garden and memories. Ma fought a feeling of hopelessness that swept over her as she stood at his bedside.

Glass vases were not permitted in the ward, so a plastic cup for the flowers would work just fine. Ma removed the plastic bag from the bottom of the stems that contained just a dab of water and placed them in the clear cup. Immediately, the fragrance essentiated the sterile air and the corners of Rodney's mouth slightly turned upward.

She ran her fingertips through his soft blonde hair; she knew these would make him happy at least for the moment.

Ma pulled the bedside chair up closer to Rodney and sat holding his hand. She could see Derrick in him. As youngsters the brothers were so close. Derrick protected and defended him when a few at school bullied him. Now, she wished that Derrick would come to visit him more often. It hurt her that, at times, he seems to act as though his brother were dead. At first, she too hated the facility Rodney had been relegated to. But over time, she grew to accept what life had offered up.

Her eyes welled up as she ran her fingers gently over Rodney's soft hand. Now was when she missed her husband the most. His strength and wisdom were essential at times when she felt vulnerable. But he's not here, and she resorted to the grim facts. She would have to deal with the pitfalls of life. She would have to produce the might required to go forth. She would have to embrace love, reject fear and trust that the messages she received from the lady in her garden would guide her in the right direction.

Ma glanced up at the wall clock. The hour she'd spent, like all of the past visits, went by quickly. She realized that her gardener had been waiting all of this time in the truck. It was time to head back home.

She leaned over, kissed him on the forehead and reached for her handbag. Just before opening the door, she turned back to him. Still motionless, his head turned toward the light, she could see an image of her husband standing next to the bed, outlined in the sunbeams streaming into the room. He would remain vigilant until her next visit.

Back at home, Ma contemplated her situation as the momentum of the rocking chair she loved squeaked back and forth in unison against the wooden slatted porch. She held close to her heart, with aged hands, *Thorn Boy*. She needed comfort, so this evening she removed it from its usual place.

The beloved statue brought her the harmony she desired after she visited Rodney today. She felt it was the most important material possession she had. It was the only tangible piece which connected her to her husband. Her emotions were evoked each time she ran her fingers down the red hairline crevasse. Her husband's blood embedded into the tiny statue served as a relic from which she had a direct connection to him.

If she had to leave her home, he would always be with her.

Strong and willful, she suffered silently. She didn't want to worry her grandson. Derrick said when he became rich and famous; she wouldn't have to worry about anything. He would take care of them all. She thought, *what a sweet boy, so kind and generous.*

So many questions ran through Ma's mind. What could she have done in the past so that his situation would be different? If her husband and son were still alive, would that have made a difference? What should she have done today to make Rodney's life more than what it is? *Would have, could have, and should have, all dead ends.* The only answer was to pray, and so she did.

She yawned; the dreams haunting her had become more frequent and vivid as she struggled with their meanings. Her visions were filled with a kaleidoscope of colors while they blended in and out of each other. The blues dominated though; the background in each segment was always a light blue. Images of the smiling lady were framed in a medium or dark blue. Everything was so serene and beautiful.

The garden had become more and more popular despite its remote location. Derrick said we should replace the front gate with a turn-stall and start charging admission—an idea that amused her. Ma knew that was the difference between older and younger generations; seniors are content with things as they are whereas the younger ones were looking for more, *nothing wrong with wanting more.*

At that moment, a blue van pulled up the gravel driveway interrupting her daydream. She leaned forward in her rocker to see who it was. A cloud of dust settled around the tires as it stopped just a few yards from the porch.

The driver slung the door open and revealed a stream of rust that originated from the window's edge leading to the base of the old door. "Good evening, Ma'am," shouted the driver with an accent as he flicked a lit cigarette from the window. A trail of smoke strung behind it as it bounced on the ground. He slammed the rickety door shut with a creek and using the tip of his leather shoe ground the butt into the shell rock. "How are you?"

Ma smiled and continued to rock back and forth as the polite man slowly approached the house. She wondered, *is he holding eviction papers.*

She tried not to gawk at the visitor's severely scarred face as she slowly stood up from the rocker and walked to the edge of the porch. There was something recognizable about him; his one good eye maybe? He had a patch covering the other. Possibly it was his manner, but she was almost sure they had never met before. Certainly she would remember such a face.

"I heard you have a fine rose garden here."

The grandmother acknowledged his remark, "And where did you hear that?"

"I was down at the garden supply store in town and spoke with the young man as he packed my order. He asked me what I was going to do with all of my purchases. I told him I loved roses, but cultivating them in the south Florida climate had been a struggle between the mold, insects and proper doses of fertilizer. He suggested that I stop by to see your garden, get some advice. He said it was the most beautiful garden in Palm Beach County."

I guess we should start charging, she thought.

"You're welcome to take a walk," Ma graciously offered. "I'll join you."

They headed for the garden. When they came upon the imposing stone structure near the garden's edge he remarked, "This is a rather impressive undertaking." He leaned in closer to read the two metal plaques mounted underneath the niche, bearing the names

CLARENCE "Stubbs" STABB

CLARENCE "L.C." STABB

There were cut stems and broken foliages tossed to the side in an indiscriminate pile. With her permission, he dug through the partially composted stack and pulled out a couple of fresh stems and foliage. "If you aren't composting these canes, I'd like to propagate them. I could use the living growth ends, the apical meristem, or growing tip, in the new canes. Cell division in the meristem is required to provide new cells for expansion and differentiation of tissues and initiation of new organs, providing the basic structure of the plant body."

"You *are* quite the expert. Of course, you may have them."

She observed as a small plastic bag appeared from his coat pocket; after some bending, he forced the plant matter into the bag and slipped it inside his jacket's pocket. He turned to make his way back, paused and noticed a sign: Please Don't Pick the Roses primitively painted on a two-by-two foot piece of plywood.

It was a good time of day to walk. The setting sun hovered just over the tips of the gently swaying sugar cane. Ma felt the firm soil under her feet along the pathway, and fortunately it was dry. She cautioned him that between the pristine rose bushes was rich, black, wet muck that could quickly oozed in between the leather strips on his fine, woven shoes. She watched as he moved with long strides through the field, occasionally stepping over the well-tended rows; the "expert-to-be" examined the bushes carefully. Abruptly he jerked and turned. It appeared that one protruding thorn ripped through his slacks and sliced his shin. She could see beads of blood had begun oozing from the torn skin.

"Oh, dear, please come back to the house so we can take care of that," she said approaching him as he leaned over attempting to dab the blood with a tissue.

"I don't think it's too bad," he replied grabbing at the cut in his pant leg and pressing it against his leg.

"What a mess I've made of things," he said red-faced as he attempted to shake the excess soil off his shoes still holding onto the fabric, but the muck stuck like tar.

Ma raised her hand to her mouth and chuckled quietly at the awkward site. She gestured with her hand again offering assistance, "Come."

Back on the front porch, he pressed the cool towel against his wounds. "I didn't realize the thorns on roses could be so treacherous. Experts should figure out a way to breed those nasty things out of the flowers."

He raised the cloth to get a closer look.

"I agree," she responded nodding her head up and down. "It looks better, but I'm afraid your slacks are ruined."

"Collateral damage, it goes with the job I guess. A thornless rose needs to be developed avoiding a problem like this.

"It's because of the thorns I've given my grandson, Derrick, a nickname."

"And what might that be?" he asked turning the terry cloth towel to a clean side continuing to hold it against his skin.

"Thorn Boy," she replied proudly. "Since he was a child, he would remove those nasty thorns from the stems for me. He became quite efficient at it, so the name stuck."

"Thorn Boy...hum. Clever," he responded.

"I won't take too much more of your time, but if you have a few extra minutes, may I ask you a couple of questions regarding your flowers? I've worked with roses in different, much cooler climates, but not here in the sub-tropics. They seem to be harder to keep healthy here."

She nodded and raised her hand to cover her mouth as she yawned. Dusk was settling in, and she was growing fatigued. She turned and smiled as the bright porch light began attracting mosquitoes. It brought an eerie dimension to his disfigurement as he leaned in closer to her.

"Tell me, Mrs. Stabb, how do you keep the foliage looking so healthy? The leaves were so green and thick I didn't notice the heavy thorns."

"Well, the watering was done early in this morning; that's one of the steps in keeping sooty mold off leaves. The plants needed the day's sun to dry. Watering them in the evening or at night encourages the development of mold in the warm, humid air."

"There are different growing conditions here. We don't have a winter season cold enough to kill insects. The right balance of fungicides and pest control along with proper fertilization is vital to keeping your roses healthy." He listened attentively, arms crossed, impressed, tapping his finger lightly against the side of his cheek.

"Well, I've taken up enough of your time," he said with appreciation. "I must be on my way. Thanks so much for the cloth. The bleeding's finally stopped."

"Good," she responded. Ma watched as he descended the stairs heading back to his van. His torn pant leg flapped. Just after he opened the door, he turned back to her, waved and shouted, "I'm going to work on breeding out those nasty thorns."

She smiled, nodded and waved back at him convinced their paths had crossed in the past.

The smell of burning sugar cane hung in the air as Ma meandered back out to the edge of her rose garden. Gazing westward over the rows of beautiful, fragrant blossoms, Ma noticed that there was a single rose bush that seemed to be taking on a unique color transformation. It appeared that its blossoms bore a hint of blue. Possibly the bees have carried pollen from other roses to hers. NO, *not possible*, she knew. It was allergy season, too; the Florida holly was in bloom; maybe her misty eyes had played tricks on her again.

The sky was turning indigo, and the sun settled below the horizon line. Grandma Ma brought her rosary beads with her to the grotto. The arthritis in her knees made it nearly impossible for her to kneel on the raised aggregate surface of the grotto Derrick built in honor of his grandfather and dad.

Ma felt a tolerable amount of physical suffering went with prayer. *Jesus suffered insurmountable pain for his believers*. She scoffed at the padded kneelers in church. Our society has put comfort before prayer. Her mind could block out any distraction because her faith was pure.

Peace settled around her as the beads she prayed with since early childhood passed through her, aged fingers. Time was irrelevant when she was deep in thought as it should be. A hypnotic state took over her mind, and what felt like an out-of-body experience occurred. Now she was in the right place spiritually.

In the niche just a few inches above her head, Ma experienced a vision as it appeared before her framed in swirls of white, puffy clouds. Now, the sky was dark except for the brightly illuminated space where the beautiful lady in blue had returned. As before, spires of bright light rose from her head while garlands of beautiful, blue roses were gathered at her feet.

Ma, mesmerized by the lovely image, continued to pray with the visitor who did not speak. This experience was mystical and yet seemed totally normal. She wondered what made her so worthy to receive a visit from such a stunning being. Her purpose was not to question but to have faith and believe. This time, she was certain; her eyes were not deceiving her.

Ma bowed her head and clutched her rosary tighter. The moment brought her peace she had never felt before. She was convinced the beautiful vision that appeared before her was there to deliver a message of hope.

After a few moments, she opened her eyes and looked up once more. As before, the lady had vanished. Ma diverted her hazy eyes to the ground. There in front of the stone kneeler was a small folded piece of paper just within her reach. It read:

A gift you possess is pure as gold

It harbors a history that is foretold

Time will reveal soon you will bask in his glow

The benefits are more than you could ever know

Perched on a stone

Attending to a need

A covering hides

What lies beneath

Claimed by many

A history untold

His heirs are near

Desired to behold

Chapter 17—Worth Killing For

Alone in his dorm room, Derrick slammed his book shut. "This is ridiculous! Hicks is either nuts, or he is putting me through some sort of secret initiation into his private little club. I'm just gonna to take an 'F' and be done with it. Guess I'm not cut out for an education in plant science," he conceded aloud in frustration.

"Hey, I'm here," Ben shouted, banging the palm of his hand on the door.

In relief, Derrick turned back and heaved a sigh, pushing his chair away from the desk. "Great! A reason to shove *this* to the back burner." He bounded to the door and flung it open greeting his buddy with a bear hug.

Ben shook his head back and forth and confessed as he entered the room, "Boy, I really blew it yesterday talking with Judy's Mom. I told her that the cops don't seem to be making much progress. It made the case sound hopeless, which isn't how I felt. Mrs. Johnson started to cry. I know answers are out there, it's just so damn frustrating."

Derrick nodded. "I can identify with frustrating, let me tell you about something else that's frustrating, this crazy ass assignment Hicks has me doing."

Ben gave him a perplexing look. "What is it?"

"I'm writing a report on soil and its affects with the color of flowering plants. I don't seem to be doing so well with it."

"That does sound like a challenge," Ben quipped. "Well, like I said on the phone, if I can help, I will. Seems he's really testing you; well, if he didn't think you could measure up, he wouldn't have given you the assignment, right?"

"Uh, I guess so, but challenge is an understatement. I have been digging around in books for hours, and this is all I came up with." Derrick tossed the bound pages at Ben.

Ben grabbed them; his eyes darted across the first page. "I don't have any knowledge of flowers and plants, but what I learned in mortuary school is that all of the elements you've got here in your report are the same that exist in the human body."

"Say what...in people?" Derrick shook his head and shot an equally perplexed look back as Ben continued.

"Yes, here you're talking about the same elements that exist in all of us. You know, in mortuary school we study science of the human anatomy. There's iron in blood, as well as a delicate pH balance. The body is a complex machine."

"What about aluminum?" Derrick inquired.

"Sure, aluminum, usually in small traces though, is in the blood. Actually high levels of aluminum in the blood can create symptoms of dementia and osteoporosis. Actually, it's the most abundant metallic element produced by the earth. It's found naturally everywhere in our water, air and soil."

Derrick's mind wondered back to his brother who lay motionless, imprisoned by a demented mind. He refocused on what Ben was trying to tell him.

"When you think about it, we are all connected together by this planet we live on. I guess that's why she's called 'Mother Earth' the Blue Planet. She is the basis of our existence. Mankind walks on her back, while she supplies us with everything we need. Not fair if you ask me."

Derrick thought, *Earth, Flowers, and People.* Then, he realized why Ben *was* his best friend. His inspiration provided a fresh start.

"Well, you'd better get to work on finishing that soil paper if you know what's good for you," Ben directed half-jokingly shaking an accusatory index finger.

Derrick rubbed his stomach. "I feel indigestion coming on." He knew time was running out. "I know. All I have is a theory. Maybe I should elaborate on that."

Ben reacted, "This isn't a creative writing class, bucko. Besides, you're not a slacker; you're a guy who does his work. You follow through."

"I'll just tell him I used a little imaginative thinking. I mean, who knows what science will come up with next anyway? TV programs that were science fiction twenty years ago are reality today. Look at Star Trek. I'm a visionary just like Gene Roddenberry!" Derrick exclaimed as he crossed his arms grinning.

"Visionary? I can envision an F on your report. I know you're a Treky, but that's probably not going to impress your professor. Let's take some time and you and I engage in a little lab work. Hey, at least you can say you've tried. Besides, with Judy missing I don't feel much like going out to a bar."

An hour later, Derrick, with Ben right behind him, slung the door open to the Hort. Building, Lab Department and flipped the light switch on. Several of the florescent bulbs flickered momentarily and finally came on flooding the room with white light.

"Where are those soil samples your teacher showed in class," Ben questioned as Derrick tossed his backpack onto the tabletop.

"Still in the classroom I guess. Let me see." Derrick departed for a couple of minutes and returned with several small jars handing one to his friend.

"This doesn't look like any dirt I've ever seen," Ben said as he shook the small glass jar, peered through the side, and then attempted to remove the lid. "It's stuck."

Derrick found a rubber grip pad in one of the table drawers, and after a few indiscriminate grunts, he finally unscrewed it.

"It's muck, not dirt. Muck is what crops are grown in around the lake region. Dirt is what you throw out," he collegiately informed Ben as he reached for a large, glass beaker from the overhead cabinet. He carefully tapped the jar against the edge of the glass spilling several tablespoons of the muck into the beaker.

After filling it with water Derrick covered the top with his hand and vigorously shook it. The flurry of varying tiny bits inside reminded him of the many glass snow bowls Ma placed throughout the house at Christmas. He and Rodney would run about shaking up each one, and then earnestly returning to the first one before the snow settled to shake it again; their little game went on for hours.

Derrick placed it back onto the countertop; he and Ben leaned in watching the particles separate. "Rock, gravel, silt and organic matter settles in layers," said Derrick his mouth so close to the beaker that his warm breath condensed on its surface. They observed the light to dark achromatic, grey layers slowly settling at the bottom of the beaker.

"There's a tinge of red in the water, see it?" noted Ben pointing into the glass container.

Derrick raised his eyebrows in question. He continued, "The lightest material would be organic matter." A few moments passed. Derrick raised himself from the tabletop pushing his tongue against the side of his mouth. "We need to let this settle a while."

"Wait! I've got another idea," he announced making an abrupt turn, darting toward a floor-to-ceiling cabinet, opening the door and removing a large apparatus with two, glass tubes mounted on metal stands."

"What's that?" Ben inquired leaning against the metal, lab top table supported by his elbows, watching Derrick maneuver the clumsy piece of equipment toward him.

"It's a fermentor or a biological reactor used in experiments with biomass—plant material vegetation or agricultural waste used as an energy source. It kind of reminds me of a modern version of one of those old stills used in making moonshine in the movies."

After positioning the piece of equipment, Derrick said, "There isn't enough substance in the beaker to put in the fermentor so I need to add some organic matter. He pulled an aluminum trash can from across the room closer, reached inside and extracted a fist full of foliage and stems.

"I'm going to use some of the sugar cane cuttings we took earlier today from the greenhouse and process it. Then, we'll mix this with more soil from the jar and put it under the microscope.

It will take awhile for the process to produce a liquid, so let's hit the vending machines."

"Whatever you say, buddy, you're the mad scientist," Ben quipped throwing his arms in the air as he watched Derrick shove the vegetation into the fermentor and sealed the lid.

An hour later, the two returned to the lab. Derrick removed a small amount of murky moss-like sludge from the glass depository. Then he took a petri dish from a drawer and mixed the sludge with a bit of muck from the jar. Next, he carefully reached for a pair of tiny, thin, glass plates from a microscope that sat on the next table. He placed a small sample of the mixture on one side and cautiously placed the companion piece on top of it. He slid the specimen under the microscope and peered though the lens.

"Let's check this stuff out...see what's in it."

Moments later he scoffed and confessed, "Well, nothing here that classifies as break-through science."

"Let me take a look. I've had lots of biology." Ben adjusted the knobs on the instrument.

Derrick glanced up at the clock waiting patiently as the second hand ticked away. A few minutes later Ben raised his head. "My earlier hunch could be right. I think some traces of blood are here. You have some luminol in one of those cabinets?"

"Why?"

"It's what investigators use to detect blood...it reacts with iron found in blood creating a blue glow."

"Let me check over here; Dr. Hicks has all sorts of chemicals here. I've caught a glanced when he unlocks the cabinets. Who knows what for, he's pretty secretive sometimes."

Derrick found a key in his professor's desk drawer and began to unlock the cabinet doors that surrounded the lab area. As he did so, he quickly scanned the contents. Minutes later, he paused. "Hey, believe it or not, I think this is what we're looking for."

Ben took another tiny sample from the jar and mixed it with the eagerly supplied luminol. He peered through the lens. "Yep, sure enough, there's blood in this," Ben announced proudly.

"Wow! Look, next to the luminol, I also found some litmus paper. It's used to detect certain trace elements." Derrick removed an eye dropper from the drawer below and placed a few drops from the beaker on the small strip of the red paper. Momentarily changing it to blue, he proclaimed, "We have aluminum here. The normal person takes in three to ten milligrams of it per day in the foods we eat. But this level seems abnormal, and it would be very dangerous for anyone to consume food grown in this soil."

Derrick pointed to the top layer formed inside the beaker. "Look at this thin coat of tiny white chips floating on the top of the water, sure doesn't look like anything I've ever seen in muck?"

Ben eerily said pointing to the particles, "Derrick, after cremations bones are put through a grinder. This looks a lot like that."

Derrick turned back to his friend. "I can give some to a guy I know studying archeology. He can run protein tests and see if they could be bone fragments. The test tells if the specimens are animal or human."

Derrick stepped aside allowing Ben to look though the microscope, again. He turned the lens to a higher resolution. "There are also high amounts of iron present. At the blood bank, this is one of the reasons donors, like Judy, gave blood, to reduce iron levels. Too much iron can be harmful to vital organs."

Derrick paused, took a deep breath. "Iron is the reason there is red in the soil, like clay, but that's usually in northern states like Wisconsin, not Florida."

Then Ben shook his head, "This is baffling. Why would there be high levels of these elements in your professor's soil sample?"

"Beats me, let's try burning it," said Derrick. "The color of the flame might tell us what other elements are in it."

"Genius!" Ben exclaimed, throwing his arms in the air. "Why didn't I think of that?"

"Okay, I know when I'm being mocked, Ben," Derrick said waving the single-fingered salute. He grinned back at Ben before removing a torch from the cabinet; he ignited the non-luminous flame and placed a small soil sample on a platinum wire. "This will prevent any distortion of color due to burning other materials." He carefully passed the teaspoon size portion over the flame. Brilliant golden flames emitted from the wire.

"Well, you're right Ben; there's iron here," said Derrick.

"Oh," Ben nodded in confirmation.

"Yes, see the bright gold colored flames show it." Behind the golden flame appeared a brilliant blue. "Ah ha, see, there must be copper present, too!" exclaimed Derrick.

"Really, how'd you know that?"

"Because a blue flame shows copper, and copper is consumed by the body through tofu, grains and nuts to name a few. A diet used by vegetarians. The missing students were vegetarians, right?"

"Yea, Judy is." Ben responded, scratching his forehead.

"This microscope is a toy...let's try another one," Derrick suggested to his friend raising his eyebrows enlightened by the idea.

"You have a better one?"

"The students don't, but the teacher does; because it's really expensive, Dr. Hicks stores it in a locked file cabinet. There should be a set of keys somewhere."

Derrick again approached his Professor's desk then stopped suddenly. He turned back to Ben who gave him a puzzled look.

"What's the problem, buddy, why the hesitation?"

Derrick pointed to his Professor's desk top. "Look, an ashtray and cigarette butts."

"What, he's not supposed to smoke in the building?"

"No! Dr. Hicks *hates* cigarette smoke. Once he caught a whiff of it on a student's breath and lectured the class ranting on about the hazards of smoking, so much so that all of the students who were smokers pledged to him they'd quit. I think they said that just to get him to shut up."

"Maybe it's not his," replied Ben.

"Wouldn't matter; like I said, he wouldn't tolerate it no matter whose it was."

Redirecting his attention, Derrick started searching the drawers on Stanley Hick's desk; one desk drawer was locked. He scanned the desk top, then spilled the contents of a pencil holder and discovered a small ring with two gold colored keys.

The second key opened the drawer that contained a plastic divider and more keys. Hopefully one of these would unlock the cabinet. Bingo. The last one worked. The secret file cabinet door was opened.

Gently, Derrick removed the Meiji Epi-fluorescent Lab Microscope from the cabinet and placed it on the stainless steel table. "These microscopes are almost $13,000, so I guess he doesn't trust us students with it," Derrick remarked with a smirk. "It would be so amazing to have one of these, but it is way out of my price range. Anyway, I'm sure the Dr. Hicks won't mind if we borrow it for a few minutes."

"Oh, yea look at this," Derrick said as he removed a small bottle from the locked cabinet next to where the microscope sat. He turned the label towards Ben. "How about we add this arsenic to the soil, too and see what happens."

He begun to mix it with another sample of green goo and muck from the jar and dabbed a minute drop onto the tiny square plate and inserted it under the microscope.

"Why arsenic?" Ben asked in wonderment.

"Arsenic has the element cobalt in it and is a byproduct of mining copper, hence the blue flame. Cobalt is used in coloring glass blue. It's a stretch, but maybe there's a connection to the color blue in flowers, too."

Derrick used a small spoon and carefully placed two specks of arsenic into a Dixie cup and mixed a third sample of the reddish soil with the olive, slimy concoction.

"Wait, stupid me; I need some compressed oxygen!"

"Okay, now, what's that?"

"It's air in a can." Derrick reached under the counter and displayed an aerosol can of compressed air. "The fermentation removed the oxygen from the substance. This caused the organic compounds to break down by the action of living anaerobic organisms. I'm going to add oxygen to our sample. Anaerobic respiration—it's what happens in our muscles when we do aerobic exercise—the process of generating energy by the oxidation of nutrients. Breathing deeper supplies the oxygen depleted during exertion. Simply put, our fermented goo, here, needs air."

"Whatever you say," replied Ben shaking his head back and forth in wonderment.

Derrick placed another tiny dab between the glass plates and put it under the high-powered instrument. Moments later he looked back up at Ben and said in a most serious tone, "I think we're onto something much more complicated than what we can understand." He paused. "Why would Dr. Hicks have a soil concoction that contains blood and possibly, bone? Complicated might not be the right word, more like sinister."

After carefully retuning the microscope to his rightful place, Derrick locked the cabinet while Ben cleaned up and reorganized the lab back to its original condition. Derrick followed behind to make sure everything was copasetic. They returned to Derrick's dorm.

Gradually, the morning sky turned bright blue as Derrick crawled out of bed alone in his dorm room. Ben left a note; he decided to head out early but didn't want to disturb "Sleeping Beauty" as he referred to him. The note continued to wish him good luck with his report and confirmed that what he had now was certainly much more interesting than before. Derrick nodded in agreement, but, again wasn't sure if *interesting* was the right word.

After working all night, he nursed a queasy stomach. He struggled to make his way to the bathroom, took a quick shower and quickly ran a comb through his thick, blonde hair. It had started to get some length and shimmered from the gel.

For just a moment, he thought of Ma and how she always rubbed his "mop", as she called it, when he greeted her. He slipped into his favorite Levi's and sweat shirt, grabbed his back pack and the completed assignment.

His report might bring up some interesting topics to discuss in class. Interesting indeed, in the report he speculated that the traces of blood and possible bone fragments were animal. They could have been, but he sensed differently.

As usual, Derrick was the first student to enter the classroom. He was taken aback to find the file cabinet door open. Nervously, he retraced his steps last night and clearly remembered leaving it just as he found it, sealed tight and carefully returned the keys to their rightful place. He was certain before he and Ben had left all traces of their work were cleared away.

Not surprising, the dirty ashtray had disappeared.

Gradually, other students meandered into the classroom. Professor Hicks entered from another door that led into the lab area. He seemed to be in a good mood this morning. Derrick breathed a sigh of relief as he waited in anticipation for him to ask the class to turn in their reports. Much to his surprise, the fifty-five minute class concluded and no mention of the reports; that is, until the students had begun exiting the classroom. "Students, please leave your reports on my desk as you leave."

Derrick was the last to depart his seat. "Mr. Stabb," Hicks addressed Derrick in his soft, feminine tone. "You have yours for me?"

Derrick quickly produced the black, vinyl binder, professionally labeled and handed it to his expressionless teacher.

SOIL ACIDITY ASSOCIATED WITH CHEMICAL

REACTIONS IN COMMON GARDEN PLANTS

Derrick Stabb

Hicks casually turned the pages in the report. "It looks like you've put a lot of work into this. I like the diagrams," he said as he pointed to the detailed sketches Derrick drew.

Derrick could feel the perspiration beads trickling down his lower back. His mind wondered back to the little jar with the mysterious contents and where his teacher could have gotten it. "I have put a lot of time in this, sir. I actually used some soil samples and did my own analysis." At that moment, Derrick realized that he had called attention to one half depleted jar.

"What samples?" Hicks inquired.

"Oh, soil from home. Muck. I had a friend visiting from South Florida this weekend. I asked him to bring some samples from the coast and inland areas." Derrick couldn't believe he had come up with such a convincing response off the cuff. He feared that his "tell-all" face would give him away, but Hicks bought it.

"Impressive. Okay, you may go."

Derrick felt the weight of his anxiety lighten as he approached the doorway. Well done for now, he thought, stepping outside the classroom door and pausing as he leaned against the refreshing, cold tiles recalling Emily's words, *a new flower someone would make millions with.* But, would it be worth killing for?

Chapter 18—A Flower Cult

A few passersby looked through the sparkling display window as Emily had begun her routine to close the shop. Taping for the project wrapped up several days ago. *That director was a real butt wipe,* she thought. She couldn't last much longer contending with one more ridiculous, dramatic episode unfolding before her.

A couple of bunches of 'Stargazer' lilies had come in today for a party next week. Emily pushed the bucket closer to the window near the light. The buds were still very tight and slightly green. These are very fresh, she thought, and probably will not start to open for at least a couple more days. She recalled the last time she sold lilies for a party when she miscalculated the time it took for the flowers to fully develop. On the day of the event, she was looking at buckets of buds, not one open flower. Customers want to see gorgeous flowers, buds are useless. The shop took a loss, and Emily took a cut in pay that month. She couldn't afford a repeat.

On her way to eagerly see Derrick, she had to make another last minute delivery. Ah, working in the retail floral business. As if it wasn't enough for her to take the order and arrange the flowers, now she had to deliver it too. *All in a day's work in the glamorous business of flowers; yea, right,* she thought after hanging up the phone and quickly stuffing the vase of bright colored blossoms into a delivery carton.

The quaint, white frame cottages tucked behind a security gate were perfect for student housing. Emily pulled up to the call box and pressed the six-digit code she was given. After several rings, a youthful voice picked up. Great! Someone was actually here. After a series of obnoxious beeps, the arm which blocked the entrance raised, followed by an opened gate.

'Janice' wound around the single narrow road to 236-B Birds Nest Lane. Every unit had its own personality, unusual for most gated developments. The trim adorning each small house along the tree covered, brick paver driveway varied with pastel colors. It was charming. She pulled into the designated GUEST parking spot and carefully removed the vase of fresh flowers from the passenger seat. As she made her way up the sidewalk trimmed in pink and purple inpatients, Emily noticed yellow, police, crime tape that surrounded the next door cottage, 236-A.,a blatant disruption to an otherwise harmonic environment. A creepy feeling settled over her.

After she rung the bell, a pretty girl with short, buzzed, blue hair bound out in front of the door almost immediately, startling her. Emily handed over the clip-board for her signature. The arrangement followed; she fumbled with it as the college girl handed back the clip-board. Unable to contain her curiosity, Emily inquired about what happened next door.

She responded handing the signed delivery roster back to Emily, "That's where Julie Rose lived."

Emily turned and ambled back down the winding walkway to 'Janice', eyeing the entrance to the innocent looking cottage next door and wondered what could have happened to the girl Derrick met in the bookstore.

Market Street Pub was a popular collage hangout that teemed with students coming and going. That afternoon Lieutenant Waites slid into the opposite side of the booth facing Derrick and Emily's stern looks staring back at him.

"This is way out of bounds with my usual way of conducting an investigation, but I'm gong to tell you that there's been another disappearance. A vacationing couple returned home in the Thornhill Estates area, and their son was missing."

"How did they know he was missing?" Derrick inquired.

"It appeared like he took his usual early morning swim and never went back into the house to get ready for class. The guy was quite the athlete, an Olympian. It was on the news today."

"Who is he; what's his name?" Derrick inquired.

"Brian Thompson."

"I know him. Swimmer, really arrogant, he thinks he's God's gift to the universe."

"What makes you say that?" Waites asked, detecting a tone of jealousy.

"He's in a couple of classes I'm taking. The type that basks in the glory of his own self-importance; he couldn't get enough attention from the girls."

"Did it bother you that he was so popular?"

"No. It bothered me that he was so rude. I hate that. The day you came to school to first question us, he and his bunch of goons, who follow him around, were talking trash about Julie Rose. I defended her; told them they didn't know what they were talking about."

Emily cut in; her expression changed to one of concern. "I made a delivery to him the day before."

"A delivery?" questioned Waites.

"Yea, an odd, little lady came into the shop and sent an order of blue roses. She didn't have the full address, so I cross-referenced it in our directory."

"You didn't find that strange that she didn't have his address."

"No, not really; you wouldn't believe it; lots of people have wrong addresses or no address at all. I really didn't think anything of it."

"You didn't ask her why she was sending him flowers?" Waites inquired with a note of suspicion in his tone.

Emily responded quickly and a little defensively. "No, I don't feel that's any of my business. We believe in a customer's right to privacy. Besides, she could have told me anything she wanted.

The card was real strange, too. It was poem, a riddle of sorts. They seem to be popping up everywhere."

"Popping up everywhere?" He questioned as his deep-set, beady eyes zeroed in on Emily.

"Yes, Derrick's grandmother has been getting these riddles from somewhere, too. She says an apparition appears to her and leaves them behind. She lives down in Belle Glade; the last time we were there, she showed us the message if you can call it that."

Waites sighed and shook his head back and forth. "I don't know about all of this, poems, riddles? You two really present an interesting challenge. Are you sure there isn't something else you want to tell me?" He tilted his head down and lifted his eyebrows indicating the he didn't quite believe them.

Derrick and Emily shrugged their shoulders.

"Hum," he murmured. Waites glanced down at his watch. "I have another meeting; otherwise I'd follow you back to the shop right now to get that customer's information. I'll stop by first thing tomorrow. I need to talk to this mysterious flower sender. She may be more willing to give me details."

The following morning, Waites paced back and forth in front of University Florist's colorful window displays holding a 'hot cup of Joe' and waited for Emily's arrival. He wasn't a patient man. He noticed the hours' sign on the door; she was late.

The shaky, Volkswagen Beetle pulled up in front of the building and slammed against the car-stop jolting the little car backwards. She gathered her belongings, stepped out onto the pavement and haphazardly slammed the door with her hip. "Sorry to keep you waiting, Detective Waites," she chuckled at the sound of it. "I suppose if your name is Waites, you would have to be patient."

He replied after clearing his throat, "Not really."

Emily randomly fumbled through her vivid, super-tote bag for the shop keys. Waites wondered what it was a woman kept in those large, handbags. "Here they are," she announced pulling out a macramé key chain as they jingled in her hand.

They entered through the shop's door as the wind chimes dangling above announced their arrival. Emily quickly leaned over and flipped the pastel, artsy, wooden sign to OPEN. The oak trees' leaves danced in the breeze as the morning sunlight flickered through the shop's eastern exposed window. Waites, a stanch Gators fan, immediately noticed the shop's whimsical display of assorted orange and blue football memorabilia displayed on the artificial Astroturf outlined with a white picket fence.

"First things first," Emily said, as she grabbed the coffee pot and emptied yesterdays cold, stale remains. She rinsed it under the water tap in the shop's utility sink and filled the carafe to the brim. In one sweeping motion, the coffee pot was set and brewed. "I have to get this going before anybody else shows up, otherwise I get attitude."

In the back room of the tiny shop, Waites noticed the splotch of blue paint on the ceiling tiles and could only imagine. "Bookkeeping for me can be a very scary situation," she said to the waiting Lieutenant. "Numbers have never cooperated with me. Either I'm short cash, or I've miscounted. What a pain the ass."

Emily jumbled though a pile of papers in a shoe box that contained the week's receipts, paper clipped together by 'day' and stacked on top of each other.

"The shop has a computer, but it's just for transmitting wire orders," she explained as her fingers shuffled through the stacks with the precision of a Las Vegas dealer. Waites nodded, unclear as to what she had referred to.

"Here we are. This was the cash order from yesterday. I thought there might be something on it you could use; no, not even a phone number. When walk-in customers pay with cash, we just take the money and run." She giggled. "Not literally; I mean we write up a receipt for inventory purposes, and off they go. It's not a big deal."

"Let me check the stack of orders for delivery. We keep those separate from cash and carry sales." Emily continued to dig back through several stacks of orders in a separate, plastic tray while Waites leaned against the lattice covered wall and sipped his coffee.

"We get as much information as possible in case there is a problem," she said after finding the receipt.

"Here it is!" she exclaimed with pride waving the creased paper in her hand.

"Well this should help you out. I have the credit card information, name and a phone."

"Did you get a driver's license number?" inquired Waites.

"No, I asked, but she didn't respond. She was strange one, to say the least. People are so funny about offering up information like that," Emily replied.

"At least this is something to start with," Waites said. "Here's a zip code that's in Broward County. I recognize it from mailing parcels to my aunt there. As soon as I get back to headquarters, I'll run this through our data base and see if something pops up. Thanks."

"I'm glad to be able to help in any way. I know if I saw her again, I would definitely be able to identify her. This state of affairs is tearing up my boyfriend and Ben, not to mention the other families, I'm sure. I'm praying that they all will be found safe," Emily said as she put the rubber banded bundles of receipts back into the shoe box.

"I do have another question for you; it's about your boyfriend."

"Derrick, what do you want to know?"

"I've heard that he's involved in some kind of cult activity."

"Yea, I heard that, too. I told Derrick about it. He denied it, told me that was ridiculous."

"In my questioning of some of the other students, seems Derrick is viewed as a bit strange. He doesn't fit in, and this story has been circulating around campus that he has this fascination with dirt."

"Dirt? You mean, soil. He's studying horticulture. Soil is part of it. The last thing Derrick would be involved in is some sort of voo-doo nonsense. He is way too logical for that; believe me, I know."

"What about this Noetic Science stuff? I understand the Johnson girl was into it along with your boyfriend."

"They were just curious. Derrick is always interested in new ideas. That's part of what makes him so fascinating, that he's unpredictable. He loves exploring scientific theories, all kinds, because he's unencumbered by hardcore facts. He's not afraid to try new things, hoping to become a better person. This cult stuff is just crazy. Some people just like to talk, maligning others, compensating for their insecurities. Obviously, since they don't know what they are talking about."

"I see. Well, if I need anything else I'll call."

Detective Waites placed the slip of paper with the customer's information into his wallet. He noticed the coffee was made and asked to refill his cup just before he headed out the door. As he exited, the shops' driver greeted him. *Interesting attire to be working in,* he thought: a guy wearing an old tee shirt with stencils ironed upside down on it, baggy nylon shorts and a blue cap.

These people in the flower business are really different, he thought pulling the door closed behind him. They could all be in a cult.

Chapter 19—Those He Controlled

Cornelius eagerly returned back to the lab in fifteen minutes from the old lady's garden. His faded blue van, still with its tail light cracked exposing the bulb and foil backing, pulled up along a few, surviving melaleuca trees standing like strong soldiers along side the rustic barn. He slid off the seat, reached into his jacket and removed the plastic bag. Lifting it up within inches of his face, he smiled with gratification. He now had one more component necessary to move forward to the next step. Eagerly, he unlocked the narrow side door and slipped through with his latest acquisition held tightly in his sweaty palm. Aside from the constant, slow, drumming, white noise of the generator, it was a quiet spot. Peace was exactly what he needed to concentrate. Other than the occasional truck loaded down with sugar cane, the road was barely used.

He proceeded at a quick pace toward the white, aluminum walls of the laboratory where he was convinced he was about to make scientific history. His science would change how people felt about the significance of roses, his roses. He was about to transform the mere idea of using a rose to reveal a sentiment with his creation—a product so elusive, until now, so unique that it could never be challenged. His impact on a billion dollar industry would certainly land his name into the history books. He would carry forth the legacy of his Docent and with it would come money and fame: the two things he yearned for most.

Now, nothing could hinder the slow-moving progress that years of labor, risk and sacrifice had offered up. Cornelius stopped in his tracks. But wait, would he have to continue killing Aryans designated with one single symbol? Yes, the blue rose tattoo was the mark that labeled them as perfect specimens.

Those specimens are an important component in the development of his blue rose and must be kept secret at all costs. As history has proven, brilliant ideas are often stolen, the inventors tricked or manipulated out of what is rightfully theirs although that wouldn't happen to him. He smiled again. No, he was too smart and picked up his pace. He related to the passion that brought men to do what others find unimaginable. He had worked too hard to let anything keep him from his goals being achieved. Everything he had done was justified.

His idol, the great Leonardo da Vinci, secretly robbed graves to study human anatomy. Today, he is celebrated as one of the world's most brilliant artists and inventors. He was convinced that, in time, he would take his place among those in history who are the *true* creators. But, admittedly, to create, sometimes you must destroy. After the laboratory accident, he chose to abandon the moral guidelines of his past and followed this diabolical theory. A conciliatory thought: Perhaps the people who gave their lives should be graced with a namesake, a rose that will live on in history.

He approached the lab door and yanked it open. Earlier, he had placed one hundred petri dishes to be used for germination. Now, cells from the plant tissue culture were placed on hot agar, a gelatinous substance derived from seaweed combined with salts and amino acids. O-Negative blood was swirled into the agar for a nutrient and turned it red. He leaned over each small glass dish and closely examined the contents' progress.

In the adjoining greenhouse, rows of white, metal containers were carefully situated on sterile, stainless steel tables. In various stages of development, small seedlings, previously cultured, gently rose toward the strategically placed, individual grow lights above. He paid careful attention as he tested the well aerated, reddish soil of each specimen. An elaborate drip-watering system had been set up so each seedling received the exact amount of distilled H2O.

The meristem rose canes he obtained from the old lady's garden earlier that evening would provide a different strain of plants, heartier, disease and nearly thorn free.

Methodically, he followed the procedures he developed subsequent to years of work and research which showed just the right combination is necessary. Each seedling was placed into the four inch, metal container that contained a unique composition. His knowledge indicated that these, immature plants would grow into the only natural blue roses known to man, not violet or lilac but a true, sky blue rose that cultivators had been attempting to develop for decades. He felt it; he knew it, and he believed *the reality was almost here.*

After the agar solidified had cooled, it was ready for the microbe laden sample. Cornelius placed pieces of the apical meristem in test tubes with agar and rotated continuously. The rotating vials help a tumor of cells to develop. He divided the tumors into small pieces and placed them in the agar inside the dishes for growth to begin. Then, days later, he would transplant the tiny, growing rose bushes into sterile, specially developed soil composition for the plants to develop and thrive. More seedlings were nearly ready for planting, but the soil had run low. He needed to produce more.

His white lab coat was secured around his waist as he slowly turned the fresh mixture, too; it had run low. Cornelius returned to the freezer; after a moment, he stepped out into the open space of the barn carrying another frozen brick of human tissue. Moments later, the drum of the compressor was drowned out by the grinding blades of the wood chipper.

After turning the muck over and blending it with the frozen matter, he scooped up a shovel full and spilled just enough potting material into the bucket to accommodate the remaining seedlings.

Cornelius carefully carried two of the growing pots into the greenhouse and placed them on the sturdy bench. He reached above and connected the watering tube that led from the pot to the main line to the growing pots. He stood, arms folded, proud and looked out over the rows of benches. A rush of accomplishment overcame him. He couldn't wait to see those first, tiny, blue buds.

He checked his watch; more time had slipped by than he realized. He had an important date at the nursing home. Cornelius turned and made his way toward a bench in the corner of the greenhouse. Neatly positioned in a long row were his prize tomato plants. He picked the luscious red fruit: perfect, ready for consumption. He held it a few inches from his face and sighed.

He removed a hypodermic syringe from his desk drawer.

In the cabinet over head, he reached for a bottle of radiator, stop leak solution and removed its cap. He inserted the needle into the bottle and carefully drew it up into the syringe. With a tomato in his other hand, Cornelius gently inserted the needle through the thin skin and injected the solution into the plump, juicy fruit. He repeated the process over and over until enough tomatoes were laced with the solution's primary element: aluminum. The corners on his mouth turned upward slightly while he turned the perfectly formed fruit side to side inches from his nose. Toxic to anyone who ate them, the negative effects were numerous: extreme dementia and eventually, death.

Careful not to bruise each perfectly formed tomato, he wrapped them in thin white foam. He carefully packed the soft-skinned fruit into a heavy-duty cardboard box and loaded it into his van.

He lit a cigarette and took a couple of deep drags blowing trails of smoke from both nostrils while smiling, thinking, *Cornelius is strong, Cornelius is worthy, Cornelius is powerful.* Keenly aware that time was ticking by, Cornelius planned his every move. His calculations had been perfectly executed most assuredly and without restraint from those he controlled.

Chapter 20—Her Next Performance

"**Dr. Hicks**! How nice to see you again," declared Sienna Hurst with a million watt smile from the circular nurses' station centrally located in Memorial's rotunda. She placed the clip-board more confidently on the counter and raised her lily white arms to the counter. "Paying your cousin another visit, I see."

"Yes, I'm in town for a couple of days, and I thought he would enjoy some nice ripe tomatoes from my special stock," he responded with a gratuitous smile. "May I borrow one of your carts to carry these? The box gets a little heavy by the time I get to his room."

"Certainly," she replied amicably.

He placed the corrugated box on top of the wired rack with a grunt and wheeled it down the gleaming hallway to Room 236-A.

Once inside the room, Cornelius removed a pocket knife from his jacket and sliced small pieces that would be easily consumed by Rodney. The corners of his mouth turned up slightly as each wedge was gingerly placed on his lips. Clearly he enjoyed their rich, ripe flavor. Cornelius stood over him and watched as the last piece disappeared. He took a paper napkin and dabbed the young man's chin.

The door eased open, and Sienna entered the room. "He really enjoys those, doesn't he?"

Cornelius responded, "You *will* keep feeding these to him everyday as I instructed?"

"Yes."

"Good, I'm glad that we're clear. It's vital that he remain in this state. Her money can't last too much longer. Not at the price this facility charges. Once her property goes into foreclosure, I can snap it up for a deal. The blue roses will have a public home."

"You've thought of everything," she said, obviously amazed at his strategy.

"I try, but we have to be careful, nothing is guaranteed. Now you will meet me there tonight as we planned, right? They don't have you on night duty?"

"No, no, I'm all set. It's just; I can't believe that she's falling for this. The whole thing seems so hokey."

"Well, Sienna, you don't know people like I do. Their faith overrides everything. She believes what she wants to believe."

The nurse shook her head and smiled back at him. He knew he had her hooked.

It was late afternoon; Sienna Hurst slid her magnetic key card through the entry device of the Psychiatric Ward and headed back to Room 136-A.

Normally a cool, level headed professional, she felt intimidated when Cornelius came to visit. There was something captivating about his intellect, and she was impressed that his deformity didn't hinder him in any way. She considered that admirable. As a matter of fact, he seemed to be able to use his unfortunate accident to his benefit, charming everyone at Glades Memorial, playing on their sympathy.

Hospital policies forbid food to be brought in from outside because of contamination. However, her credibility enabled her the flexibility she needed to carry out her duties. She sliced into the fruit, allowing the scent of the ripe tomatoes to waft by Rodney; he perked up. As she sat on the edge of his bed and followed through with Cornelius's instructions, Sienna took solace in the monetary promise he made to her. Her parents struggled physically and financially.

Adoringly attentive, she frequently stopped by to help her mother care for her ill father.

Rodney's bright blue eyes sparkled as he looked up to the nurse's angelic face. She offered the last helping and wiped the corners of his mouth. Dusk had settled in; her shift was over. She slipped out the door, the clock hanging above the nurses' station read 7:45. She had a little over an hour to stop by her parents' house before meeting Cornelius and giving her next performance.

Grandma Ma's life was quiet even with all of the unusual, recent activity in the rose garden. Now in the solitude of her lovely home, Ma reflected back on the memories of her full, rich life.

Where have the years gone? She still clearly remembered the day in 1941 when she and her husband drove to the bus station for his deployment to the military. What a time filled with so much emotion, doubt and love. The last impression of him was burned into her memory. It replayed over and over: his strong figure as he stepped onto the bus. Just as the door was closing, he turned, gave a smile and wink. That was the last time she ever saw him.

Raising her son alone wasn't easy; however, love got her through everything life threw at her. One thing was for sure; her faith guided her down the right path. Ma's unshakable beliefs galvanized her against anything. Now she was experiencing doubt. She knew there was a reason God had put these obstacles before her. What should she do?

Now with everyone gone, she was faced with new challenges; all alone with her thoughts. She was in a situation she never would have imagined a few years ago. So it is true: the things we least expect sometimes do happen but for a reason. Perhaps to test our faith, to see what kind of character we have...the stuff we're made of.

Dealing with life's uncertainties was indeed character building. She could never go back, only forward with what she knew. Everyone would make different choices if they had a crystal ball showing the future. Since that was totally unrealistic, she could only rely on intuition, experience and prayers.

Ma knew that the surprises in life, good and bad, are what happen. She wasn't naive. The challenge was how she should react to those surprises. Should she allow fear to dominate or choose love? It all boiled down to these two emotions. Love or Fear, God or the Devil; whatever she chose as her guidance...her behavior would be governed by it.

It was time for her walk in the garden. The cool, night air and sweet fragrance called to her. This was the best place to be. On this evening, Ma felt the desire to walk all the way out to the grotto, probably because she'd been thinking so much of her, beloved husband and how much she missed him. The wedding vows they took had deep meaning to her. Honoring those vows was beautiful. It gave the brief period of time with him so much significance as he enriched her life more than she could have ever imagined.

She gently touched the lovely, full blossoms on the rose bushes along the path's edge. Occasionally she stopped and guided her hand down the sturdy stems; she felt the prickly, large thorns. Surely, as she approached the grotto, there was a noticeable difference in the amount of thorns on the plants, the ones nearest the grotto seemingly thorn-free...interesting. Maybe her visitor's idea wasn't so far fetched.

The rosary beads she had since she made her first holy communion were woven through her, arthritic fingers. Ma stood before the stone and mortar shrine and prayed the Hail Mary and the Our Father.

A calm feeling surrounded her as the beautiful lady in blue appeared once again high above the grotto. Her experience was like a beautiful dream; she'd shown out-stretched arms guiding her to heaven. Barefoot, the vision stood on a bed of blue roses. Ma sensed the lady's reappearance was a sign. She needn't question her faith or fate; just believe, and she would be shown the way.

This time she spoke in a soft, almost inaudible tone. Ma heard the faint words: "Trust in those around you." Was it permission to let go of her property and let God take care of the rest? That thought had crossed her mind; maybe it was time to concede. She griped her beads more firmly considering the divine guidance presented to her. This *must* have been the answer she was waiting for.

Then Ma genuflected slowly on her wobbly knee and kissed the crucifix.

As she precariously stood, regained her solid footing, the lady in blue had vanished once again into the darkness. Ma looked on the ground before her feet for another message, but the visitor didn't leave anything behind this time. She turned and headed back to the house.

Sienna ran across the grassy field as fast as her legs could carry her heading for the waiting car. Her blue and white robe flapped wildly against her, bare legs. Those wicked rose thorns she stood on during her amazing performance at the grotto's ledge sent shooting pains through the bottom of her blue-dyed, stained feet.

She ripped off the veil and grasped it in her hand enabling her to see better through the thick, evening fog. A set of rosary beads swung wildly in the other. She approached the blue van grasping the door just above the window and said as she gasped for air, "I don't know how much longer I can go on with this charade."

"As long as I tell you," sternly replied Cornelius as he slumped behind the wheel taking a final deep drag from his burn out cigarette.

She responded, "Sooner or later she is going to recognize me. I don't think the woman is as delusional as you think."

Cornelius adjusted himself sitting straight up in the driver's seat asserting his authority over the diminutive nurse. His one steely eye bore a hole through her. "I have one word for you, Sienna...*chloroform*. Remember those missing bottles from the hospital's pharmacy? How I came up with the excuse to get you off the hook when the other doctors had you on the hot seat? They thought that no one else had keys to that cabinet except you until, well, I confessed to have found an extra set hanging inside a cabinet. They are still looking for the culprit. So let's not forget that you owe me. You owe big...your license...your job would have been down the drain if I hadn't stepped in."

"It was *you* I got the damn chloroform for!"

"Right, so let me worry about the old lady's psychological wellness. You just do as you're told. We are in this together. One slip up by you, and we both suffer. Understand!"

Desperate, she sighed deeply and wondered how she allowed him to manipulate her into tricking the sweet Mrs. Stabb into believing that she was a divine presence. Using the grandmother's unwavering faith to get him what he wanted: her property, lock, stock and barrel.

"It's not enough that I feed her grandson those aluminum-laced tomatoes you show up with, now this."

"Don't worry, Sienna; when all of this comes to fruition, you will get more money than you can count. You won't need the job. You can spend all of your time taking care of your sick parents."

She slumped down in the seat, folded her arms under one another and contemplated her predicament. Torn between her values as a human being and greed, this man had a hold on her that defied explanation.

Chapter 21—Growing Florida Roses

In his Gainesville office, Lt. Robert H. Waites rubbed his forehead with the back of his hairy hand. His rickety chair creaked as he leaned forward feeling the pressure of his stomach against his belt. Hopeful, he scooted up to the keyboard and typed Hazel R. Craig in zip code 33019 into the new, state-of-the-art computer system recently installed at police headquarters. *Hazel Craig, let me see if she's here*. Sure enough, *bingo,* Hazel R. Craig, 4015 Johnson Street, Hollywood, FL 33019. He knew that a face- to-face meeting was better than if he attempted to contact her by phone. *Catch her off-guard,* he thought.

He picked up his phone and dialed Palm Beach County Sheriff's Office. "I need to speak with Detective Bruce Sistrunk."

"Hold on, I think I just saw him walk by."

Waites drummed his fingertips against the desktop.

"Sistrunk here."

"Sistrunk, this is Robert Waites with the Gainesville Police Department. I got your name from the records on the missing person's case of Judy Johnson. I have, what I believe to be, a connection to that case up here. I need for you to check out someone who lives in Hollywood.

"What makes you think she's involved?"

"She sent flowers to one of the missing victims here."

"Flowers?"

"Yea, and as of now, she's the only link we have to this case."

"I need you to check her story out. What was she doing up here? And what is her interest in this young man. Here's the address."

"Well, that's quite a drive from here. Don't you have someone in Hollywood that can check her out?"

"Not anyone who's familiar with the case. I don't want to dilute the investigation by bringing in more people and opinions. The whole situation is strange enough. I think the investigation should be kept as tight as possible. No more hub da bub than necessary. OK?"

"I'm not really clear on that."

"Just indulge me."

"I'll drive down this afternoon."

"Great, call me back as soon as you can."

Waites replaced the receiver to its cradle, stared at the address and hoped that Sistrunk's efforts would yield clues bringing him one step closer to a resolution.

Sistrunk eagerly scooped up his wallet and shoved it into his back pocket. By the time he arrived at the Hollywood police station from West Palm Beach, it was 4:00 pm. A buddy from the police academy worked on the Hollywood force, so he called him to join in. Sergeant Tomas Pass took his jacket from the hall tree and slipped it over his broad shoulders. "Are you driving, or am I?" he asked as Sistrunk stood in the corridor.

"You drive. I've been in the car all day. I need a break from the wheel. I hope she's there. She's the only lead we've got."

The FEC railroad tracks boarded the east side of the modest concrete block and stucco house on Johnson Street. Three citrus trees graced the front yard. As Sistrunk walked up to the front door, he noticed three painted Mexican pots, each filled with a tomato plant, rosemary and a little rose bush.

Sistrunk firmly knocked on the front door with no response; they sauntered their way around to the back of the house. The driveway led to a garage and upstairs apartment. Pass continued to knock on the back door while Sistrunk ascended the stairs. He rapped on the shaky, white framed, screen door. Several paint chips flecked off and drifted to the floor. A lace curtain hung over the four, framed windows. He pressed his cupped hands over the glass panes and gazed inside to see. No one was home as far as he could tell. Disappointed but unwavering, he made his way back toward the car. Just as he rounded the corner of the little house, a car hummed quietly into the driveway. Peering over the steering wheel was a woman with tufts of gray hair that puffed out from under her knitted cap.

The driver's side door opened. "May I help you, officers?" She called out with a grunt as she rocked back and forth gaining enough momentum to exit the car.

"Are you Hazel Craig?" Bruce Sistrunk asked.

"The one and only," piped back the stout, little lady as she bumped the car door closed with her elbow and limped along the edge of the driveway. She approached the gentlemen confidently and extended her hand with a wide smile that showcased a mouthful of crooked teeth. Slightly taken aback by her rueful appearance, Sistrunk shook her hand.

"I am Deputy Bruce Sistrunk, and this is Sergeant Tomas Pass."

"What is this about? Did my tenant get into some trouble?"

"We don't know. That's what we're trying to find out. We've come to ask you a couple of questions," replied Sistrunk.

"About what?" she said slightly defensive.

"Perhaps we could go inside," suggested Pass.

The little lady nervously fumbled inside her purse for a set of house keys. She unlocked the door, and the two officers entered behind her. The room was dark despite the fact it was mid-day. All of the blinds were closed, and shades drawn.

"I like my privacy," she said while she removed her cap and scarf and hobbled her way about the room as she opened the window shades that revealed the true color of the periwinkle walls. “I just love this shade of blue. You know blue suppresses the appetite. As you can see, it hasn’t worked that well on me,” she said smiling as she stroked her hands along the contour of her rounded hips attempting to make a joke.

“May I offer you some coffee or tea, officers?” They shook their heads no. She gestured toward the sofa offering them a seat.

Sistrunk began, “Ms. Craig, you made a purchase at a florist in Gainesville earlier this week. The recipient of those flowers has been missing for two days. Do you know anything about the disappearance of Brian Thompson?”

The chubby woman gave both officers a noticeable look of disbelief and responded, “I placed the order to the florist for my nephew, Casey. He hasn’t any credit, so I used my credit card.”

Sistrunk had his steno pad opened, writing down every detail. “Please have him contact me when you speak to him,” Then he leaned forward and handed Hazel his business card.

She took a quick look at the card in her tiny hand and responded, “Certainly, officers; what could have happened to this young man up there?”

“We don’t know; that’s why we are here,” Sistrunk replied as he looked directly into her eyes. “There have been three disappearances of young people in the Gainesville area and another disappearance involving a young woman from a nightclub in West Palm Beach. We have reason to believe that the cases are linked together.”

Hazel glanced down toward the floor.

The deputy continued, “This young man was quite an athlete and apparently went missing right after his morning swim.” Sistrunk leaned forward to show her a photo of him in a diving position, the Olympic logo clearly displayed on his Speedo.

“I see, an Olympic swimmer; impressive. Have you tried the International Swimming Hall of Fame in Ft. Lauderdale? See if your missing person has been seen there.”

"Swimming Hall of Fame, never heard of it. No, but thanks for the tip," responded Sistrunk feeling a little inept. "I also have some head shots of the three others." Hazel took the pictures from the deputy.

"Oh, what a shame, they're all so beautiful; uncanny resemblances. You say they're not blood related?"

"No, we need to talk to your tenant. Let me know when he returns," he ordered and then flipped over the cover closing his note pad and tucked it into his shirt pocket.

"Certainly officer," she responded to his command as they stood and headed for the door. The three paused for a few minutes on the front porch allowing the deafening noise of the train to fade.

"I've been living here for a long time and have gotten used to the noise."

Detective Sistrunk, a foot taller than Hazel, looked down at her and reiterated, "We appreciate your time. When you hear from your nephew, please call us immediately."

The two cops were a safe speaking distance from her house when Sistrunk said, "She's not telling us everything she knows. She kept fidgeting with the card I handed her. I was waiting for her to start cleaning her nails with its corner. And did you notice the funny thing that she was doing with her mouth? Like she was wearing uncomfortable braces, God knows she needs them. What really aroused my curiosity most was her callused hands. How many office workers do you know have hands as rough as a farmer? I'm definitely gonna be back here. She's got something up her sleeve, and I'm gonna find it."

***What** had she gotten herself into,* thought Hazel as she watched the cruiser pull away from the curb from behind the sheer curtains? It was all because of Cornelius; he lured her into this.

Pacing back and forth, she recalled the very moment last summer when she met the mesmerizing Dr. Cornelius Hicks. It was at a Florida Garden Club June conference in Tallahassee; he was the keynote speaker. She walked over to the bookshelf in her living room and removed the book he had published. She opened it; his bold signature leaped off the page. She ran her fingers over it and allowed her imagination to carry her back to the beginning of their relationship. She romanced the moment when she eagerly stood in line for hours patiently waiting for him to sign it.

As though it happened yesterday, she remembered approaching the signing table, stacked with books, as she tried to think of something memorable to say. Then he looked up, smiled and complimented her on the blue, floral print dress she was wearing. She was so taken; she almost forgot how to address him. Red faced, she regained her composure expressing her appreciation particularly for Chapter Six, GROWING FLORIDA ROSES.

"Oh, you like roses?" he inquired then with genuine interest. She placed her hands on the table and leaned in closer detecting the odor of tobacco on his breath.

"Yes, they are my favorite flower. I'm just sorry they don't come in blue because that's my favorite color." She was embarrassed; what a silly thing to say she thought. She quickly clammed up.

"Who do I sign the book to?"

"Oh, uh, Hazel, *please*."

The palms of her hands were moist. She wiped them on her skirt and watched closely as he flamboyantly signed the book with broad, sweeping, hand strokes, as though he were conducting an orchestra.

"Well, never give up hope, Hazel. I'm working on a break-through process that may grant you your wish. What do you do when you're not gardening?" he inquired.

"I am the director of the Central County Blood Depository."

"Interesting, you must meet all types of people."

"I do, and each has their own reasons for donating blood."

That instant happily provided her the opportunity to share some of her world with him.

He closed the book, handed it back to her as he glanced past her to the next person in line.

The professor extended his hand. She hesitated, and then shook it. Her moist palms persisted. She moved on.

The moment was still unsettling; maybe it was because she was lonely, but she felt there was a "connection" between her and this Dr. Hicks at that moment. He was so worldly and sophisticated. Captivating, she thought, despite his facial deformity. The eye patch added a mystique to his intriguing character. After she returned to her seat and gathered her belongings, Hazel noticed his hand writing on a business card inserted into Chapter 6; it said, *call me*.

She waited several agonizing days before she could drum up the courage and dialed the number. She couldn't imagine what this man would want with her. Who was she? A retired school teacher who loved to garden and worked in a blood bank. Hazel couldn't get him out of her mind. A smile came to her reminiscing about his throaty, foreign accent. Hazel could instantly feel her heart race. A woman of her years shouldn't be having these feelings, she thought, as she continued. But he must have felt a connection, too, or had she allowed her imagination to play tricks on her? It didn't matter, she thought. Risky business, but she was willing to play along keeping the volley of conversation going.

She was thrilled at his suggestion they meet again where she worked. The fact that he was taking interest in what she did was titillating. That evening, months ago, they walked through the halls of the blood bank.

"I have a request," she clearly recalled him saying. It was a turning point in her life.

"I need a few sample vials of O-negative. The blood samples from specific donors, those who observe a strict vegetarian diet, and they must have blonde hair and blue eyes."

At that moment, she was so immersed in him that she would have provided gallons of the crimson liquid upon request. She was thrilled that he thought enough of her then to invite her to join in on this amazing experiment, a collaboration of sorts, she thought.

"I can do that for you; when?" Hazel responded.

"Can you get them for me now?"

Hazel checked her watch.

"Right now, I don't know it's rather late. It would take some time. I have to search the files for the records on each donor."

"I can wait," she recalled him saying in his deep, persuasive voice.

Hazel entered through her office door. She took the small step ladder from the corner of the room, carried it over to the rattling air conditioner and elevated herself to adjust the temperature which had been set at a higher setting for the night. She then began to yank out the massive, metal file drawers. The act of divulging confidential information divided her between the moral values she held and the man who fascinated her.

That was four months ago. She slid the book back into its glorified place on the shelf in between NATIVE FLORIDA PLANTS and GROWING FLORIDA TOMATOES and thought. Now she was too involved. There was no turning back even if she desired. In retrospect, she knew it was all planned. He had her right where he wanted her.

Nervously, Hazel dialed the pizzeria where her tenant, and nephew, Casey Craig worked. "Casey dear, I have a little job for you."

"Job, Auntie?"

"Yes, tomorrow morning early I need to for you to go to the Miami airport for me. I have a friend, you remember me introducing you to Dr. Hicks; remember, he's the one who grows roses."

"Yes, Auntie."

"Well, he's expecting a shipment and needs someone to pick it up. He's agreed to pay you handsomely for your efforts."

"I don't know, Auntie. That guy *really* makes me nervous. I mean, he creeps me out with those scars and that eye patch."

"Now dear, he can't help that. And let's not forget about the money he's willing to pay."

How much, Auntie?"

"Two-hundred dollars."

"Wow! Two-hundred bucks, sure I'll do it."

"Wonderful, dear; I will have all of the instructions for you when you get home tonight."

Chapter 22 –There Is A Way

Dawn hadn't yet arrived. Casey thrashed about in his twin bed convincing his beleaguered body to meet the floor. Finally, he stood in an upright position and made it to the bathroom splashing south Florida's tepid water on his face. He returned, got dressed and sat on the bedside to tie his sneakers. He checked his watch. This was about the time when he was usually coming home from a night in the Ft. Lauderdale bars. After he checked his pockets, took a quick inventory of his wallet and the explicit directions crafted by Cornelius, he headed down the stairs. It was about a ninety minute drive to the airport.

Customs at Miami International was bustling early in the morning, and today would be no exception. Delivery vehicles, jockeying for position, backed up to the docks claiming product that arrived from around the world.

Jet engines rumbled overhead while Casey found a convenient parking spot near a dock. He looked around the confusing, unfamiliar assembly of concrete and steel, low-lying buildings—referred to as the land slide—for a sign indicating where to go. Down the loading dock, past several huge overhead doors, Casey spotted what appeared to be the right entrance, marked B-10 on his directions.

He emerged from his car looking about, intrigued by all of the activity and wandered up to the counter. On the other side of the glass partition was a serious- looking, Hispanic fellow whose biceps bulged from under a crisp, blue uniform. His lapel, photo I.D label read, Juan Rodriguez, Customs. With his thick, jet-black hair neatly combed back, the man's steamy looks immediately caught Casey's attention. He waited patiently as he studied the Latino's dark, striking features while the official quickly scratched his pen over documents.

The plexiglas window had a small slit at the base just above a recessed pocket in the counter, through which people claiming product, Casey assumed, could slide their paperwork under. Juan retrieved the documents Casey produced and indicated with a hand gesture his return in a few minutes.

Casey paced back and forth on the cement dock observing the hustle and bustle around him. He watched as flower shop delivery trucks, refrigerated vehicles and tractor trailers backed into the docks. He had no idea this part of the airport existed, let alone the tremendous amount of perishable products that came through here. Ever curious, he stopped an attractive woman in a grey suite and stilettos as her heels clicked against the concrete.

"What's in all of these planes, people?" he asked smiling sweetly. Casey knew how to get what he wanted.

"Oh, no, not over here; most of these are cargo planes," she answered as she pointed to one of the 747s slowly edging along.

"These stripped-down jets come in from South America and bring in the majority of the flowers and produce into South Florida. Nearly eighty percent of all cut flowers that entered the country came in through Miami. Sometimes passenger jets transport goods in their cargo area, which is why travelers are limited to only one free, checked bag. Transporting perishable commodities is more profitable and less trouble for the airlines. I've got to run, " she concluded checking her leather wrist band. She smiled at Casey and quickly made her way down the dock, obviously in a hurry.

Casey paced back and forth in front of the door marked B-10. Suddenly, it opened, and the Latino agent appeared carrying a long, skinny, white box secured with clear packing tape. Unmarked except for a small 4" X 6" Avery label that read...

ISRAEL GOLDEN FARMS

DR. C. HICKS

MIA#74639

GOLDEN CANE CORP LABORATORY

CLAIM TAG BG10528

Without uttering a word, Agent Rodriguez handed Casey a release form and a pen, pointing where to sign. Pen to paper, Casey's hand trembled in excitement as he signed the document while trying to figure out the strikingly handsome guy's background, who, he noticed, was not wearing a wedding ring.

"That's it?" Casey questioned after he scribbled his name on the paper.

"Si," he responded in a rather short tone tearing apart the triple copy document and handing Casey a duplicate copy followed by the box. Abruptly, he made an about-face and disappeared though the thick, metal door, slamming it shut.

Friendly guy, Casey thought sarcastically...*gorgeously typical attitude*...

Slightly disappointed in his ability to score one for the team, Casey dropped the carbon copy into a plastic zip bag, sealed it and shoved it into his shirt pocket; he then toted the lightweight box back to his car. Killing time as he drove back to the lab, he entertained fantasy thoughts about the beefy, customs agent.

The ride back to Belle Glade wasn't expected to take too much time, depending on traffic. Since he knew where to go, the only problem was the early morning rush hour traffic on State Road 836, known as the Dolphin Expressway.

So far, Auntie Hazel would be proud of him. The difficult part of finding the pickup location was behind him. He shouldn't have any problem meeting his delivery deadline where Cornelius, and his money, would be waiting.

Casey found a pay phone just before he reached the ramp to the highway. With traffic speeding by, he dropped a dime into the slot and dialed Hazel's number. He got her answering machine. "Hey, Auntie, I just picked up the box and headed out toward West Palm."

After an hour into his trip to West Palm, the flapping of the flat tire vibrated Casey's small car. He yanked the car over, crossing two lanes, to the road shoulder. Two drivers laid on their horns. Unaffected by the comotion he caused, he exited the car and made his way down the ramp to a pay phone. He dug into his pocket for his last coin. He didn't have a phone number for Cornelius, so he called Aunt Hazel; her answering machine picked up again.

"Hey, Auntie, it's me again. I got stuck on the freeway with a flat tire, and wouldn't you know it, not one person would stop to help me. I'm gonna get it plugged, and I should be on my way soon."

Casey hoofed it back about a half mile to a nearby service station, bought a can of tire-fix and headed back to his car sitting tilted on the roadside. The heat from the black pavement radiated the can. He quickly filled the tire, tossed the empty can onto the back floorboard, and started his car hoping his rim wasn't damaged.

A few miles down the road, the plug didn't hold and the tire went flat again. "Damn it!" Casey yelled aloud. "I knew I should have bought a new tire. Auntie is going to kill me! Auntie? No, it's that loon Hicks that I need to be worried about. What could be in that box anyway that's so freakin' important?"

Stuck on the outskirts of Wellington, an equestrian community, he was still about a half an hour away from his destination. He decided to leave the car, grab the box, and hitch-hike.

State Road 80 was almost a direct shot into Belle Glade. There was just one turn. So he could get someone to drop him off, and he'd walk the rest of the way. Being the cute guy he was, he was confident that it shouldn't be too difficult to get a lift.

His hunch proved true; several minutes later, two girls from the coast were headed west. They spotted the young man with a wide smile and big dimples on the roadside.

"Hey, what's in the box?" one hollered as she yanked the car to the roadside and pulled up next to him.

"A delivery for a friend," Casey responded with pleasure. "Can you give me a lift?"

"Sure. Hop in."

"Are both of you in some sort of cheering squad?" Casey inquired still grinning with appreciation.

"Yea, we're headed to Belle Glade to a practice, so you lucked out."

"I sure did," he responded gratefully envisioning the two hundred bucks in clean, crisp twenties.

The cheerleader in the passenger seat leaned back, placed her arm, bearing a blue rose tattoo, over the seat and asked, "You have no idea what's in there?"

"No, and I don't care. All I want is the money I'm promised for delivering it."

"Money...how much are you getting?"

"I'd rather not say," Casey responded a little paranoid that his ride might want a cut.

"Well, since this is a money-making proposition, maybe we should charge a little transportation rate to get you where you need to be with your secret cargo."

"Oh, come on girls, give me a break. Don't you just want to do something out of the goodness of your hearts?"

"Well," replied the passenger in the front seat. "We could figure out some other form of payment."

Casey gave the girl a questionable look realizing that his self proclaimed "cuteness" might now be his ticket to Belle Glade although doing it with two girls wasn't high on his agenda. "Make the next turn; we'll find a private spot."

Thirty minutes later, the girls hopped over the seatback and the three headed west shielding their eyes with the tops of their hands, blinded by the giant fire ball sitting just above the horizon. Thick rows of sugar cane lined the highway and canals in the rural areas of the western county.

Barreling down the partially paved roads, dodging pothole after pothole, the pretty girls laughed and shouted to their passenger. In the back seat, Casey could barely make out what they were saying. Then his attention was diverted to the directions and scribbled map Hazel provided, and he thought that the turn to the barn was just ahead.

"Turn here, now!" Casey hollered as they practically missed the road; the driver made a sharp right. The front left tire jumped a small pile of stones at the intersection, scattering them everywhere.

"Slow down!" he barked another order to her. Against the setting sun, the silhouette of a huge barn appeared. Finally, they had arrived at his destination. Lacking the time to walk up the winding gravel trail, Casey persuaded his two girl friends to deliver him to the door step...what could it hurt? He'd get the stupid box there that much faster; besides, they wouldn't remember where they were out here in the boonies. Now the convertible cautiously approached looking for an entrance. Casey noticed an old van on the opposite side from where they entered. He recognized it belonged to Cornelius.

"Keep your voices down," he whispered disciplining them. After he grabbed the long, white, cardboard box from the back seat, limber Casey, unencumbered by a roof, jumped over the side of the convertible and headed for the door. "This won't take long. I'll be back in a few minutes."

Hazel stared at her phone after she retrieved Casey's message. She quickly dialed Cornelius's phone number.

He sneered on the other end on the phone line. "I didn't like that kid from the moment I met him. If he screws this up, he's finished. Where is he?"

"He should be close," Hazel responded worriedly. "He left the message over an hour ago."

"If you hear from him, call me, understand?" he shouted.

"Yes, I will. I'm sure he won't let us down," she pleaded.

"Let '*ME*' down!"

Click.

His frustrations mounted; Cornelius ripped at the cellophane into a fresh pack of cigarettes. He had spent most of last night and this morning looking for the hair follicles he safely tucked into his pants pocket, or so he thought; he couldn't find them anywhere. Without the specimens, the next test would be impossible. He'll have to get his hands on more.

He paced back and forth inside the lab. He thought as he contemplated his next move. I need that fresh tobacco to proceed forward.

Through many trial and error attempts, he discovered that when the tobacco was composted with other organic matter that included specific levels of iron, acid, aluminum and sulfur containing cobalt, astounding fundamental changes occurred in the plant tissue feeding from the mixture. Chills went up his spine.

But this process involved more than tobacco and soil. His theory was that there was a direct connection between the blue color gene in roses and people. He was convinced that people with specific traits were vital to his experiment. Once the process had been perfected and patented, the roses will be mass produced most likely by a Dutch or South American grower. The product needed to be hardy enough to travel distance by air and still perform, lasting two or three weeks. He'd make a fortune. There was a lot at stake, and no sacrifice too great. Then all those souls who forfeited their lives would live on immortally.

Although time was growing short and his benefactor was anxious to see results, Cornelius could taste success.

The expenses had already exceeded what was projected, but he knew it did not matter as long as they got the intended results.

Not to worry; I'm close.

The adrenaline still rushed through his body as Cornelius pushed open the heavy, insulated, steel door to the walk-in freezer, emerging with two bulging plastic bags filled and rock solid. Just then, he heard a car pull up the gravel road. Good, the kid had finally shown up.

The girls giggled and chatted about how cute their new friend was and who would end up with him, again, later. Minutes seem like hours to them since they had to be somewhere. The driver checked her watch; she was mindful that time was running short, and she didn't want to be penalized for being late for cheerleading practice. "Should we leave, or wait?" she asked. It was a trying question for two young girls who just found a "hottie" on the side of the road.

Finally, time had gotten the best of them. The daring, blonde one decided she would go in and find out what was taking their friend so long. By now, it had been over fifteen minutes, longer than they had anticipated. Her friend was apprehensive about trailing behind her and remained at the wheel.

More time passed; now the driver was in a real pickle. She could have justified leaving their freeloading friend here, but now her fellow cheerleader was missing. She decided to wait a few more minutes hoping the two of them would appear soon.

She wondered why they couldn't have just driven by *him* and stayed on course. They would have been there by now. Angry, she got out, slammed the driver side door and headed for the building. The side door was open. In the pitch black, she slowly walked toward a light at the far end of what seemed to be a mammoth shelter. Getting more and more pissed off, she slowly stepped up to the white, shimmering building.

Well illuminated from inside, she cautiously gazed through the large plate glass window into the white, metal structure. Before her appeared to be a test area for plants; rows and rows of potted, small, leafy stems stacked on gleaming, metallic shelves, were situated one above another. It looked like some sort of high-tech potting shed. A variety of sizes, plants in white containers were lined up like soldiers. She leaned in closer. Her breath created a perfect circle of condensation on the glass.

A light fog passed beneath another door on the opposite side. A cooler? The door was ajar.

Staring intently, captivated by the spectacle of plants and intriguing layout of the room, the cooler door flew open. A tall, slender man in a white lab coat soaked in blood drug her friend by the arms into the room. Her lifeless body flopped about. He dropped her next to another body on the lab floor. In a second, she recognized their cohort. He, too, appeared dead. The man in the coat turned; his eye patch added a creepy aspect to the spine-chilling circumstances. Now they were eye to eye. He dropped the body and ran back through the door into the freezer.

In the darkness she heard a heavy thud, a door opening, and then quickly it slammed shut. Frozen in fear, a tingling sensation emerged from every nerve ending in her body. Before her was an imposing figure with a disfigured expression the likes of which she had never seen before. A tiny glow from the end of his cigarette brightened and dimmed with each puff.

She recoiled into a ball on the ground and protected her head with her hands. The last thing she remembered was him pulling her up by her bleached locks.

Cornelius stood at the laboratory sink washing the blood from his hands. His sense of gratification was expressed in a deep inhale, then exhale. His competitors would have done anything to get their hands on the highest grade of tobacco that existed in the world. He removed the air-tight, plastic wrapping and held the verdant, aromatic foliage against his face as he deeply inhaled again. He stood in place for a few moments content with everything that surrounded him.

He returned to real time and checked his watch. He had to report in; he hated it, but necessary if he was to continue receiving the much needed funds. He picked up the slick, white phone receiver to the left of the lab door. Cornelius felt belittled constantly checking in like a child working on a high school project, who had to explain every detail to his mother. He dialed the memorized number.

"Yes, madam, I am proceeding on schedule. I know I told you that earlier, but there was a little problem with the delivery here from your farm in Israel.

Oh, no need to worry, the tobacco is in the lab now, and I am proceeding forward. Oh, please don't say that. Your money isn't being wasted. I know. I know. You've put out a lot for this, and you've been patient. Now, *wait,* please don't threaten me. Please, please don't spoil how far we've come. I need for you to be a little more tolerant. I know I've said that before, but I am getting real close to success. I'll have some updates for you real soon. And there's been a recent discovery...what? Oh, let's just say a *new* breakthrough that I'm certain you will be very, very excited about. Please be open-minded; I guarantee it will be worth the wait."

He slowly returned the phone to its cradle and pursed his lips. Damn her, he thought. I can't let her back out now. Women...could never trust them. Now what do I do? He paused, sighed and begun reciting the words that brought him comfort. "Cornelius is strong, Cornelius is worthy, Cornelius is powerful"

Hicks glanced through the window into the specimen room. Hundreds of plants in various stages of development slowly inched up towards the grow lights suspended overhead.

His progress lay out before him. He placed both hands on his desk top drumming his finger tips against it and leaned in closer to the window continuing to study the seedlings displayed on the rows of benches. His reflection appeared back. There's got to be a way to appease her, at least for awhile. He thought and thought, and then the corners of his mouth turned up. Yes, there is a way.

Chapter 23—The Moment Of Truth

"What did the critical Professor Stanley Hicks say about the report you turned in?" Emily prodded her boyfriend.

Derrick sat back in his chair and cupped his hands behind his neck responding.,

"I haven't gotten it back yet. After it was turned in, he casually flipped through the pages and nodded seemingly in approval, maybe a positive sign? But all I can do now is wait. In the short amount of time I had with Ben, we put the soil sample through every kind of test our imaginations allowed. We burned it, blew air into it, and added some arsenic. We also found iron and high amounts of aluminum in the sample."

"Arsenic? Where in the world did you find arsenic?"

"There was a small jar of it in the locked cabinet where Dr. Hicks kept his precious microscope. Obviously it was not for the students to get their hands on." Derrick continued, "In the end, most of what I included in the report was theory, really, because I don't have any scientific proof yet on how the elements of aluminum and iron affect plants collectively. After Ben and I found the keys, we pulled out Dr. Hick's pricy, high powered microscope from his locked, storage cabinet; then we started making some interesting discoveries. We found traces of blood in the soil.

"Blood!" exclaimed Emily.

Derrick nodded, enjoying his girlfriend's reaction. "That's not all," he continued. "Things got really interesting when we decided to add sugar cane."

"Sugar cane!" exclaimed Emily. "What in the world is that suppose to do?"

"Fermentation, sure enough, there were subtle changes in the composition of the soil. Well, I'll find out soon enough what Dr. Hicks thinks of my theories. He'll probably say its all hocus-pocus."

"Of course it's real science," Emily responded defending his work. "I think this is all very interesting. What will you do with this information?"

"I have to wait for the verdict from Dr. Hicks tomorrow. Right now, I guess I'll just add it to my library of meaningless information."

"I don't think it's meaningless. You're on to something. I know it."

"Well, I had a great time with Ben. He's one smart guy, very philosophical. He helped me see how closely related we are to all living things. When you look under a microscope with an open mind, you can see that Darwin had the right idea; another really smart guy."

"What it all boils down to is that we originated from a single source, Mother Earth. And it's that source that still joins us together, physically and spiritually. Ben shared his viewpoint with me while we were peering though the microscope. He's right, we're all evolving. Think about it; if God has always been and will always be, then the creation of Earth in six days would relate. What would have taken billions of years seemed like only minutes when time is infinite."

Derrick added, "As advanced, scientific human beings, surely we can think creatively and interpret ancient, meaningful words into a modern message. We're all creators of our own thoughts and actions. Whether people choose to take responsibility for their actions or not, we each have what we each created; seems if more people took that attitude, the world would be a much better place."

"Now you're starting to get 'out there' on me," Emily kidded with him before her tone turned serious.

"Derrick, there's something going on that you need to know about. That detective, Waites, stopped by the shop creeping around; he thinks you're involved with some sort of cult."

"What! Where in the world did he hear that?"

"Sorry, I thought you knew. The rumor that has been circulating around campus, obviously he caught wind of it. I traced it back to that Thompson guy and his friends. They used some crazy-ass story about you and your fascination with blood and soil as a basis for seeking out victims with a certain blood type for experimentation. Now that he's missing, too, I'm afraid the cops will be focused on you."

"Geez, don't know what to say about that. People sure do have empty lives if that's what they need to do to feel good about themselves. Tear down someone else's reputation."

"It's hard fighting rumors. They're so destructive. Derrick, I'm worried. This is serious if the cops think you're somehow involved."

"Great, now this; thanks. Do you have any antacids?"

In class the next morning Derrick slipped into his seat just before Stanley Hicks entered the room. He barely slept the night before as thoughts of what the professor might say haunted him. He knew Dr. Hicks wouldn't pull any punches if he thought his science experiments were stupid. Derrick watched the second hand on the classroom wall clock sweep through the minutes as Hicks initiated the day's lesson. He wrote in broad strokes on the board.

SOIL CONTENT AND ITS IMPACT ON PLANTS

Nervous, Derrick had begun to squirm in his seat. It was the moment of truth. He watched as the professor, without uttering, made his way through the rows of chairs handing each report back to its author. Derrick observed the expressions on the faces of his fellow classmates while each nervously retrieved their work. Some had a hint of a smile, but most displayed a look of failure. It was apparent to Derrick that Professor Stanley Hicks didn't pull any punches when it came to marks of disapproval.

The student seated behind him burst into tears after she open the first page. It was as though the class was lined up in front of an intellectual firing squad, and Hicks was calling the shots, literally.

Derrick could feel the hair on the back of his neck standing, signaling the moment of truth, as Hicks approached him. He braced himself for what he anticipated to be the mental equivalent of a kick in the groin, but he was passed over. *What could this mean,* he thought as he sat motionless?

Throughout the room were sighs and murmurs. All reports, except one, had been returned to their rightful owners. Derrick waited; the perspiration accumulated under his muscular arms and trickled down his sides.

"Mr. Stabb, please come to the front of the class."

Derrick stood and approached Dr. Hicks making every attempt to ignore the subtle, involuntary twitching of his left eye lid that beleaguered him when he was extremely uneasy. He dared not look at the class. He faced his professor.

"I don't know where you accumulated this information from, but it is a brilliant piece of exploratory science. Your theories on a flower's genetic code and mutations are thought provoking and challenging. You attention to detail is very impressive. The experiments were intriguing and intelligently executed. I found this to be one of the most comprehensive and complete reports that I've ever reviewed, and it is the only one that has earned an A. Congratulations, Derrick!"

"So, what happened?" Emily inquired as she looked intently across the library table into Derrick's sparkling blue eyes. "I'm dying to know what Hicks thought of you hard work."

"I got an A; couldn't believe it. Stanley Hicks has a reputation for *never* giving A's. I was the only one in the class to earn one." Derrick sat tall and proud protruding his muscular chest outward imitating a dandy rooster.

"Impressive, but not a surprise. Everyone knows you're brilliant."

"I think *'the everyone'* you're referring to is *you* and *Grandma Ma*."

"You're too modest. Have you called Ben yet since he was so instrumental in this project?"

"Not yet, but I will. I can't wait to tell Ma; she will be so excited."

"Are you still going home this weekend?"

"I plan to and take my report with me. Not that I need proof; they would believe me, but I want to show it to Ma and Ben."

"Can you come with me?" Derrick requested in the endearing tone he knew worked on Emily. But to no avail.

"No, I don't think so. I have a wedding. Remember my bride who wanted the blue roses. She's using the Florida Gators colors as her pallet. I tried to talk her out of those hideous, blue, painted roses, but she was determined they be carried in her bouquets. Yuck. The irony of it is that this wedding is one of the largest the shop's ever done. Usually people with no taste are cheap, too."

"Don't judge, there's always an exception," Derrick responded in defense of a bride he had never met. A lesson his Ma taught. One of many lessons he'd learn from her.

Chapter 24—A Bloomin' Bash

Ma proudly stood at the edge of the porch and stared out over her spacious garden. At this point in her life she thought, *what was an old lady to do but enjoy her memories*? Over the years, caring for the garden had become a life support in some ways. As Derrick and Rodney grew, the time she spent with them between the rows of perfectly cultivated rose bushes was cherished. The flowers bonded them together.

Placed on the kitchen counter were the two urns from the church. Today, she had to fill them with flowers for weekend services. Ma made the trek into the garden with her pruners; she wished Derrick were home now. He made her job easier, carrying the thick stems back to the house and systematically de-thorning each one.

The midday sun heated up the garden quickly and shortened her time pruning the largest bushes. Ma swung the basket filled with the luscious blossoms over her arm and walked slowly back to the house. She took the V- shaped silver plated urns over to the kitchen sink and filled each one, which didn't hold that much water. It was a labor of love for her as she had begun to prepare each stem.

Ma guarded herself against the treacherous thorns with heavy gloves. The needle-like protrusions have been known to draw blood; as in the case of her recent visitor. Interesting, she noticed this batch of roses didn't seem to be very thorny. Typically, her preferred ones for church were covered with thorns but also were the sturdiest stems guaranteed to draw water. The sturdy variety was perfect.

She used the half-opened flowers so the arrangements would last for several days. Ma opened a can of sugary soft drink to add to the water, which kept the arrangements lasting longer.

If the arrangements were for a wedding, she forced extra flowers into the narrow vessels to make them more special. One of the buds was opened too far to use in the arrangements. She recut the stem, gently placed it into a special bud vase and placed it next to the *Thorn Boy*. Afterwards, she paused and studied the collection of memorabilia that surrounded the statue. The area had evolved into an indoor shrine where she paid homage to her fallen solider.

Ma made certain that in her will Derrick would get the little statue. Everything she had was modest in value, or so she thought, but the statue's sentimental meaning and history were priceless. She envisioned *Thorn Boy* passed down from generation to generation with its story told each time. She taught Derrick an important lesson. "We must never forget the lives that have been sacrificed so we can live free."

She returned to the kitchen, cleaned and cut the remaining stems and placed them in the urns; she stood back proudly with folded arms. This is what the beauty of nature is all about, she thought. We are here to enjoy and respect it. The flowers, to her, were a direct connection with a higher power, a testimonial to the lady who appeared to her in the garden.

After she finished, Ma thumbed through the calendar tacked to the wall opposite the back door. Last month her group of garden club ladies had talked her into holding a flower arranging class in the church's fellowship hall. At first she had been apprehensive. She enjoyed arranging, but was uncertain about showing others.

The notices had already gone out to the members and some guests that lived on the coast. The event was entitled a "Bloomin' Bash", which, Ma thought, sounded more like a party of society ladies lifting a cocktail, or two, than a church fundraiser. Some of the women in the club wanted to include a wine tasting, but she discouraged the idea. She wasn't going to be responsible for a bunch of drunken women with sharp instruments whittling at rose stems.

The ladies social in Belle Glade drew a broader variety of people than Ma had anticipated. Originally, Ma planned on the twenty ladies who reserved, but two more showed up unexpectedly, who were not members. Turned out they were invited guests of a prominent member. There were plenty of tables in the fellowship hall, and one of the other volunteers found two extra vases in the pantry. She was relieved that she had thought to cut more roses than needed from the bountiful harvest in her garden. Luckily, everyone had been told to bring their own tools.

Portraying herself as an expert, Ma paused for a moment to reattach the barrette in her hair before demonstrating to each of the participants the proper way to cut each flower on an angle with a knife. The room was filled with chatter as the women cautiously followed her detailed instructions and arranged their bouquets.

An hour later, as they sipped their coffee admiring the completed arrangements, Ma noticed the two latecomers sitting apart from the rest and said, "Ladies, please introduce yourselves and share something about you with our group."

Gracefully, one stood from her chair and addressed the group, "I am Tchelet Goldstein-Smith and this is my sister, Varda Goldstein-Blackman. We just moved to Palm Beach from Philadelphia where we had been involved for years in the Pennsylvania Horticultural Society. We loved it. The Society hosts the annual Philadelphia Flower Show, one of the most outstanding flower shows in the nation. After coming to Palm Beach, we joined the garden club there but found it difficult to break the ice with many of its members. We appreciate the invitation to join your class." She smoothed out her dress and took her seat.

Ma watched as, obviously, the blue-bloods were unaccustomed to being in such humble surroundings. One had placed a starched white linen handkerchief on the chair before she sat. They each had a pair of floral print gardening gloves that matched their cloth tool pouches.

After the meeting, Tchelet paid Ma a gracious compliment on the flowers. She said holding her arrangement proudly, turning it from side to side inches away from her scrutinizing eye, "We can hardly go wrong when we've got flowers this beautiful. They must have been touched by God because each stem is perfect."

"I mentioned it to Varda and we would be so honored if you could give us a tour of your garden, Mrs. Stabb."

Initially, Ma was surprised by the self-invitation, but her love of flowers replaced the bolt from the blue as she expressed glee.

"Oh, I would be delighted, and you will have to see the stone grotto my grandson built in honor of his father and grandfather. It really is the centerpiece of the garden. I live just a short distance from here. Please, after we disperse, follow me back."

Ma hurriedly swept the leaves and rose stems into the trash can. The heavy, woody stems made a bang as the ends hit the metal bottom. She glanced over to the two guests and watched Tchelet as she assisted her ailing sister. Clearly, she was the one in charge. Ma noticed Tchelet motioning Varda to sit while she tidied their work space. Tchelet pushed the vases of roses to the side as she forcefully scooped the thorny stems into a pile at the end of the table. "Ready," Ma said as they loaded up there car. Ma smiled at the site of the two neatly quaffed women as they situated their bouquets on the back floor board, again Tchelet in charge of the process.

Ma's workman took the empty buckets, as well as her arrangement, and placed them in the truck. "Now, don't go too fast. We don't want to lose them," she instructed him just before they slowly pulled away from the fellowship hall. Occasionally, Ma glanced back through the back window checking. Tchelet was right on their tail.

Thirty minutes later the three ladies stood in the center of the garden of waist high rose bushes. They walked through the rows of fragrant, blooming blossoms toward the grotto that Derrick built last summer reminiscing about The War.

"We are survivors of the Holocaust," said Tchelet gently touching the edge of several petals. "After the liberation and war's end, my sister and I left Germany for Holland. Varda met her husband, married and moved to the states. I stayed in Amsterdam for several years before following her to Philadelphia where I met my husband at a flower show of all places."

Ma paused and faced her, "My husband was part of the liberation movement. Sadly, he never made it back home, but I take great solace in knowing he fought for freedom. You'll have to see my statue he had sent back to me. My most cherished possession. It's the only physical connection I have with him now."

Inside the house, Tchelet stopped and took notice of the *Thorn Boy* statue. "This *must* have an interesting story."

"My husband's army buddy brought this back to me. He told me that my husband took it from one of Hitler's offices. Sometimes I try to imagine the settings *Thorn Boy* must have been in the presence of, as the saying goes, 'if only he could talk.' The blood on its base tells me it must have been with him when he died." At that, Ma tilted her head downward. She walked her guests out onto the front porch. "I've enjoyed our time together," Ma said as she extended her hand.

"Thank you, Mrs. Stabb, for your time and sharing your beautiful garden with us. We enjoyed hearing about the statue, too; very, *very* interesting."

Ma caught the extra "*very*" in Tchelet's acknowledgement.

"Please include us in your next lesson. We loved the class."

"Did you register with our secretary? We can add your names to the mailing list."

"We did, thank you again."

Ma stood on the steps as the two women approached their car.

She shouted to them just as Tchelet reached for the door handle, "What kind of automobile is that? I don't think I've ever seen one before."

Tchelet turned, opened the door for her sister and said, "It's a vintage Bentley. A 1960 Continental Flying Spur. My husband and I collected them. After he passed away, I couldn't bare to part with any of them. I store them in an old barn not too far from here. I must say they do draw attention. Anyway, good-bye, hope to see you again."

Ma watched as the two-toned, classic car backed away from the house and crept down the long, shell rock drive towards the highway. A gentle breeze wafted the loose strands of hair unrestrained by her rose barrette. She put her hand up to her face and caressed the corners of her mouth saying aloud, "People are seldom what you imagine them to be."

Chapter 25—A Well-Staged Hoax?

Bernice Johnson kept the bedroom exactly the way Judy left it; each photograph and nick-knack was meticulously placed. This morning she had discovered her daughter's diary tucked under clothing in the top, dresser drawer. She fought the urge to open and read it. The pages bound together in white leather were the only pathway into her daughter's deepest thoughts. She hesitated, then raised back the soft cover and ran her thumb over the edge of the pages creating a slight breeze as they pressed through. She hesitated feeling guilty, replaced it and descended the stairs.

The sun was just beginning to peek over the pine trees in Boca Raton. Eight days had passed without her daughter, and she was straining under the pressure. She turned as the clamor of the kitchen wall phone demanded her attention. Dreading its sound, which could bring good news or bad, she paused for a moment, and then gave in to her belief in hope. Relieved, it was Ben. "How are you Ben?" she inquired.

"Torn, I'd like to stop by today if you're going to be at home. I was in Gainesville. I spent the last couple of days with Derrick. He was working on a report about soil."

"Soil?" she questioned.

"I'll explain when I see you."

"When?"

"I'm in the car now. Dad has me on a business call in Boca, so I should be there in half an hour."

"Alright," she responded and replaced the receiver. Bernice turned and faced out through the window wondering if Ben was picking up a body, but he politely chose to keep the details of his mission secret. Surely not; oh, the idea of a body in the back of his van, sitting in her driveway, was unnerving to say the least.

She sighed with a little relief when she saw Ben pulling into her driveway in the black Cadillac and not the white van. She stood in the open doorway as Ben stepped from the car. His dark brown bangs parted in the middle against his forehead. Dressed in his grey suit, no tie, he approached her. His arms wrapped against her in a warm hug. She returned the embrace looked into his eyes and said,

"Living with not knowing is the hardest part. I don't know what to think or how to react when friends inquire. All I can say is that their prayers and expressions of love bring some comfort but not much."

"I know the police are working hard," Ben offered carefully not to make the same insensitive blunder as the last time they spoke.

"So what's this about soil?" She inquired closing the door behind him.

"Oh, yes. His horticulture professor assigned it to the class. We worked on it together. I know Derrick was very nervous. I guess his teacher is rather intimidating...holds very high standards for his students."

"How were you able to help?" she questioned, a little perplexed by the topic.

"Well, let me try to put it simply."

"Ben, just tell me; if I have a question, I'll ask, okay?" she said in a slightly defensive tone.

"Okay, basically, he had to break down the soil's components and identify what was in it. In mortuary school, I learned that the human body has the same elements that exist in soil. And it's those elements that affect the plants grown in them. For example, if you add iron to a plant that is showing sign of yellowing, it will help green it because of its role in the production of chlorophyll."

She sat back in her kitchen chair interested but couldn't imagine where he was going with the conversation.

"Ben, what in the world has that got to do with humans?"

"There's more; what really threw us was, as we analyzed the tiny specs of soil, we discovered blood and bone fragments were in it."

"Blood...bone fragments!" she exclaimed as the statement caught her off guard.

"Yea, I know. The last thing we were expecting to find. Derrick had a test done and found out they were human."

"Did you take this to the police?"

"Oh, no, no, not yet; Derrick is worried because he caught wind of this rumor going around campus that he's involved in some sort of cult that does weird experiments. Weird, I know, but he's afraid that what we've discovered here will add to the rumor and implicate him in the student disappearances. To make it worse—"

"Make it worse?" Bernice interrupted.

"Yea, I took a tiny sample back to the blood bank and had it tested. It turned out that it's the same type Judy and the other missing students have, O-negative."

She couldn't believe what he was telling her.

"What! Ben, we've got to tell Deputy Sistrunk about this. Where did this blood tainted soil sample come from?"

"That's another really bizarre part of the story. Derrick's professor brought it in. He said something about acquiring it in the Lake Okeechobee region."

She persisted in trying to convince Ben that this was the time to involve the police regardless of how Derrick felt. Any clue that might lead to Judy was her only concern. "I know the two of you have been like brothers to each other, but you have to tell the police."

"I agree, but I have to think of Derrick's situation, too. I don't want to get him into any trouble. I mean, it was all harmless. We were just exploring, and now this."

She blurted out, "Well, if you don't confide in Sistrunk, I will. I don't care what might happen. If it is a lead to my missing daughter, I want it checked out."

Bernice regained her composure, leaned across the table taking Ben's hands and cupping his fingers around her. "Sorry, Ben; *no,* I'm not sorry. I'm desperate!" Her head bowed down for a moment, and then she looked up and made eye contact with him. "All of this experimentation you boys are doing isn't going to solve anything. We need action, and we need it now!"

Ben looked back at her. She could see it in his eyes. He was torn, too. He slipped his hands from her and stood taking a deep breath.

"Well, I have to run. I have an appointment," he said glancing down at his watch.

Indicated by his gesture, their visit had come to a definite end. Nothing else was exchanged, verbally anyway. She followed him to the door. Ben didn't turn around. He headed straight toward his car, got in and backed down the driveway without as much as a glimpse or wave toward her. His departure left her even emptier.

Crazy, crazy, crazy thoughts raced through her mind. Haunted by her secrets, *could this be some sort of punishment for who my parents were?* She thought. Over the years, she was able to hide her history with cleverly crafted stories about her childhood. Most people thought she was adopted. She would say, "I have no memory of my father and mother." The phrase provided a quick ending to any future questions.

After years of marriage to the man she truly loved, even he didn't know the truth behind her past. If he did, she wondered, would it have made a difference? She would never know because the fear of telling him was stronger than the courage it took to reveal the truth. She felt that lies weren't the worst thing in life; sometimes the truth can be far more hurtful.

Her thoughts turned back to her daughter. What would Judy say or do if she were here and this was happening to someone else? Bernice pictured her daughter's beautiful, blue eyes and thought. Perhaps *I* should have tried to instill more skepticism about people in my trusting daughter. I might not be having these thoughts now. But how could I have kept my daughter from her ideas?

Believing in people the way Judy did; this was what everyone loved about her. She glanced back up the stairway fighting her unyielding, curious desire.

Moments later, she stood again before the chest of drawers in Judy's room. Bernice regretted the argument they had about her becoming a funeral director. She was a big girl now and could make her own decisions. She realized it was a mistake for her to interfere; when Judy returns, she *would* honor any choices she makes. She lifted the little book from the drawer; for an instant she hesitated, but decided, due to the circumstances, it was justified. Apprehensively, she opened it.

According to the dates, Judy had begun writing several years ago when she entered grade school. Some of the pages were just a few lines—thoughts for the day. Her eyes darted across line after line of text about her feelings toward her mother and the death of her father, thoughts Bernice didn't know her daughter had entertained. She sighed; it was private, at least until now. She looked up from the page and wondered if her mother had ever read her diary. How would she have felt about that? Fighting off a sense of betrayal, Bernice pressed on.

Seeing her daughter's handwriting caused tears to well up immediately in her eyes. She could barely read the words as she sat on the bed and began to turn the pages. Her eyes darted from left to right skimming down each sheet exposing Judy's intuition. She couldn't comprehend the words fast enough; it was like an addiction. The time passed without notice until she reached the last entry. Judy mentioned a party she attended without Ben, where she met a man who captivated her. Bernice read on thinking that this man could've been a rival for Ben's affections, but what he possessed, his gift, was what Judy was curious about. Her passage read:

> *I spent most of the day curled up in bed struggling again with a panic attack followed by another bout of depression. Hours passed; the emotional weight that felt like a ton of bricks on my chest gradually lifted. I had begun to feel better and pulled myself together before heading off to a party at my sorority sister's apartment.*
>
> *The evening was rather dull until this tiny, old man entered. He was hunched over supported by his cane that had an ornate ivory handle carved into the shape of a rose. I don't think anyone in the room took him seriously because of his comical appearance. Wisps of thinning,*

grey hair danced about his head as he hobbled into the room. Several of the girls giggled while he fiddled with his hearing aid emitting a high pitched, squealing sound. Annoying, it reminded me of fingernails drug across a blackboard. Then, I remembered him as a visitor to the blood bank.

My sorority sister and fellow, rose tattoo bearer, hosting the party, led him into the room and then introduced Giles Van Cormack, a well known psychic—well known to everybody but me. She had invited him to give readings.

He took his seat at the only table in the small room. One-by-one, each of the girls sat before him, and Mr. Van Cormack placed a white handkerchief over his face, appeared to go into a deep trance and deliver a poetic riddle. The experience lasted only a minute or two leading me to think that he was wetting their pallets for more. An ingenious way of marketing his skills, certainly in hopes the girls would book private sessions for a fee. The ploy seemed to work beautifully, for he struck an interest in each one of them using some sort of esoteric riddle.

I waited, arms folded across my chest, until last, skeptical about what I had seen. Our hostess urged me to sit; obviously, she noticed my hesitation. I relented and took the chair across from the odd, little man. He had already placed the white cloth over his face and leaned against the back of his chair. Like with the others, there was moment of silence. Then, the thin cloth began to move in and out with each breath he took.

I didn't have anything to write on, but I remembered a few of the words...blue, rose, blonde hair, sky and divine. It didn't mean anything to me, but the hair on my arms stood up as he spoke the words Aryan and Satan's children. I couldn't for the life of me make out what this eerie, little man was saying. Then, his head dropped forward, and the handkerchief drifted onto the floor. He glanced up at me with clear blue eyes and said the strangest thing. "My dear, you behold a fascinating legacy that will draw two people with a unique agenda to you and cause you great harm. Be very careful."

Bernice turned the page, but it was blank. She clutched the tiny book and after a few moments replaced it back in the drawer, pulled an article of clothing over it and headed back downstairs.

Hum, Giles Van Cormack, she thought.

She tapped her finger tips against the kitchen counter top struggling to keep her sanity while the investigation proceeded seemingly at a snail's pace. Her intuition indicated that she shouldn't tell the police about Ben and Derrick's discovery, not yet anyway.

Bernice wondered if psychics listed their services in the Yellow Pages. On hands and knees, she pulled the heavy book out from under one of the end tables in the living room, sat on the sofa and thumbed rapidly through the thin pages. *Where to start*: psychics, tarot card readers, spiritualists? He's in business; he must be listed somewhere. No, not psychics; noone by the name of Van-anything listed under tarot card readers either, only Madame Vicky and somebody named Eleuthera in Delray Beach. Bernice imagined a woman dressed for Halloween holding a crystal ball. She moistened her index finger and put it back to work quickly turning the pages backwards to spiritualists. There was only one listing, in Hialeah, Giles Van Cormack. Nervously she dialed the number.

She glanced up at the kitchen clock. Luckily, he had an opening in an hour. Without anytime to waste, she quickly got dressed, applied a little lipstick and headed out the side door remembering to lock it behind her. Their non-gated community had some reports about suspicious looking people lurking about after dark.

She stopped at the corner gas station. While the attendant filled her tank, she stepped inside to pick up a road map. Hialeah was a suburb of Miami that she wasn't familiar with, but she could read a map. Back in her car with an overwhelmingly large page unfolded on the seat next to her, Bernice studied the best route. After he finished applying the windshield fluid and with even strokes masterfully squeegees the liquid leaving crystal clear glass, the attendant confirmed her directions. "Looks like a plan to me, Mrs. J.," he spoke as she handed the cash through the open window. She smiled at him, "Thank you."

Hialeah was a charming community that sat on the edge of Miami. Bernice struggled to follow the map as she turned down one street after another. She glanced at her watch; the time was nearing. Maybe she should resort to the logical thing and ask someone. She had to be close. Ambling down the tree lined street, she notice a man working in his yard. This was her opportunity. As she approached, she called out from the car window to him hunched over behind a knee-high Eugenia hedge. He didn't respond. She thought, too far, maybe he didn't hear her. Frustrated, Bernice pulled up forward, leaned out the car window; a little closer now, she called louder to him, "Excuse me!"

Obviously startled, he lost his balance and tumbled to the ground. Bernice threw the gear into park, shut off the engine and darted from the car to assist him back onto his shaky legs, then apologized and noticed he was wearing wooden shoes. "I'm so sorry. I didn't mean to catch you off guard." He pulled off his glove and reached for the volume button on the now visible hearing aid.

"Sorry, I usually turn it way down. I hate the street noise," he said as he fiddled with the tiny knob.

Bewildered, Bernice glanced up and down what appeared to be a pretty quiet road. She showed him the slip of paper with a street address. "I'm looking for this address."

"Are you Mrs. Johnson?" he inquired.

"Yes," she responded, feeling a little foolish.

"I've been expecting you," he said as he pointed to the neon sign in the front window. She turned her attention back to him as he reached into his soiled, pant's pocket and produced a folded, mud smeared business card.

GILES VAN CORMACK

SPIRITUALIST

PSYCHIC & TAROT CARD READER

305-666-0660

How could she have missed the glaring neon sign, SPIRITUALIST, prominently displayed in the window? Where she lives, in Boca, city codes prohibited such signage outside of the building in residential areas, but she guessed that they couldn't touch it since it was inside.

She followed him to the door and then stood on the porch admiring the tiny, blue flowers that sprang up sporadically in the damp garden. Several paint chips flaked from the screen door and fluttered to the floor as he tugged on the rickety door handle.

He closed the solid-looking, inner door behind her sealing them inside the dark, quiet foyer.

Standing at the doorway of what appeared to be his parlor, he looked up into her eyes. The subtle light had shown years of life's experiences in the deep crevices on his sagging skin. His eyes were sunken in with rings of dark circles just above protruding cheekbones.

"May I offer you some tea before we get started? I only use caffeine free, herbal tea." He spoke in a raspy voice barely above a whisper as he gestured to the chair at the table.

"Yes, that would be nice," Bernice answered nodding as she made herself comfortable in the Victorian style chair with an embroidered seat and back overstuffed with mohair.

Bernice could hear the rattling of what she guessed was a tea pot in the other room. Moments later, the whistling sound came to an abrupt stop. Van Cormack made her nervous as he shuffled unsteadily toward her. One small slip and she would be wearing scalding hot tea. She sighed with relief as he carefully slid the tray across the table and took the other chair.

The room was perfectly silent illuminated by a few votive candles and a low wattage lamp in the corner. "I'll begin," he said as he placed a white linen handkerchief over his head. Moments later, he appeared to be in a trance; he began to softly speak poetic verses, as subtle breaths pushed the delicate fabric back and forth. Captivated by his mystique, Bernice leaned in as he delivered in an elevated whispered:

"Beds of blue roses,

Blonde hair so fine,

Look to the sky,

She is divine."

"Aryan features grace them all,

As Satan's children they will fall,

The sacrifices made may be in vain,

Because his fate is not to gain,"

"A soil's composition is his path,

Its elements contained will expose his wrath,

Blood and bone are hidden within,

He will be judged by his twin,"

"A young man's gift is his bane,

The truth he seeks could be in vain,

Words on a page lead the cause

Confronting those who abide the laws,"

She waited as his head slowly tilted forward allowing the white cloth to fall onto the tabletop. He gradually came about as his eyelids fluttered, then he staged whispered—moving his lips without sound. "That's all".

Her obvious expression of disappointment initiated his response. "I have no control over this. I'm in under a spell, and the words follow. There could be more later, but for now I'm afraid that is all I can offer you."

Fighting her feelings of disillusionment, she stepped onto the porch after her all-to brief session ended. She looked up into green leaves of the tree's canopy and took a deep breath. She attempted to make sense of the poetic stanzas portions replayed over and over again in her mind. She wondered what lay in their meanings, if anything. Or, was he some old crazy kook, who had lassoed her emotions and money into thinking this was a divine pathway to her daughter?

Whether it was the stress or her shear determination, she began to recall the conversation with Ben earlier, his experimentation in the lab with Derrick, and Derrick's soil report leading to blood and bone fragments. She had to get in touch with Ben, now.

Traffic along the I-95 wasn't too heavy at mid-afternoon. In less than half an hour, Bernice pulled into her driveway. After she dropped her bag and keys on the kitchen counter, she noticed the flashing light that signaled a message on her answering machine. It was Ben. "Call me back," he said short and sweet. She fervently dialed his number.

"Hi, Mrs. Johnson, I felt bad about the ways things ended. I called to see how you were doing."

"Can you meet me at my house right away, Ben?"

"I think so, why, what's—"

Before he could complete his inquiry she responded, "I'll tell you when you get here."

A half an hour later, Ben stepped onto the front porch of Judy's house eager to find out what Mrs. Johnson had planned. "Ben, I want you to come somewhere with me this afternoon," she commanded seconds after she opened the door.

"Mrs. Johnson, I really don't want to tell the police about what Derrick and I found in the lab."

"I know. That's not why I asked you to come here. I want to take you to see a man that I think can help us."

"Help us, how?"

"Just trust me."

Ben, curious, followed her to the doorway. Apparently, she wasn't revealing any details until they got there.

"I'll drive," she insisted snatching her keys and purse. Ben keenly grasped that she was taking control of this situation, and he should just go with it.

Ben was surprised at her little heavy-footedness on the gas pedal, which pulled him slightly to the right as the car hurriedly exited the road. They were in an old part of Hialeah he wasn't familiar with. Charming, heavily tree-lined streets, wide side- walks and plenty of parking, if one didn't mind the bird droppings.

She said, "So many of the old South Florida neighborhoods had fallen into the hands of slum lords, gangs and violence, but this place is the exception." There wasn't a person to be seen anywhere. Bernice drove slightly over the 30 MPH posted speed limit. Wherever they were headed, she was determined to get there fast.

The leaves in the street swirled as the car pulled to a sudden stop along the curbside at their apparent destination. Ben's chest momentarily pressed firmly against the shoulder harness. With great earnest, Mrs. Johnson unhooked her seat belt, grabbed her purse and was out of the car while Ben was still struggling with his. She delivered a sharp glance through the windshield indicating he needed to hurry. Fumbling nervously for the release on his belt, he finally located it and slung open the door bounding from the car. Instantly, the neon sign of rainbow colors in the front window caught his attention.

Where is she taking me? Ben thought, as he followed Mrs. Johnson's quick steps clicking up the wooden steps onto the grey, slatted, wooden porch. After she knocked firmly, a hand appeared and slowly lifted the heavy blinds. Ben saw a pale face peering thorough the dust covered window pane attempting to see who was outside, followed by a series of locks disengaging, each with a loud clack, down the inner door.

Ben, always a gentleman, held the door and then stepped over the threshold behind Mrs. Johnson. The old, frame house smelled musty, a common odor in tightly locked up, humid environments. Memories flashed through his mind of one occurrence where Ben and his father had to pick up a body. An elderly man, who lived alone, had been found by a concerned neighbor.

It was a standard practice. The coroner called Mr. Freeman to retrieve the body. It was his first call, and Ben could never erase the stale smell from his memory. The minute he stepped into the spiritualist's parlor, Ben could visualize the scene where a covered body lay on the floor.

Along with his father and the coroner, the three men picked the old man up and placed him on a gurney. The warm body had turned blue but rigor mortis hadn't set in, yet. Ben was surprised how heavy the little man was substantiating the term, *dead weight*.

He brought himself back to reality, confused, as the typically pragmatic Mrs. Johnson introduced Ben to the psychic. Van Cormack acknowledged the introduction with a slight nod. Extending his hand, the frail man shook Ben's while he adjusted his hearing aid with the other. Ben followed Mr. Van Cormack and Mrs. Johnson into a parlor labeled READING ROOM scored in a handmade, wooden sign.

The floral print wallpaper was dark blue with a cream and brown, rose pattern meandering through it. Thick, horizontal blinds that blocked out the daylight were surrounded by fabric window treatments that echoed the pattern on the walls. As far as he could tell, the room had been professionally decorated. After years of designers working for his father to create the perfect atmosphere of pink and peach highlights in the funeral home, he recognized a "decorator's touch". He thought interesting that Mr. Van Cormack would appreciate such a talent once upon a time.

A crystal chandelier, in dire need of cleaning, hung from the center of the ceiling. Cob webs, strung together from arm to arm, moved gently in the air's current. Its condition was understandable since the frail man would have had a difficult time reaching it in his unstable condition.

In one of the corners, an antique grandfather's clock stood. Its pendulum expectantly swung back and forth silently as the second hand ticked through the minutes.

As he took a chair in the corner, Ben shifted back and forth in the well-cushioned seat and crossed his legs trying to get comfortable. Bernice took her usual position at the little table across from Mr. Van Cormack. At this point, Mrs. Johnson hadn't disclosed her relationship with him to Ben. He was wondering what was yet to come.

Nervous and curious, Ben, well trained from childhood, remained respectfully silent as Mrs. Johnson said, "The riddles you shared during our last session, now, have a clearer meaning." She said to him, "I need to hear more."

He spoke softly as he once again fiddled with the tiny dial in his hearing aid.

"As I said earlier today, I can't promise you anything, Mrs. Johnson. The words just come to me as I speak them. Usually, I do not give two readings on the same day, but since I had the time available, well, here we are." He gestured upward with both hands and then turned his attention toward Ben. "And, who, might I ask, are you?"

Before he could respond, Mrs. Johnson chimed in as though she was responsible for everything and anything that concerned those in the room. "This is my son," she delivered convincingly. Ben managed to contain his look of astonishment. "He agreed to join me when I told him about our earlier session. He's, well, a bit skeptical of those with your rare talents."

"Well, let's see what he thinks after the reading," said Van Cormack confidently.

Van Cormack seemed to buy her story despite the fact he was supposed to hold inner talents that would have told him otherwise. This was a side of Judy's mother Ben had never seen. She was manipulating their relationship as an excuse to get more out of the frail, but most certainly up-to-the-challenge psychic. She continued to prod him with whatever flattery he'd buy into. "Your words, so far, are the only thing we have to go on that mean anything. I was hoping there was something else that you could share with us which might lead to the truth."

A votive candle, emitting a trace of vanilla fragrance, in the table's center flickered against Bernice Johnson's flawless, peachy complexion as she made her plea. He slowly stood and approached a small wooden cabinet next to where Ben was seated, opened the top drawer and removed a white, linen handkerchief and several pieces of paper.

He returned to his seat at the table and unfolded the delicate fabric with his aged and spotted fingers. "I will apply a skill I've been perfecting. I'll write the words as I speak them." He removed his glasses and closed his eyes. He gradually lifted the cloth, tilted his head back and placed it over his face.

He sighed; slow breaths were now visible underneath the material that gently moved back and forth.

Hands folded on his knee, Ben thought, *what a crock* as he waited patiently for what was to come next.

Giles Van Cormack sat upright, slightly trembling, and tilted his head backwards. He had begun to breath deeper and deeper. Ben's eyes occasionally wandered about the room. He didn't know if spirits were supposed to come out of the walls next or what.

Cautious, not to miss anything, Mrs. Johnson removed a small pad and pen from her handbag. Her eyes didn't leave the little man. She sat patiently in anticipation of what was to come. Ben couldn't imagine what drew his girlfriend's mother to this man in the first place. He'd soon see.

An ever so slight, high pitched, squealing sound entered the room. Van Cormack raised his wrinkled hand and adjusted a tiny dial on his hearing aid under the cloth, ending the annoyance.

Van Cormack's breathing had begun to increase, indicated by the white linen cloth draped over his face. The trembling suddenly stopped. Pen in hand, he scratched in narrow strokes as he deliberately spoke in a barely audible tone...

"A hideous face he receives sympathy from all.

Blind in one eye hidden anger will appall.

His brilliance is concealed behind a scarred face.

Some involved will die in the chase."

"His plan has been for decades long
Blood type, blue eyes, they all belong.
Manipulation is his key tool
Under stress he keeps his cool."

"Evil exists where good deeds once thrived,
Sacrifices are made at a time justified,
Intentions appear honorable but not so,
What is to result he will not know,"

Ben, stupefied, glanced over to Mrs. Johnson, her eyes remained fixed on their clairvoyant host. Van Cormack paused for a few moments then, he spoke again...

"Life from their veins completes the test,"
There are no limits set to achieve the best,
No matter who has died or survived,
Success it seems has just arrived,"

"A sweet grandmother's garden is a delight.
She holds a secret, you've created her plight.
Your success will soon be realized.
In the end her flowers will be prized."

"A tissue of blonde hair is a treasured gem.
It is entwined in a thorny stem.
Discovered by a man you'd least expect.
His powers guide you to redirect."

"Science will reveal the one who is gone.
The modern needed tests will drag on,
It appears the answer is in a piece of foil.
But the substance you seek is in the soil."

"Rows of roses reach for the sky,
Their blossoms pure white no stain or dye,
Untainted stems can jab like horns,
But those manipulated will not have thorns."

"A tiny tag symbolizes his prey,
Though its image is subtle they cannot stray,
Etched on their arms detailed in blue
Each victim presents a rose tattoo."

Ben, unconvinced, struggled to quell any outbursts bubbling deep inside of him. Could it be that the man he met at the door was not the same one now seated at the table? Someone or something may have entered Giles Van Cormack's body, messaging through him. Or this was a well-staged hoax?

Mr. Van Cormack removed the cloth from his face and opened his eyes. His breathing and tremors resumed. *Is this what we came for?* Ben thought as he remained seated.

"I can only tell you what the Spirit shares through me," he said, continuing to fumble with the volume on the miniscule instrument in his left ear. "Sorry. I've been having problems with this thing. It's new. I preferred my older one, but my audiologist persuaded me to try it."

"We need more clarity, Mr. Van Cormack," she expressed glancing over to Ben, wrinkling his bow. "My son is confused. This doesn't mean anything to him."

He answered sliding the pages of automatic writing across the table to her, "They don't mean anything to him now. It's up to him to decipher the messages. As you discovered before, Mrs. Johnson, there is significance in what you were told. It will be your journey to find their true meanings."

He slowly rose, indicating their session had ended. Van Cormack scooted his chair back under the table. Bernice and Ben followed him to the front door, her expression indicated that she felt a little short-changed. They stepped back over the threshold onto the paint chipped porch. The faint, high-pitched sound gradually faded as the door handle slowly clicked shut behind them.

Chapter 26—A Rose Tattoo

Derrick entered the large open area cluttered with desks and chairs, duly lit with fluorescents at the Gainesville Police Department, and looked about. Sitting alone in the corner, Detective Waites returned the phone's receiver, looked up and motioned for him to come over. Derrick fondled the last few tablets of antacids in his jean pocket as he approached. He pulled out the fax sheet Ben sent earlier and his remaining cherished antacids tumbled to the floor and rolled under the desk. *Damn it,* he thought. "This is what I wanted to show you, detective."

Waites unfolded the tattered piece of paper and glanced down at the neatly arranged words in four-line groups. His eyes darted back and forth over the page. "What is this?"

"My best friend is Judy Johnson's boyfriend. He and Judy's mother visited a well-respected psychic in Hialeah. This is the reading they got from him. I think the psychic is showing us something."

"And *exactly* what is he showing us?"

Derrick knew it would be a tough meeting. Waites would expect hard core evidence.

"That there are clues here. The search teams need to check out my grandmother's rose garden. Something, I don't know what, but something is there that is important in solving these missing persons cases."

Waites gave him a cold stare. Derrick, unwavering, continued.

"Look...blue roses, blonde hair, and blood types; weren't these missing people all of the same type of description?"

"Yea, so?" he said bluntly.

"Well, that can't be a coincidence!" Derrick blurted out exasperated. "Someone dangerous is targeting, maybe sacrificing specific people, I think Aryans, for some kind of process that involves creating a blue rose."

"You do, do you? Don't you think that is a little far fetched? I'm mean, what are you getting at? That this, what is he...a psychic knows something we don't. I mean, come on, this is a waste of my time." Waites dismissed the stanzas waving his hand over the pages and with a laugh shaking is head back and forth. "You can't seriously expect me to waste valuable, police time following through on this. Besides, as far as I'm concerned, only kooks and nuts put faith into this crap."

Derrick persisted pointing to one of the stanzas, "Detective Waites, look at this. There's reference to science and foil. I told my buddy, Ben, that I think the soil should be tested for abnormalities. Check out the rose stems that grow in it. See what's in the plant that shouldn't be there. Hey, foil, maybe it's an indication of a high level of aluminum. What would that do?"

Determined, Derrick pressed on as Waites resisted, "Look, here, it says rose tattoo. Judy has a rose tattoo. Her mom hated it. And the others, Julie Rose, she had a rose tattoo. That's tangible. Doesn't that mean something? Come on Detective."

Aggravated with Waite's condescending attitude, Derrick pulled out his last chance at garnering the detective's attention. He'd disclose what he found in the jar.

"I have more information, something substantial," he spouted. The cop looked up at him with glaring green eyes that said stop bothering me. "I was researching soil for class and found blood and human bone in a sample jar. My friend, the same one I mentioned, was with me. I had this report to do, and it involved a little experimenting. After several processes we made this discovery."

The blunt confession didn't seem to faze Waites in the least, seems he was going to chalk this one up to a creative mind as well. "Look Sonny," he said interlocking his fingers behind his head, leaning back in his chair discharging a subtle squeak. "Bones and blood in soil, what makes you think it's not animal?"

Derrick fired back, "Because we had it tested. That's what researchers do; we test things for accuracy. And the tests produced certain trace elements, too—aluminum, iron and copper, as well as proved unusually high and potentially dangerous levels of said elements should they be consumed."

The cop snorted, "But you're just a college kid, not a *real* professional. Tell you what kid, bring me some of this soil and we'll test it in our lab by the pros. They'll tell me if I need to pursue it more."

Feeling the detective was only placating him, Derrick conceded, "Sure, you do whatever."

"We will, son. And as I said to you before, let the police do their job. You focus on your studies. Now, I have someplace I need to be."

"Officer, it is because of focusing on my studies that I've come to you with this. Behind what seems to be a crazy notion *is* real science. I'm certain."

Derrick turned to make his way to the door, but not before one last word. He turned back on his heel and faced him. "When all of this comes to light, and hopefully it will before too many have died, you will see what I have been getting at, and it will blow your mind."

Derrick dropped the paper onto Waites' desktop. He marched across the room toward the doorway like a soldier marching into battle. He pulled the door shut with a slam and thought, *I'll prove him wrong. He'll see.*

Waites watched through the marbled glass as Derrick's image disappeared. He grabbed the paper, folded it and shoved it into his shirt pocket. He stood, picked up his keys, tossed them high into the air before grabbing them and moments later left the parking lot responding to a recent call.

In a vacant lot a few miles north of the U of F campus, a group of law enforcement officials were gathered. He stepped over the crime scene tape and approached the sight amidst the commotion of police. A photographer snapped pictures of a young woman's naked body lying facedown in the grass. Her smooth skin, void of color, shimmered in the street light. Her golden blonde hair was tossed about with bits and pieces of leaves and twigs tangled through it. Waites stood over her for a few seconds before he knelt down to get a closer look at a small tattoo on her, right, upper, arm. It was a rose.

Besides the indentations in the skin around both ankles, the body looked as though it hadn't suffered any trauma: no bruises or broken bones, no sign of blood, not a drop, anywhere. He sighed and thought, *strange*. Then, barely visible on her neck were two puncture wounds three centimeters above the clavicle. Her jugular vein had been tapped and her body drained seemingly of every ounce.

He stood, crossed his arms and pinched his chin with his hand before making his way back through the teeming activity of cops while the images of Danny Rolling's victims again penetrated his memory. Back inside his car, he grunted and pulled out the crumpled paper Derrick adamantly dropped on his desktop. The words bounded from the page...a rose tattoo.

Chapter 27—The Glades Are Filled With Secrets

A thick fog drifted over the Glades as tiny water beads glistened on the narrow blades of sugar cane. Later in the day, the fog would have burned off, but Sistrunk didn't want to wait, too much time had already passed. He paced back and forth along the side of the shell rock road flanked by stalks of cane waving at the sky. He glanced down at the fax Detective Waites sent last night. He sighed, frustrated by the mysterious riddles that didn't mean a thing to him, or to Waites, which pushed his suspicions about Derrick's involvement.

He stood on his toes and peered over rows of tall cane that edged the many small, dirt roads creating a labyrinth sending those unfamiliar with the area into endless circles. This search for a body, for anything was a job that required people who knew the Glades.

A cloud of dust settled around the truck of the first volunteer to make an appearance. He stepped from his muck incrusted pickup and approached Sistrunk, who at first didn't know what to make of this bald, wide-grinned, black man. Hand outstretched, he greeted the deputy with a firm handshake throwing Sistrunk off balance and nearly tumbling him to the ground. Sistrunk felt the callused hand as the two men shook. Obviously, he was used to hard work and now gave his time to volunteer in the community; this impressed the deputy. There must be a reason this man stood before him.

The stout man in overalls and a tee shirt helped him regain his stance. "Howdy, I'm Sonny Locke," he said. He appeared to be an affable man. "It's nice to meet you, uh, deputy? I guess."

"Yes," replied Sistrunk straightening himself up.

"I grew up here in the Glades. My papa and mamma were field workers picking sweet corn and beans. I know every inch of this land, and if someone's gotta be found, I'm gonna find 'em. Let me ask you something, deputy. Why are you searching way out here? You got some sort of clue because this is a mighty large area to cover."

Sistrunk glanced over at Sonny's rusted-out pickup, which, apparently, also had seen every inch of the land. He reached inside his car window and pulled out a folder. Inside were photos of the four missing students and a fax. He handed it to Sonny and said, "Besides finding a handbag of one of the missing in the area, all we have are these riddles."

Sonny took the open folder and turned the photos over studying each one. "Nice lookin' kids," he offered. Then he took the worn fax in his creased, dark hands. His eyes darted across the lines. He closed the folder and handed it back to Sistrunk, shrugged his shoulders, looked him in the eye and wrinkled his forehead. "This is why you're searching the cane fields hoping to find something or someone, because of these riddles?"

"There's more to it than that. I know it's strange, but I think there are clues hidden in these. So far, the only person who's been able to make any sense of them is a college student named Derrick Stabb."

Sonny interrupted pointing east toward the sun rising high into the noon sky. "I know him. His grandma lives over there, just a short distance down that road. Nice folks, everybody likes Grandma Ma. She's known for her beautiful flower garden and delicious apple pies. She's raised those grandsons alone since her son died in Vietnam and the mother disappeared. Heard tell she had mental problems and one day just left. But you know how people like to talk."

Darting out from behind Sonny was a large, slobbering bloodhound that vigorously encircled the two men. Sonny gestured towards her, "This here's my dog, Rosie."

The canine's large drooling jowls suddenly reached around to her backside and started nibbling in retaliation against annoying fleas. Sistrunk took a look at Rosie, smiled and wondered why he named his bloodhound Rosie...a cocker spaniel, a Chihuahua, a dachshund, another cute dog but not a bloodhound. Clearly, Sonny Locke was a distinctly different thinking person.

“Once she gets the scent, she won’t give up,” He informed Sistrunk.

“Well, welcome to the team, Rosie. Okay Sonny, let’s get started.”

Sistrunk pulled his rain gear from the back of the car, realizing that he was inappropriately dressed for the elements. As he pulled the heavy latex jacked over his shirt, another truck pulled out with three more men inside offering their assistance. Sonny leaned over and whispered into Sistrunk’s ear, “Folks out here are real neighborly. If they think they can help they show up.” Sistrunk looked back at him as Sonny smiled and nodded his head in pride.

“Howdy,” one of the men said to Sonny and Sistrunk. The deputy thought “Howdy” to be a popular acknowledgement when meeting someone for the first time in the Glades. He said indicating with a hand motion, “We were just getting started, thought we’d fan out over this area first.”

“What are we lookin’ for, a body?” inquired one of the men glancing down at Daisy.

Sistrunk replied handing the folder of photos over, “Maybe, but anything that can help us locate where these four young people might be.”

He nodded and returned it back to Sistrunk, who instructed, again, “Let’s get started.” The search had begun as they slowly made their way through the heavy vegetation firmly rooted in the rich, black, muck soil.

Into the hunt about thirty minutes, Sistrunk was hit by a pungent odor. He immediately turned his head as the stench burned the lining of his nostrils and shouted to the other men, “I think we have something over here!”

Clearly something was dead; it could have been anything since there are all sorts of wildlife deep in the Glades. Reportedly, even the Skunk Ape had been sighted there.

Sistrunk, used to nasty smells, was becoming nauseated from this particular stench that hung in the air. Sonny was the first to appear through the cane, and then the men slowly made their way toward Sistrunk’s voice as the disgusting odor grew more intense.

Surprisingly, Rosie followed happy go lucky. Sistrunk wrinkled his forehead. If each of them could smell it, why wasn't the bloodhound charging forward? Placing one foot slowly in front of the other, he crept closer and closer. The sun had slowly burned through the thick haze revealing the source of the obnoxious smell, a surprise no one expected.

Sistrunk and Sonny stood awe stuck in front of an alien plant. Something Sistrunk had never seen before; its stalk was approximately six feet tall with a large purplish flower resembling a space ship. The blossom seemed to measure a foot tall by two feet wide.

"What in the hell is that?" shouted Sistrunk.

"It's a Corpse Flower! They have *one* nasty smell. It's to draw the bugs in," instructed Sonny as he pinched his nostrils closed distorting the sound of his voice.

"I know that now!" Sistrunk broadcasted waving his had in front of his face, attempting to fend off the disgusting odor.

Rosie galloped up to the strange plant curiously sniffing. As she made a quick turn, her sturdy tail struck the thick stalk and sent a swarm of tiny flies into the air. Sistrunk was disappointed yet somewhat relieved as he slowly trekked on, behind the team through the moist vegetation. Their search continued.

About a half an hour later, Sonny wiped the sweat from his brow with the back of his hand, looked up and stopped suddenly. He said to Sistrunk, "Let me see that paper again. I'm getting a feeling that we're in the wrong place."

Sistrunk reached inside his raincoat and handed the wrinkled fax over.

"So, there's a mention of beds of roses here. Grandma Ma is the only person in the Glads that grows roses. When my mama died, Mrs. Stabb, everybody calls her Ma brought the most beautiful bouquet of roses I'd ever seen to the funeral home. And you say she's been getting messages sort of like this. We should check out her place, don't you think?" Sonny suggested as he stared directly into Sistrunk's eyes.

Sistrunk replied, "Yea, but I think it is all a bunch of baloney."

"Well boss, you got any better ideas?" He said convincingly.

"No, not really," Sistrunk replied sinking in desperation.

"Well, let's see what's in the rose garden besides flowers. Follow me," Sonny said as he waved Sistrunk and the three other men back toward the road.

"I think you guys should start to search that area. We all don't have to go. The day is wearing on, and we need to make as much use of the sunlight as possible," Sistrunk told the other men as he pointed in the opposite direction.

Sonny stared over the dashboard through the mud smeared windshield as he seemed to drive aimlessly on the maze of two-lane dirt roads. After several minutes, crowded in Sonny's truck with Rosie on the floor resting her drooling jowls on Sistrunk's lap in the front seat, Sonny took a sudden turn and drove down a winding path. He stopped in front of a gravel road marked with a single mailbox and the name *STABB* stenciled on it.

"This is it," Sonny said as he threw the gear shift into park and slung open the truck's rusty door. Sistrunk hopped out onto the rock driveway and faced a modest, white framed, wooden house displayed before them.

"Let's see if Mrs. Stabb is at home," said Sonny.

Sistrunk followed, walked up onto the neatly painted front porch, approached the door and knocked. He knocked again, a little more persistent the second time.

"No one's home, let's go around back."

"Let's get searchin'," said Sonny as he hopped over a short, chicken wire fence and headed toward the garden. Sistrunk followed.

Sonny turned back and said, "My motto is successful searchers don't take anything for granted, or make assumptions. Often, what we're seeking is right under our noses. We just choose to not see it."

Sistrunk thought it was a rather profound statement that didn't match the appearance of the person who proclaimed it. Of course, who was he to question anyone? Its mid afternoon now, and he's in a stranger's rose garden searching for something, but he has no idea what it could be.

Sistrunk checked his watch; two hours had passed and he was battling the feeling that he was on a wild goose chase with Sonny Locke at the helm.

"I think we need to wrap this up."

"Don't be so impatient, deputy," Sonny replied as he noticed footprints in the neatly raked muck. The prints seemed to follow a short path then hop over the planted rose bushes and resume on the next row. Sonny followed the trail, which brought him to a place where the muck was stomped and packed as though someone had been dancing about on one foot. Several of the stems from the rose bushes were broken over but not severed from the plant. He turned and bent down on one knee. Something wrapped in a piece of aluminum foil, that was nestled in between the protruding thorns at the base of the stems, reflected upwards. Inside, a small tissue, damp from the morning dew, was clinging to the foil. Sistrunk watched as Sonny unfurled the delicate layers; inside were several curls of blonde hair, the roots with tiny specks of dried blood still attached.

"Wait! You'll contaminate it. That could be evidence, let me take it." Sistrunk pulled on a pair of latex gloves over his hands and removed a small plastic bag from his jacket pocket. He carefully took the foil and tissue from Sonny and secured it inside.

"Amazing the birds didn't get to it first to use it as part of their nest," Sonny said scratching the top of his head.

Sistrunk looked back at Sonny in wonderment. "Why would this be here? And how did it get here? I have to talk to this woman as soon as possible. What did you call her, Grandma Ma? I have some questions. And her grandson, maybe Waites is right. Maybe he is involved, and all of this mystery about him deciphering riddles *is* a bunch of bull.

"Like I said, boss, sometimes what we're seekin' is right under our noses. While you're checking out Derrick, you might want to check into the source of those riddles," Sonny replied as he yanked open the rusty pick up's door. "The Glades are filled with secrets."

Chapter 28—Something's In the Soil

The next day, Sistrunk kicked the mud off his shoes before entering the front door of the Criminal Justice Complex. He pulled the dog eared fax from his pocket, inserted it in the manila file folder and plopped down in his office chair.

He hesitated and looked at the phone on his desktop. In the folder was Detective Robert H. Waites' card. He picked up the black receiver and dialed.

"Waites? Sistrunk here; we have a clue, although a small one."

"What have you got for me?"

"I was part of a search team in Belle Glade yesterday. One of the guys named Locke found a few strands of blonde hair wrapped in foil and tissue in a garden in Belle Glade. I'm waiting for DNA to see if it's one of the missing students."

"You sure the evidence wasn't planted."

"No, I'm not sure of anything, but I know what I saw. He found it in a garden owned by an old woman named Stabb near Belle Glade.

"Did you talk to her?" inquired Waites.

"No one was home, so we looked around the house and garden. Just when we were about to leave, this guy, Locke, caught a glimpse of something shiny on the ground; inside was the tissue with the hair. I took it to forensics."

Waites interjected, "Another body's been found; a college student same description as the others right down to the rose tattoo. The body was intact but all of the blood had been drained out of it. There were two hole punctures in the side of the neck. Now, I guess we have a vampire on the loose. Her name hasn't been released yet, gotta notify the parents."

"And, oh, by the way, as if things couldn't get stranger, Derrick Stabb stopped by my office a few days ago. He was trying to convince me about some nonsense of tainted soil. He mentioned about his buddy seeing a psychic and some poems. He thought there were clues hidden in their meaning. I've never come across anything like this before. I thought the Danny Rolling case was as strange as it could get. I think this is even weirder. I think this kid knows more than he's letting on. I think he's playing us."

"How so," responded Sistrunk swiveling his chair around and faced out the window.

"I think that he's involved. There could have been some sort of jealousy issue between him and his buddy, who knows, but I don't like the smell of this at all. He might be trying to set up somebody else, taking the attention away from him. Anything else you got for me?"

"No, not now."

"Let me ask you a question, Sistrunk. Why are you spending so much of your own time on this case? Procedure is what a detective is assigned, let them do their job."

"I'm too involved to pass this case onto someone else. I know it's not my job, but I was there at the nightclub, and then after meeting with the odd, little lady down in Hollywood, and now more clues are taking me back to the Glades. I'm waiting to see what bizarre thing happens next."

"I see, well this really isn't up to you, but I understand when there's a vested interest. Keep me posted."

"I'm making another trip out there this afternoon to meet this Locke guy again and go back to the garden. Maybe I can find out something more. Meet the old lady and dig around some more.

Sistrunk had never been as far west as the Glades before this case evolved. He'd read about Lake Okeechobee, referred to as "Big Lake O". The road heading west seemed to be endless. Miles and miles of sugar cane, sky and water was all he saw as his cruiser barreled west on State Road 80. An hour later a billboard appeared before him.

WELCOME TO BELLE GLADE

HER SOIL IS HER FORTUNE

Sistrunk turned his head backward through the side window, grinned and thought as he drove past the rows of rundown, tenement houses. Dark skinned women dressed in tattered, mismatched tops and dresses sat in old, dirty chairs on the catwalk watching their children play in the parking lot below littered with papers and cans. *Yea, fortunes for a few.*

They agreed to meet at the police station. His hand drawn map on the dash indicated two left turns and one right. As the cruiser came to a stop in front of the Belle Glade Police Headquarters, Sistrunk took a quick, second look as Sonny emerged from the building with something strangely affixed to the side of his shiny, bald head. Looking oddly at him, head tilted sideways, he said, "Uh, what's the deal with that," as he pointed to what appeared as fishing tackle.

Sonny with his broad-faced grin replied in a deep, southern drawl. "Oh, uh this," pointing to the tiny collection of pseudo flies, bees and worms. "I was in a rollover a number of years ago. I have a metal plate in's my head. Sometimes, I use magnets to attach my bait and other stuff. It works great for grocery lists, too. I know it's a little odd, but then I don't forget. It started back when my wife yelled at me for forgettin' stuff. I'd come back home with half of what she needed. Not good, not good at all, if you know what I mean. She already yells too much at me for other stuff."

He continued as they approached Sonny's truck.

"One day, one of the kids was playing with some toys, little magnets. I was sleeping on the couch, and they discovered the things would stick to my head. You know kids; they went crazy from there, but I haven't forgotten anything since. See, it works."

"That doesn't hurt you in any way?"

"Gosh no, only if you had a pace maker; pace makers and magnets don't work together; doc says the magnet screws it up, I guess."

Sistrunk nodded his head thinking, *folks out here really are different.*

Sonny offered to drive. Since the dirt roads would have trashed his car, Sistrunk was happy to oblige him. His rickety truck squeaked its way passing huge flat bed trucks hauling sugar cane along the narrow roads; Sistrunk mostly asking the questions, Sonny mostly answering.

"What brought your family to his area?" inquired Sistrunk killing time while Sonny drove back to the garden.

"A big share of the nation's vegetables in the winter grows here. Most of the fancy people on the coast have no clue what exists beyond the city limits of West Palm Beach. It's another world out here, a few very rich and many very poor, with a few middle class folks sprinkled in."

Sonny's muddy pickup turned off the main road and headed down a winding path Sistrunk was familiar with, toward a two-story, pristine, white frame house. Coming to a quick halt in a cloud of dust, each released their seat belts as they gazed about.

The sound of their heels on the wooden steps announced Locke's and Sistrunk's arrival. This time no one needed to ring the bell. Standing at the open door was an elderly lady wearing a floral print apron with a dusting of flour on the front.

Sistrunk showed his WPB Police badge introducing himself and Sonny. The search warrant remained folded inside his pocket. Sistrunk quickly learned that no introduction need be made for Sonny Locke. Obviously, Grandma Ma certainly knew who he was, and it seemed his association with the officer from the coast had drawn a warm, immediate welcome into her home.

Hot apple pie combined with the rose's sweet fragrance drifted through the open windows. The two men stood politely in the front parlor as the family matriarch fetched three cups of coffee. Sistrunk glanced about taking in every detail. The house was warm and inviting and reminded him of his own grandmother's home. Even the smells were the same. He wondered if grandmas have a secret scent bottled up and distributed only to them.

Sistrunk got down to business. "Mrs. Stabb, we found some evidence in your garden. Clues possibly point us in the direction of one of the missing college students."

"Oh dear, that's strange. What did you find, deputy?" Ma responded bewildered.

"I'd rather not get into details now, but there were some foot prints in the muck, and it seemed strange since the rest of the rows were so neatly raked. We'd like to take another look."

"Of course," she responded wrinkling her forehead obviously confused.

Sistrunk and Locke entered the rose garden. Bruce followed Sonny back between the rows of bushes where he found the foil. "This is the spot, Boss."

Sistrunk looked around puzzled then remarked, "It's amazing that you were able to find this."

"I just followed the foot prints, Boss."

An hour passed as Sistrunk walked through several more rows of the large garden. He signaled back with a quick head jerk to Sonny he was ready to go.

Frustrated, he said to Sonny, "Let's see if she has anything to tell us. Maybe a visitor, I don't know; it's all very, very strange."

Back in her parlor, Sistrunk sat patiently while Mrs. Stabb guided him through her daily routine; he waited for something, *anything* he could work with.

"Mrs. Stabb," he interrupted.

"Please, please call me 'Ma'. Mrs. Stabb sounds so formal, and out here in the Glades, well, we're not formal people."

"Alright, 'Ma'", he conceded. "Anything that you can remember, possibly something unusual that happened to explain why this foil was found in your garden. Would your grandson know anything? Has he brought anyone new to your home?"

"Just his girlfriend," she replied.

"Who is she?"

"Oh, a lovely girl he met in school. She's a florist."

"Yes, they were here a few weeks ago. It was the first time she had ever been to the Glades. She was captivated by the roses and Derrick's impressive grotto. I hope to see her again."

"She didn't say or do anything that seemed strange to you?" he inquired persistently.

She stood and replied showing her disapproval of his line of questioning. "Deputy, I don't know what your implying, but my grandson would never bring someone here that he thought would be a threat to me. She is just a nice girl he has an interest in, and he wanted me to meet her."

Grandma Ma turned, seemed to quickly compose herself and added, "Now, can I interest you two gentlemen in a piece of apple pie?"

"I didn't mean to imply anything like that, but I'm trying to cover all of the bases. If my questions offend you, I apologize," Sistrunk responded feeling that he had just been scolded by his own grandmother.

"Apology accepted," she said approvingly.

"I will have to pass on the dessert, but thank you."

He stood reaching for his card inside his pant's pocket. Sistrunk handed it to Ma.

"If you think of anything else, please give me a call."

The three made their way through the open door onto the freshly painted, gray porch. "Everything here seems to grow like crazy," he said. Just below the porch railing, Sistrunk noticed a grouping of cherry tomato plants hung low with ample clusters of bright red fruit.

"My grandson, Rodney, loves tomatoes. Those were planted specially for him. He's in the hospital, but he'll be home soon."

She spoke the words head downturned with sadness in her eyes.

"Sonny, you mentioned footprints. There was a very polite gentleman by here several days ago asking about roses. He was different from most of the tourists who usually just wander around. He snagged his slacks on the thorns of one of the rose bushes. As he was hopping around on one leg and his other leg was bleedin, he tried to compress the wound with a handkerchief. That was the reason the soil was disturbed. But his questions were very intelligent, inquiring about the soil and types of fertilizer I use. Not the usual inquiries I must say. I tried not to stare at the hideous scar that deformed half of his face. What a pity. I'm sure before he was a very handsome man."

She paused for a moment, thinking, and then continued," As we spoke, there was something that seemed familiar about him. At first, I thought we may have met in the past, but I couldn't place him. His voice was familiar, and something about his eye, the one that wasn't covered with a patch. Normally, I have a good recollection of people. I didn't think anything of his visit until now with all of the comings and goings of company."

Sistrunk said, "What, who was he? Mrs. Stabb, the only trace of physical evidence associated with our, missing person was found in your garden in that spot. The question was how did it get there and by whom? These questions he was asking about the soil leads me to think that there had to be a reason he was here. He wanted something ...but what? That's what we need to find out."

Once again, Bruce Sistrunk and Sonny Locke reentered the garden, this time more studiously. They cautiously walked through the rows and rows of sterling, white rose bushes.

"Ouch!" exclaimed Sistrunk as he suddenly pulled his arm up from one of the bushes. A few dots of blood oozed from a tiny puncture along the inside of his arm. He removed his handkerchief from his pants pocket and wrapped it around the wound.

"Hey, Boss, it might not be nothing, but look at this," said Sonny as the two men got closer to the stone grotto.

Sonny's keen eyes took note of a subtle detail as he cautiously reached down between the stems of each bush. The rose stems on the plants closer to the stone structure had fewer thorns, way fewer.

"So?" said Sistrunk as he shrugged his shoulders holding onto his bandage.

Sonny responded, "I don't know for sure, but didn't you say Derrick thought the riddles told something about the soil. Maybe that was the reason the stranger was here, to collect a sample, and, in the process, he cut himself on a thorny stem and dropped the foil."

Sonny's theory was the only assumption Sistrunk had to go on, as bizarre as it sounded. Amazingly, from all directions, as the two men approached the grotto, the thorny stems seemed to disappear.

Sistrunk took sample stems from the back of the garden, closest to the grotto, and compared them to the samples near the house. The difference was astonishing. One was covered in sturdy, needle-like thorns as he discovered earlier. You could barely touch it while the other was thorn free. *Could it be something in the soil?*

After he showed the stems to Ma, it was as much a surprise to her as it was to him. She hadn't noticed. But now that the subtle oddity had been called to her attention, she, too, was perplexed.

"Maybe a closer look under a microscope will provide some answers. There's a lab at the sheriff's office in West Palm Beach I can take these to."

Ma placed the dozen, or so, stems into a brown paper bag and handed it over to Sistrunk.

In Sonny's pickup, Sistrunk opened the tattered paper with the poetic stanzas scribbled on it and said, "Sonny, take a look at this. It mentions a man with a scarred face and a decades-long plan that involves blood types and blue eyes. All of our victims have blue eyes and O-negative blood."

"Yea, Boss. So what are you thinkin'?"

"I'm thinking that her grandson knows more than he's letting on to the police. Why is he the only one who seems to come up with what these poems mean? Waites up in Gainesville feels the same."

"So what you gonna do?"

"I going to have these rose stems analyzed, and then I think I need to focus my attention on one Derrick Stabb."

Laboratory technician, Delores Dawson, had been with the Palm Beach Sheriff's Department since graduating college, majoring in forensics. She typically analyzed blood and human tissue in the painstaking DNA connection with evidence. Her attention to detail was known throughout the force. A new challenge awaited "Laborious Delores", as she was referred to, as Sistrunk entered the lab.

After handing over the rose stems, he eagerly watched as she took out a large, sharp knife and cut slivers from several stems; she then placed the tiny pieces under the microscope. He was close enough to smell her clean, aromatic fragrance rousing the secret crush he had on the saucy technician.

"I don't know anything about plants except how to kill them. What am I looking for?" she said suddenly turning around, then reared back, startled to find Sistrunk inches away from her.

Sistrunk responded also pulling back sharply, "I know it is going to sound strange, but I want you to check for the level of aluminum in the stems if that's possible. I have reason to believe that could be affecting the amount of thorns on each stem."

"Why are *you* interested in thorns on a rose stem?" she inquired thoroughly puzzled.

"Let me just say that for some reason a suspicious person has been visiting the garden these grown in. And while that person was there, I believe that he or she dropped the evidence you analyzed for me earlier. It's the only evidence I have to go on involving a missing person's case. If the DNA connects the hair follicles with one of the missing people, then I have a link. And if I can find out why he was there, maybe I can find out who he is. I know, it's a backward way of investigating a case, but it's the only route I have."

"Hum," she uttered and placed the crushed, stem particles under the microscope and peered through adjusting the small dial on the instrument. Sistrunk took the opportunity to get closer and leaned in.

After a few moments, she removed one plate and inserted another. Several minutes passed; then she said, "Well, I can tell you that the thorn free stems show a higher concentration of aluminum in the cells than the thorny ones, whatever that's worth."

Sistrunk fought the urge to scratch the bald spot on the back of his head. He'd just gone through an expensive procedure of hair transplants. The tiny incisions were healing now; he knew that if he picked at the scabs, he would damage the hair plug. *Why did I do this?* he questioned. Answer: *He did it for her.* He turned his desire from scratching back to what Delores was telling him.

"So you think a higher concentration of aluminum affected the development of thorns on these roses?" he inquired pointing to the stems.

"I don't really know. I'm not a horticulturalist, but it was the only thing that was different. You say all of these roses were of the same variety. The cellular make up of all the stems are the same. This was the only difference. I'd check out the kind of fertilizer she used. I don't know what goes into that stuff. Like I said earlier, I just know how to kill them. However, I can tell you that if this product was used on produce, it would have a very bad affect on consumers."

"How so?" Sistrunk asked, taking advantage of the banter between them by moving in slightly closer, leaning one arm on the countertop.

"High concentrations of aluminum can cause dementia; deterioration of mental faculties combined with emotional disturbances, all resulting from organic brain disorder. Since people aren't eating the roses, the results seem to be beneficial; the stems won't prick you."

"That's it?" Sistrunk stated wrinkling his brow in disappointment.

"Not according to what I can see here, but I'm not a plant expert. Granted, we're all connected through science, but this was the only connection I could make sense of. I'm afraid after this you are on your own."

He sighed, reluctantly accepted her finding. Additionally, he was disappointed in the fact that he didn't have substantial reason to see her again, at least professionally. Getting up the nerve to ask women out had always been one of his weakest personality traits. He stammered and stalled for time, holding the last two stem samples in one hand.

"Thanks for your time, Ms. Dawson," Bruce extended his hand.

"Please call me Dody," she replied shaking his hand. "We've been working together all this time. I think when it's just the two of us, we can be less formal."

Surprised by her candor, Sistrunk felt much more confident now. "Join me for coffee?"

"Sure. I was just going to take a break. Coffee would be great."

Maybe starting these hair transplants wasn't such a bad idea after all.

Chapter 29—What Do The Riddles Mean?

Derrick flung his bag of laundry into his pickup, wiped his brow and checked his watch; it was nearly three o'clock. He hadn't returned home since that terrible night...the sequence of events plagued his mind since. He fought the idea of blaming himself for what had happened to Judy. After all, *he* wanted to go to the last club. *He* wanted to stay out later. Now, what could *he* do to solve the puzzle of Judy's disappearance? Ma had instilled a sense of confidence in him since he was little. She would say, "Derrick, you can accomplish anything you set your mind to."

He climbed into the front and turned the engine over. He meandered down the tree lined lane through the campus toward the Florida Turnpike. His mind wandered back and forth between Emily and concern for Ben.

Half way down I-75, past acres of orange groves, he stopped at his usual place, a Stuckey's Pecan Shoppe. It had become a little tradition of his. He savored the pecan logs sold there. He needed gas and a pay phone to call Emily.

"Can't talk long, babe; I'm working on my wedding flowers."

"Don't tell me. This *is* your blue rose bride, isn't it?"

"Yep, she's getting painted roses and lots of complimentary flowers. You know how I hate painting flowers. Thought I found some real blue roses, but they turned out to be lilac. Not the same. I'm tellin' ya, if someone came up with the real thing, they'd make a fortune."

"I gotta go, too, just dropped in my last dime." He hopped back into his car, peeled back the wrapping on his pecan log, took a bite and started the car. As the sun slowly settled behind the pine trees, he sailed down the road aiming for the long east-west stretch of SR 80, a familiar route to Belle Glade.

An hour later, he stepped his long legs onto the shell rock driveway and hopped out of his truck. A tingling sensation indicated the blood was moving more freely. Glad to be home, he grabbed his battered suitcase and headed up the porch steps.

Usually Ma was at the door with a warm welcome when Derrick arrived, but it was late and the house was dark. She must have had a busy day and decided to retire early.

Derrick was careful not to disturb her as he tipped-toed up the wooden steps and slipped through the front door. His stomach had started growling, so he made a bee line for the kitchen and started rummaging around the refrigerator quietly for ingredients to make a sandwich. Hungry enough, he'd eat most anything now regretting he didn't grab something at Stuckey's.

He grabbed his loosely piled assortment of cold cuts, bread and a glass of milk and headed for the dining room. Ma had stacks of paper from her garden club on the kitchen table. He was careful not to disturb them as he carefully guided the loose pages to the corner of the table. As he did, a tiny piece of folded paper made its way out from the bottom of the paper stack. Curious, he opened it and found an inscription similar to the one Ma showed him and Emily during their last visit.

"A thorn boy's past is about to unfold.

The symbols revealed his true owners are told.

Upside down they subtly appear.

Blue roses are the connection they hold dear."

"The Führer wife is the connection.

Follow a blood line it will guide your direction.

Her past and present are soon to be revealed.

They hold the secrets decades have concealed."

He pursed his lips, paused, and then finished his milk and sandwich. He leaned back in the chair and stared at the *Thorn Boy* statue.

He had paid little attention to it over the many years as it sat on the side board. It was just always there, always a part of their family. When he was a boy, Ma forbade his small hands from touching it concerned that it could be broken. Her words lingered into adulthood. He glanced down at the paper again; the poetic words puzzled him. He rose and examined it closer gently raising and lowering it. For its small size, the statue was quite weighty.

He ran his fingertips over the thin meandering lines of his grandfather's dried blood deeply embedded in the crevasses as he felt a bit creepy. Slowly, he turned it upside down and noticed a tiny inscription. He squinted. Much too small to read clearly without an aid; he fetched a magnifying glass from Ma's desk in the front hall and returned to take a closer look.

Faint were two lines of tiny characters he wasn't familiar with. Derrick turned on the overhead light and held the magnifying glass closer. Barely visible were two symbols.

וַרְדָּה

תְּכֵלֶת

Derrick ran his fingers over them curiously. He sighed and replaced the statue wondering where it really came from, what the symbols meant and who originally owned it. His late night snack had begun to settle in his stomach bringing with it fatigue. He'd look into the images later.

He stretched, picked up his plate and glass and headed for the kitchen. Time to hit the sack; he was exhausted.

Sunrise was 6:30, but Ma was awake long before that. Sleep always came and went with so many uncertainties that constantly haunted her. She threw the comforter back on the bed and scooted over to the side getting a firm grip on the mattress. She glanced out her bedroom window just as the sun was just beginning to kiss the tops of the pine trees. Today's worry was wondering how she would be able to keep Rodney in the hospital when she couldn't pay the bill.

The phone calls and registered mail had come more frequently now. She knew time was growing short, and all that she and her husband had worked for was in great jeopardy...what a dreadful thought.

Ma kept her problems to herself. Even if Derrick could help, she didn't want to burden him with her troubles. He needed to focus on school.

As rays of sunlight streamed through the windows of her kitchen and dining room, she took a seat and arranged the crumbs from Derrick's evening snack on the table with her index finger contemplating her dilemma. She had to put it out of her mind. Derrick was home; his visit made everything better, for awhile at least.

She stood and picked up the statue and looked warmheartedly upon the *Thorn Boy*, memories of her lost love replayed clearly. The day her "Stubbs" boarded the train for training camp now seemed like a foggy scene from a black and white movie. They stood on the platform as the rail cars slowed to a screeching halt; they locked in a tight embrace. She could still smell his, husky aftershave.

Ma recalled the expression on his face as he gently wiped the tears streaming from her eyes. And traces of her red lipstick on his neck and collar were as clear today as they were forty-five years ago. It was amazing how vividly her mind recalled the details from so long ago, and yet, sometimes, she couldn't remember what happened yesterday.

The sky grew brighter. She slowly placed *Thorn Boy* back onto the side board and headed for the kitchen. The arthritis in her joints was a constant reminder of her slowly failing body. Ten years ago, she could go all day in the garden and still have energy to prepare an evening meal.

Now it was time to make Derrick his favorite breakfast—Eggs Benedict. Later, it would be time for them to visit Rodney in the hospital.

After breakfast, Derrick placed the plastic container of ripe, red tomatoes in the car. It had been a couple months since he last saw his brother. Witnessing Rodney's decline as his motionless body lay trapped in bed was something Derrick dreaded. *Life sucks.* He had to put on a brave face for Ma. Derrick started to feel guilty. It wasn't right of him to be angry with his brother. Rodney couldn't help his situation.

He took a walk around the house waiting for Ma. Every time Derrick looked at the rose garden, she so loved, he was in awe. Emily was right; this place needed to be open to the public, he thought. The grotto in the distance was one of his crowning achievements, as well as a testimony of love and commitment to his family.

Following Ma's instructions, Derrick cut a dozen roses in a bud state, so the flowers would last. He removed the thorns one by one and wrapped them at the kitchen counter in brown paper he found in the pantry.

He waited patiently by his truck as Ma pulled the front door behind her and carefully made her way down the wooden steps. Careful not to express any uneasiness in visiting Rodney, Derrick held the truck's door open for Ma. The pair was down the gravel road as the truck left a trail of dust behind.

"Are you seeing Ben while you're home?" Ma asked after several minutes of strained silence clutching the straps of her handbag as it rested upon her lap.

"Yes, I plan to," he responded as he eased the truck onto the main road.

"No word on what is happening with the investigation?" she inquired.

"No, Ma. I wish that there was something that I could do. So far all I've done is annoy the police."

"It's strange, but I think there is something to those riddles Ben and Judy's mom have gotten from a psychic."

"Riddles from a psychic, dear? Well, if anyone can figure out anything, it's you, Derrick."

He glanced over at her, smiled and said, "Thanks, Ma."

Derrick anguished about the visit during the ten minute trip from home to hospital. He dropped off his grandmother under the portico saving her steps from the parking lot. By the time he parked the truck, Ma was down the hall past the nurses' station. Derrick picked up his pace to catch up with her.

Sienna Hurst, the nurse, was on duty. She greeted Ma with a smile and gave Derrick a quick, flirtatious wink just before they entered the ward housing Rodney. "How nice to see you again, Mrs. Stabb, and I see your handsome grandson is escorting you today."

Derrick forced a smile. It was obvious the woman had a crush on him. Pausing, he noticed her eyes tracing him.

"You look great in that shirt."

"Thanks." He thought, *in the future I'll throw on a baggy flannel one.*

Derrick rushed to catch up to Ma as she was about to enter Rodney's room.

This visit seemed a little different. Usually Ma cooed and carried on over Rodney regardless of his reaction, which was always the same, nada.

One of the custodians entered the room with a plastic pitcher from the utility closet. Derrick was holding the usually large bundle of roses they always brought.

"Ms. Stabb, you should be a professional rose grower."

She responded, "I think they make him happy. They're a reminder of home. Just like the tomatoes he loves."

She waited until Derrick dropped the flowers into the container and then peeled back the plastic lid and scooped a puréed spoonful. As she leaned in to serve the red, ripe fruit, Rodney suddenly jerked his head away startling her.

"He'd never done that before. He always ate every bit I brought...what is going on?"

"Maybe he's just not in the mood, Ma," Derrick said in a consoling manner.

As she attempted to redeliver another spoonful, Rodney's reaction was the same; this time was more violent as he shook his head back and forth. His bright blue eyes expressed something she had never seen: terror. He attempted to speak, but nothing came out.

"What is it dear, what's wrong?" Ma responded. "Tell me what are you trying to say, Rodney?"

Ma urged him again and again as Rodney seemed to struggle with forming the words on his lips. Derrick shook his head back and forth grimacing. "Ma, I don't think he's able to tell you."

She began to sob. Derrick gently placed his hands on her shoulders, which seemed to offer her little comfort. The scene as it unfolded left him feeling hopeless. Ma retreated, sealing the container and leaned back into her chair, motionless as the tears trickled down her cheeks. Rodney had finally fallen asleep. "Let's go, Ma," said Derrick.

They quietly left the room approaching the nurses' station. Ma turned, reached up and pulled Derrick down closer to her quietly mentioning, "I like that young lady. Her face is so angelic, like I've seen her before."

She continued as they stepped out onto the driveway, "She resembles the lady I've see in my garden. We pray together."

Derrick smiled as he held the truck's door for her. "Ma, Ben's coming over tonight. He said he's got something to show me."

"Show you, what?"

"Some inscriptions, I think he said something about some riddles from a psychic Judy's mother had seen. He thought that maybe I could make sense out of them."

"I told him that I wasn't psychic, so I don't know how much help I could offer."

"Riddles," Ma repeated. "They seem to be popping up in lots of places," she mumbled.

"What did you say, Ma."

"Never mind dear."

"How did your visit go at the hospital?" Ben asked entering through Ma's front door.

"Not very well, my brother seems to be getting worse," replied Derrick in a tone which sounded more like Rodney had died.

"Sorry to hear that. You know," Ben said looking about making every effort to cheer his buddy up, "I've actually never been to your home during the daylight hours. I'm eager to see this work of art you created for your grandmother. I didn't know you were so handy in masonry skills."

"Well, Emily sure was impressed. She thinks we should open it up to the public for weddings and make some money. Ma's already getting visitors who heard about her garden from people in town. Just in the past few weeks, she's had a slew of folks through here asking all sorts of questions."

"About what?" Ben inquired as the boys headed out the back door into the garden.

Derrick responded as they meandered through the rows of rose bushes, "I haven't gotten into the details with her. Her mind seems to be elsewhere. I guess it's the stress with Rodney. I noticed that she's praying her rosary almost constantly. Ma's never been one to burden anyone with her problems. She keeps them to herself, but I can tell something's really bothering her."

"Wow! Impressive!" exclaimed Ben as he and Derrick stood before the stone grotto. "How long did it take you to build this?"

"Practically the whole summer; I stayed committed to it once the project was started. I felt there was a divine presence constantly pushing me. And now look at it.

I am proud of how it turned out, considering I've never done something like this before."

Ben leaned in closer and studied the plaques dedicated to Derrick's father and granddad. "This is really cool, Derrick. Just think, for many years down the road, this will be a testament to the feelings you have for these men. Maybe you *should* open this place up for ceremonies. I'd pay to get married here."

"Well, so far Ma isn't so keen on the idea. I don't think she wants people trampling her roses. I told her, with all the money we'd make, she could replace them. But she's not buying into it."

"You'll have to say hi to Ma before we head out," suggested Derrick.

"Oh yeah, I want to. Has she asked about Judy or the others, or if the cops found anything?"

"Sure, she asks. But since there isn't much to tell, it's a short conversation," Derrick replied. "I know they are part of the reason she prays so much. Let's get back to the house."

Ma descended the stairs as the two young men came in from the garden.

"That's quite an impressive job Derrick did on the stone grotto. I didn't know he was so talented," Ben offered smiling

"I know. I love it. If his father and grandfather were here, they would be so proud, I'm sure," she said.

"Can I make you boys some dinner?"

"No, Ma. Ben and I are going to West Palm, not sure where; we just want to get out of Belle Glade."

"Well, you be careful. I think that highway is the most dangerous road in Palm Beach County with those canals that run along side it and no lights."

"We will," Derrick assured her.

She turned heading back upstairs.

"Before we take off, I want to show you something," Derrick whispered. "Last night I got in late and was sitting here eating. I was moving some of Ma's garden club stuff over to make room, and this slipped out from under the papers. I don't know where it came from, but it isn't the first riddle she's gotten. In the truck on the way to the hospital, I mentioned the riddles you and Judy's mom had. Ma mumbled something, but, for whatever reason, she didn't repeat it. See this one stanza; it mentions the statue," Derrick said pointing to the four lines.

"Yea, they seem to be in the same style as the ones I have," Ben responded.

"Anyway, I got to thinking about Ma's statue, so I brought it back over to the table while I finished my sandwich."

"First of all, the weight, for stone it seems really heavy."

Ben took the statue from Derrick and motioned up and down with it.

"Stone's heavy. We have granite slabs in the cemetery and they weigh a ton."

He handed the statue back to Derrick.

"Yeah, but take a look at this." Derrick carefully turned the sculpture upside down and revealed the small characters barely visible underneath.

"What are they?" Ben inquired as he gently ran his finger over the inscription, "Arabic?"

"I don't know," replied Derrick. "Granddaddy's army buddy brought this back after the war at granddad's request to make sure Ma got it. It was pretty special to him. He was in Germany, not the Middle East."

"Well, it could have traveled," Ben added. "Could the symbols be Hebrew?"

"Maybe, but how can I know? I don't think she's gonna let me take it back to school."

"Do a rubbing."

"Say what?"

"Put a piece of paper over it and gently rub it with a soft pencil; it'll make an impression of the image. We did that on old grave markers when I was researching genealogy for a class project. I was all over South Florida and even went to Ireland and took impressions of tombstones there. Some of them weren't in English; they were in Gaelic, the native language of Ireland. Anyway, that way you can take the image back to school and research it."

"I'll do it later tonight. Let's go before it gets too late." He returned the statue to its spot and headed out the door behind Ben just as the flickering sunlight disappeared below the tops of the sugar cane.

"I have some late-breaking news to share with you," Ben said in the car as he and Derrick continued east toward West Palm.

"What's that?"

"A search team headed up by a group of locals found basically what amounts to a needle in a haystack; some blonde hair wrapped in foil and tissue."

Briefly, Derrick took his eyes off the road and glanced at his friend hopefully.

"My hunch was right," Derrick said.

"Explain, buddy."

"That fax you sent, I called the detective in Gainesville and showed it to him. I told him about Ma's riddles and suggested that they send someone over to search her garden. That's amazing; that skeptical Detective Waites should be thanking me instead of patronizing me. He treated me like I was some dumb kid. Well, now they have another clue."

"Oh, there's more!" Ben continued. "Mrs. Johnson didn't give me all of the riddles. Apparently she has more. Here are three of them. I can read them to you if you have a flashlight."

"There's one in the glove box."

Ben popped open the lid, clicked on the small but adequate light and began to recite the words as Derrick steered through the verdant farmland.

"Cutting through the night with wheels ablaze,
He eagerly pursues those with a blue-eyed gaze,
Blatantly ignoring a simple repair,
Will end the chase with much despair,"

"The rhythmic sounds of the rails at night,
Guide the rescuers in their plight,
To rows of presidents charted about,
Sworn into his post after three shots rang out,"

"His legacy was tarnished by an unpopular war,
Gripping the nation for many years from a far,
Riots and protests banish the purpose,
The people have spoken the cause seemed worthless,"

"These are the two I already have," Ben said.

"Beds of blue roses,
Blonde hair so fine,
Look to the sky,
She is divine."

"Aryan features grace them all,

As Satan's children they will fall,

The sacrifices made may be in vain,

Because his fate is not to gain,"

Derrick diverted his eyes away from the road looking at Ben and inquired, "So, how many riddles does that make? Ten, Twelve?"

Ben responded, "About that. Now we have some hair in a tissue that miraculously turned up in a garden. And Mrs. Johnson is going nuts. She thinks this guy is offering clues. We just need to figure 'em out."

"This is the one he recited today," Ben rearranged the pages in his hand.

"Perched on a stone,

Attending to a need,

A covering hides,

What lies beneath,"

"Claimed by many,

A history untold,

His heirs are near,

Desired to behold,"

Derrick analyzed the poetic phrases. After a few moments of silence, he said,

"Hey, Ben, have you ever heard of a guy named Nostradamus?"

"No, not really, I mean, I've heard he was a prophet or someone who made predictions hundreds of years ago that had come true. Is that who you mean?"

Derrick chuckled at his friend's ignorance, then responded, "It's not like I am any kind of expert on sixteenth century French history, but you're kind of correct." He continued, "Nostradamus has been credited with all sorts of predictions ranging from the French Revolution and the atom bomb to the rise of Adolf Hitler."

"Sounds like you know a lot about him."

"I did a paper on him in high school English literature."

"I hope that report went as well as the one Professor Hicks gave you."

"Very funny, actually I got an A on it, I'll have you know."

"Of course you did," Ben quipped back, "I wouldn't have expected anything else."

Derrick gave Ben a smug expression in response to his sarcastic reply and then continued just as the truck hit a pothole in the road rocking the two violently back and forth. "Man, I hope that didn't knock my wheel out of alignment!"

"Seems okay, but you should get it checked out tomorrow," Ben suggested cinching his seatbelt tighter.

Derrick continued, "Good idea, I will, and for your information, my friend, Nostradamus was known as an apothecary."

"What's that?"

"A pharmacist," replied Derrick, feeling quite like the authority by now.

"According to history, he created a 'rose pill' that was believed to protect against the plague. He's best known for a series of books he wrote, *'Les Propheties'* or The Prophecies published in 1555, consisting of hundreds of quatrains."

"Qua-what!" exclaimed Ben?

"Quatrains, from quadrant, meaning four," answered Derrick. "They're stanzas or poems of four lines." At that, Derrick pointed to the page indicating the verses Van Cormack recited to Judy's mom. "Some people thought Nostradamus was a servant of the Devil. Some of the upper class thought his quatrains were spiritually inspired prophecies. Anyway, he developed quite a reputation that continues to this day. Are you going back to see this guy?"

"Maybe, I don't know. But I'm certain Judy's mom will. Who knows what she paid him, but the sessions aren't free. This is how he makes a living. When we first got there, he told her that he couldn't guarantee anything. She was obviously hooked. It's possible this is how he does it...feeds you just enough words to keep you coming back for more all the while saying, 'I can't promise anything.' It could all be a great gimmick that he uses on a lot of people. Pretty smart when you think about it."

"I'd go back. If for no other reason, than to make sure Judy's mom isn't being taken by this guy playing on her emotions."

"She doesn't need me. If Mrs. Johnson wanted to go back, with or without me, she'd do it."

"That's what I mean. The chances are pretty strong she will, so you make sure to tag along, and when you do, take a recorder and capture every word. At this point I wouldn't rule out anything."

"Okay, you're right," Ben agreed and continued. "Hey, if this horticulture career doesn't work out for you, you can always become a P.I.; sounds to me like you have the stuff for it."

Derrick glanced over at his friend. "I know we can be The Hardy Boys. You wanna be Shaun Cassidy?"

"Sure, whatever you say, buddy."

"Read those to me again, Ben..."

Derrick's mind churned over the passages as he steered his truck. After a few moments of silence Ben said, "So, what do you think, a bunch of hooey?"

"No, I don't think so. This must have a connection with Judy and the others, with Aryans. Someone is doing something dastardly, maybe an experiment creating a blue rose. And I think there's a connection to Hitler. That's what I interpret from Satan's Children. They're used in some sort of sacrifice."

Derrick paused for a moment then continued, "Maybe this stanza about a president and an unpopular war; as far as wars go, they're all unpopular, but one of the most turbulent was the Vietnam War during the Johnson Administration. My Dad died in that war. The whole nation was in an uproar. Presidents charted about could mean anything, possibly streets. You live on a street named after someone famous, right?"

"Yea, Flagler Drive, so I see what you mean, like down in Hollywood. Many of the streets are named after presidents," Ben added.

"The only connection I can make to perched on a stone is Ma's statue. He sits on a rock, but what that has to do with anything is a mystery. Hey, maybe somebody's looking for it. *Thorn Boy* could be important to somebody other than Ma, like he's part of their history or something. That's who the symbols represent. That's what the riddle means."

"Derrick, I think you've got some puzzle pieces that need to be put together."

Derrick glanced over the gear shift at his friend. "Ben, I think you're right. He isn't gonna like seeing my face again, but I'm gonna bug that Detective Waites some more when I get back."

A couple of creaks faintly announced Derrick's arrival back home as he tip-toed up the wood steps onto Ma's front porch. Once inside, he took a number two pencil his friend had in the car's glove box, grabbed a piece of note paper and headed for the dining room.

He held the weighty statue upside down precariously between his knees and placed the thin sheet of paper on the bottom, and then he gently brushed the soft lead tip over the symbols. Just as Ben told him, the images appeared on the paper. To be sure he did it right, Derrick took another impression of the tiny characters on a heavier paper stock. This time the detail was better, but he'd keep both. He replaced the statue.

He removed a can of aerosol hairspray from Ma's hallway cupboard and lightly sprayed the images, sealing the soft lead onto the paper so it wouldn't smear. The spray quickly dried after waving the pages back and forth. *Mission accomplished*.

He stared at the tiny impressions for a moment thinking the spiritualist's poetic riddles had made their way into his and Ma's lives for a reason. His words certainly had meaning that he was obsessed to figure out. Derrick headed upstairs to his bedroom. He stretched, yawned, threw the covers back and crawled between the crisp sheets fearing that Thorn Boy's past would soon come calling.

Chapter 30—Serendipity

***Bloody** work,* thought Cornelius as he lit his second cigarette and took a deep drag, still wearing his blood splattered lab coat. He reached into the white, corrugated box, scooped up a handful of dried, dark green tobacco and pressed it against his mutilated face. Fortunately, the box Casey was sent to fetch in Miami made it unscathed to the lab. Unfortunately, the same couldn't be said for Casey and his two girly sidekicks who delivered him.

Cornelius steadily drew the vials of blood from each victim sprawled on the laboratory floor. He was pleased to see the first one would work fine, then the second. *Well, look at that*, he thought, two of the three are O-negative. He'd dump the third body, along with the convertible, far from here in the gator infested canal. He couldn't run the risk of accidentally contaminating the soil he had carefully and scientifically created by mixing a foreign substance.

Time was now of the essence. He had to produce results soon, or he feared the funds would be cut off. His benefactor didn't understand that science needs time; it's not on a schedule.

This should do it, he thought again, dangling the dark leaf inches from his nose. The rarest of rare tobacco, high in the elements he needed: cobalt, aluminum, iron, and the right degree of acidity, mixed with the special soil he concocted. The rose seedlings, germinated from the most exquisite bushes he'd ever seen, grown in the one-of-a- kind soil composition he created, would produce the first authentic blue rose. She will be very pleased. And he would be famous.

He sighed for a moment, exhaled and pondered the hair follicles he had lost. There's always a solution; he knew where to get more. The scientist picked up his lab phone.

"Hazel, this is Hicks."

"Oh, Cornelius, I just got this crazy message from Casey. Did he—"

"Yes, he delivered the box. I have my precious goods, just a little late. No harm though, everything's fine."

"I am so relieved. I was thinking he screwed up again. I would have been so disappointed after we had our little talk setting him straight, so to speak. What about his car, did he get the tire plugged?" she went on to say.

"I guess so; he didn't mention it. He just dropped off the package, I gave him some money, and he left happy. It was a win-win for everybody."

"I have a request," he asked.

"Sure, anything," said Hazel, relieved, cordially obliging him.

"I need you to get me some more of those hair follicles from our victim."

"When do you need them?" she responded.

"Now," he replied.

"Right away," she said obediently.

Hazel Craig was pleased to be in a position where she could help the man she had grown to love. Now she was in a position to be a part of cutting-edge science. The feeling sent chills up her spine.

The lock on the door to the spare room clicked open; Hazel entered. The second bedroom in her little CBS house had become her hobby room. Packed away in the dark, cramped quarters were shelves of books on crafts and gardening.

Her favorite book was signed by Cornelius. She removed the bound pages from its prominently displayed place and opened it to the inside, front cover that displayed his signature. Slowly, she ran her fingertips over the black swirling lines. The tingling sensation raised goose bumps on her arms confirming her motives. After a few moments of self indulgence, she returned his book to the shelf and turned to the matter at hand.

Strapped down and blindfolded on the bed was the motionless body of Judy Johnson. She had been drugged into a semi-catatonic state. The only life saving source was an intravenous feeding tube.

She felt pride to be a part of the abduction Cornelius masterminded from the West Palm night club. Although, Hazel was baffled at the hesitation Cornelius had with this victim. He extended immunity this one time sparing her life, for now.

She pondered momentarily. Why was this particular young woman the only victim, identified by name, which Cornelius's benefactor insisted be part of the project. Her qualities were no less or no more valuable that the others as far as Hazel knew. But Cornelius didn't see any rush to commit her body to the project, at least not now. Most assuredly her days were numbered, though.

Hazel took several strands of Judy's long, silky, blonde hair and gave a forceful yank, releasing the locks along with miniscule pieces of blood and tissue. In her semi-conscience state, Hazel knew that she didn't feel a thing. After she placed the samples into a plastic zip lock bag, she compressed a cotton ball soaked with hydrogen peroxide on the donor area, a practice she used many times at work after drawing blood.

Hazel pulled the door closed behind her and turned the key until she heard a click. Cornelius should be here soon. She longed to see him. He was like a drug, and she needed a fix. It had been several weeks since they worked together on the last abduction. She took the hairs, wrapped them in foil and dropped them into a clear, plastic bag just as a vehicle pulled into the driveway.

Cornelius had three reasons to drive to the coast on this sunny, clear afternoon. A man who desired to make good use of time thought, *I'll kill three birds with one stone.* He had scheduled at ten a.m. to meet with Hazel—bird number one.

He had grown to appreciate Hazel's absence. She had become so annoying: clinging to him, pestering him, wanting to know every detail of his work. Obviously, she adored him, a huge stroke to his ego. But, as time progressed, his feelings changed. He was no longer amused with her eccentricities and had grown disgusted at the site of her.

This won't take long, he contemplated as he pulled his van into the driveway. Cornelius slung open the heavy van door with a creak. He slid down from the vinyl seat, turned and took several swipes dusting the dry, red soil from his pants. He had to play it cool with Hazel, though. He needed her until he figured out what to do with his live donor she harbored. His appointment in Palm Beach would serve as an excuse to get in and out quickly. Hazel wouldn't *do* anything to jeopardize the project. His excuse that he was meeting with the project's benefactor was perfect. He stepped onto the front porch noticing the small pots of herbs and flowers near the door. Hazel waited on the other side of the door and immediately opened it with a welcoming gesture.

"Is she still comatose?" Cornelius inquired as Hazel handed over the plastic bag with streaks of blood smeared against its inside.

"Yes, but I don't think we can keep her this way much longer. Her body is dehydrating and starting to show signs of distress. You'll have to make a decision soon."

"I'll let you know," he responded.

"Have you heard from Casey?" Hazel asked. "I haven't heard a word from him since he was on his way from Miami to deliver your package."

"I'm not surprised," Cornelius responded with a sneer. "Who knows who he had decided to take up with? I was relieved that he actually delivered my box. I'm sure you will hear from him. Well, got to run; the money source is waiting for me."

Her disappointment was clearly visible. "But I thought we could spend some time together. Please stay for tea. You always seem to be in a rush lately.

Things aren't the same between us as they used to be. Cornelius, I'm...I'm starting to feel used."

He pressed his tongue again his cheek, looked at her and said, "Oh, not this again. Hazel, I don't know why you think our relationship is more than business. I thought I made that clear from the beginning."

She clinched her fists responding, "The only clear thing I see is *you* getting what *you* want. Using me, that's what this seems to be adding up to. I don't have anything in writing. Up to this point, I've trusted you. I want an agreement that spells out what's in this for me. You said it from the beginning, 'Without my help this would have taken much longer or not possible at all.' Remember those words, Cornelius? I certainly do. You don't want me going to the police do you? They've already been here you know, asking questions, following a paper trail from the flowers I sent to that Olympian's address you so badly wanted. Fortunately for you, I'm a good liar. "

He turned and approached her; towering over her stoutness and responded with force, "Fortunately for *us,* you're a good liar. You're just as much a part of this as I am. If I go down, I'm taking you with me, remember that. All in time, Hazel dear, you will get exactly what's coming to you. Now, if you will excuse me."

Standing in the front entrance, she backed down noticeably defeated, for now.

"Good, I'm glad we're in agreement." He nodded approvingly, and then slammed the door in her face.

His next stop, Hialeah—bird number two.

Cornelius headed south on I-95 picked up the Dolphin Expressway and barreled west toward Hialeah. It was in the opposite direction from Palm Beach, but he had to see Van Cormack this morning. He glanced down at his watch carefully monitoring the time. With each reading came a clearer message. They had become his guiding light.

Cornelius pulled up in front of the unassuming, old, frame house and checked his watch once again, right on time. He sighed a bit of relief when he saw the spiritualist's sign was still illuminated. Sometimes Van Cormack had inexplicably changed his mind and refused to see clients indicated by his sign turned *off*.

Without wasting a minute, Cornelius approached the front door. He banged hard on the rickety screen door reverberating it against the wooden frame. Moments later he heard the old man's cane tapping against the floor, soon followed by his frail hand that slowly raised the window blind. A series of locks disengaged, and the door opened with a creak. "Come in."

"You don't' look well, Giles. Has the arthritis been getting worse?"

The unexpected, piercing squeal from his hearing aid penetrated the scientist's ear drums. Van Cormack scrunched up his face indicating his annoyance with the inquiry then fiddled with the tiny dial. The noise stopped. Hunched over, he looked upward directly in the scientist's good eye and said, "I'm getting by."

Cornelius knew not to show any pity on the old man. He wouldn't tolerate it. A trait among many he admired in him.

"I'm ready for you."

He followed Van Cormack down the long, narrow hallway, past the Van Gogh, into the reading room. As they entered the space, garlands of cob webs waved every so gently in the subtle air currant.

"Giles, why don't you get someone to come in and clean for you, maybe help with small duties?"

"Don't worry about me."

A tinge of regret settled onto Cornelius. He knew better but still succumbed to his feelings of concern for the little man he had enormous respect for.

Gesturing to a chair at the table in the center of the room, he said, "Sit down."

Cornelius took his place at the table where he had sat many times before. Again, he fought his desire to assist the old man as he watched Van Cormack hobble over to the dresser and open the top drawer. He took his place opposite the scientist, who sat erect in his chair with both hands placed palms down on the table top.

Van Cormack reached across the small table top and gently brushed his fingertips over the surface of the disfigured tissue on each hand.

"These scars haven't shown much improvement over the years."

The scientist quickly jerked back. Time hadn't eased his sensitivity regarding his deformities. He had worked hard for years putting the memory of that awful accident behind him. Van Cormack's remark brought his insecurity to the surface in a way only he could do. Something Cornelius couldn't seem to control; very unnerving for a man who was always in control.

"It's only cosmetic, Cornelius. What matters is the man inside. What he does with his life."

The scientist slowly placed his hands back onto the table's surface. It was just one more way that Van Cormack demonstrated his ability to take someone's emotions and twist them anyway he wanted to.

"Well, let's get started," he said while he placed the fragile cloth over his face and tilted his head back.

Cornelius sat motionless. His good eye focused on the white cloth that had begun to gently move back and forth. Momentarily, a few soft, garbled words emerged from under the handkerchief. Cornelius leaned in closer; his chest touched the table's edge. Then, he heard:

"The prize you seek is an old soul,
He is the one you need to meet your goal,
You will know him when you first meet
Without him your success will be incomplete,"

"A garden's grotto has been an inspiration,
You and he share the same determination,
You cannot persuade him alone with your charm
A beauty's assistance will do you no harm"

"At first the sign is unclear,
He is endearing to you, he is sincere,
Intelligent and kind, eyes of bright blue,
He bears the sign of a rose tattoo,"

"His talents in science are just the key,
Within your reach he would be,
Between the pages scored an excellent mark,
Vital signs needed, a path to embark,"

Van Cormack paused, his head tilted foreword as Cornelius eagerly waited for more. This was the most difficult part of their relationship to tolerate. He fought the urge to stand and slam his fists on the tabletop, knowing full well that if he did the spiritualist would cut their ties like a cane knife slicing through a meaty melon.

Cornelius wrung his hands over and over each other under the table with anticipation. He must hold on, he told himself. Van Cormack will deliver, he always has. At that moment, the handkerchief moved, his head raised and he spoke:

"Aryan qualities have been the root,

You need to challenge her and refute,

An argument develops to an assail,

You have the power to prevail,"

"The partnership you have has been mired"

Her goals differ from what you've desired,

The challenges you face can tilt the scale

The blue rose you desire should not fail,"

"Approach those you deal with very carefully,

They can disrupt your success fearfully,

The road is long and unclear,

Don't allow her to manipulate your career,"

Van Cormack's head dropped forward again and allowed the white cloth to drift to the floor. His eyes blinked several times before he appeared alert. Cornelius, still with pen in hand, had scratched down his final words before he forgot them. After he had driven so far, he'd hoped for more but knew how the readings worked.

"Cornelius, use your gift to understand the quatrains. As in the past, in them are important messages.

If you don't heed their guidance, you'll regret it."

He leaned back taking a deep breath. "They seem to indicate that there's another person important to the project." Cornelius stretched his arms across the table. "Give me another reading, Giles. Tell me when it's going to happen. Who's manipulating me?"

Van Cormack's eyes diverted toward the wall clock and suppressed a yawn.

Cornelius read his actions; he knew.

He gripped the steering wheel of his rattle-trapped, blue van and gunned the engine aggressively keeping up with the traffic. He struggled to be calm and collected for his meeting with her—bird number three; he veered off the interstate to take the relaxed ocean road up to Palm Beach.

As he edged along the seacoast, a thin coat of salt spray covered his van as he approached the town of Palm Beach. Known as "America's Breadbasket", the island's inhabitants are some of the nation's wealthiest. He passed mega mansions that dotted the coastline behind manicured, three-story ficus and ligustrum hedges. North of Sloan's Curve was the prestigious Beach and Racket Club. Its membership included the islands wealthiest gentiles. He was only minutes away from Tchelet's condominium building.

Cornelius pulled into the condominium's circular driveway. After the suited and white gloved valet slid behind the wheel of his van, Cornelius made his way through the grand foyer. Soon he was standing in the luxurious, gold accented and mirrored elevator. As he watched the numbers climb, he couldn't fight his anxiety nor deny it. Certainly by this time he would have been able to conquer the nervousness, but no.

He had developed a relationship with Tchelet as he felt she was nearly his equal. Something he never felt about a woman before. Always the consummate professional, Cornelius had rehearsed what he was going to say. He had to get more time. Play on her ambitions. Convince her it would work. He was so close to success. He couldn't allow her to pull the funds now.

He took a deep breath and tried to relax. Minutes later the door opened into a private foyer of polished marble and inlaid onyx. His eye squinted at the dazzling room. The type of home he dreamed of living in one day. Once he refocused, a rotund butler stuffed into an undersized suit greeted him.

"Mrs. Goldstein-Smith will be with you shortly, sir. May I bring you something to drink?"

Still taking in the details of the beautiful, penthouse apartment, he responded, "Wine, please."

Moments later she entered the room. "Cornelius, darling, how wonderful to see you!" exclaimed Tchelet. He made an about-face in the direction of the shrill voice. Before him was an elegant lady 'dressed to the nines' in a gorgeous, black and white, tailored Chanel suit. Light spires radiated from a dazzling, prodigious diamond ring adorning her right hand.

She escorted her guest to the living room and its panoramic view of the ocean. By this time the butler had rejoined them; he presented the wine from a silver serving plate. Just the thing he needed to calm himself.

"Your scars have improved with time, Cornelius. Cosmetic surgery is so amazing. I am due for a little lift myself," she said glancing in the mirror, placing her fingertips against her temples, pulling back gently.

"Thank you Tchelet. I've grown to focus on what is possible—the future, rather than what has happened—the past. After our project is successful, I hope to have more done," he said as he clutched the leather attaché closer to his chest.

"I am sorry to say my sister Varda, will not be able to join us. I almost postponed our meeting because she was admitted to the hospital late last night."

"I'm sorry to hear that. What's wrong?"

"Cystic Fibrosis, most are dead at an early age, but Varda has held on much longer that any of us could have imagined. Thank God we have the best doctors money can buy. However, this time her exertions were too much. When we returned home from a benefit last night, she began to feel very ill. I called our doctor, and he immediately admitted her to Good Samaritan."

She continued, "I am the stronger, more determined one, Cornelius. Varda has accepted this disease as her fate. Even though I encourage her to fight, I feel that in her heart she's let go."

"I'm sorry to hear that."

His show of sensitivity—uncharacteristic of him—was an unrehearsed scene. In the forefront of his mind were the funds he needed.

"Now that this turn of events has happened, I'm more eager that our project see results *soon*. What have you got for me?"

He reached for the leather attaché case, released the buckle, and pulled out the documents and photos. She noticed a bound manuscript in the papers and called attention to it.

"Interesting, what's this?"

He replied, "A research paper one of my twin, Stanley's, students completed. It happened to contain vital information pertinent to our project. I took the liberty of photocopying it while he was down here. Look, he gave him an A on it. Stanley never gives A's. The discoveries this very bright young man made was just the information I," he hesitated momentarily, "I mean, *we,* need to move forward. Happening upon this has accelerated the process. Without it our success could have been delayed."

"Well, we can't afford that! You have a twin brother, Cornelius? I've known you for a long time; you've never mentioned a twin before."

Cornelius took a deep breath, leaned back against the soft material regretting he mentioned Stanley. "He's a professor at the University of Florida. The only thing we've shared is an interest in plants. We've never been close. It's always been a rather contentious relationship. I know most twins are close, but not us; we're polar opposites. He was the athletic one, swim team in school, and all that—got the girls—you know the type. Me, after I gave up trying to compete, I relented and buried my head in my books, that is, when I wasn't avoiding the bullies. They seemed to zero in on me like a heat-seeking missile. I got tired of

Stanley coming to my rescue...it was embarrassing. I'd rather have gotten beaten up."

He regrouped. "Well, I didn't come here to hash over the past. I know you're interested in the progress." He scooted closer to her on the sofa with the folder neatly resting in his lap and pointed to the open pages. "This part is of particular interest to you. It shows how the blue roses genetic mutations created in the flower's pollen could have profound affects on the respiratory system of Aryans."

"Genetic mutations—respiratory system?" she questioned, straining to understand the scientific lingo. "In plain English, Cornelius, I don't need to be impressed with your education. I know you're brilliant."

He paused, smiled and responded respectfully, "It's possible that the flower's pollen, inhaled when an admirer is attracted to its scent, could trigger symptoms similar to TB in them."

"Tuberculosis, isn't that highly contagious?"

"No," he responded confidently. "Similar symptoms, it would only affect them because of the genomes encoded in their DNA. Although, that could pose somewhat of a problem if all of the Aryans died. Then where do I obtain the victims needed for the soil composition to produce the roses in?"

"Cornelius, Cornelius, silly, magnificent Cornelius. I know you will figure that out. Besides, we don't want to get rid of *all* of them, just six or so million."

He continued, "Oh yes, to even the score. Well, you see why I said I have some exciting news. See, fate is on our side, and it's secured by the rose tattoo."

"Rose tattoo?" She questioned wrinkling her brow.

"Up to now all of the Aryans have had a blue rose tattoo stamped somewhere on them. I'm certain that's a sign of our fate, that these particular first specimens are required to secure our success."

"Serendipity!" she exclaimed. "And the young lady, Judy Johnson, I told you about who would be so important to the project. Do you have her?"

"Yes, and she's marked with a rose."

"I'm not surprised. Good. Well, Cornelius, combined with these latest revelations of yours, I'm convinced that her essence will provide the blue rose with something very special. I've been thinking." She paused, arms folded, tapping her French manicured index finger against her cheek. "I've come up with a new word to describe our original blossom's scent."

"A new word?" he queried.

"Yes, 'Essenciate', the rose will 'Essenciate' and delight all those who experience it. After our blue rose is successfully created, I'm thinking of developing a perfume with that name and marketing it in a cobalt bottle in the shape of a rose. It's another opportunity to secure the brand and generate revenue. I'm certain I can get one of my celebrity girlfriends to endorse it. What do you think?"

"Essenciate, fabulous; I like it," he responded with a grin nodding approvingly.

They laughed wildly followed by a startling crash. A pelican flew into the glass door. They turned to see the winded creature struggle on the balcony. "That has been happening more lately," Said Tchelet. "I've complained to the condo board, but seems they can't do much about it. I suggested an open season on pelicans, but that seemed to fall on deaf ears. Several of the residents are also members of the Audubon Society and didn't appreciate my suggestion. Oh well, the price one pays to live in paradise."

Once composed, she took a deep breath. Then Tchelet turned the pages of the report. Her eyes darted to the four eight by ten photos of the Aryan specimens. Obviously very pleased with what she saw and heard, she reached for her checkbook, opened the leather flap and said, "How much?"

Cornelius earnestly made his way to the exit. He turned, smiled and shook her hand noticing the brilliant large diamond once again.

"I feel that we're getting close to producing our blue rose."

"I will look forward to that success."

Inside the four, descending walls he folded the generous check and slid it into his wallet. After the elevator's doors opened to the foyer, he hastened to the exit relieved he was able to bluff her. He hopped into his old, blue van and pulled out of the parking garage onto Ocean Blvd and thought, *The toxic pollen and fragrance scheme was pretty believable, if he had to say so himself. That should buy me more time now that she's got something else to look forward to: Essenciate, huh, more money in our pockets.*

The thought of driving up to Gainesville and dealing with that rental property situation was the last thing he had time for. He'll manipulate Stanley into representing him. He was already there. He'd been so accommodating to his needs in the past. Cornelius tapped the steering wheel. He sensed he was approaching his limit with his brother, but he'd take the chance anyway. It's much more important he get back to the lab, to his work.

Everything had fallen into place, proof that coincidence doesn't exist. Fate had brought him and Grandma Ma back together again, seeing her exquisitely produced roses, knowing they would provide the root stock for his perfect, blue rose. Certainly this was his reward for delivering the statue back to her so long ago.

Derrick's research paper filled in the missing links so perfectly. It was a stroke of genius breaking down the natural compounds in just the right portions to give the soil proper levels of cobalt, aluminum, acidity and iron. *I really owe that kid.* Cornelius thought: the timing, background, connections; everything worked out. Confident that he had figured out how to manipulate nature in such a cunning way, surely there was an honor for that. Didn't matter, he'd be very satisfied with the payout. Growers from around the world would shell out almost any amount of money to have their first opportunity for a totally unique product. He deserved this achievement.

Charles Darwin's theory that all life forms stem from the same origin was an inspiration. We are all connected, not only on this planet, but in this universe. Nothing happens by mistake.

Tchelet was right, "Serendipity."

The following morning, Tchelet's shoulder length auburn hair was pulled back behind her head and fastened with a gold beret. She fumbled with the buttons on her blouse quickly dressing. *Where is my handbag?* She leaned out her bedroom door calling down the hallway, "Charles, I can't find my purse. Help me, PLEASE!"

Her butler hurried into the bedroom holding the leather Gucci clutch she demanded. "Madame, here it is, on the console table outside the door." Without a word, she grabbed it, exited and headed down the elevator. It was 8 a.m., summoned to Good Samaritan Hospital by Varda's doctor; her pulse had grown weaker and weaker. She had stopped taking food.

Minutes later her ink blue Bentley had crossed the Flagler Memorial Bridge into West Palm and pulled up under the portico of the hospital. Before her chauffer could exit the driver's seat, she had the car door opened. She approached the entrance and then turned about abruptly facing him.

"I'll call you later," she instructed him, and then entered through the automatic double, glass doors. A mammoth granite slab hung in the generous foyer. Etched, it bared the names of the principle benefactors of the hospital, listing hers as one of them. She paused before it and thought, *I've given them all of this money and they can't save my sister.*

Tchelet took the elevator to the fifth floor. The upgrades to the hospital's rooms on this floor were specifically approved and paid for solely by her. Another acknowledgement graced the wall opposite the elevator, which bared *only* her name. When residents of the Island, across the bridge, were admitted to the hospital they would be surrounded in the luxurious atmosphere they were accustomed to. She wanted her name to be the one they remembered at their time of need.

Bedside, Tchelet held her sister's delicate hand as memories replayed inside her head like an old fashioned reel to reel projector. Their years together had raced by. She was thankful for the time they had together celebrating their sisterhood. But, sadly, now it seemed that Varda would never know of their blue rose. A precious gift for her precious sister, this was the most honorable thing Tchelet could do for Varda. What better way to pay tribute to someone special than with a flower that is as unique and beautiful as they are?

A tear streamed down Tchelet's cheek. She stood heroically as her sister took her last gasp. Now she was alone and more determined than ever to accomplish what she'd set out to do. *Death is so final,* she thought.

Chapter 31—Ma's In Danger

Emily returned the shop's phone receiver back to the cradle. After her successfully busy Saturday, she was excited to see Derrick. Distance did make *her* heart grow fonder. As she put the last of the left-over, blue dyed, rose stems into the cooler, she entertained visions of her own wedding. What would she carry? She scrunched up her nose in disgust. One thing was for sure—it wouldn't be painted roses. But she did what her bride wanted, despite the girl's appalling taste. She checked the wall clock; yea, time to close. She grabbed her bag, flipped off the shop lights and locked the door.

Emily noticed the posted, tattered flyers of the missing students tapped to the gas pump flapping in the evening breeze as the attendant squirted solution on her, dirty windshield. Rewards were offered for information leading to the arrest of individuals responsible for the kidnapping of Brian Thompson, Julie Rose, Kelley Puria and a newer looking, recently posted flyer that showed the picture and stats of Judy Johnson. At the bottom of the tattered flyer was a post script: each of the missing bore a rose tattoo.

Emily gazed at the faded, colored, photocopied pages, each bearing an uncanny resemblance to the other, wondering what could have become of them. So much time had passed. How four people could go missing without a trace, and no one seemed to know anything.

She handed a few dollars through the window to the cute, male attendant, smiled and said, "Thanks, what a relief to be able to see the road again!" She turned over Janice's rackety engine and edged away from the pump. Fifteen minutes later, she swung into her usual parking spot across from his dorm. Emily threw Janice's gear shift into park and yanked the emergency brake. Once she forgot, and her little, blue bug rolled down the hill.

Fortunately, it came to rest on a grassy mound. She grabbed the bottle of welcome home vino and darted up the dormitory steps.

Anticipating her arrival, Derrick left the door ajar. He was sitting at his desk flipping through the tattered pages of an old book as Emily quietly surprised him from behind.

He jumped as she carefully leaned over and crossed her arms around his neck. She gently whispered into his ear, "Hi handsome, I've missed you. I brought us some wine but forgot the glasses. Have you got something we can use?"

He opened his desk drawer producing a couple of plastic cups from his desk drawer. "Will these will do?"

She glanced over his desk top and noticed the two small pieces of paper shaded with pencil lead.

Picking one up for closer examination she asked, "What's this?"

"I'm trying to find out. During this last visit home, I made a little discovery on the bottom of the *Thorn Boy*. These two lines of faint characters were there all the time. Ma mentioned that she thought it was a maker's mark, but I'm not convinced."

"I showed it to Ben. He suggested I do a rubbing with paper and pencil to capture the images." Derrick pulled a book from a stack sitting on edge of his desk. "Now I'm aimlessly researching for more information starting with this old book I found at a book shop across from campus."

"Wow, that's really interesting. Well, I love a mystery," Emily replied in solidarity pulling a second chair up to the desk. "Let's put our heads together and see what we can come up with. I'm more curious than hungry. With this bottle of Chianti, I think we're all set to do some exploring."

"With that bottle of wine, our explorations could take a turn towards something else."

She grinned back.

The next morning in his dorm room, Derrick's feet dangled from the bottom of the cramped twin bed. With her sweater wrapped tightly around her, Emily grabbed the loose covers and pulled them closer. Derrick reached for his glasses and glanced down at his Sleeping Beauty. He shivered after his feet touched the cold floor. His anticipation about today's class stirred him up earlier than usual. Since *his* paper was the only one in the class Stanley had awarded an A, he'd put Derrick in charge of documenting all of the information from the students' lab work. The trust factor felt great. After splashing cold water on his face, a quick brushing of his teeth and hair, he threw on a sweatshirt and jeans and darted out the door.

Derrick felt he had developed a special connection with Stanley Hicks. There was something about the man he really admired. Maybe it was their mutual respect for nature and science, or the fact that Derrick never had a father figure, and this man showed a unique interest in him. Whatever it was, he was grateful.

This morning the class was divided into teams conducting experiments on how plants responded to different components in various soils that the students collected.

Always the first to arrive in class, Derrick dropped his backpack, took his front row seat and began to retrieve his research paper from his backpack. Moments later, Dr. Hicks entered the classroom. His body language seemed to indicate that he was annoyed, mumbling to himself.

Should he approach him? Derrick felt resistance, but decided to ignore it. He seemed to startle his professor, whose attention was focused on rifling around in the side desk drawer.

"Good morning, Dr. Hicks."

"Oh, good morning, Derrick, I didn't see you there," he spoke in his soft voice.

Derrick could see the dark circles under his eyes, and his hair was not its usual neatly combed style.

Wrinkled jacket and pants, actually, he looked like he'd just crawled out of bed. Feeling the need to ease whatever concerned his professor, Derrick respectfully asked, "Is there something I can help you find?"

"No," he replied abruptly. "It's, it's not that important."

Something told Derrick it was, but intimidation prevailed, and he didn't push the issue. Dr. Hicks paused and closed the desk drawer, catching a few of the disheveled papers in its track. He pulled it out again, attempted to fix the problem, and then abruptly halted. Something seemed to have caught his attention. He shoved the papers down into the shallow drawer and slammed it shut.

"I have something for you," he said to Derrick. "Come with me."

Dr. Hicks produced a set of keys from his pants pocket; he unlocked and opened the door, revealing the high powered microscope Derrick was very familiar with.

"I want your team to use this in the lab today. It's my personal microscope. I earned this many years ago in college." Derrick sensed his pride as Stanley continued, "I placed first in a national science competition."

Stanley reached in and removed the pricey piece of equipment, covered with a plastic sleeve, from its secured spot. Carefully, he placed it on the counter and removed the cover. Derrick noticed the small engraved plate he'd seen before.

First Place Honors

Stanley Hicks

A smile appeared on the professor's face. "I bought this with the prize money I received and had the side engraved. You should have seen the expression on the face of the engraver when I took it to him. Fortunately, he was able to remove the side plate to engrave it. Clever man, I knew he would figure out something. He did. It's a timeless piece of equipment. Despite its age, it still performs as well as any new one could."

"I admire people who can figure things out. That's what I like about you, Derrick. You're very bright, which is why I am lending you my most cherished possession."

Derrick took a big gulp. If Stanley knew that this was the very microscope he and Ben had used for their soil research earlier—without his permission—he might not be so trusting.

The students had begun assembling in the lab. Stanley turned his head back to Derrick and leaned in speaking just above a whisper, "Let's just keep this little conversation here to ourselves, shall we? I don't want the others to think I am showing you any favoritism, although I am." With the end of the remark came a quick wink.

Derrick nodded in agreement, at the same time feeling incredibly honored and a little weird about what just happened. The two lifted the heavy microscope transporting it into the lab area. Derrick winced.

"What's wrong?" asked his professor

"My shoulder's sore, I got a tattoo a few days ago."

Derrick pulled up his shirt sleeve.

"A tattoo, Derrick, why did you do that?" Stanley asked, seemingly to disapprove.

"To show courage; it's known that the missing all had rose tattoos. I want everybody to know that I'm not afraid. I believe that Judy and the others will be found, and until that happens, we have to be brave."

"You are an exceptional, young man, Derrick."

Derrick pulled his sleeve back down and grinned with pride. Stanley turned observing the students as they entered. Then, he looked back at Derrick and said, "Remember, just between you and me."

Stanley hurriedly distributed instructions for the lab as the students congregated before he returned to his desk and retrieved a piece of paper. He shoved it into his pants pocket and left the room.

At the end of classes that day, Derrick eagerly got back to his investigation of the unsolved tiny characters on the base of Ma's statue. Derrick loved history. He spent one particular weekend during high school at the VFW in Belle Glade listening to veterans' stories for hours researching information for a history assignment.

On that day, he discovered details about his granddaddy's tour of duty from the men. His grandfather was on the heels of what remained of the Third Reich during the final stages of the war liberating concentration camps.

According to one of them, Grandpa Stabb and his company were just hours behind the enemy, searching and securing the former homes and offices of the diabolical Fuehrer. Could this be where the little statue originated? Did his grandfather slip it into his army pack as a trophy? Questions he would never know the answers to. It was amazing that the delicate statue made it back to Ma in one piece by way of granddad's army buddy.

Driven by his obsession to discover and learn, Derrick held the piece of paper with the mysterious images up to the light and studied each curved line with an intense curiosity.

"I see you've started without me," Emily said standing at his dorm room doorway.

"Just got here, where should we begin?"

"I think we should start here with this book I brought, The Meanings of Flowers." She held the copy with both hands up to Derrick's face. "I picked it up at the library."

"How would that have anything to do with this?" Derrick responded, pointing to the pencil images in his hand.

"It may not, but it's a place to start. You got any better ideas since you're the history buff."

"No."

Emily continued as she flipped the pages through her fingers. "You know, since like forever, flowers have represented man's feelings. Take for example, all of the names that people give their daughters that are also the names of common flowers, like Daisy and Rose. Not so much now, but I know several older ladies with names of flowers; although, there is a girl in my class with the name Petal."

Derrick leaned back in his chair with his arms folded behind his head and stared directly at his girlfriend as he struggled with where she was taking this train of thought.

"Just humor me, Okay?" she said reading the expression on his face. "Let's get to work."

The minutes turned into hours as they burned through page after page of the books Derrick accumulated. In frustration, Derrick pushed the stack of books off his small desk onto the floor startling Emily.

"Hey, what's up, why did you do that?"

"I think we're heading nowhere with this."

"Oh, come on, you were the one who always preached faith. Time you showed some."

He paused, looked down at her seated amongst the piles of hardbacks and responded, "Glad you're here, Emily. I needed someone to give me a kick in the butt about now."

"Derrick, how about we go back to that old bookstore you mentioned. Those places are filled with cheap books. Maybe we can find something on symbolism. What you have here doesn't seem to be offering much."

They pulled into the angled parking spot designated by two cracked painted lines directly in front of Vintage Books. The old store had been a fixture in Gainesville for decades. Wooden framed, glass panels displayed some of the offerings inside. Derrick held the front door as Emily stepped back in time.

"May I lend some help?" an employee asked, who appeared to have a vintage look going on herself, white hair pulled back in braids tied with yarn and corresponding beads that matched her hand-made woven vest.

"Were looking for books on names and what they mean," responded Emily.

"All the way to the back of the store on the right, you'll see some wooden slatted racks that might have what you're looking for. Honestly, we don't get too many requests for that." She paused for a moment tapping her finger against the side of her face. "But there was a little man here awhile back who also made the same request. I remembered him because he had this annoying hearing aid that sent a high pitched most irritating squeal through the store. We try to keep it as quiet as a library in here so shoppers can concentrate. Anyway, good luck."

Emily turned toward Derrick and said, "Well let's get cracking."

At a small desk in the corner, they accumulated four small books that looked to fit the bill. After an hour or so into flipping through pages and sneezing from dust, Derrick said, "Hey, look at this; it's written in Hebrew and shows symbols of names and their meaning. This is interesting. This symbol shown here kind of looks like the ones I have."

He turned the opened book toward her displaying the page.

Derrick placed the book on the desk, took the edge of the paper with the image on it and methodically went down the pages, exposing each character, their English name and meaning. Line after line his eyes followed the text, occasionally pausing to take in a flower meaning. He stopped, holding the paper under one particular line and exclaimed, "Look at this!"

Examining his finding closely, Derrick observed the identical image of what was on his penciled paper and the book's page.

תְּכֵלֶת Tchelet—

Azure, sky blue, pale blue

He continued down the page using the paper's edge, exposing line after line of more characters and their meanings. He paused again and said, "I might be onto something." He discovered the second identical character on the paper.

וַרְדָּה Varda—

Rose

He looked up at Emily and said, "Uh, I think Thorn Boy is telling us, together, these symbols mean 'blue rose'."

"Whoever carved this statue did it for someone special. Obviously the marks on the bottom would be some sort of way to identify it should it get lost. The marks would make it one of a kind. They have meaning to someone."

"There's a folded piece of paper here marking this page," said Derrick removing the yellow tattered paper. "It looks like someone used it to mark the page."

He unfolded and read it.

"Blue and pure is the rarest rose,

Its namesakes yearning to expose

Sisters pray for their treasure returned

Decades have passed as they yearned."

Derrick looked up at Emily and said, "With all that's happened, I feel that Ma's statue and a blue rose have a connection. I have this suspicion that Ma's in danger. Thorn Boy's giving me a sign. Emily, I have to go back to Ma's."

Chapter 32 – Hebrew Names

Derrick apprehensively stepped from his truck in front of Ma's house. He braced himself for the scolding she'd deliver in disapproval of him leaving school to follow some foolish hunch. The front screen door creaked as he opened it. From the back of the house, Derrick saw the shadow of Grandma Ma as she worked in her kitchen. He pondered the words he would use to convince her that he wasn't wasting his time.

She turned abruptly. "Oh, Derrick, what brings you back home so soon?"

He could tell when she wasn't her usual self. There could be many reasons, visiting Rodney's hospital room, or just "old age" as she would often reply.

"I've got something interesting to share with you about your little statue," he eagerly told her.

"You do, what's that dear? Was it so important that you had to make another trip back home so soon? With the cost of gas, and what about your studies, it couldn't wait?"

"No, Ma, it couldn't. Have you ever noticed those two little marks on the underside of *Thorn Boy*?"

"Yes. I thought they were a maker's mark."

"Well, when I was here on my last visit, something told me to bring the statue closer to me. So, I picked him up and took a close look at the underside of the base. I saw two faint characters, symbols of some sort. Ben suggested doing a pencil rubbing of them, creating an impression on a piece of paper. I brought the paper back to school with me."

"And what did you discover, Derrick?" Ma responded arms folded clearly skeptical.

"Emily and I researched it through some books I found at an old book shop in town. It turns out, they are in Hebrew, and translate into' blue rose'. Whoever was the past owner of this statue had it engraved to represent something significant about blue roses."

"Well, that is very interesting, Derrick. So you think someone Jewish had it a long time ago?"

"I guess so. When you think about it, I mean, granddaddy's involvement in the liberation movement, there could be a connection."

"Well, that does bring something to mind, now that you're telling me this," she said taking a seat at the kitchen table.

"You remember the ladies' group I had here a few weeks ago? We held a flower arranging class in the church's fellowship hall."

"Yes, sort of, I remember you said you met some nice people."

"Two of the ladies at the meeting were invited guests of a member. They had just moved to Palm Beach from Philadelphia. The one was much more talkative than her sister. I brought them back here and showed them the garden. They were very impressed with the grotto you built. They said if they didn't live in a condo, they'd hire you to put in a garden for them. After our stroll through the roses, we came inside for some tea. They noticed *Thorn Boy* on the side board and asked about him. It was getting late, so I gave them the shorter version of the story. You know how I love to tell granddaddy's story, dear."

"It was sort of odd though, that they kept staring at it. Usually people don't make such a fuss over him, but they had lots of questions, questions about his history. I didn't really know the answers, so I think they were disappointed. I think I let them down, but they were polite about it. We're supposed to see each other again. I told them the next time I came to the coast we'd have lunch together. They seemed to like that idea. And their names, they, they were so unusual. Names I'd never heard of."

"What were their names, Ma?"

She replied, "Oh, I can't remember, isn't that silly of me. Well, probably because they were so out of the ordinary. But I need to, so if they call, or I call them for our lunch date, I won't look foolish. They're on the roster for the church luncheon. Our treasurer is very good at collecting money and contact information. Let me see, I think I put it here in this stack of papers on the dining room table. Hold on a minute while I look for it."

"No, Ma, that's—" Too late, Ma left returning a few minutes later.

"Oh yes, here it is. I'm so glad she kept such good records, and her handwriting is still perfect. Isn't that amazing for her age?"

Derrick knew he'd get more than he bargained for when he asked the question.

"Let's see here," she said as Derrick observed her fingers going down the page, abbreviating the list of names: "J. Mangin, F. Janmiczky." she continued with a dozen more as Derrick propped his head up with one hand drumming his fingers on the tabletop with the other.

"Oh yes, here they are. Their names were hyphenated. We've never had anyone with hyphenated names before."

"V. Goldstein-Blackman"

"T. Goldstein-Smith"

"Their first names are unique: Varda and Tchelet."

"Would you repeat those again, Grandma?" requested Derrick, as he scrambled for the paper in his pocket Emily jotted the names on.

Paper in-hand, Derrick listened as his grandmother repeated and spelled clearly:

"Varda, V-A-R-D-A and

Tchelet, T-C-H-E-L-E-T"

"Ma, this isn't a coincidence. The marks on the bottom of your statue represent the Hebrew names for blue rose. The marks must have some relevance to the original owner. The owner, that is, before the Nazi invasion."

"Did your lady friends see the symbols on the bottom?"

"No dear, they didn't get that close to it. After all of these years, we learned something new about *Thorn Boy*. But, now what do you think my new friends are going to come back for it?"

"Ma, that's okay, we don't have to solve anything right now—or for that matter—at all. You know granddaddy had it sent back to you as a token of his love; that's all that mattered. *Thorn Boy* had been yours all these years, and it will stay with you for the rest of them. I guarantee that."

As he spoke the words, his stomach knotted. Ma and her treasured *Thorn Boy* were now in jeopardy.

Chapter 33 —Clues To The Puzzle

The early morning light flickered through the sheer fabric of the blousy, window trim and bounced off of the soft blue wallpaper in Bernice Johnson's bedroom. She stood on her toes and reached stretching for the small but sturdy fire safe box kept on the top shelf of her closet. Finally, she managed it to her bedside and began to systematically shuffle through the rubber banded stacks of letters and newspaper clippings she had secretly locked away since her mother's passing at eighty-five years old. Like her mother, she was a keeper, a caretaker of guarded documents to be passed on from generation to generation. She thought about destroying them—burning away the past, but fought the urge even if some would consider her history a curse. She took a deep breath as she glanced through the black and white photos, for her, reminiscing was painful.

She paused at one picture briefly. Posed, sitting on her mother's lap, both of them were neatly dressed in blue satin embellished with white ruffles. Their shimmering blonde locks—perfectly curled, arranged upon their shoulders—glistened.

She had protected the family secret for forty years ever fearful of what the media would broadcast. She envisioned *The National Enquirer's* trumpeting, 72 pt., bold, front page feature below the currently scorned celebrity of the week. The devastation on Ben's trusted, family, funeral business would most certainly affect his relationship with Judy in the worst possible way. Her eyes welled up; what she feared was so ugly.

After World War II, it was easy to get a new identity with so many, displaced souls. The Dutch government was liberal and pretty much took your word—or certainly the word of an influential person—with whom they said you were.

Gratitude wasn't enough to express the feelings her mother had for the photographer, a seemingly kind, young, Jewish woman who took them in—a safe place to stay as long as they needed it. There were so few angels in the world; fortunately, they'd found theirs. With the Jewish girl's important connections, their true identities were concealed and new ones created. A debt so great that it could unquestionably never been repaid, or so Bernice thought. She tucked her memorabilia safely back into its hiding place and descended the stairs into her kitchen.

Where is that contraption? she thought as she turned boxes over on the lower shelf of the hall closet. *Finally, here it is.* On her next appointment, she'd go back to Van Cormack's alone armed with a tape recorder.

Bernice stepped up onto Van Cormack's front porch and tapped on the rickety, wooden, door frame. Recalling the hearing aid, she knocked again, much harder.

"We need to get started; I have another appointment," he said insistently after opening the door.

She clutched the recorder and followed him past the painting in the hallway and paused briefly to examine it more closely. The bold, unusual, brush strokes were a technique she recognized and had appreciated many times before. She loved Van Gogh's work and pitied the tormented artist for his, psychological illness.

The tiny plaque underneath read, *The Ravine*, and there was an inscription. *The best way to know God is to love many things—Vincent Van Gogh.* Van Cormack turned around and approached her.

"Oh, reproductions are so amazing today," she said complimenting the artwork. "You have such an interesting home, Mr. Van Cormack."

"You like this painting?"

"Yes," she responded.

"Observe the tiny blue roses nestled in the crevasses of the ravines."

She tightly covered her mouth stifling a giggle and then responded. "Blue roses, hum... maybe it was notions like that which landed him *in* the mental hospital."

Van Cormack frowned, clearly not amused. They continued down the long, narrow hallway. He turned back to her and remarked, "Oh, incidentally, it's not a reproduction."

Back at home, she replayed his recorded voice over and over again while writing, scratching over it and rewriting. She shouted aloud to herself in frustration slamming her hands against the tabletop. "Why doesn't he just speak in plain English?"

She heard a car pull into the driveway and glanced out of window. It was Ben looking every bit the funeral director his father was grooming him to be in his blue suit, but he wasn't alone.

"Come in," she said wondering who the tall, good looking blonde fellow was behind him.

They stepped over the threshold into the kitchen. "Mrs. Johnson, this is my best friend, Derrick Stabb. He's the one I told you about, the guy who was able to shed some light on those riddles of yours."

Derrick extended his hand and smiled broadly. "A pleasure."

Ben continued, "Derrick was visiting his grandmother in Belle Glade. I was surprised by his call telling me he was down from school, *again*." The two youths exchanged grins. "Derrick, you seem to be *here* more than in school."

"It's not *that* far away. Besides, I like to drive, and I miss my Grandma."

"Have a seat you two," she instructed directing their attention to the small round table in the center of the kitchen.

Once they were all seated, she went on in a tremulous voice, "Derrick, I'm a desperate mother.

The police aren't working hard enough, as far as I am concerned, to find Judy. If you think you can help find her by translating these rhymes, I would be forever grateful."

She pressed the ON button and scooted it closer to them. The tape had begun to turn inside as Van Cormack's feeble voice recited each stanza. The three of them leaned in closer straining to hear.

"Evil exists where good deeds once thrived,

Sacrifices are made at a time justified,

Intentions appear honorable but not so,

What is to result he will not know,"

"Life from their veins completes the test,

There are no limits set to achieve the best,

No matter who has died or survived,

Success it seems has just arrived,"

"There's a young man in your midst,

With his talent he will persist,

His knowledge of plants and flowers, elements and soil,

Will guide those forward in hopes an evil mission will foil,"

"A beauty is captured held against her will,

She's imprisoned in a tiny cell,

Not the obvious place as one might think,

The walls are light blue and soft pink,"

"The compassion she has will be her salvation,

Touching cold hearts filled with determination,

Acceptance and love so pure and good,

Will triumph in the end as it should,"

"A stamp upon her arm seals a fate,

It has captured his attention one more trait,

Etched and dyed into her skin not just any rose tattoo,

The one she bares is pure blue,"

The tiny wheels on the recorder stopped. Bernice reached over and brought it closer to her. She gently pressed the rewind button and said, "I know. He's a strange one. What do you think, Derrick?"

Derrick rubbed his jaw with his open hand, "I'm convinced he's referring to Judy. Her love, compassion, rose tattoo, and her Aryan characteristics."

"Aryan characteristics, what do you mean?" she echoed in alarm. "Are you calling my daughter a Nazi?"

"No, not at all!" the youth exclaimed waving his hands, his expression dismayed. "I just think that she fit the profile, just like all of the other missing kids. It's a subtle connection, but all of the victims have traits associated with Hitler's Master Race. The tangible link is the blue rose tattoos each one had, too. I believe Judy's alive, and she's imprisoned somewhere, maybe on a street named after a president. Ben showed me this after one of your earlier readings." Derrick removed a folded paper from his pocket and handed it to her. Bernice scanned the familiar words, her lips pursed. Then she looked up. "We've got to take this to the police."

"**Do** you think we can convince the police?" Bernice said to the boys just before Ben gave a light tap on the thin glass of Bruce Sistrunk's office door. Sistrunk motioned for the three to come in. "Have a seat." He pointed to a couple of chairs that faced him over a little, metal desk in his cramped, office quarters. Derrick stood behind Mrs. Johnson's chair as she placed her tape recorder on the desktop.

"Listen to this," she commanded and pressed the start button. Appearing to yield to his curiosity, Sistrunk leaned forward resting his arms on the desk top. After a few minutes of straining to hear the scratchy, barely audible tape, he leaned back in his swivel chair and put his arms behind his head.

Ben slid across the desktop several pieces of folded paper with some text written on it.

"What's this?" the deputy asked with a smirk.

"Please, just hear me out," she said.

"You may think I am a little strange telling you this, but I've been seeing this clairvoyant. I had to do something. Since Judy's disappearance, I haven't been able to function."

"Yeah, I was there for one of his readings," Ben piped up nodding his head up and down confirming her story.

Sistrunk stared at them, looked down at the recorder, then at the papers he was holding, and then back at them again. "Mrs. Johnson, really, do you *really* believe that this man's, what do you call them, 'readings', have any bearing on this case?"

"I don't know what to believe, *sir*. So, do *you* think this a bunch of malarkey? Well, I'm not interested in the police trying to appease me. I've had enough of that.

I suppose that you're going to chalk this up as a desperate mother seeking advice from some weirdo?"

"Mrs. Johnson, I know you're stressed, but when I tell you that we are working every angle of this case, we are."

She stood, placed both hands on his desktop and looked him straight in the eye saying, "You're not working *this* angle. Sure, it's a stretch, but it's a clue your office needs to look into."

"Well, let me photocopy these," he said picking up her notes, tapping the edges on his desktop before leaving the room.

Sistrunk returned to the cramped, office space. He shuffled in sideways past them, little by little maneuvering his corpulent belly around their chairs and file cabinet, back to his utilitarian desk. The wobbly chair gave a loud squeak as he plopped back in it and scooted up closer.

"I need to make a call and do some follow up. I'll get back with you. I don't know what to say right now, but we will talk later. Is that okay?"

"Do what you have to do, but *do* something," she said in a slightly more convinced tone while taking her seat.

Ben added gesturing towards Derrick, "One more thing, Deputy, my friend here said that he thinks this stanza has a clue in it as to where Judy could be, see...presidents streets, Hollywood?"

Sistrunk stood, nodded and reached over the desk to shake their hands. He concluded, "Thanks for taking the time to drive up. I know this is a tough time. Everybody always expects us to say this, but we *are* going to do everything we can to find out what happened to your daughter, Mrs. Johnson."

He watched as they departed down the hallway. He closed the door and, again, glanced down at the photocopies. They could prove to be the most challenging clues he'd ever seen if, indeed, they were clues.

He hesitated, thought for a moment, then, intrigued, he picked up his office phone and dialed Robert Waites.

"Detective Waites, this is Sistrunk. I just met with the Johnson girl's mother, boyfriend and Derrick Stabb," he said after the two exchanged greetings.

"I'm sittin' here lookin' at some more of these damn riddles. The mom and those kids are convinced that they hold some sort of clues."

He heard Waites snort. "They're nonsense!"

Sistrunk privately agreed with that determination; still, he persisted, "We don't have much in the way of clues at this point, so I figured what the hell. I'm thinking of making a trip down to Broward County again to see if I can make some sense out of this. The three of them are convinced she's held somewhere down there. The mother thinks Derrick Stabb has an ability to read into what these riddles mean. Damn if I can figure them out, or how he deciphers this stuff."

"He comes up with this because he has it all staged," replied Waites.

That had occurred to Sistrunk, as well, but he'd learned over the years never to jump to conclusions until he had all the facts at hand.

"Well, I'm headed down there again. After my experience in Belle Glade, well, I need to find out if there is anything to this."

"It's up to you. It's your time and gas," Waites scoffed into the receiver.

Sistrunk heard a final snort from the detective as he replaced the handset. Sighing, Sistrunk sagged back into his chair and gazed out his tiny office window at the trees and flowering plants. Talent escaped him when it came to growing anything. Sistrunk admired those who not only didn't kill the poor things, but they flourished under the TLC that people like Hazel Craig provided.

A breeze carried the train's sound against the tracks, a few blocks away, through his opened window. The obnoxious noise jolted his memory from a few days ago of the odd little lady who was abruptly interrupted by the screeching sounds of the Florida East Coast Railroad.

As they stood on her front porch facing Johnson Street, Hazel paused to allow the insufferable clamor of the same train to pass by just a block or so from her house. Sistrunk, once again, glanced down at the stanzas.

The words leaped from the page and smacked him square between the eyes.

"The rhythmic sounds of the rails at night,

Guide the rescuers in their plight,

To rows of presidents charted about,

Sworn into his post after three shots rang out,"

"His legacy was tarnished by an unpopular war,

Gripping the nation for many years from a far,

Riots and protests banish the purpose,

The people have spoken the cause seemed worthless,"

He carefully scratched at his hair plugs remembering Hazel's position as Director of the Central County Blood Bank. Then, he realized, the woman must have known Judy Johnson, since the girl worked there part time as well. Sistrunk's eyes glanced back down at the poetic verses on his desk.

"A beauty is captured held against her will,"

"She's imprisoned in a tiny cell,"

"Not the obvious place as one might think,"

"The walls are light blue and soft pink,"

Could Derrick Stabb be right? Could the words here be a connection, guiding him to the location where Judy Johnson was? he thought. With nothing else to go on, Sistrunk did something he' done before—follow his intuition.

He gathered the papers, grabbed his side arm and headed for the courthouse calling in an old favor from a judge. He needed a search warrant.

He stood drumming his fingers against the wall next to the annoyingly slow, elevator doors. With no time to waste, Bruce Sistrunk decided to opt for the stairs.

In the stairwell between the fourth and fifth floors, he nearly collided with Delores Dawson, the luscious, forensic technician Sistrunk surreptitiously lusted over.

"Hey, where's the fire?" she jokingly said to the hurried deputy.

Catching him off-guard, he apologized for practically knocking her down the stairs. "Sorry. I'm on my way south following a lead on the case you and I worked on. Remember those rose stems you analyzed for me?"

"Oh yeah, I have the afternoon off, may I join you?"

Surprised, hesitant, but delighted by her request, he responded enthusiastically, "Sure! I might need the advice of a scientist."

She wrinkled her forehead obviously perplexed. "Great. Let me get my bag; it's just inside the door."

Combing his fine, dark hair plugs with his fingertips, he waited patiently.

"Okay, let's go," and the two headed down the stairwell. As his belly jiggled over his belt, he resolved to get back to the gym or at least resort to the stairs more often.

Feeling energized by his theory and the surprise accompaniment of Ms. Dawson, they sprinted to the parking lot. Within a few minutes, the pair headed up Dixie to the Palm Beach County Courthouse. "It would be impossible to get a warrant with the evidence I have, but I have an in with a judge. A couple of years ago, I stopped a car speeding down Poinciana through Old Northwood. Needless to say, when I approached the car, it was, well, let's say a pretty prominent lawyer. I could smell booze on his breath. After I checked his license, I saw that he was just a couple of blocks from home. So I gave him a police escort. He told me that if I ever needed anything to just ask. He was elected circuit court judge last year."

Sistrunk pulled up to the car stop in the courthouse parking lot and opened his door. "Give me a minute."

Later, they were headed east on Southern Blvd., then turned south onto I-95 just slightly exceeding the speed limit. It might be just a bit too much to put on the blue lights and siren; he didn't want Delores thinking that he was trying to impress her. That would come later if his crazy-ass hunch proved to be true. If it turned out to be a wild goose chase, he would only have her to explain to.

Once exiting the interstate at Hollywood Blvd., he followed the familiar streets, over the railroad tracks, to Hazel Craig's charming, stucco and cinderblock house on Johnson Street.

Pulling into the driveway, Sistrunk looked around for another car. The property appeared to be vacant. He slung open the car door and headed up the sidewalk. Delores followed the eager detective onto the front porch.

Sistrunk knocked hard on the front door calling out, "Sheriff"; no answer. He banged harder a second time. "Sheriff"; he thought he'd heard a faint voice. "Stand back," he ordered Delores. He threw his body against the wood frame door. Surprised that the little Florida house was much sturdier than it looked, he made a more powerful second attempt. This time the front door flew open, rocketing splinters of wood and part of the door jam into the living room. He turned to her, "Let me make sure the coast is clear." As he remembered, pastels of pink and blue wall coverings were everywhere.

He called out again, "Sheriff, is anyone here?"

What appeared to be a little house from the street was actually much larger. The pair quickly made their way down a long hallway to three shut doors at the end. The first two bedrooms were neatly arranged with pretty needlepoint and crocheted work displayed on the walls. Windows allowed natural light to flood the room.

He tried the third door, locked. Not sure if his shoulder could take one more door bashing, he threw himself against it with as much power as he could muster up. The thin, wood door splintered in half, allowing light into the pitch dark room. Delores reached for the light switch and flipped it on.

To their surprise a motionless body wrapped in a blanket was lying on the bed. The woman had long, blonde hair trailing out from under the covers. Her face was turned towards the wall. Delores immediately reached for her wrist to check her pulse. "She's alive." A blood stain was on the pillow near a bandaged area on her head.

Sistrunk, rubbing his aching shoulder, picked up his radio and called for backup.

"Who is this?" she asked.

"If my guess is right, it's one of our missing persons, Judy Johnson."

"No identification, how do you know?" asked Delores.

"She fits the description, and this." He turned Judy's arm displaying her rose tattoo. "I have to contact a very anxious mother."

Carefully selecting his words, Sistrunk called Bernice Johnson. "We found her."

In the hospital, Bernice Johnson sat up in her chair and stretched. She had spent the night next to Judy's bedside. She left the room to take the elevator downstairs to the coffee shop. As she walked through the lobby, past the front desk, she noticed Sistrunk's cruiser driving up under the hospital portico.

Thinking, he could have waited until this afternoon to question her daughter, Bernice remained in the lobby. He appeared through the door and approached her.

"Is she responding?" he asked in the most compassionate tone he could muster up, careful not to ruffle her feelings like he did during their last encounter.

"Yes, I had a few words with her this morning," answered the doting mother. "Deputy Sistrunk, she's still foggy about what has happened to her. I don't think this is a good idea to press her for answers right now."

"I understand, Mrs. Johnson, but we have some missing people out there, and Judy may be able to help us find them. We have a warrant out for the Craig woman, but we need more."

Bernice Johnson certainly knew how it felt to have a child missing, not knowing whether they were dead or alive. She relented, and the pair entered the elevator together.

She quietly pushed open the door to Judy's room as Sistrunk followed her in. Judy seemed to be responding to the activity around her. She smiled at them.

"Judy, this is Deputy Bruce Sistrunk. He is the man who saved your life."

Sistrunk stepped up to her bedside.

"Judy. Hi, can you remember anything about what happened to you?"

She blinked her long eye lashes at him. The officer stood over her and smiled patiently. Time was of the essence.

He said, "There are three, other, young people missing, and I feel that their cases are related to yours. Anything you can tell me, any minute detail could maybe help us find them."

A few moments passed before she responded, "After coming out of a haze, I remembered being bound and crammed behind the seat of a van. There were two people in the front—a man and woman, I think."

"I was able to inch my back up against the side of the van and catch a few glimpses out the side window. It was covered with a piece of cardboard, but it was ripped. The seat backs were high; they couldn't see me. The man driving commented on some of the buildings on route. When I was a little girl, my father took me fishing out there on Lake Okeechobee. It was our time alone. Mom would never come along. She couldn't stand touching the worms."

"We would head to the shallows of the big lake off Torry Island Road. I knew the quick turns on the bumpy road well after so many trips there.

The van then seemed to head west on Lake Road and crossed over the dike. We passed a small marina and Slim's. Dad and I would stop there and rent a boat. Anyway, we turned off the road onto a small lane and headed toward a huge old barn. It must have been a dirt path because the van rocked and rolled over lots of pot holes. The man pulled up to a side door, and the woman got out. I could peer through the torn cardboard flap; she sort of walked with a limp. After that, a man opened the side door of the van and covered my face again with a cloth soaked in chloroform."

"Well, you've been a big help, young lady. Now all I need to do is find this barn you're referring to. There are probably lots of them out there."

Sistrunk paused for a moment and took a deep sigh. "Suppose I should revisit those riddles and see if Derrick can offer more clues into this puzzle."

Chapter 34 –What's The Next Step?

From her upstairs bedroom, Grandma Ma heard an unrelenting knock on the front door and reached for her housecoat. *Who could that be at this hour*, she thought, quickly buttoning up her house coat.

After descending the stairs, Ma yanked the door open to a sweet, smiling, little lady and robustly said, "Yes?"

"I'm a process server for Palm Beach County. I have some legal documents for you."

Ma sighed; she'd grown weary of the harassing phone calls from the bank.

"Please sign here," she said handing over a pen. "Now, you have twenty days to respond to the court, but you do *need* to respond," she advised then offered, "Do you have legal representation?"

Ma shook her head back and forth indicating no.

"For what it's worth, Mrs. Stabb, you may want to fight this. Think about getting yourself a lawyer."

The server retrieved her pen. "Stay and fight, Mrs. Stabb, the banks are cheap, and it costs them money to evict people. I wouldn't leave until I saw the whites of the sheriff's eyes."

Ma managed a gratuitous smile before the woman turned and headed down the steps. She closed the door and returned to the kitchen holding the inch thick stack of fastened papers. This was it, now she had no choice.

Must she tell Derrick of her dilemma?

She stood at the kitchen sink and looked out into her beautiful, rose garden contemplating her choices. Ma was disappointed in herself and her choices; she felt she'd let her grandsons down. She reached up and opened the door to the cabinet right of the window. Inside were bottles of prescription sleeping pills the doctor recommended.

A fist full of the little, blue tablets would cowardly resolve all of her problems. She popped open the cap and dumped a pile of pills into her creased palm. Her tiny fingers enveloped them. She filled a large glass of water and set it at the edge of the sink.

She glanced backwards through the door leading into the hallway and wondered if she could make it back up the steps before the pills took ahold of her. She'd rather be found in bed appearing that she had peacefully drifted away in her sleep.

She recalled the virgin who appeared in the garden and her message: "Ma had earned her reward." She took solace in the thought of seeing her fallen soldier again. His warm smile would welcome her. They would be together again throughout eternity.

Ma, head held low, gradually raised her fist full of pills toward her mouth. She thought of the relief the end would bring. She reached for the glass of water and stood, strong hands outstretched, with her fate symmetrically balanced between both arms. She faced east just beyond the sparkling clean window pane at the blue sky and white puffy clouds.

In their forms she recognized Derrick's profile; his strong jaw and wavy hair. Could she abandon him this way? She bowed her head staring into the sink. What she was about to do would fly in the face of everything she believed and taught her boys? She had to practice what she preached, set an example for her boys and learn to live with whatever happened.

Ma took the pills and forcefully flung them into the sink, and then she flushed them down the drain with the glass of water. She flipped the switch on the disposal. The grinding sound jolted her, determined that this would *not* be her fate; she *would* stay and fight. Now it was time to face reality and be the example her husband would be proud of.

Papers in-hand trembling, Ma headed for the stairs but not before she stopped to pay homage to *Thorn Boy* scrutinizing the minute lines of dried blood her husband shed embedded into its surface. Her statue was with her for a reason. There had to be more to the story of his long voyage back from Germany. She prayed. *Thorn Boy, please rescue me.*

Returning from Varda's service in Philadelphia three days later, Tchelet raised the back of the leather seat to an upright position in her private Gulfstream jet as it circled precariously over the Atlantic Ocean and made an eastern approach into Palm Beach International Airport. She replaced her fashion magazine into her Hermes tote and observed through the jet's window the surf's frothy white caps below as the plane slowly descended with the runway clearly in view.

She grinned. PBIA had been a bone of contention with her, and a few other Palm Beach residents. The enormous thrust from larger passenger jets, as they made their way into the sky, interfered with her phone conversations, television programs as well as annoyed one trying to take in a tennis or golf game. They proposed building another airport farther west, a cause she hadn't given up on. First things first.

She glanced down just as her jet was directly above the Beach and Racket Club's manicured property. The thought of its exclusive, gentile membership still gnawed at the pit in her stomach.

Turbulence kicked at the jet. Tchelet, a seasoned flier, had never gotten a grasp on her fear of falling. She held the armrests with a firm, white-knuckled grip and imagined that she was in control.

What's the next step? *Thorn Boy or the blue rose.* She thought. Tchelet thumbed through her check book mentally totaling the amounts written to Cornelius in exchange for her name on the patent. Now that Varda was gone, simply having the flower named after them wasn't enough. As a contractual sole owner of this new cultivar, she would be able to call the shots. *Oh, the power,* she thought.

Relieved to finally feel the landing gear as it touched the runway, Tchelet could already feel the blood returning to her hands as she released her clench.

The band from her prodigious, Canary yellow diamond left a deep impression in her ring finger.

She shook her hands stimulating the circulation. Eagerly, she reached for the jet's phone to notify her chauffeur. The second call went to Mrs. Clarence Stabb. She could hardly wait to see those magnificent roses again.

"**Mrs.** Stabb? Is this Mrs. Stabb? This is Tchelet Goldstein-Smith. I would love to come back to see your garden again."

Ma's voice chimed through the jet's receiver. "Why, let's plan to spend Thanksgiving together. I make a great turkey dinner. My grandson will be here. I'd love for you to meet him."

Tchelet paused tapping her manicured nail against the armrest. "Your grandson, would he be interested in a group of ladies talking about roses? I would have thought that boys his age would only be interested in their music and sports."

"Oh no, Derrick is one of those boys who really enjoys meeting people, especially those who are enamored by his work."

Tchelet hesitated a few more minutes. "Well, okay then, if you're sure it's not an imposition."

"No, no not at all, this is a time for giving thanks. We all have something to be thankful for."

"Great, then we have a date."

Tchelet could feel the satisfaction of getting closer and closer to recovering *Thorn Boy*. She returned the receiver as her jet taxied to the private hanger. *Thanksgiving, isn't that something*, Tchelet thought. *I wonder how thankful she'll be when I pull out my law team's big guns.*

Chapter 35—The Price Paid For Science

Sonny Locke was a religious man often praying aloud as he walked the narrow paths along the canals' banks that fed into Lake Okeechobee. He connected to God in the midst of nature through the grasses and birds of the Everglades.

Big Lake O, as the locals referred to it, was known for bass fishing tournaments that drew people from around the world. Sonny occasionally attended, but he couldn't afford the registration fee for the tournament; maybe one day. For now, he liked to catch some bass for dinner. Sometimes, when he was standing on the water's edge casting his line, he would fantasize the huge crowds of people watching from the shoreline or boats.

He paused on the lake's bank and imagined the roar of the horde as he reeled in the "First Place" catch. Later, standing proud and tall for pictures that appeared in sport fishing magazines around the country. He dreamt big for a small town guy.

Today he'd try some new "phony bait", as he called it, recommended by Slim down at the fish camp tackle shop. Normally, he used his cane poles, cork bobbers, hooks and night crawlers. The store owner convinced him to try some new magnetic fishing flies he just got in. Sonny jumped right on that because he constantly misplaced his favorite fishing lure. These easily affixed to the metal plate in his head just below the skin's surface, granted an unusual solution, but effective. Within easy reach, he knew exactly where his bait was at all times.

Dawn on this day in the Glades was serene. A gentle breeze glided over the lake's surface, which had a span so immense Sonny couldn't see the other side. The sun's rays pierced the strips of clouds hugging the horizon as he watched the flocks of heron fly overhead just before the birds located a stop to rest and feed. Sonny, smiling with satisfaction, began casting his line out into water sending concentric rings from the point of entry outward toward the shore. The first two casts were warm ups as the line whizzed overhead cutting through the air. On the third cast, Sonny hooked something big. He yanked his pole backwards, the fiberglass rod bending practically in a U shape. Beads of sweat trickled down his brow into his eyes. The line was quivering as Sonny again pulled back pacing from side to side on the shore line. "God Almighty," he proclaimed as he felt as though he was being pulled in. *I guess that bait shop owner knew what he was talking about.* He had never hooked this big a catch with live worms.

He wasn't giving up; one of his many qualities, Sonny wasn't a quitter. As he fought with his unseen catch his curiosity grew. What could this be? After a few taxing minutes, he considered cutting the line and let this monster swim away, but the thought of the newspaper's heralding headlines the next day, LOCAL MAN SNAGS LAKE'S BIGGEST CATCH, spurred him on.

Now, through the murky water, he could see what appeared to be some kind of immense dark creature: a largemouth bass, long nose gar, a bull head catfish? Whatever it was, it was putting up one hell of a fight. Sonny pulled and pulled with all of his strength, relieved when he felt his opponent was slowly tiring. It looked like he was going to win this fight. The anticipation mounted inside him as the giant catch slowly relented. Gradually it emerged from the muddy depths.

In his exertions to pull his catch to the edge of the lake a few feet away, Sonny slipped and fell backwards. "Sweet Jesus!" He shouted. He stood, sighed with relief and wiped his brow with his long shirtsleeve. "Thank God!" he shouted, fearing that he'd lose his trophy, although the fall did knock the wind out of him. He gradually regained his ground, continued to recoil his line and with great anticipation walked to the bank.

Steadying himself in a wide legged stance, Sonny, dismayed, leaned in closer to catch a glimpse of what were seemingly the remnants of a blue jacket bearing a logo, WHS, *Wellington High School*. Sonny reached in, grabbed the sleeve and shook his head in disgust. All that effort just to retrieve some kid's, lost letter jacket. Might as well clean it up out of the water so no water birds got tangled up in it, he thought as he pulled the sodden garment closer. It was only then that he realized the sweater wasn't empty. Its seams abruptly snagged open to reveal a bloated white torso. Eyes widened, he yelled, "Lord Almighty!"

He released it and fell backwards onto the ground. Appearing to have been in the water for days, fish and turtles fed on it. Sonny rubbed his eyes. He stumbled back up the deep embankment to the road and his truck. He cranked the engine, stomped the gas and then headed back up the shell rock road to the main highway. His destination was an intersection a few miles away and the lone pay phone he'd passed many times on the roadside.

Sonny slid to a stop next to the phone, reached over and popped open his glove box. After their search, a few days ago, which yielded some hair follicles wrapped in foil in Ma's rose garden, Sonny kept Bruce Sistrunk's business card tucked inside. He frantically dug around in the compartment, found the card and bounded from his truck. Sonny's sweaty hand got stuck in his pocket as he approached the phone; he eagerly tugged and finally pulled out some change. After the dimes dropped in, he punched in the numbers hoping to find Sistrunk at his desk.

"B-b-b-boss!" he stuttered, "I just found something awful."

An hour had passed, Bruce Sistrunk and Sonny Locke stood with their arms folded on the lake's muddy bank and watched the divers bobbing up and down combing the bottom. The wrecker's hoist pulled the convertible from its watery grave. While the taut chain held the car on the bank's forty-five degree angle, lake vegetation and a few small fish gushed, flopping onto the marshy, muck soil splattering Sistrunk's new slacks.

He snorted, jumped back a foot or so, turned to Sonny and said, "I received an APB a couple of days ago describing this car. Two girls, cheerleaders, were reported missing by their parents. I'm dreading telling them what you found, lousy news to be getting over the holidays."

He took a deep breath, paused and continued, "It was probably dumped here. Maybe the other girl is alive, but I've got a gut feeling she isn't."

Sistrunk approached the car; he reached inside and found a gym bag whose strap was tangled around the emergency brake. He struggled for a few seconds with the zipper but finally opened it. Inside was the laminated identification of both girls. He signed, handed the bag to Sonny and continued his search leaning over the front seat. Stuck between the back seat cushions, he found something else mysterious in a sealed plastic bag. He opened it and carefully removed damp signed documents indicating a parcel had been retrieved from Miami International Airport. Smeared but legible, the signature read *Casey L. Craig*.

Sistrunk walked back to his cruiser and retrieved his little steno pad. He flipped through the notes he had taken during his earlier interviews. He looked at Sonny and said, "I've got to find Hazel Craig."

"Who's she?" Sonny questioned wrinkling his forehead.

"This signature belongs to her nephew."

That same morning Hazel returned to her office at the Central County Blood Depository greeted by a staffer inside the front door who said, "Mrs. Craig, the police were here looking for you."

"Me, my dear, what in the world would the police want with me?"

"They didn't say, just that they'd be back."

Hazel proceeded to her office and quickly shut the door behind her. The palms of her hands had begun to sweat. She sensed it; something had gone wrong. Did Cornelius betray her? Casey, what happened to Casey? She should have heard from him by now. True, the kid was a pain in the ass, but he was still her family, her only, blood relative. She cared about him, and she *was* the one who got him into this. She stood by her desk and thought for a moment.

It was time to pay the illustrious Dr. Cornelius Hicks an unannounced visit.

Hazel peeled out of the blood bank's parking lot gripping the steering wheel. She pushed the gas petal nearly to the floor and aimed toward Route 27's winding road destined for the Glades in western Palm Beach County.

She replayed her past conversation with Cornelius. She didn't like the way he had spoken to her. He'd been so illusive, so rude. She was sick of it. She deserved some answers and some respect. She had begun to feel used. She had been doing all of the grunge work. His demands on her had been endless:

She was the one who went through the blood bank files and researched the young Aryans he needed with O-negative blood. She was the one who had set up situations for him to nab one more victim. She was the one who stuffed their lifeless bodies in bags and lugged them in and out of his van. She was the one who froze her ass off while he barked orders to her as she retrieved the packets of frozen body parts. She was the one who jeopardized losing her hands as she fed them into the wood chipper. She was the one who scooped and shoveled the bloody, disgusting mixture of human tissue and muck. She was the one who harbored Judy Johnson in her home until he decided what to do with her.

Forty minutes later she was in the heart of the Everglades. After she passed several large cane trucks that rumbled past her, Hazel turned onto Torry Island Road heading for his, secret lab.

Aware that her noisy muffler would give away her surprise visit, Hazel made a decision to park far enough away from the building and walk the last fifty yards. She struggled with her limp up the narrow pathway, but finally entered through the small side door where she noticed his parked van. This was perfect; she could quietly slip in and surprise him.

Hazel slowly made her way across the generous expanse of barn, past the line-up of vintage Bentleys, their chrome grills glistened as she passed, toward a light. Her leg was beginning to ache, but she trudged forward edging up to the window of the white, metal building and then peered through.

She could see inside were rows of gleaming white containers of plant seedlings.

"These must be it," she said aloud to herself. She followed the outside parameter of the laboratory and found a door. After entering, she scoped out the lab. His progress was impressive, but so far, not a blue rose in sight. No one around, Hazel wandered through the rows of steely, shiny racks thinking he must be here somewhere.

She paused; mounted on the wall next to another door was a two by four wood plank. In it large hooks were securely screwed to hold five, huge cane knives. It was common knowledge they were used to harvest the thick stalks of sugar cane; with one fell swoop, a worker could sever a number of the substantial trunks at once. One of the hooks was missing its blade.

Her leather sole shoes slipped in something spilled on the floor's, smooth surface. Hazel rounded the corner finding Casey's lifeless body and the source of the spill. "Blood, oh my God!" She ran to him, stooped over the body and saw a huge gash in his head. She quickly removed her scarf and attempted to stop the bleeding. He was dead.

"I told you not to come here," he shouted from behind her in a thunderous voice. Hazel Craig fumbled to her feet, nearly falling again. Behind her was Cornelius Hicks. The vessels in his neck bulged. He was holding the fifth cane knife; its massive, blood-stained blade gleamed in the laboratory light as he tilted it back and forth.

"You monster, what have you done to my nephew?"

"He finally got what he deserved," he said, seething. "You're both fools. You can't follow simple instructions either. I've warned you about coming here alone. Now you will get yours."

He approached her swinging the enormous blade in broad strokes as though he was directing an orchestra. She ducked. As Cornelius turned around back to her again, Hazel scurried past the rows of specimen tables. She could feel her heart beat thumping in her chest.

She turned back; Cornelius's lab coat's button had gotten caught in the wire shelving on one of the tables. She had a chance. He gave the coat a yank with both hands ripping the fabric, freeing himself. She knew she couldn't outrun him. She had to think of something, something clever.

She picked one of the specimen containers and hurled it.

Cornelius dodged the flying, metal container before it hit the wall sending soil scattered through the air. He laughed and said, "You stupid, old woman, where do you think you're going?" Then he leaped up on the tabletop and came at her swinging the knife as he kicked the aluminum cylinders, sending seedlings flying in all directions. Hazel ran through a doorway into a larger windowless room. She turned in circles. Its walls were covered in mirrors. Cornelius entered and ran down the middle aisle holding the blade overhead. "I've got you now!" he shouted and swung the huge cleaver downward striking her reflection. The blade cracked the glass and bounced backwards, his face contorted in confusion.

Hazel stood and ran past him toward the door; he stuck out his foot tripping her. She hit the floor with a thud. Dizzily, she rolled over to see him standing overhead with the blade raised in both hands high above. She raised her arm shielding her face and took her final breath.

Blood covered nearly every square inch of the lab floor. A watering hose hung nearby. Cornelius turned the pressure up as the handle squeaked to its fullest and washed the blood down a drain in the center of the floor.

After replacing the hose, he turned catching a glimpse of himself in the splattered laboratory mirror. A whitish, scraggly beard partially covering his face was once full, but that was before the accident. The reflection haunted him with memories of the explosion so long ago. He chanted, "Cornelius is strong, Cornelius is worthy, Cornelius is powerful." He turned the sink's facet on and adjusted the water temperature to suit him. Steam rose from the streaming, hot water and slowly accumulated on the mirror's border. It framed a distorted, ghostly image that gazed back at him. He deeply sighed, the price paid for science.

Exhausted, Cornelius, in his blood drenched lab coat, fell backward into his office chair. No Thanksgiving dinner for those two. He lit a cigarette, and then realized he had never typed their blood. Oh, too late, now it was tainted. Unfortunately, Hazel and Casey Craig's final contribution to the blue rose project will never be appreciated.

Chapter 36—Vegetarian Students

Lt. Robert H. Waites was confident in his ability to solve this case while the constant reminders of Danny Rolling's victims filtered through his brain. He tapped his index finger against the steering wheel waiting for Julie Rose's parents. Her mother had called daily since her daughter's disappearance. He hoped today would be a turning point; the three of them were meeting Julie's mysterious landlord. Through county records, Waites was able to track down the property owner, Cornelius Hicks.

Moments later, Julie's parents pulled up behind him. Waites glanced in his rear view mirror. The emotional stress showed on their faces, yet another rerun of the awful things people do to each other. He stepped from his car, approached them and extended his hand.

"He should be here momentarily," referring to the landlord, said the detective. "Hopefully there will be something inside that will provide some clues." Waites was searching for words that would ease their apprehension. He realized that no such words existed.

After a few minutes, a van meandered down the winding road towards the three waiting on the sidewalk. It pulled up to the curb behind their cars. A tall man, his face disfigured, emerged sporting a tweed jacket and khakis; he approached them, presented a slight smile and nodded. "Good morning, I am Dr. Stanley Hicks, Cornelius's brother. He called me early this morning to tell me about your meeting with him. He's been detained and won't be able to make the drive up from Palm Beach County. He asked that I assist you in any way I can."

"Looks like your van has some serious issues; you should get those bald tires replaced and that tail light fixed."

"The police will stop you for it," Waites advised turning his attention back to his vehicle.

Stanley took a deep breath. "I know. It belongs to my brother. I had some car trouble, and he lent me this piece of junk. His work takes precedence over just about everything else. Sorry I'm a little late; I couldn't remember exactly where the place was, and I had to scramble through my desk drawers to find the key and directions Cornelius sent to me." His tone changed showing frustration as he continued, "I try not to get involved in his business."

Waites reached into his coat pocket and presented the search warrant. "I have this to show we are official."

"My brother wants to be cooperative, detective. It wouldn't have been a problem getting into your daughter's residence," Hicks responded in a soft, breathy tone turning to the parents.

"It wouldn't have been a problem if we could have made contact with your brother earlier. We didn't want to take any chances on delaying this longer," snapped Mrs. Rose.

Stanley defensively responded, "Ma'm, my brother is a research scientist; most of the time his work takes him to Holland. I've encouraged him to sell these rental properties. Again, I apologize for the stress this has caused you. Shall we?" he said, signaling for Julie's mom to proceed forward up the sidewalk, dotted with broken fragments along its edge. She obliged. A torn screen in the door flapped in the breeze. On the porch, Stanley handed the keys to Lt. Waites who unlocked it. They entered.

The interior of the wood frame cottage showed signs of neglect, too. Waites walked through the living room; the wooden floor creaked under his footsteps. He noticed a few areas of pealed paint before heading into the bedroom, Julie's parents followed.

Waites opened the door to what he assumed to be the bedroom. A bright flash of light blinded him momentarily, quickly disappearing, after which he imagined blood smeared everywhere. The flashbacks were relentless. He leaned over supporting himself against the door's frame and rubbed his eyes.

"Detective, are you okay?" Mrs. Rose asked.

"Oh, yea, sorry; yesterday I had some bad Mexican food, and it's still haunting me."

The kitchenette was next where a leaky facet steadily dripped. Mrs. Rose shook her head and said, "Julie told me the place was cheap. I can see why." He opened the cabinet doors one-by-one noticing that they were filled with an array of healthy foods, mostly jars of dried fruits, seeds and nuts. He remarked, "She must be very conscientious about her diet. I don't see one junk food item in here."

"Julie is a vegetarian; she has always been careful about what she eats," answered her mother leaning through the doorway.

"The other missing students were vegetarians, too," Waites added as he removed a jar from the cabinet, turned it back and forth, reading the label. After replacing it, he opened his canvas bag and took out a fingerprinting kit. He glanced up at Mrs. Rose. "Fingerprints can linger for a long time."

He started with the obvious places: window ledges and door handles hoping the dirt that had settled there wouldn't hinder him. Experienced in his task, Waites quickly moved from room to room as the parents stood by. "I'd prefer that you not touch or move anything right now. Let me finish; then we can go through things."

Waites noticed a framed photograph on the tabletop next to the window of Julie arm-locked with Derrick Stabb. They were squinting in the sunlight between the rows of plants. He towered above her. She appeared to be smitten with Derrick; her head turned upward at him smiling broadly. Raising an eyebrow, Waites stared at it for a moment. "Hum," he uttered to himself.

After the forty-five minute process, the detective allowed the parents to take a few extra minutes inside the cottage while he and the professor walked to the curb. In a stern voice he said, "I would need to speak with your brother soon. Tell him that he has an obligation here. Doesn't he realize the seriousness of this situation? All I'd need is a body to put out a warrant for him. "

"I'll try to get ahold of him, but he hates the phone. He told me once that too many people spend too much, wasted time yakking needlessly on it. He had more important things to do."

Waites condescendingly replied, "Well, this *is* one of those important things, professor. Tell him I will be anticipating a call from him soon, real soon. His little flower experiments will have to wait."

Stanley Hicks glared back at him for a moment pursing his lips. Then, he yanked the driver's side door open with a creak. It seemed about ready to fall off its hinges. A puff of black smoke and a backfire blast shot from the tail pipe after he turned the ignition. He turned back to Waites and gave a military salute. A weird gesture Waites thought.

As he edged away from the curb, Waites reached inside his pocket for his new 35mm camera. In that second, instinctively, he snapped a shot of the back of the van.

Chapter 37—Proving His Innocence

Derrick finished up his last class; he rushed cramming another pair of old jeans into his bulging suitcase. Gotta get back home; Ma had him on another one of her projects...painting. The "sprucing up", as she called it, was what "one" needed to do before guests arrive; of course the "one" she was referring to was *him*. He worked for food before. *Life was looking brighter though,* thought Derrick. The holidays were around the corner, and Ma's planned a special Thanksgiving dinner to celebrate Judy's, safe return.

Derrick rubbed his upper arm that itched from the new tattoo he just got as a symbol of solidarity with Judy after he'd heard the news about her recovery, and hope for the others, too. There was optimism in the blue rose he painstakingly sat through as the tattoo artist carved it into his skin. He removed a tube of ointment from the medicine cabinet and applied it.

In the bathroom, Derrick heard a knock on his dorm room door. He replaced the ointment's cap, pulled his shirt sleeve down and shut the cabinet door.

"Derrick Stabb?"

Before opening the door, he recognized the voice; his stomach churned with dread. Seems someone else had taken interest in Derrick's unusual ability for deciphering riddles; but Waites clearly wasn't so convinced that it was purely Derrick's talent. He took a deep breath and opened the door.

Waites stood in the hallway glaring back at him and said, "I'm following up after a search of Julie Rose's residence yesterday. May I come in?"

"Uh, sure." Every time Derrick spoke with Waites, he felt like he was on the hot seat, and it was getting hotter.

"How much about her did you know?"

"Not much, really; our teacher had us working on one field project together, shortly after that she was missing."

"So, *no* love affair huh, Derrick?" responded Waites, head tilted down leaning in closer to Derrick, looking over the rim of his glasses, his voice softened with suspicion.

"Gosh, no, Lieutenant, I have a girlfriend!"

"Well, sometimes having just one girl isn't enough. You know how it is when girls show interest in us guys." Waites gestured up and down Derrick's tall frame with his hand. "Come on, you're a healthy, good looking guy; girls must be falling over themselves to be with you. You have to admit it is tempting knowing what *they* want is so readily available, and they're so willing. You're going to tell me that you haven't thought about it. I don't know one straight guy in your position that wouldn't go for it. And you're the exception. Is that it?"

Derrick crossed his arms; his expression conveyed that he couldn't believe what he was hearing. "It sounds like you think I was involved in some sort of love triangle."

"Well, college campuses are breeding grounds for all sorts of affairs with all those hormones in high gear."

"Well, I am not your typical collage freshman!" Derrick disputed taking a stand against the lieutenant's accusation.

"He who cries out the loudest is often the biggest offender, Derrick". I saw the photograph of you and Julie at her cottage. You two looked pretty chummy."

"We shared a love for horticulture. That's all."

"It looked like more than a little plant fondling was going on to me."

"I assure you Professor Stanly Hicks wouldn't allow one extra minute of free time for us to do anything but stay on task. He is a tough teacher."

"Stanley Hicks, is your professor?"

"Yes, and he's a committed one. Why?"

"I met with him yesterday. His brother is Julie's landlord."

"Yes, he has a twin."

"A twin, he didn't mention that, but it doesn't matter." Waites raised his one eyebrow and paused for a moment.

Derrick continued, "Well, you can ask him about all of the homework he gives us. He'll tell you that there's no time for anything. And he expects his students to deliver his assignments on time."

"OK, I will."

"I gotta go," Derrick said.

"You run along. We will chat again later."

Derrick shut the door and leaned against it holding his stomach; just when he thought his situation was better. It's clear that until he could prove his innocence and get Waites off his back, his situation would never be better.

Chapter 38 –A Web of Deception

Sienna Hurst eagerly filled in the patients' charts finishing her shift at Memorial Medical Center. Today was her mother's birthday. She looked up and sighed, recognizing the disfigured face walking towards the nurses' station. Surrounded by her colleagues at the front desk, she spoke carefully not to reveal too much about her guarded relationship with Cornelius.

"How nice to see you again, Dr. Hicks," she said unwittingly knocking the clipboard from the countertop onto the floor sending patient files flying across the gleaming tile. Cornelius bent over and retrieved it along with most of the scattered papers.

"Thank you," he replied down on one knee with unfaltering composure. She watched as Cornelius returned the mess of papers to the countertop attempting to put them back in order. "There you are; no permanent damage." In her peripheral vision, she could see the others staring at him. He could be so charming when he wanted to be.

"You've brought your nephew some more tomatoes, beautiful!" she added.

"These were getting ripe quickly, and I didn't want them to go to waste. I figured that Rodney was running low by now."

Sienna replied, "You have been very committed delivering these in a timely fashion. I don't think we have had one other family member who is so attentive."

"Well, I just want to make sure he has this little bit of joy in his life. In his condition, it's the small things that count."

"I noticed that it seems to be the one thing he counts on most," she added knowing Cornelius was a master at deception.

"I'd like to see him. I had hoped he wasn't sleeping."

"I don't think so," Sienna replied. "I was just in his room, and he was alert."

"Good and I have a couple of questions for you. Stop by before you leave, please." Cornelius winked, picked up the box of fruit and made his way down the hallway.

Sienna took a deep breath and glanced at the wall clock; she'd hoped that Cornelius's plans for her had come to an end, but clearly not.

"Goodnight," she said to her fellow nurses, picked up her bag and headed towards Rodney's room.

Moments later she paused and then gently rapped on the heavy wooden door with her knuckle. "Yes," he said; she stepped into the room just as Cornelius scooped up another spoonful and brought it to Rodney's mouth.

"I'll have another small assignment for you. This shouldn't be too difficult since it involves the *one* you have such a crush on."

"Crush on?" she responded stepping up to him, raising her eyebrows.

He turned away from Rodney glancing up at her. "Oh, come on Sienna, you don't think anyone notices how you coo and flirt with Derrick Stabb when he's here. The staff talks; I know what's happening even when I'm not around. Can't say I blame you. He is a fine Aryan, specimen."

Sienna continued looking puzzled," Why Derrick?"

"The mark," Cornelius responded.

"I don't understand."

"The blue rose tattoo on his shoulder. I considered him, but I was hesitant. Now, knowing he has the mark, I'm certain he's another one who's also been selected. It's so clear to me. The signs are everywhere.

The links he provided in his research paper were just what I needed. And now this, naturally; Derrick Stabb would be the perfect specimen. He is the last scientific puzzle piece I need to accomplish my dream. And you're going to help me achieve that."

Sienna dropped her bag onto the floor and folded her arms in defiance. "Haven't I done enough? The charades you've put me through with his grandmother. I thought you were finished with me."

"Almost, we are going to arrange a little meeting: you, Derrick and me. I have a few questions for him, and I need a distraction."

"What does that mean?" she said wrinkling her forehead.

"You'll see. You'll benefit from all of this, too, Sienna. I assure you that when my plan comes to fruition, all those who have obeyed," He paused, "I mean, cooperated, will be rewarded. That's all for now; I am about to leave, myself."

He gradually stood up from the bedside chair and ran his hands through Rodney's golden hair. "I have plans for you, as well, young man."

He turned to the nurse with a cunning smile. "I'll be in touch. You don't have any out of town plans for the holiday, do you?"

She shook her head back and forth, "No," picking her bag up. She looked at Rodney lying face up. His clear blue eyes seem to plead with her. What had she done, entangling herself in Cornelius's web of deception?

Chapter 39 – Notice Of Foreclosure

The first thing Derrick spotted as he walked through Ma's front door was the six cans of paint soldiered strategically against the wall. He grinned; he should have known it would be blue, two shades, which he could tell from the drippings down the side of the opened cans. Ma obviously couldn't wait until he got home to start.

When he and Emily entered the kitchen, everything was in its place. He took a deep breath; the house smelled so clean, cleaner than usual, if that was possible. Derrick was well familiar with life in the Glades, dealing with the muck dust and cane ash. Ma certainly had been busy. There wasn't a speck of anything anywhere. *But where was she?*

After running his finger across the tabletop, he turned to Emily and said, "I suspect she's out buying Halloween candy. She doesn't get too many trick- or- treaters out here, but Ma wouldn't want to disappoint any of the town's kids, even if it's just a couple that show up."

A crash followed by broken glass came from upstairs. Derrick turned towards the stairway. "What the heck was that?" He left the room to investigate, Emily followed.

Entering Ma's bedroom, he noticed the source of the ruckus; a lamp that sat on the reading table by the open window had blown over from a wind gust. It was still on the floor with its crumpled shade a few feet away. A pile of disheveled papers flipped and blew across the floor.

Derrick picked up several of the pages and begun reading. The words NOTICE OF FORECLOSURE leaped from the pages. Soon his expression changed; he looked at Emily and said, "Ma has been keeping a secret from me apparently for quite some time."

Emily picked up the remaining papers on the floor. "Look at this," she said showing the summons to Derrick. The date it was delivered on was past the twenty-day notice to reply. The foreclosure process had already begun.

They heard a car door. Emily glanced out the window and then turned back to Derrick. "She's back."

With an ashen face and papers in hand, Derrick descended the stairs to confront his Grandmother.

"Honey, I didn't want you to be worried about this," Ma said sitting in her chair in the front room looking at her forlorn grandson's expression. "You have way too much on your mind with your school work."

Derrick anxiously rubbed his forehead with the back of his hand. He felt a bead of sweat trickle down from this temple. "Ma, this is way serious. You are going to lose this place. Have you called an attorney?"

"No dear," she replied. "I've just been praying to your grandfather and to the Virgin Mary in the garden for a miracle. You know miracles can happen everyday."

He leaned in close to her, looked urgently into her eyes, sighed and said a second time, "Ma, you're going to lose your home. Why have you done this?"

She took a deep breath, paused a moment and softly replied with that expression that would melt him, "When Rodney became ill and could no longer stay with me, I had to find a place that would care for him. At first there was some money in an insurance policy, but that was quickly used up. I hoped his condition was only temporary, so I turned to the only source of money I had, the equity in this property."

"I prayed that he would get well soon. Instead, he went deeper and deeper into dementia. The doctors and nurses were baffled by what was happening to him. They diagnosed a poison in him—excessive amounts of aluminum—but they couldn't figure out the source. They didn't know what to do."

"The time passed, and the money was gone before I knew it, leaving me in this dire situation. The reason I was having this last Thanksgiving dinner was I knew my time here was coming to an end.

I wanted to have a celebration remembering all of the good times."

Derrick sat there and stared at his sweet, loving grandmother, trying to figure out what to say or, more importantly, what to do. He rose from his chair and approached her. "Ma, on Monday I'm calling an attorney. We have to see what options you might have. There must be something that can be done to hold this foreclosure off instead of wasting time painting. Why redecorate if you're not staying? It doesn't make any sense."

A peaceful smile graced Ma's face. "Honey, there isn't anything left to be done legally. I've conceded to the inevitable, so let's make our limited time here memorable. And, as far as the painting goes, as long as I'm still here, I'm going to have a pretty home I feel good living in."

Emily took a deep breath and said, "Mrs. Stabb, if there is anything that I can do for you, please tell me."

Ma turned toward her, "Dear Girl, yes, there is. You can get busy with this painting. We have a job to finish. I am going to have a get-together in just a few days with lots of happy people giving thanks for whatever is important to them: being rescued, finding lost loves, solving mysteries or making new friends. The day will be a celebration of love, and we will deal with what lies ahead tomorrow."

Derrick looked down shaking his head back and forth. Obediently, he picked himself up off the chair and walked back over to the awaiting paint cans.

After an hour into their project, void of conversation, the kitchen phone rang. Derrick, once again, put down his paint roller, entered the kitchen and picked up the receiver, "Stabb residence."

"Hello, this is Sienna Hurst at the assisted living center. Who am I speaking to?"

"This is Derrick Stabb, Sienna."

"I need to see you. It's your brother".

Hit a second time with disturbing news, he sounded an alarming tone into the receiver. "Why, what's wrong, has something happened?"

"No, no, no, it's nothing like that, he's stable. It is more of a financial matter." She continued, "Can you come over *now*."

"I'll tell Ma. We'll be there as fast as we can."

"No, we'd rather talk to you alone."

Strange, he thought, but maybe in light of Ma's financial dilemma, it was best he'd go alone.

"Give me thirty minutes."

"Good, I will meet you in the Admissions Office."

Derrick hung up the phone and attempted to quell the uneasy feeling deep inside his gut. He needed to put on a casual face and come up with an excuse quickly.

"I thought I heard the phone. Who was that, dear?" inquired Grandma Ma.

"Uh, oh, it was the auto body shop. I had them take a look at Emily's car the last time we were here to get an estimate on repairs. They want me to bring the car in." Derrick grinned, rather pleased with his cunning tale. Of course, leave it to Emily to throw a wrench into his plan, he thought.

"What repair? It's just a small dent and the bike rack was damaged, a minor scrape. I had buffed out."

"I know, honey, but I didn't want to spoil my surprise. I had ordered a new rack, an early Christmas gift. The shop is installing it this afternoon. I will only be an hour or so."

"That is so sweet. Do you want me to go with you?" she said beaming from ear to ear.

"No, you stay here with Ma; I won't be long."

"Okaaayyyy, you're right as always," she responded grinning, swaying her body back and forth.

Derrick grabbed his wallet and keys and darted out the door before any other inquiries could be made. Moments later he's headed down the dirt road in Emily's Bug leaving a trail of dust behind 'Janice'.

It only took Derrick ten minutes, or so, to reach the hospital. He pulled into a guest parking spot along the neatly trimmed curb; Derrick bounded out of the little, blue Volkswagen Beetle. He quickly paced himself past the thick shrubbery encircling the blacktop parking lot.

He entered through the main foyer making long strides toward the Admissions Office. He glanced down the lengthy halls, which usually were teaming with activity. He noticed the wall clock. It was close to lunch time. *Maybe everybody was in the cafeteria*, he thought, nothing more. Politely, Derrick knocked on the heavy ajar door.

"Please, come in," Called Sienna Hurst's sweet, angelic voice from the other side. Derrick opened the door wide to find the petite nurse in her scrubs sitting behind the massive desk. The sunlight streamed through the sheer window treatments illuminating her blonde hair. He stepped all of the way into the office.

From behind the door a powerful hand grabbed Derrick's arm forcing it behind his back. Another hand placed a padded, foul-smelling cotton cloth over his nose and mouth. His body fell limp.

Sienna opened the side office door leading into the physicians' private parking lot. Army trained Cornelius Hicks slung Derrick's weighty body over his shoulder. In minutes Derrick was in the back of the van, where so many other victims before him rode. Hicks removed the STAFF sign from the dash board and tossed it onto the floorboard. He turned back to Sienna and ordered, "Get back to your duties, and don't arouse any suspicions."

He hopped into the front seat, looked around and then unnoticed he departed the impeccably landscaped parking lot he had designed.

Chapter 40 – A Miracle And Rats?

A maze of bumpy back roads was etched into the rich farm land that surrounded Lake Okeechobee. This surely *was* a test for Sonny's sense of direction, Sistrunk thought from his vantage point in the truck's passenger seat as he braced himself against the dash in anticipation of yet hitting another pothole. Someone would have to live here for a long time to understand the lay of the land. He knew the man had been born here which provided Sistrunk with a hopefulness that positive results would arise from this hot, torturous investigation, soon.

Dried muck kicked up from the worn tires of Sonny's pickup and drifted through the truck's open windows as Sistrunk fanned his face with the card stock folder from the missing persons' file. Together again, they were following Judy's sketchy leads to the mysterious barn where her abductors supposedly had taken her.

"Is this the way to Slim's Fish Camp?" Sistrunk asked with a tone of frustration.

"Sort of," responded Sonny, as he wiped the sweat from his brow.

And what the hell did that mean? Sistrunk shot the man a sour look. Another day's end was approaching. If Sonny's talents didn't yield any results soon, he'd have to fast-forward to his next plan. The problem was he didn't have a Plan B. This was it and a miracle. As Sonny turned down one more winding dirt path, Sistrunk let out a deep sigh, staring out the truck's dusty window at the seemingly endless miles of sugar cane before him.

He had already witnessed one phenomenon, so he was counting on a second.

"Where in the hell are we?" Sistrunk said in a huff jostled from one side of his seat to the other.

"Welcome to the Glades," Sonny responded with a big grin as the cane tops lashed against his truck's windshield along the narrow, gravel paths.

Sonny pulled his truck to the roadside, opened his door and slung his legs out. "Let's take a break. I need a minute to get my bearings again." Off in the distance they heard the clamor of the sugar cane, harvesting machines.

"Someone could really get lost out here forever," said Sistrunk scratching his semi-bald head with the folder's edge. "I've got some more of these damn riddles that Stabb boy studied." He fanned away an annoying fly, then flipped it open and pointed to one of the verses. "He told me that he thought this one referenced a location where harvests were taken for processing, but now the facility could be abandoned. And, it has something to do with rats...lots of them."

Sonny frowned. "Let me see those." Sistrunk took another swat at the irritating insect before handing the page over. Sonny read the stanzas aloud.

"Harvests brought here have come and gone,

A new purpose it will spawn,

A botanist's dream is in progress,

To the entire world he will profess,"

"Tiny eyes have watched his deeds,

Silent witnesses as he proceeds,

They scurry inside seeking shelter from fire

Across the vast fields of soggy mire,

"The vermin within exist in packs,

Breeding and feeding in between the stacks,

They live and thrive no fear from cats,

Running from the field are packs of rats,

He looked up, stared back at Sistrunk and responded, "Is that what he thought that meant? Oh boy, Ma Stabb's grandson really is *one* weird dude."

"I know. It's like me reading Shakespeare back in high school lit class. I couldn't figure out was *he* was saying neither," Sistrunk responded with a wry grin.

Sonny thought for a moment, took a deep breath, and then continued. "There are new packing houses in the region where vegetables are taken for grading, packing and shipping. The winter harvests here supply the country with much of the vegetables consumed. That's a lot of processing. Somewhere out there must be an old barn that's no longer used, but where...sure beats me."

Sistrunk kicked a large stone from the roadside into the field. "Oh, come on, Sonny, I was real impressed with your discovery back in the rose garden, so turn on your thinking cap under that metal plate in your dome, and let's solve this case. We've been up and down these roads until I can't feel my ass."

With that said, Sistrunk yanked the truck's, squeaky, passenger door handle and leaped out. He grabbed his waistband and hiked up his pants easing his discomfort from the moist, sticky fabric. He awkwardly walked to the roadside shaking his legs stimulating his, blood circulation and grabbed a stalk of sugar cane. "So they turn this stuff into what I put in my coffee every morning, huh?"

"Yea, there are three big cane mills in the area." Sonny pointed outward into various directions. "The field workers burn the undergrowth and then use sharp cane knives to cut it. Sometimes they use a harvesting machine; that's what we heard off in the distance. You should see the gazillions of rats run out of the field when they get those fires going.

It's like they're on steroids following the Pied Piper."

Sonny paused wiping the sweat from his forehead. "Wait, let me see those riddles again." He studied the stanzas and looked back up at Sistrunk. "That Stabb kid might not be as weird as I thought. I *do* know of an place we haven't checked out. I don't know why I didn't think of it earlier. This muck dust must be clogging my brain."

Sonny paced back and forth in front of his truck fanning himself with the folder. "At one time there were a bunch of old barns over near the shallows of Lake Okeechobee, off Torry Island Road, by the marina and Slim's. Most of them have been torn down, major rat infestations. They love the water and there are a million places where they can hide and breed. There could be one barn left."

Sistrunk shivered forgoing his usual manly façade admitting, "I hate rats. When I was a kid, I faced down one in our garage. The thing just looked at me, like it was defying me. A miracle and rats somehow don't seem to go together."

Sistrunk wiped his brow and once again perched his sunglasses on the bridge of his nose shielding his sensitive blue eyes from Florida's blinding sun. The two climbed back into Sonny's dusty pickup and proceeded toward the illusive barn somewhere near Slim's.

Another hour has passed and now the sun flickered just below the tops of the sugar cane. Sistrunk took a deep breath rubbing his hands industriously up and down on his pant legs as he and Sonny sat in the truck at the intersection of Old Vandergrift and Belle Glade roads. Dusk had given way to twilight. He was ready, once again, to call it a day glancing down at his watch. Its florescent dials indicated the evening hour as his thoughts engaged his upcoming rendezvous. He had another date with Delores Dawson. Thoughts of her were a pleasant interruption as he painstakingly pushed forward in discovery of the said, rat infested, mysterious barn. Their relationship had gained some traction, and he was eager to get back to West Palm.

A procession of cars and other pickups passed through the intersection as the men waited for the signal to change. A faded blue van with a busted tail light, tailed closely by another car, were the last to squeak through just before they got the green light. The van caught Sistrunk's attention.

He reached for his brief case on the floor board, popped open the latch and removed another file folder. "Would you turn on the interior light?" Beneath the faint glow of the dome light, he swiftly flipped through photos Detective Robert Waites recently mailed to him from Gainesville. He stopped at one and gave a tight, satisfied smile.

"Follow them," he clipped out, pointing to the left.

Sonny, obligingly, turned his muddy truck and gunned the engine trailing at an inconspicuous distance. "You thinking something?"

Sistrunk held up the picture of a van identical to the one ahead. Its left tail light winked back at them. "You don't see too many old vans like that on the road. Let's see where they take us."

They slowly approached the big lake and crossed over NW 17th Street then turned left onto Harris Road, which paralleled the Herbert Hoover Dike. "This earthen dam was built around Big Lake O after the 1928 hurricane, which wiped out Clewiston and drowned thousands." Sonny offered as his truck struck another pothole slamming Sistrunk into the passenger door, again. He rubbed his scoured shoulder and deigned, "Thanks for the history lesson."

The caravan now turned onto Torry Island Road and headed back north towards Pelican Point. They were near this area several days ago, but like so many roads, they came upon one dead end after another and gave up. Sistrunk's pulse was amplified by speculation as Sonny turned and followed the two vehicles down a remote path even Sonny mentioned he wasn't familiar with.

"I've never seen this trail," Sonny said squinting through the windshield as he killed the truck's lights trusting his gut to guide them. A perfect full moon on a clear night shed a bluish, ambient light on a winding pathway leading to the silhouette of a large building.

The van and car's brake lights just ahead of them illuminated indicating a sudden stop. Sonny quickly yanked his truck off the path and parked. After a few hesitant moments, they exited, armed. Sistrunk reached for his revolver in a shoulder harness on the floorboard. He fastened it snugly, pulled it out and removed the safety lock. Sonny had a pair of nun chucks or Nunchaku—known as chain sticks—he kept tucked in the back of his truck next to the spare tire.

Sistrunk gave him a strange look. Sonny leaned in closer and with a nod said, "I don't like guns, so learned how to use these in a martial arts night class on self defense. Once I even defended myself with them in an alligator attack."

Sistrunk nodded and thought, *Too many Bruce Lee movies.*

As the two readied themselves next to the pickup, Sonny looked past Sistrunk and reiterated, "I've lived all my life in the Glades and didn't know this barn was here. Apparently, at one time it was a processing facility just like that Stabb kid said." They slowly proceeded up the pathway on foot, Sistrunk trailing behind Sonny, the crunch of shell rock felt under their heels.

The car and van they followed were parked along the north side of the building. Sistrunk pointed ahead to a small wooden door slightly ajar. He cautiously approached and peered through. "You hear that?" Sonny gave a submissive nod. Two distinctly different voices echoed across the cavernous space of the barn's interior. One sounded low, a roaring tone of voice. The other was feminine; Sistrunk assumed it to be a woman's.

A foul odor, reminiscent of the corpse flower they found growing in the muck weeks ago, wafted through the opening. Sonny pulled a handkerchief from his back pocket and covered his mouth and nose. Sistrunk, used to fetid smells, braved on without protection. They crouched, shuffling along the gravel floor about ten yards leading up to a single light coming from a gleaming white building on the far side of the barn.

Stooped underneath the glass window, Sistrunk slowly raised himself sliding against the glossy, orange peel, textured wall. He could feel his knees cracking. Sonny remained bent down. He whispered to Sistrunk, "What do you see?"

Sistrunk rapidly raised his palm pausing Sonny's question. Then he hand gestured for Sonny to follow as the two entered through a door. They stooped close to the ground, a few moments later resorting to slithering on their bellies toward the voices. They rested on their elbows beneath a row of metal tables about twenty feet away from a man in a lab coat.

Sistrunk heard a scratching sound and turned to shoot Sonny a disapproving look. Instead of the planned scorned expression, his eyes widened beholding a dreaded sight, *No*! he thought...a rat. Its fury, grey body wiggled past Sonny and was quickly approaching him. Sistrunk clasp his hands together, shut his eyes as tight as he could, and buried his face in his knuckles. He shook as beads of sweat tricked down from his temples. *If that thing get close to my face I'll freak*, he thought fighting the horror. His stomach begun to churn; he couldn't even read about rats Edgar Allen Poe wrote of in high school lit class. Once, his teacher assigned one of Poe's novels, and he had to request another after segments of the story made him nauseous.

Drawing in heavily, he filled his lungs to capacity attempting to squelch the queasiness inside. Sistrunk labored to think of something else, something pleasant for God's sake, but with the shouting going on a few feet in front of him, and knowing the little critter possibly could be only inches away, his thoughts were stuck somewhere between A and Z...Anxiety and Zen.

Sistrunk jerked; he felt something tugging on his pant leg imaging the rat had grabbed ahold of it. Raising his head and turning back, he discovered it was Sonny doing the tugging and motioned toward the direction of the pest. Thank God, it has jiggled off away from them ducking under a door. Sistrunk gulped and refocused on the episode unfolding a few feet away.

His face was severely scarred, and he appeared engaged in a heated argument with himself gesturing wildly, pacing back and forth before a full length mirror. He stopped and said to his reflected image in a voice Sistrunk originally mistook for a woman's. "Cornelius, are you mad? What in the hell is going on here with that contraption out there and this horrid smell?" He turned and walked several paces away from his image.

Then, seconds later he made an about-face, approached the mirror, placed both hands against it with his head down, responding in an low, intimidating voice, what sounded like a mantra. "Cornelius is strong, Cornelius is worthy, Cornelius is powerful".

He continued, his head raised, glaring at his reflection, "Stanley, I've been waiting a long time to prove to you that I am capable of great innovations. What I am on the verge of is creating a flower so unique, so magnificent that all of those in the horticultural world, who've shunned me, will now take notice and recognize me for the genius I truly am."

The scientist threw himself against the mirror. It wobbled back and forth from the force. Sistrunk clenched his fists expecting it to shatter at any moment. The mad man's cheek was pressed against it; his breath was visible as he then slumped to his knees and balled up on the ground breathing deeply, exhausted.

Seconds later, emerging from a fetal position he crawled back up to the mirror. He stood precariously on shaky legs, turning back to his refection responding, "Cornelius, Cornelius, your science is all wrong. This isn't going to get you anywhere but committed to a padded cell. What you are doing here is mad. Why would you think that this kind of crazy science, murdering innocent souls for God's sake, grinding them up, would achieve this insane idea of producing, what did you say, a flower? Why? It's crazy!

He then swung his body away from the mirror. He stooped over as he held his temples tightly between both palms appearing to squelch a migraine. Seconds passed and he returned, once again, to the confident Cornelius personality glaring back into the mirror.

"Others believe in me. You see, Stanley, no man achieves greatness alone. My docent—the man I admired since the beginning of my career—has guided me from the beginning when we started in our little make-shift lab beneath the flower auction in Aalsmeer. He believed in me; he had confidence in me, and he was there when I needed him. He has been my most trusted and loyal friend. It is his inspiration and belief in me that has propelled my vision. He recognized my gift for creation. And like those before me: Da Vinci, Hitler, sacrifices had to be made."

He backed away, threw his arms into the air, turned around continuing as spittle fired from his mouth. "Understandably, research requires lots of money. There's a benefactor with deep pockets who also believes in my science, and when she sees the results of my work, I will be very, very rich, too."

Cornelius stood as still as a rock. He stared upward toward the ceiling momentarily, and then turned away from the mirror once again. He took several steps closer to where Sistrunk laid with his belly hugging the ground under the specimen table unable to miss the tips of his blood covered shoes inches away from his nose.

"You see, I've spent years planning this, Stanley, and all of the pieces have come together. Serendipity. A long time ago, I befriended another rose expert. Our relationship went back to when I was in the army with her husband. When we were on the battle field, he asked me to honor him with one wish should he die. I delivered a statue to her, a boy removing a thorn from his foot, he had taken from the Nazis, so she could have a memory of him. I made good on that promise, and she was indebted to me. I've laid out a plan to get her property, a home in the rich muck where my blue roses will survive healthy and strong. "

"All of these people have played a vital role in my life," he continued, shaking his head with pride. "You know that even your star undergraduate provided me with some of the key elements I needed! You bragged about this brilliant student you had, and the insurmountable task—the soil report—you assigned to him for which he earned an A. An A grade from the professor who *never* gives A's. So, I had to have a copy. Indeed, it included some missing links."

Cornelius turned and grabbed a bound stack of papers on the edge of the counter. "See for yourself Stanley," he said, as flung the bound documents striking the mirror.

His alter ego grabbed the bound pages and recklessly fumbled the documents around in his hands to take a look at the cover. He slumped, turned and questioned into the mirror, "Derrick's paper, where did you get this?"

Cornelius's intimidating persona returned, "From your briefcase. Actually, *he* has turned out to be a valuable link, as well. I needed one more victim with those perfect, Aryan features."

With that remark, Cornelius flung open a heavy, silver door exposing a freezer compartment. A frigid, cold fog drifted from the open cubical across the ground toward Sistrunk, propped up by his elbows; he stifled a cough and fanned it away. Sistrunk witnessed a sight thought unimaginable; gagged and bound to a chair was Derrick Stabb's, motionless body. He was blue, his head tilted to one side. Like all the others, he had been frozen.

Chapter 41 – Genetic Karma

"**Sheriff**, freeze!" Sistrunk hollered rising over the aluminum shelving, rotating his arms and pinpointing his gun directly on the botanist's head.

Cornelius turned toward his voice, grabbed a cane knife from the rack next to the freezer's door and turned the gleaming blade toward him.

Sonny lunged forward, slinging his nun chucks at Cornelius, just missing his head. The force of the heavy chained sticks threw him off his feet. In another sweeping motion, as though he was directing an orchestra, the botanist whirled the heavy blade striking the side of the black man's cranium. Blood began spewing from the open gash on to the freshly painted, white floor.

Sistrunk fired. The bullet ricocheted off the heavy, metal door and struck the mirror shattering it into a million pieces. Sistrunk ducked under the specimen table dodging the glass shards piercing the air like ice crystals.

"You're doomed!" Cornelius yelled as he threw the cane knife whirling past him. Sistrunk raised himself up and fired again, but Cornelius had slipped out a side door leading into another freezer.

He followed his assailant into freezing, pitch black darkness. The cold was so biting Sistrunk had to cover his face again. He heard the thud of another door and followed the sound into a separate chamber. He reached frantically, found the knob and pushed, only to meet resistance. The handle must have been secured from the opposite side. He made his way back through the opposite door into the lab area, precariously stepped over Sonny's still body, surrounded by a pool of blood, and ran through the immense barn toward the small, open door at the far end. His chest was pounding as he felt the blood surging through his veins. He looked in all directions. Gone?

Sistrunk reentered the barn and ran back toward the laboratory. He pulled his police radio and breathlessly said. "I, I'm Deputy Bruce Sistrunk; please send a couple of ambulances to the end of Torry Island Road. Look for a pickup truck parked there, and make a right turn up a gravel road. There's a barn; we're inside."

As Sistrunk heard the dispatcher muffle a few inaudible words into the radio as he laid it down, he ran toward Sonny. He approached, but he assumed it was useless; he was too late. His attention was grabbed by Derrick Stabb in the laboratory's freezer sitting unconscientiously upright in a chair, his hands bound behind.

He took one of the cane knives from the rack and cut the restraints, and then he pulled Derrick from the frigid room. He hoped the ambulance would not get lost.

Once outside the freezer, Sistrunk searched through the cabinets for anything he could cover Derrick's body with. On the top shelf was a stack of terrycloth hand towels, small, but better than nothing. As he pulled them from the shelf a coil bound note pad placed on top fell open to the floor. "Where could they be?" he asked himself aloud after placing the last towel over Derrick's still, cold body.

He reentered the freezer and turned to a shelf unit containing what seemed to be plastic, pint jars, each designated with a freezer taped label, including a date and name. In the front row were five jars; affixed to each was Derrick's name and yesterday's date. *Blood*, he thought. Sistrunk knew the human body held ten pints. He found a cardboard box in the lab and returned to the freezer loading the pints into it. He placed the box on the metal table and returned to Derrick.

Kneeling next to Derrick's body, he picked up the note pad and begun to flip through the pages. At the top of each page was a date. The pad was filled with four-line stanzas scribbled in a poetic form. They read:

"Her enamored view supports your plan

With contributions made you know you can

Although challenges ahead may cause beset

A position she holds is your best asset"

"The sky is blue calling your fate

The time is now you mustn't wait

Sacrifices made are surly justified

After all their names will be immortalized"

"An unearthly goal is yours to by right

Clouds in the heavens are blue tonight

A bright young man has a secret prevention

He holds the knowledge requiring your attention"

"A sweet grandmother's garden is a delight

She holds a secret, you've created her plight

Your success will soon be realized

In the end her flowers will be prized"

"A pure blue rose is yours to hold

This gift is deserving, its pure as gold

Because your commitment is unwavering

You will pick the blossom of your favoring"

"She is the path for your financial success

Her requests are simple non the less

Follow the dream you both dreamed tonight

The lime light is yours at the end of this plight"

His eyes darted across them flipping page after page, too much to comprehend. He looked up from the notebook and wondered where their rescuers were. Sistrunk felt like he was in some sort of a time warp. The room went silent; seconds seemed like minutes. As he raised his head, Sistrunk heard a faint, annoying, high pitched squeal that reminded him of feedback from his grandmother's hearing aid. Still on his knees, he turned around in the direction of the irritating sound to find Giles Van Cormack propped up with his cane in one hand and a revolver, aimed directly at him, in the other.

"I didn't expect to find the likes of you here," said the old man.

"Who in the hell are you?" the deputy demanded.

"I don't think you are in a position to ask questions, but since this is the end of the road, I'll tell you. I am the spiritual guidance, advisor and, referred to by some as an oracle to many important people, including the world renowned botanist, Dr. Cornelius Hicks."

"So these are yours?" Sistrunk inquired waving the flapping pages at him.

"Yes. My relationship with him goes back many decades. We met when he was a student of mine in Amsterdam.

I am his docent, or as you might be more acquainted with, teacher. I knew he was brilliant. He was the only one who could decipher the riddles. That is until that young man came along. Van Cormack turned his head toward Derrick and nodded.

"I thought Cornelius's concept was brilliant—a perfectly formed blue rose. Brilliant!" He shouted again, extending his arms overhead, cane and gun in-hand. "Impossible to achieve by natural processes; only a man, as daring as he, could develop a plan to achieve seemingly the unattainable. Van Gogh, our idol, he, too was a genius; he painted blue roses. If anyone could bring to life something as rare and beautiful as Van Gogh made famous in his work, well, it was this man. Unfortunately, an explosion in the laboratory long ago left him torn in two. What do you Americans call it, duo-personality disorder? Over time the disease got in his way.

"So these weird riddles are yours? What was their purpose?" Sistrunk demanded struggling to make sense of it all.

"The stanzas, or riddles, as you refer to them, are a test channeled to me from a higher power. They will guide anyone who can figure out their meanings. The only two so far are Cornelius and Derrick Stabb. But, unfortunately Cornelius developed other plans for Derrick."

Sistrunk shook his head back and forth. "I know a little something about artists, and Van Gogh was crazy! You're all freakin' crazy!"

Van Cormack defiantly responded shaking his cane at the man. "No crazier than Da Vinci digging up bodies to study the human form. No crazier than Giovanni Aldini performing electric shock on executed prisoners. No crazier that the Nazis performing experiments on expendable Jews. No crazier than developing a Master Race. No crazier than killing thousands of Japanese with a couple of bombs. This isn't any crazier, as you say, my good man, than many other, unimaginable deeds enacted by ambitious men. Besides, it was a collaboration of sorts. I tapped into the universe; Cornelius took the necessary actions. As you can see, its not exactly incriminating evidence; it would be very hard to pin it to me. Do you think some 'poetry', as you refer to it, would hold up as evidence in court?"

"You're not getting away with this," said Sistrunk.

"I already have, sir," sneered Van Cormack. "You've insulted geniuses, Van Gogh, Da Vinci, Aldini, Hitler, Cornelius and me, because you don't understand. Your simple brain cannot begin to understand!"

Suddenly, Sistrunk heard a whirling pair of nun chucks rotate through the air magically wrapping around Van Cormack's neck; his gun fired simultaneously as it was knocked from his hand before the old man slammed against the floor with a thump.

Sistrunk grabbed the weapon, turned around and from behind saw, crouched on the floor, still bleeding, Sonny. Sistrunk ran toward him. It seemed the blunt end of the cane knife made contact with the metal plate in his head. Once he came to, he again instinctively performed.

Sistrunk tore off his shirt and tied it as tight as he could around the gash. "POLICE!"

Sistrunk called through the open laboratory door through the dark space. "We're over here, follow the light." He heard feet running across the gravel floor.

"Here, here."

Sistrunk pointed to Derrick on the floor who was immediately lifted onto a gurney by the medics. He left Sonny's side and ran toward the freezer removing the jars with Derrick's blood and handed them to one of the lifesavers. "I think half of the blood has been drained from him and possibly replaced with saline." The EMT nodded.

Next, Sonny was placed on a stretcher and followed Derrick out of the laboratory with the paramedics.

Van Cormack was lifted to his feet by the cops, arrested and read his rights. But before his furrowed body was handcuffed and hauled out of the lab to the waiting squad car, he took one last look at Sistrunk and offered one more piece of his view point: "Deputy, I know that this must be quite a stretch for your microscopic brain to handle, but here is how I see it. We are all linked to our pasts by genetic karma. Cornelius Hicks is a man controlled by his predetermined destiny. His inheritance was responsible for his, innate talent in understanding horticultural science as well as his propensity for obsessive, unrelenting exploration of what others considered insane, extreme concepts, even if it meant killing to satisfy his theories.

The young lady you saved from Cornelius's freezer has her own dark karma to face, too. She isn't free from her fate."

"Genetic karma rules our lives; its past down generation to generation. We may think that it can be ignored but not so. However, it can be altered. You see, we choose what we have. For most people, their programming is too deeply ingrained to change; the solution is, and please excuse the cliché, to turn a blind eye. But, in reality, that isn't the key that unlocks and removes generations of dark karma because it will surface again with devastating results. Unfortunately, Cornelius shares the equivalent, negative, genetic karma as his wealthy benefactor does. And, as you might imagine, two with the same tendencies cannot survive together for long."

"As for that young man," Van Cormack continued, as he turned his head toward the open lab doorway through darkness of the vast barn. "His soul's choice of where and when to incarnate is a mystery, however I believe that the synchronistic moment of his birth was also the pathway to his unique talents. His karma, just as the intentions of his ancestors, is to do good things. He will persevere until he succeeds."

"After all of my years in the spiritual world as a teacher and oracle, I've learned that there are some—granted, very few—who would out shine all others in every way: physical appearance, intelligence, intuitiveness and determination. They are—as Hitler desired to build—a masterful breed."

"With that said, would you give this to the young man?" He handed Sistrunk a folded piece of paper, and then continued, "If he is to survive this ordeal—and I believe that he will—I think he will know what to do with this, and how to handle what it brings."

With a wrinkled brow, Sistrunk took the paper from Van Cormack. After that, the two policemen, with firm grips under Van Cormack's frail arms, drug him out the door.

Sistrunk shoved the crumpled paper into his pant pocket and hurriedly stumbled down the dark pathway back to Sonny's pickup. Fortunately, for him, Sonny left his keys dangling from the ignition. He jumped into the truck and followed the speeding emergency vehicles.

Sistrunk followed the gurneys through the ER doors. He explained to the doctor on duty, in between sporadic breaths of anxiety, the events as they unfolded and what he had found in the freezer near Derrick. "I know it's been done with animals, but could it be possible that he was injected with a saline solution and placed in suspended animation?"

"I've never heard of anything like that," the young doctor replied.

"We'll hook him up and very slowly return the blood to his body."

Among the endless tubes and machines', humming sounds, Sistrunk rubbed his hands over and over each other as the procedure progressed. His eyes widened as, next, the physician took two paddles and rubbed them together before delivering Derrick an electric shock. Finally, his heart begun to beat.

Chapter 42 –A Bitter Pill

The following morning Sistrunk felt satisfaction phoning Robert Waites with a follow up clearing the suspicions Waites had about Derrick. The detective was the most stubborn man he'd ever met, but he finally conceded that Derrick was probably not involved in some cult.

Sistrunk said, "Actually, without the kid's talents for decoding these riddles and your photos of the van, I think we'd still be out there looking, and one more person would have been dead. In a way, you partnered with that kid. It took both of you, and your insightfulness, to lead us to the place of the crimes. Huh, probably the last thing you would have ever expected." Silence.

Grinning, Sistrunk clichéd to himself; he knew that remark was a bitter pill to swallow.

Just before he hung up the phone, Waites snorted mentioning the Rolling's case again. Sistrunk figured it was still eating away at him and didn't want to take any chances on letting another sicko get away with victimizing innocent, college kids on his watch. Sistrunk understood...being a cop is tough business.

Later that morning, he received a call from the tending physician. Derrick was showing signs of coming to as Grandma Ma kept her vigil at his bedside. "She's been here all night long," said the doctor. "I'd recommend you allowed him a few more hours of rest before drilling him." By his use of words, Sistrunk wondered if he had past issues with cops. Sistrunk thought he was a bit more sensitive than that; he didn't look at himself as some sort of drill sergeant. "Uh, sure, doc. When do you think I should see him?"

"Doctor, not doc," he replied tersely. "And, I'd recommend a couple more hours of rest."

Now certain of his earlier doubt, Sistrunk replied, "Will do, doctor."

That afternoon, Derrick jerked his head back and forth signaling some alertness, the deputy leaned in closer over the hospital bed, "Can you hear me, Derrick?"

"Yes...yea," the youth responded groggily. "What, what happened, was I in an accident?"

"Not exactly, but you're very lucky, which is more than I can say for the others. There must be an angel in heaven looking over you."

"Lucky, what do you mean? What happened to me? Does my grandmother know where I am?"

"Yes, she was here all night. When the doctor said you were in the clear, he nearly physically forced her out the door, recommending that she go home and get some rest herself. He told her he was concerned about her ending up in the hospital, too. After that remark, she finally gave in. She'll be back later this afternoon."

"What is the last thing you remember?" Sistrunk asked so he knew where to start.

"Uh, I was at the nursing home. I walked into the administrator's office and that was it, blanksville."

Sistrunk nut shelled what took place after that. "I have to hand it to you, Derrick, I don't know how you managed to figure out what these weird poems meant, but they rattled my search companion's memory. After days of hunting, we were headed in the right direction and it turned out our suspect lead us the rest of the way. We found the frozen remains of the other missing people. This guy is one sick dude. And, he's still out there."

Derrick's blue eyes widened. "Still out there," he muttered.

"We've got our sights set on him, Derrick. We'll get him." Sistrunk hoped his confident words would bring the youth a little comfort. "You need to focus on getting better and helping us solve this. So, here's a start. I have another riddle for you. It's from that crazy, old man, the creator, who called himself a spiritualist. He gave me two more stanzas before he was hauled away and booked.

He requested that I pass them onto you."

"What do they say, sir?" Derrick asked in a muffled voice now slightly more alert.

Sistrunk unfolded the note paper and read it to Derrick.

> *"You're no doubt exceptionally bright. I suggest you take closer look at your statue. Believe me, when I say, that there are more hidden clues."*

Beneath the message written were three more stanzas.

"Crimson lines on the statue's base,

Do not symbolize a grandfather's loving embrace,

Witness to a demon's self demise,

He wears the truth beholding a greater surprise,"

"Retaliation is sought to avenge her ancestors' pain,

No blue rose can truly replace a great loss so insane,

She's held a secret so rare so prized,

History will be changed if it's ever realized,"

"Your best friend's girl holds a secret past,

Soon she will face it at long last,

Her mother's fear has suppressed her choice

She's forfeited her freedom, she has no voice,"

Chapter 43—Posthumous Liberation

Days later, Derrick sat quietly at the dining table with the crumpled piece of paper in hand that Van Cormack had scribbled the stanzas on. These proved to be the most challenging so far. Derrick thought the soothsayer was getting revenge delivering a final rhyme that couldn't be figured out, thus shattering Derrick's reputation. But, as Ben once told him, he wasn't a slacker. Think; think, oh, Derrick paused, and then looked up from the paper at *Thorn Boy*. His eyes traced the meandering blood lines on the tiny statue's base. He glanced back down at the stanzas, and he suspected that what Ma was told and believed after all these years was actually a lie.

One of the benefits of being in a small town was everyone was listed in the directory. He needed to know how to get in touch with someone who didn't think he was some, crazy kid with an even crazier notion. Derrick picked up the phone and called his high school guidance councilor; fortunately, he was home. "I'm helping my girlfriend on a school project, and we need an expert we can contact about the details of Hitler's involvement in World War II. Where should I start?"

His teacher answered, "The German Consulate General in Miami."

Derrick thanked him and checked the kitchen clock; the library should be open by now.

An hour later, he was going through a stack of consulate reference documents the librarian handed to him. Patiently, he flipped through them and found a name, number, address, phone number and picture of Jürgen Schmitt. He had begun his career in Foreign Service twenty years ago. The man was tall, blonde, blue eyed and presented a facial bone structure not unlike Derrick's, Aryan.

Back at home, Derrick's convincing tone on the telephone got him further than he expected with the consulate as he struggled to condense Ma's story about *Thorn Boy* and the reason for his call. "I need to know where I can send some evidence to be tested."

"Tested?" replied the German's guttural voice on the other end of the line. "Tested for what?"

"DNA," Derrick responded. "I understand the Europeans have far advanced the scientific progress over the United States, and I have some blood on a statue dating back to World War II. I believe its history would be of interest to your countrymen."

"I see," he responded. Although, Derrick suspected he really didn't, but the man's curiosity was aroused. He continued, "I can give you a name and address of a colleague in Berlin. He speaks English. Write him and tell him that I directed you to contact him. He might be able to assist you. But you need to know that what you're requesting is expensive and will take time. Your petition most likely will not be granted."

Grateful, Derrick hung up and returned to the dining room. He took a needle from Ma's sewing kit and tediously picked at the flecks of dried blood on the statue. Carefully he dropped them into a tiny white wrapper and folded it.

Afterwards, he returned to his upstairs bedroom, removed a larger, more official looking envelop. He then placed the contents and enclosed a letter and photo of the *Thorn Boy* into the self addressed, postage paid envelope, and headed off to the post office mailing it to the German Historical Museum in Berlin.

Ma relished the closeness of family and friends. It was Thanksgiving Day; everything had to be perfect; she didn't see any problem in accomplishing that. After all, this was her entertaining reputation on the line. She thought, *for heaven sakes, a guest from Palm Beach would be in attendance.*

Looking so much like his grandfather, Derrick descended from upstairs and sat expressionless at the table, obviously still unnerved by her pending foreclosure. The moment reminded Ma of when he was a little boy and unhappy about something. Even at a young age, he wanted to control everything, make it all better.

"Now we must hurry and get ready, the guests will be showing up starting at four," she ordered.

The mouthwatering aromas filled the kitchen as Ma leaned over, opened the oven door and checked on her turkey. Like clockwork, she bumped the door shut with her hip, grabbed a large spoon from the overhead rack and dipped it into the gravy; then she raised it to her lips for a quick sampling proclaiming, "This is the best gravy I've every made!"

Emily bounded down the steps announcing, "I'll cut some roses for a few places throughout the house. It will be a real treat; pretending I'm in a French rose garden."

An hour later Derrick sat dutifully with her on the edge of the porch, picking each thorn from every stem. Ma glanced out the window and watched them together. It was so sweet that now he was doing for his girlfriend what he used to do for her. Like Ma and her 'Stubbs', they were a good fit.

Wondering how the evening would unfold, Ma completed her preparations and went upstairs to change. *Anticipation is the best part of life* she thought, putting the final touches on her ensemble. There were the pearl necklace and matching earrings from her late husband that were just the right accent. The time was flying by. Soon the guests would be arriving. She must get back downstairs. It was time; she loved it when people were punctual.

This is going to be one first-class Thanksgiving dinner, thought Ma proudly as she watched through the living room window the first car to pull up the driveway. It was Ben Freeman with Judy and Bernice Johnson. Ben was driving his dad's Cadillac. Ma was looking forward to meeting Judy's mother, such a strong woman.

Once inside her home, filled with commotion, Ma took great delight in watching the four interact once again. Derrick couldn't stop smiling; he was thrilled to see Ben and Judy together again. The glow of joy filled the room. Judy seemed back up to par with her quick wit. The positive energy and sheer happiness exuded from them.

"Follow me," said Ma to Bernice Johnson as she led the way down the back stairs to show her the roses. "Careful," warned Ma pointing toward the ground so Bernice didn't get her shoes caked with Glade's muck. They slowly made their way along the path's edge, out to Derrick's masterpiece grotto at the far end.

As the ladies approached the impressive stone structure, Bernice remarked on the two plaques paying tribute to Derrick's grandfather and father, "What an amazing young man he is to have erected such a remarkable tribute to his family."

Ma turned to Bernice and said, "I have never told anyone this before, but on several occasions I experienced an appearance from Our Lady in this spot."

She replied, "I think that's beautiful. It clearly shows what a special person you are. I believe in miracles. Just look at what happened to my daughter. She was gone, now she's back. My prayers were answered."

Tchelet carefully steered her Bentley with one hand while occasionally glancing down at the hand-written directions, fluttering in the car's air conditioning, in the other. She opted to drive herself and generously gave the chauffer the holiday off to spend with his family. They had such a tough year, and this is what Thanksgiving was all about.

Sitting against the background of sugar cane waving in the breeze was the modest, white frame house with blue trim elevated on cinder blocks. The tires kicked up muck dust depositing it on her beautifully detailed car. Tchelet turned on the wash-wiper, clearing the view through the windshield as she approached. She pulled along side the black Cadillac, turned the ignition off, gathered her purse, a gift—professionally wrapped at her favorite Worth Avenue boutique—and stepped out of the sedan wondering how many guests Mrs. Stabb had invited to her party. With a house full of people, it would be a challenge for her to discretely examine the statue, but she had been faced with more difficult tests in the past.

Inside were sounds of glasses clinking softly and light laughter.

Humble abode, she thought standing on the freshly painted front porch, glancing about before tapping on the wood framed screen door. Moments later, a tall, blonde haired, handsome, young man, with a perfect smile appeared and opened the door. His prominent, Aryan profile immediately drew her into a past she'd sooner forget.

"Hi, welcome; I'm Derrick Stabb, Ma's grandson," he said as politely as any well-bred gentleman she'd ever met in Palm Beach.

She stepped through the doorway and responded with a strained smile. "Good afternoon, I am Tchelet Goldstein-Smith. I met your grandmother at a church social."

"Oh, I remember Ma telling me about you. Grandma Ma, that's what we call her sometimes. Come in, please. Everyone has gathered in the kitchen for some reason. I suppose that's because the food is in there."

Tchelet presented a tight smile. As she followed him through the house, she took a subtle glance at the little statue that sat on the sideboard in the dining room. Her smile quickly diminished as she refocused on her reason for being here. Thoughts of Varda stayed with her, and she'd hoped her mission would not be in vain.

"Ma and Mrs. Johnson are in the rose garden," he said as they entered the room. "In the meantime, allow me to introduce you to my friends." Derrick gestured toward Emily and Ben who acknowledged her with a nod and shook her white-gloved hand.

Tchelet grasped Judy's hand only to have her suddenly yank it back. She addressed the young lady, "You remind me so much of someone I knew many years ago, after the war, back when I lived in Amsterdam." Judy stood motionless.

At that moment the back door flung open, and Ma entered accompanied by another woman. "I am so happy you could join us!" Ma exclaimed with a big smile. "I suppose you already met my, gorgeous grandson and his friends," Ma continued. Derrick blushed.

"Yes I have, thank you," Tchelet responded.

"This is Bernice Johnson, Judy's mother."

Tchelet gazed slyly at her as her past flashed by. The corners of Bernice's red, painted mouth turned slightly upward then she said, "You remind me so much of a friend of my mother's back when I was a little girl. We were living in Holland."

"Amsterdam?" questioned Tchelet.

"Yes," Replied Bernice.

Déjà voo, thought Tchelet.

Redirecting her attention, she took in every detail of the picturesque interior and complimented her hostess on how quaint her home was.

Ma offered, "You don't need to have a lot of money to make something look good. Keep it simple and clean is my motto."

Tchelet thought, *no, unless all one wants is simple and clean. Money buys options—like a cleaning staff.*

The smell of just baked apple pie permeated the kitchen. With grace, Ma opened the oven door and removed the picture-perfect confection, suitable for a magazine cover. "Part of being the perfect hostess is not looking like any effort was made—everything just magically appears."

Tchelet checked herself in a wall mirror; yes, the smile was still there, and then she thought, *a personal chef makes it effortless, too.*

Everything was served on white china plates with fresh linen napkins; Tchelet, pleasantly surprised, half expected paper plates.

After dinner, Tchelet requested, "I'd like to hear about more your little statue, Mrs. Stabb."

"Here we go again," remarked Derrick. "She jumps at the chance to tell the story."

"Well," Ma said, pausing for a moment seeming to gather her thoughts. "My husband, Derrick's granddaddy's army buddy, actually we called him Corny, but he was Cornelius Hicks. He brought the statue back to me after the war."

Tchelet fought a tendency to gasp; she thought, *Cornelius, he sure got around; she should have known that somehow he'd be involved.*

She rose from her chair and approached the statue. She turned back to her hostess.

"May I?" she addressed Grandma Ma.

"Certainly," Ma responded smiling approvingly.

Tchelet picked up the statue and ran her fingers over its surface, studying every crease and crevasse on its small surface. "What a beautiful remembrance this is," she remarked carefully turning the sculpture over to examine its underside. *There they were*. She thought. What she and Varda had been seeking for nearly sixty years, the marks.

Tchelet, clutching the statue, closed her eyes momentarily and envisioned the last time she'd set eyes on it just before they were rushed from their Berlin home. It all happened so suddenly; her only clear memory was of her father holding the statue.

Ma asked, "Tchelet, dear are you alright?" The others sat in silence in the flickering candlelight, exchanging glances, awaiting her response.

Tears began to stream from her delicate face trickling onto the statue she gripped. Tchelet took a deep breath and labored to compose herself. Internally, she was fighting to comprehend everything that had been stolen from her.

Ma stood from her place setting and approached her from behind. She placed her hands gently on Tchelet's shoulders. "Tell me what's wrong, dear."

"Mrs. Stabb, you have your story about *Thorn Boy*, may I tell you mine?"

Grandma Ma quickly removed her hands. "Yes, we'd all like to hear it. I'm sure," she said, as she turned encouraging the others approval seated around the table.

Tchelet rejoined the group bringing the statue with her placing it in the center.

"This statue is mine."

"Yours?" Ma questioned.

"*Thorn Boy* was a gift to me and my sister from our father.

We were planning our bat mitzvahs. Since we were so close in age, a joint celebration seemed appropriate although we would each have our own day. They would just be back-to-back. Our beloved father, a very successful businessman in Berlin, commissioned a local goldsmith to cast a statue of our favorite work of art, Spinario, or Boy with Thorn. You see, of all the works of art we saw when we visited the Palazzo dei Conservatori in Rome that year, we were captivated by the bronze statue of the young boy who sat stoically, carefully removing a thorn from his foot. There was something about its charm that enticed us. It was all we talked about for days, and we would have brought it home if the museum would have allowed it.

Wanting to do something very special for us, he decided that this was it. But this statue would be truly unique to us, for it would have the marks in Hebrew bearing our names, stamped on the underside by the goldsmith." She turned the underside of the statue toward the guests.

"The marks translated into the meaning of our names, Tchelet, for blue, and Varda's, for rose."

"Blue Rose."

Tchelet reached for her handbag that sat on the side board and opened it. She removed a newspaper clipping, yellowed and dog-eared from age. The society page article was in German, but clearly showed two young girls at their celebration, sitting on either side of the beautiful little statue. The caption below read their names, location and date.

After looking at the aged photo, Ma inquired, "But, dear, this statue in the picture is gold, the one I have is white."

Tchelet reached back into her handbag and removed a nail file. She took the edge of the sharp instrument and scraped the back of the statue, peeling a fine line of white paint. She did it again and again exposing a gleaming surface.

"Our father had this statue created for us of pure eighteen karat gold. It was a symbol of his love for us. Although he would tell us that we were worth our weight in gold, this was all he could afford; still a very valuable gift, about $50,000. He had it painted to protect it during the invasion. Mrs. Stabb, your brave husband brought this back home probably as a souvenir. My sister and I have been looking for it ever since, it meant everything to us."

Emily glanced over to Derrick and nodded.

Derrick removed himself from the table and left the room returning a few minutes with a note pad. He flipped it open and tossed it into the table's center next to *Thorn Boy*. Before Tchelet were the stanzas Van Cormack recited.

"Perched on a stone,"

"Attending to a need,"

"A covering hides,"

"What lies beneath,"

"Claimed by many,"

"A history untold,"

"His heirs are near,"

"Desired to behold,"

"A thorn boy's past is about to unfold.

The Symbols reveal his true owners are told.

Upside down they subtly appear

Blue roses are the connection they hold dear.

"Where did you get these?" Tchelet inquired.

Bernice Johnson answered, "A spiritualist I'd met after reading my daughter's diary. As it turned out he had more to do with all of this than any of us imagined."

"Mother, you read my diary?" Judy asked wide eyed.

"I was desperate, Judy. Sorry. I would have done anything to get you back."

"Then you know," Judy said with a wry look.

"Judy, not here," her mother pleaded.

"Why not, Mother. Obviously, we're not holding back any secrets tonight. Why shouldn't my friends know of my periods of depression and those awful panic attacks you told me were just in my head. These women here are suffering; why shouldn't we suffer along with them?"

"Well, well", said Ma. "It looks like you have found what is rightfully yours, Tchelet."

Judy leaped from her seat, "You can't just give up something that you've treasured all of these years, Mrs. Stabb. This is your only tangible link to your husband."

"I know, but I cannot, in clear conscience, keep what is not mine."

Judy looked back at Tchelet. "This isn't fair. She invited you here; she thought she'd befriended you, and this is how you treat her? You plotted to take this. You suspected the first time you were here that *Thorn Boy* was yours. That's why you manipulated an invitation out of Ma. Is this how *you* people live? You think you have a right to everything."

"Judy, what's gotten into you?" said Bernice. "I'm sorry, I'm so sorry, everybody. It seems my daughter has not fully recovered from her ordeal."

Judy stood responding, "For your information, it is because of my "ordeal", as you call it, I've decided to stand up and speak my mind. I've suppressed these feeling for long enough." At that, she turned and marched out of the room.

Fumbling for words, Bernice Johnson said, "Again, I'm sorry. Judy needs some professional help."

Tchelet sat straight. In silence, she looked around the table at five remaining sets of eyes glaring at her, feeling not quite certain that she would be able to carry out her mission. She thought of Varda and her sweetness.

She looked back at Ma, and then said, "Yes, I admit I was fully prepared to fight anyone tooth and nail for this once I found it. However, I feel there is something that I need to do for you."

Again, Tchelet reached into her hand bag, she removed her checkbook, flipped it open and signed a blank check. She tore the document from its binding, and handed it to Ma.

"Please fill in any amount you wish. That young lady is right, everything comes at a cost, and I realize that this has cost you dearly. I could have spent a great deal of time and money recovering him, but you made it possible, and for that I owe you."

"I am leaving for Europe in a couple of days. Please keep the statue a while longer."

Ma gazed at the figurine in the table's center and then back up at her grandson. "See, Derrick, miracles do happen; my home is saved!" She looked upward. "Stubbs, my husband, must be looking down; he probably never imagined that he would once again be a liberator." She paused, and then continued, "posthumously."

Chapter 44—The Power Of Revenge

***How** would he tell her?* Cornelius contemplated. His sweaty palms nervously gripped the steering wheel inching the van alongside the curb of a narrow, side street. He knew the reputation of the Palm Beach Police for stopping service vehicles in town after working hours. Tchelet warned him about the unwritten rule, without written permission from their boss, workers must be off the Island after six.

Suspecting he'd be recognized by the cops, he reached behind the seat, rifled inside a paper bag and pulled out a wig, blouse, heavily padded bra, a skirt and pair of high heels. He exited the van, looked up and down the quiet road and then quietly clicked the door closed. He thought it best to walk the next few blocks stopping behind a Jasmine vine covered, wall to make a quick change. After ditching his bloody, dirty lab coat and pants, he then headed toward a side entrance leading into the condo's garage.

Desperate, but convinced he'd see their blue rose to fruition, there was no one else to turn to except Tchelet. He hoped she would understand. It would require them making a new plan, but he would convince her that he could recover and start fresh someplace else. He'd done it before.

Minutes later, he approached the perfect spot to wait; a vantage point, where he hunkered down in between the flourishing, pittosporum hedge and the condominium's sea wall waiting until she returned home. Through its woody branches, he could peer at the fancy cars arriving and departing from the driveway leading into the garage beneath the prestigious residences.

He quickly ducked down, rustling the plant's green leaves as a cop's cruiser slowly rolled past the driveway. His heart pounded. He looked upward and took a deep breath. The ocean breeze felt good on his sunburned skin. Rays of the setting sun flickered through the palm tree's waving fronds in the darkening sky, overhead.

Finally, she arrived. He emerged from behind the plants, awkwardly tiptoeing through the grass careful not to sink a shoe heel into the soft, uneven, recently laid sod. Once on pavement, he slinked along the inner wall of the garage, entering after the last of several cars pasted. He watched from the shadows as Tchelet pulled the Bentley into her, designated, parking spot. The engine's hum echoed against the concrete walls. Cornelius waited until the car went silent and then approached her carefully from behind a Rolls Royce positioned next to her. He caught a glimpse of himself in the tinted windows and thought his costume was rather clever.

She jerked from his sudden appearance and leaned back against her car's muck dust-covered side putting her hand over her heart. Quickly regaining her composure, she looked about to see if anyone had noticed them. "You smell like a pig. What is this mess you're wearing?" The disguise would have fooled everyone else, but Tchelet was more clever than most.

"Why are you here?" she drilled him in a restrained voice, demanding answers. Then, grabbing his arm, she ushered, what appeared to be a rather unattractive, tall woman to the service elevator. Their heels clicked against the concrete floor. Fortunately, they appeared to be the only ones around. "There are too many, nosy neighbors, and this would be a tough one to explain," she said with an angry shake of her head. She whispered, "In case someone spies us, I'll have to tell them I'm interviewing a new maid. Now, why are the police after you?"

As the elevator climbed, he confessed what had happened days ago. "I've been hiding from the cops in the swamp, camping out in my van. I had no where to go."

She wrinkled her brow in an effort to comprehend what he was telling her. The doors opened up in the foyer and then closed behind them again. Once inside the condo's sound proof walls, she unleashed her fury on him. "You're a fool! No amount of explaining can justify why you allowed someone in the laboratory. Everything is ruined! Everything!"

Cornelius followed her inside the apartment determined to make her understand why he did it. "I was trying to prove to Stanley that he wasn't the only one who succeeded. I was sick of his condescending attitude. I was trying to show him that I was worthy of success, too. I was going be the one to create something big, really, really big."

"What in the hell are you talking about, Stanley, who is Stanley, and why was he in the lab?" Cornelius hesitated. Would she understand, or would she laugh at him, just as Stanley always had?

He shouted, "He's my twin, I've told you about him, the Professor." He confessed, his words coming at a rush, "He was always better, smarter than me. I've spent my career proving to him that I could be successful. I could create something that the world would take notice. He would take notice. I-I just wanted to show him."

Cornelius shrank back as Tchelet's expression twisted, morphing from puzzled to disbelieve, to angry and then her rage exploded. "You've sabotaged our project with your silly idea of proving something. God! Why did I get suckered into this?" She threw her arms into the air and swung hard backhanding his, tortured face.

Cornelius whipped a hand to his stinging cheek. He crouched as her voice continued to excoriate him. "I'll tell you why, Cornelius; because my parents, my people died on account of the idea that they didn't fit the image for the 'Master Race'. I swore on their graves that I would seek retribution. That's why I agreed to fund the venture, knowing every time I held a blue rose, every time a blossom was sold, admired and cherished around the world, it justified sacrificing their Aryan souls. Just like the Nazis justifying murdering six million of *my* people."

Tchelet stared at the botanist quivering before her, wanting nothing more that to smash his ugly, scarred face.

Gradually, her tone faded replaced by his comforting mantra, "Cornelius is strong, Cornelius is worthy, Cornelius is powerful", replaying over and over, in his head. When she finally paused for a breath, the botanist stood and faced her. In a light and feminine voice he asked. "Who are you? Where am I? "

Tchelet shook her head. "What!" she shrieked. "What in the hell are you doing, trying to fool me? It won't work, Cornelius Hicks. You're not getting away with this charade. We're in this together, and if I go down, you go down with me."

"Cornelius?" He turned a mild, puzzling expression to her. "No, no, my name is Stanley Hicks. How do you know my brother?"

"You are crazy!" she realized in disgust. How had she ever been stupid enough to partner up with someone like him? She speedily walked away toward her Louis XVI desk where they reviewed his progress a few weeks earlier. She turned back to him. "You're a sick man, whatever your name is." She slammed both hands on top of the desk listening to more of his idiot garble.

His eyes widened. "Lady, I don't know what you're talking about. You're the sick one. I've never seen you before in my life."

Tchelet covered her ears with both hands and shook her head back and forth. She looked up, grabbed a heavy, crystal paperweight from the desk and hurled it striking him in his solar plexus. He doubled over as the weight crashed and shattered against the marble floor.

Tchelet fought to deal with what she was seeing as she watched him regain, and, once again, Cornelius returned. In a booming voice he cried, "You bitch! You're gonna join all of those ancestors soon."

Tchelet opened the desk drawer, removed her revolver and steadily drew it on him. Suddenly a pelican crashed into the window, causing the winded bird to land on the balcony's floor. Tchelet turned, flabbergasted by the noise and flapping commotion. Cornelius, quick to react, took advantage and lunged for her gun.

One of the large sliding glass doors was open. They struggled through it onto the balcony that overlooked a serene ocean. If she fired the gun, building security would be at her door in minutes. She had to do it. She couldn't let him get ahold of it.

He finally broke the weapon from her grip after slamming her wrist, twice, against the balcony's, concrete railing. Wrathfully, Tchelet backhanded him again across his mutilated face with her other hand, so hard his wig flew off sailing into the night sky. Her diamond ring left a deep gash.

Cornelius hatefully reacted, picking up the petite woman in the same fashion he hauled Derrick's unencumbered body from the office and threw her over the balcony's railing, trailing his hair piece onto the manicured lawn below.

For a few seconds, he took deep breathes, grasping the railing and looked over it down at the swimming pool's, reflective water and massive, concrete apron surrounding it, knowing her body was somewhere down there, and he needed to be somewhere else, now.

He descended down the elevator. The doors whooshed open; he cautiously peered out and looked both ways. "Whew," he murmured, the expansive lobby was unoccupied. The hour was late and most Palm Beachers were already tucked in.

He made his way toward a door with an engraved brass plate marked *SERVICE CLOSET*. He took refuge there for several minutes, peering through a crack. He sighed. *Now, or never,* he thought. He inched out into the foyer and crept along, near the floor, past six, massive marble columns behind the security desk. The guard's attention was occupied taking a phone call. Past the desk, he paused and peered through a tiny window in a door that led into the garage. All clear.

Yards away from the building, he kicked off his heels tossing them into a trash can neatly positioned behind by a perfectly trimmed, Eugenia hedge. The van was just a couple of blocks. As swiftly as his stocking feet could run, occasionally turning back to see if anyone was following, he approached, opened the rickety door with a squeak and climbed in. A light rain began to fall. He cranked the engine and engaged the wipers smearing dirt across the windshield, momentarily obscuring his view. He turned the wipers' knob to a faster speed. He had to get off the Island. Struggling to see through the smeared windshield, he navigated a few blocks south along Ocean Blvd.

Minutes later, a cop's flashing blue and red lights signaled for him to pull over. "Damn it!" he said out loud striking the steer wheel with is hand, remembering. "That tail light, I knew that I should have had it fixed."

Cornelius's heart raced as he floored the gas pedal. He made a sharp right turn, skidding on the wet pavement onto Royal Palm Way, nearly missing a few tables and chairs for outdoor seating. He rapidly headed west toward the middle bridge, which was just a mile, or so, away. Knowing the cops would radio ahead and raise the bridge, he hoped he could get across. In West Palm, he plotted to hide in the maze of warehouses on the other side of the waterway.

He gunned the engine with the police in hot pursuit. Just ahead, he saw the bridge beginning to rise. Did the cops get the better of him, or was it a boat, hopefully a small one? Why don't these, rich people keep their big ass yachts docked long enough for me to get the hell out of here?

Confident he would make the bridge before it fully opened, he gripped the steering wheel in the ten and two positions and set his sights on the road ahead. Cornelius floored the gas pedal soaring past the Society of the Four Arts garden and building complex. On his tail, the screaming siren of the cop's car reverberated against the tall, bank buildings that lined the street. He was almost there.

The bridge's caution gates had lowered, but he ignored them and crashed his bumper through sending splintered pieces of wood and metal flying overhead. He was feet from the opening confident he could jump it. Freedom was awaiting him on the other side.

Unexpectedly, the bridge's span halted, and then began to close unevenly; Cornelius was staring straight ahead at the blunt end of the bridge's other side. He slammed his nylon covered foot against the break pedal but couldn't stop in time. The van skidded to the opening and hit propelling his chest against the steering wheel. His padded bra absorbed some of the impact. He rocketed back against the seat, gasped, took a deep breath and felt shooting pains across his ribs. Winded, he flung open the driver's door and hurriedly two-stepped toward the bridge's sidewalk opening hoping to jump it. His stockings slipped on the road's, wet surface sending him to the ground, skidding toward the opening. His skirt caught on the sidewalk's, jagged, metal edge as his lower body fell through the space; now his feet dangled above the dark, brackish water.

Exhausted, he struggled to get his waist through the opening but his hands kept slipping on the wet pavement. He took one last gasp, looked up as the bridge's metal teeth slowly met, and cried, "Cornelius is strong, Cornelius is worthy, Cornelius is powerful."

Chapter 45—Family History

UNIVERSITY OF FLORIDA

6 AM

Ugh, that alarm clock.

Derrick reached over Emily and tapped the snooze button, then rubbed his eyes struggling to wake up. He had class this morning and was trying to put all of the madness behind him focusing on his two passions...horticulture and Emily.

Late yesterday, he received a memo, slipped under his dorm door, to stop by the dean's office. After all that had happened, he anticipated the obvious...a change in professors. What else?

He pulled on his favorite pair of blue jeans, slipped on a black tee shirt and a U of F sweatshirt, kissed Emily on her forehead and headed for the door. She stirred a bit and opened her eyes. He said to her softly, "You stay and sleep awhile longer."

He carefully closed the heavy, wooden door and headed down the stairway. Winter had arrived early with the brisk, morning air hitting him smack dab in the face. The administrative offices were midway between his dorm and Fifield Hall. He yanked open the metal double door with a grunt. The fresh faced receptionist greeted Derrick with a smile. "He's waiting for you, Derrick."

After Derrick entered through the frosted glass door to the dean's office, he immediately noticed the microscope on his desk top. The shimmering, engraved plate on its side made no mistake as to whom it once belonged. The dean stood next to it holding a paper.

"Stanley Hicks had this notarized document in his file leaving this piece of equipment to you should anything ever happen to him."

Mouth agape, Derrick said, "Why?"

"Apparently he felt you would be the right person to make the best use of his most valued possession. It's without question he thought very highly of you."

"I don't know what to say."

"There really isn't anything for you to say. I would suggest honoring the man's wishes by doing your best work with it."

Derrick paused for a moment and then turned back toward the dean and said, "You know, it's impossible to comprehend someone's insanity. I can't stop thinking about Dr. Hicks and what had happened to this brilliant man that led him down such a destructive path. Was it the fire, was it his ego, was it his brilliance, was it fear, or maybe it all of those things? My Grandma Ma said, 'It's the emotions you hold deep in your heart that rule your life. Any choice that is rooted in fear—in the end—is always the wrong choice.'"

Derrick took a deep breath, hoisted the heavy microscope and carefully replaced it in its padded case.

"Thank you," he said after clearing his throat.

In his dorm room, Derrick set the case with his new acquisition inside on the small desk where he found Emily's note. *See you later tonight, babe.* He smiled at the squiggly loops she made at the end of each word.

Wondering if his much anticipated response had arrived from Europe, he eagerly ran back down the steps to the bank of mailboxes near the entrance and unlocked the door to his mailbox. His heart began to race; he glanced into the box and sighed, finally, the letter he had expected arrived from the German Historical Museum.

Anxiously, he tore into the beige, official looking envelop and carefully read it's contents.

He pondered the information while tapping the edge of the stationary against his hand. Derrick wasn't sure how to approach his best friend, Ben, and his new fiancé, Judy, or if he should at all.

The news he held in his hand offered some explanation about Judy's behavior. Ben confessed her mood swings, bouts of depression and even panic attacks. Could it be that her heritage haunted her? Could the actions of her ancestors have inflicted emotional and physical pain on her to the point of possibly destroying her own life? And, a bigger question, if so, can she heel? Should he intervene? Could she resume the ranks of people with content lives, or must she live with this inner conflict forever?

Some things are best left unsaid. There were so many things about *his* Father's past that he would have liked to know. Some people don't care about their family's history, but Judy and Bernice Johnson's family history wasn't *like* most peoples'.

Chapter 46—Unbreakable Bonds

Ma awoke and sat on the edge of the bed thinking of her, fallen soldier. If he were here, she'd have so many questions to ask. Could he have predicted the future, somehow know that she'd be in a financial mess? Why did he take *Thorn Boy* in the first place? Were his actions only because of her love for art, or something more? Questions that could only be answered the next time when they met.

She stood, feeling dizzy, pulled her nightgown around her snuggly and ambled to the bathroom's medicine cabinet. Her doctor prescribed "a little pill" he said would help ease "the spells" she had frequently experienced.

She returned to her bedside and sat. Minutes later, she felt a little better; she slowly descended the stairs now focused on her coffee percolator. On the counter was the check Tchelet left Thanksgiving night. She picked it up and wondered what amount she should fill in, enough to cover the bills, or more? What amount would be enough to replace *Thorn Boy*? Ma reached for a pen and completed the signed document. Satisfied.

She stepped onto the back porch holding a coffee cup in one hand and her statue in the other. Gazing out over the rows of beautiful roses, she took the last sip, set it down, and preceded toward the garden's grotto with a firm hold on her, beloved statue wondering if the lady would appear to her again. No, instead blurry images of blue roses were presented in all directions before her.

Facing the grotto, Ma sat on the stone bench; the dizzy spell returned and intensified. She turned, let out a deep sigh, and placed *Thorn Boy* on the bench. Sitting next to their little statue was Stubbs dressed in his army uniform. He smiled at her, reassurance that what she had done was right. She no longer should question her actions about Rodney, about borrowing against their house, about anything. He reached out to her, and she took his hand. The spell subsided, and she was gone.

BACK AT HOME ON CHRISTMAS BREAK

Derrick took her hand lovingly and walked Emily toward the end of the rose garden. The grotto, he built, was silhouetted against the late afternoon, blue sky. Feather shaped forms of white, soft, puffy clouds overhead contrasted with the heavy stone monument as mockingbirds greeted them in song.

Emily enjoyed the touch of Derrick's strong hand as it gently enveloped hers. She looked up into his clear blue eyes and smiled. "Derrick, I know that this is a very difficult time losing Grandma Ma so unexpectedly. She was a beautiful woman."

He responded head tilted as tears meandered down his cheeks. He wiped them away with the back of his hand and said, "Her doctor said there were signs of earlier strokes; guess that explained her visions of blue roses and the Madonna. Ma was such a strong person she wouldn't have shown any weakness, probably fearing that I'd abandon my studies to take care of her, which, of course, I would have."

Emily rubbed his back and offered in a tone of condolence, "You can find peace in knowing that she died in the place she loved most, right here in her garden among these beautiful roses." As the words left her lips, she sensed they brought him little comfort.

They traversed through the rows of white, fragrant rose bushes. Emily began to playfully swing their cupped hands back and forth as she did a little dance kicking up the rich muck. Derrick looked at her and smiled. "I know I've been withdrawn over the past several days, but I want to say thanks for sticking with me through all of this, Emily. There really wasn't anybody else, besides Ben, who I could have turned to."

Emily paused, squeezed Derrick's hand a little harder and pondered her words before she spoke.

"That day I saw you on campus, my intuition said that's a guy I want to know. And, my intuition wasn't wrong. You only mentioned the darkness, but what about the love, the light, the goodness? I'm getting really deep, I know, but it was how you handled all of that with grace, well, most of the time. You were under a lot of pressure. I think most guys would have freaked, gotten drunk or drugged out, but you faced the darkness head on. You weren't afraid, or at least you didn't show it. You stuck by Ben and Judy and her Mom when all of the weirdness was surrounding you. The cops, that whole cult business, talk about pressure. And, as they say in the movies, 'We made it through the hard part first.' I think that I might be in this for the long haul. What do you think?"

Derrick glanced back at the grotto and took a deep breath expanding his chest beyond its usual impressive size. He raised Emily's hand and kissed it. A simple gesture that spoke more than any words he could say to her.

Emily was influenced by Grandma Ma over the short period of time she knew her. She set the bar high for the next woman in Derrick's life. "Are you going to be alright going the Ben and Judy's engagement party tonight?"

He hesitated for a moment and said looking her straight in the eye, "There's something else I want to tell you."

Emily's insecurity, once again, wrapped around her squeezing her gut; she had to get over thinking the worst every time he uttered words of concern. She took a deep gulp. "Yes."

"You might think that what I'm telling you is real weird especially after all that's happed with Ma's statue."

Emily's anxiety lessened a bit; she stopped clenching her jaw. At least it was about an inanimate object. She tiled her head and questioned, "*Thorn Boy*?"

"I've been thinking really hard about this, and, well, after witnessing Judy's emotional attachment to the statue that night when she first saw it, her curiosity, and then later defending Ma's ownership when that woman wanted to take it, I decided to give *Thorn Boy* to Ben and Judy."

Emily pursed her lips and stared a puzzled look at her boyfriend. "But, Derrick, your Grandfather, his blood is on the statue, I don't mean to second guess you, but don't you think Ma would *really* want you to keep it in the family, pass it down. What about it its value? Gold, it must be worth a fortune! Seems to me that what happened Thanksgiving night secured your right to—"

"—and my right to do with it as I see best," he interrupted. "Sorry babe, I didn't mean to cut you off like that, but I have my reasons."

"What reasons?" she asked as the curiosity mounted inside her.

"I'd rather wait and tell you all together tonight. Sorry, again, for the secrecy, but I have to choose my words carefully. Besides, I don't care about its value. It's not like I'd melt the thing down. I want you to know that I am doing this of my own free will. My interest in the statue was because of Ma's connection to Granddaddy through it, but now that's changed, not only because of her passing, but because of something deeper."

Bernice Johnson was grateful that Judy hadn't had any incidents since her ordeal; she half expected Judy's panic attacks and depression to amplify after going through what she went through. She felt blessed as she busied herself clearing the table after her special, German feast. Ben, Judy, Emily and Derrick retired to the sofa in the living room.

A Christmas tree was positioned in front of the large picture window. Red velvet bows, various hand-blown ornaments and multicolored lights festooned it bathing the room in a warm glow.

Derrick, always able to carry a conversation, inquired of Bernice after she entered the room, "Where did you learn to prepare such delicious, authentic, German cuisine?"

"My Mother," she responded. "She was a wonderful cook."

Derrick continued with the questions, "Where did you live?"

Bernice struggled with an uneasy feeling when the conversation focused on her past. She never liked to talk about it. She ignored the question and faced her daughter inquiring, “Judy, have you and Ben set a date?”

“No, Mother, it’s no rush. We’ll take our time. All I know now is that Emily is doing our flowers.”

Bernice faced Emily and eagerly inquired, “What kind of flowers are you planning on using?”

Emily put her hands in the air. “We haven’t gotten that far, but Judy was emphatic that there wouldn’t be a blue rose within ten miles. Fine with me, I said, I hate painting flowers.”

Derrick’s persistent curiosity—one of his trademark qualities—brought the conversation back to food and German ancestry. “Did you eat primarily German food, or did your mother prepare other types of dishes?”

“Yes, and I have a lovely *French* dessert planned.” It was an opportunity for her to spring to her feet and head back into the kitchen. Moments later, Bernice returned with a tray of petite fours. “I have coffee brewing.” She continued, “Judy, I suppose this would be the perfect time to open the beautifully wrapped gift Derrick brought you and Ben.”

Judy turned in the direction of Emily and Derrick. “You guys, you didn’t have to bring anything.” She picked up the gift lifting it up and down. “Well, for such a small box it sure is heavy. What’s in here a brick of gold?” Ben smiled as he sat next to Judy while she ripped through the ribbon and paper. The heavy clear packing tape didn’t hinder Judy from her curiosity. “Mother, would you grab a pair of scissors for me? You guys, we haven’t even started planning this yet.” Moments later, Bernice returned with the requested tool, and Judy pierced the clear packing tape with a pop. She reached in and pulled an object mummy wrapped in bubbled plastic. “God Derrick, the way you have this wrapped, this thing must be worth a fortune!” She exclaimed with humor and excitement as she took the scissors and determinedly broke open the covering.

Resting on her lap, as the final pieces of plastic came off the object, Judy halted. She brought her hands to her face placing her fingertips on each of her delicate cheeks.

The room fell silent. She picked up the statue and held it close to her chest. "Oh my, Derrick, why, why would you give this to me?"

He reached inside his coat pocket and pulled out a small, beige colored envelope. On it the return address was clearly marked, GERMAN HISTORICAL MUSEUM, BERLIN.

"What's this?" inquired Ben.

"Since all of this madness had transpired, I've been doing a little detective work. You know how I love solving puzzles, Ben, especially where history is concerned."

Derrick removed the letter from the envelope and handed it to Bernice. She began to visibly tremble. For the first time in her life she was faced with her past, present and future all at once. The feeling was almost more than she could handle, nearly trumping the dreadful thoughts that went through her head when Judy was missing.

Derrick said, "This letter confirmed an exact DNA match between that of Judy and Adolph Hitler. The blood stains on *Thorn Boy* are those of the Führer. The museum officials, who substantiated this, ascertained the statue must have been on the desk at the time he shot himself."

"DNA?" questioned Ben.

"Yes, a new science, much more advance in Europe. It links people through their blood lines. I contacted the German Consulate in Miami and got in touch with the authorities at the museum. I picked a few tiny samples of blood, which we had always thought was Granddad's, from the statue and sent them off to the museum's laboratory in Berlin, along with another sample, a tissue, Judy used at Grandma Ma's Thanksgiving night."

Bernice composed, gracefully rose from her chair. Eyes forward, without saying a word, she made her way upstairs, then returned a few minutes later with a small, wooden box unfamiliar to her daughter.

"What is that Mother?"

She unlatched it and carefully lifted the lid. Inside was a locket, several aged photos and a number of letters neatly bound with rubber bands.

She removed the locket and handed it to Judy. With a perplexed expression, she took and opened it. Inside were small, time worn, but two clearly identifiable black and white photos.

They were of Hitler and Eva Braun. Mrs. Johnson confessed. "These are my parents. My mother survived Berlin's invasion and the war."

"She obviously didn't take the cyanide capsule. Since so much mystery surrounding Hitler's death, it was easy for my mother to create a new identity in Amsterdam. The woman who assisted and protected her until after I was born was Tchelet Goldstein. She set my mother up in an apartment and supported her until she could get a job and sustain us. The reason she did this still remains a mystery. I like to think that it was from the goodness in her heart, but, according to Mother, she was the type of woman who always had her own agenda. Derrick, when I met her at your grandmother's Thanksgiving night, she wouldn't have recognized me as an adult, but I knew who she was. The events that unfolded there that evening were shocking to everybody but me. Tchelet was generous but cunning. She was a woman who would die before she failed."

Judy stood and faced her mother. "Mother, this explains it. I'm convinced this explains my condition, my behavior. I've been struggling with this dark, genetic, karma my whole life. You saw me suffering. You medicated me to deal with the depression and those awful panic attacks. At times, I thought I was going crazy. I've carried this with me all along and tried as hard as I could, alone, to rid myself of it. Mother, you thought you could wish it away. 'Ignore it', you said. If anybody asked why I was in one of my moods, you told me I should say 'it's none of their businesses.'"

Judy tossed the statue to Derrick; he grabbed it with both hands. "Take *Thorn Boy* back, Derrick. I don't want it!" She gasped; then Judy clutched her chest and collapsed to the floor.

Ben leaned over her. "Judy, my God!" He looked back up in horror at Bernice. "I think she's had a heart attack!"

"Stand back!" Derrick shouted. Bernice stood over him as Derrick had began chest compressions. He turned to her. "Mrs. Johnson, call an ambulance!"

Derrick, Ben, Emily, and Bernice Johnson stood together as the doctor entered the hospital's, cardiac care waiting room. "Who administered CPR?" he inquired.

"I did," Derrick answered.

"You saved her life. She will be able to see you in a few minutes, Mrs. Johnson, but we're keeping her here for a few days. I'll be back."

Mrs. Johnson turned toward Derrick. "I want to thank you not only for what you did tonight—saving my daughter's life, again—but for forcing me to face something I have tried to ignore and feared my whole life. At first, I didn't buy into this dark energy, genetic karma nonsense, but now, well. I now know that what we hold in our hearts can emerge physically with disastrous consequences. It makes sense that illnesses are referred to as dis-ease. Judy is proof."

She paused looking at the floor, and then continued, "This second chance is a gift. When Judy is well enough, we will start addressing this issue together, beginning with better understanding of something that's foreign to me. I know it won't be easy, but she's my daughter, I love her and I want her to be happy. Hopefully, there is therapy that can help us."

Bernice turned toward Ben. "Ben, I hope you will not abandon Judy. She's not an evil person, just one that carries the sinister burden of her ancestor."

Derrick concluded, "I believe Judy is everything that symbolizes goodness and purity, inside and out. Ben and Judy have an unbreakable bond. She was placed on this earth to do good work, which was why her life had been spared. You have been given a second chance, and I pray that you're all going to be okay."

The doctor reentered the room. "She's alert. You can see her for a few minutes."

Bernice turned back to Ben, extended her hand and said. "Are you coming?"

Before they exited through the intensive care doors, Bernice turned back to Derrick, smiled and said, You're right, Derrick; we *are* going to be okay."

Epilogue

CHRISTMAS DAY

It was midmorning as Derrick sat at the dining room table thinking of Ma while captured by *Thorn Boy's* shimmering gold service. He had the white paint removed. The radio in the kitchen played Elvis singing *Blue Christmas.* He heard the steps creak as Emily bounced down the stairs and approached him from behind wrapping her willowy arms around his neck. "When are you supposed to go and pick him up?" she inquired softly into his ear.

He turned toward her. "The hospital said he would be discharged at noon."

Emily looked up at the clock on the radio. "It's almost time. I'd offer to go with you, but I think this is something you should do on your own. I can get lunch together for when you two get back."

Derrick hopped into his pickup and made his way to Glades Memorial grateful that Rodney had made a full recovery. As mysteriously as his disease came, it went. Derrick's faith proclaimed it a miracle. His scientific mind said something else.

He passed a wide variety of holiday decorations in route. He could never figure out why people displayed those plastic snowmen on lawns and deer with Santa's sleigh on rooftops when it was Florida, and there wasn't a speck of snow anywhere.

He smiled, remembering that Rodney loved them. The snowman was his favorite. He begged Ma to get one when he was a little boy. She relented.

It was so tacky, but he insisted on dragging it down from the attic after every Thanksgiving eager to display it.

After he'd gotten sick, Ma finally threw the faded, dingy thing away.

He pulled up in front of the hospital doors under the portico. Sitting on the bench with his knees together neatly dressed in a flannel shirt and corduroys was his little brother. His thick, blonde hair tossed in the breeze as he smiled a bright and perfect smile at Derrick's arrival in such a way that reminded him of Ma.

Derrick reached over and cranked down the truck's passenger side window calling out, "Hey bud, you ready?"

Rodney picked up his small, vinyl sided suitcase, tossed it onto the truck's bed and opened the passenger door. "Thanks for coming to get me, Derrick."

"No problem man, that's what brothers are for." He said poignantly, placing his hand on Rodney's shoulder, smiling. "This is how Ma would want it, us together."

Derrick maneuvered the pickup down the circular drive. As he turned onto the road heading home he said, "Rodney, I'll be back at school after New Year's. I'm trusting you with *Thorn Boy*."

ABOUT THE AUTHOR

John Klingel AAF, AIFD, PFCI (photographed with his Thorn Boy statue) began his career in 1973 at his hometown florist in Southern Indiana. Since that time, he has owned a retail shop, traveled to Amsterdam as a guest of the Holland Flower Council, judged the Interflora World Cup Design Competition in Shanghai and has taught students worldwide. He lives in Palm Beach County with his camera shy dog, Felix and continues inspiring lovers of flowers. His motto is: Imagine...Create...Believe...

Visit his website at www.centerforfloralstudies.com

Made in the USA
Charleston, SC
11 October 2014